Praise for Lis
Stunning Works of
Romantic Fiction

"[Lisa Jackson] fires your imagination and stimulates your senses. You'll hear the clamor of armor, the hiss of arrows, and whispers of treacherous men. . . . Passionate, you bet. Entertainment I couldn't put down."

—*Rendezvous*

"Lots of action, romance, and atmosphere; not to be missed!"

—Linda Lael Miller

"Her books are compelling, her characters intriguing, and her plots ingenious."

—Debbie Macomber

"A bright star in the medieval romance galaxy."

—*Affaire de Coeur*

"With a deft hand and lyrical pose, [Lisa Jackson] spins a spell-binding tapestry of Medieval Wales, drawing the reader ever deeper into the vibrant drama enacted by richly crafted characters."

—*Romantic Times*

Also by Lisa Jackson

KISS OF THE MOON

ENCHANTRESS

LISA JACKSON

Outlaw

Previously published under the author name of Susan Lynn Crose

POCKET BOOKS
New York London Toronto Sydney

POCKET BOOKS, a division of Simon & Schuster Inc.
1230 Avenue of the Americas, New York, NY 10020

ISBN: 978-1-5011-5242-9

This Pocket Books paperback edition December 2005

10 9 8 7 6 5 4 3 2 1

POCKET and colophon are registered trademarks of Simon & Schuster Inc.

Manufactured in the United States of America

Outlaw

Prologue

Wales
Winter 1295

"Hurry!" Megan ordered, her breath fogging in the frigid air as she leaned forward in the saddle. Her horse, a headstrong bay mare with an urge to nip, galloped through the forest as night closed in. "Faster, you beast, faster!" Megan glanced at the sky. Through the bare branches she saw clouds, thick and dark and menacing, ready to spill a shower of sleet over the countryside near the castle of Dwyrain, her home.

At least she hoped it was still her home. Her father might just banish her this time. "Please, God, no," she whispered, suddenly frightened and contrite. Why had she been so foolish as to let her younger sister Cayley goad her into an argument? Wouldn't she ever learn?

"Run, Shalimar, 'tis a good girl you be." The encouragement she gave slid through teeth that chattered.

The wind picked up. Megan shivered. Her gloved fingers turned to ice as she held the reins. The forest surrounding Dwyrain had always been an enchanted place in the summer where she'd ridden, hunted, laughed, and waded in the meandering streams. She'd picked berries and nuts, dug for herbs, and plucked wildflowers and ferns from their stalks.

But this afternoon, only a few days before the Christmas revels were to begin, the woods were gloomy; the dark-limbed trees with their naked branches appeared to be forgotten soldiers guarding secrets that no mortal man dared unearth. How many times had her mother warned her that the forests around Dwyrain were sinister, haunted by the spirits of ghosts, people who had believed in the old ways rather than the lawful teachings of the church?

Megan had always laughed at her mother's silly warnings, though Violet of Dwyrain was not the only one who believed in spirits boding both good and evil. Many servants in the castle professed Christianity and knelt on the cold stone floor of the chapel each day, but clung to the faith of their forefathers—the ancient ways. Even old Rue, the nursemaid, trusted the runes and spells of her elders. Megan had spent years watching her, learning quickly, though knowing instinctively that she should never let anyone realize just how much of Rue's pagan magic she'd planted in her mind.

Gathering her cloak to her neck, she squinted as the first icy drops began to fall. The sky was nearly black, and again Megan cursed herself for her foolishness. Her father, Baron Ewan, would be furious with her and would probably send her to her chamber without food and order her to spend hours in the chapel on her knees while begging forgiveness of the Blessed Mother and Holy Father.

Saints in heaven, why had she been so foolish? Frozen cobwebs brushed her cheeks as she rode, guiding the animal down the narrow deer trail. The mare's quick hoofbeats echoed in the quiet forest. Gripping her hood about her neck with one hand, Megan leaned forward and the horse took the bit, running faster and faster along the narrow trail. " 'Tis good you are, Shalimar," Megan cried as a branch slapped her face. They weren't far now, just around the next bend and up a hill and—

The earth seemed to shift. Megan flew forward as Shalimar stumbled.

"Oh!" As she slid sideways in the saddle, leafless branches spun wildly in her vision. The slick reins slid from her fingers as she hung upside down. Her cloak fell over her face and swept the ground. Gamely, the horse plowed forward, limping. "Stop! Shalimar! Halt!" she commanded, scrambling to pull herself back into the saddle. The mare went down on one knee and Megan, barely astride again, pitched forward.

The ground rushed up at her. She landed hard on her shoulder. Pain screamed up her arm and she felt dizzy as she tried to sit up. Shalimar stood, sweating and mud-spattered, favoring a foreleg, her liquid eyes rimmed in white, her dirty coat trembling.

Gritting her teeth, Megan climbed to her feet and made her way to her horse. "What is it, girl?" she asked, but the mare shied and limped farther away.

"Your mount's lame." A deep, soft-spoken voice shook the rain from the leaves of the ivy that clung tenaciously to the trees.

Megan nearly jumped out of her skin. She whirled quickly, her boots sliding in the mud, her eyes narrowed as she squinted into the thicket. "Who are you?" she asked, her horse forgotten, her fingers searching through the slits in her cloak for the knife she had strapped to her belt. "Show yourself."

A soft chuckle followed and an owl hooted from the higher branches of a great fir tree.

"I said—"

"I heard you." A man appeared from the shadows. Tall, broad-shouldered, with a ragged cape that nearly touched the ground, he stepped forward with a noticeable limp. His face was hidden by the hood of his cape, and for a second, Megan shivered in fear. "What are you doing out here alone, Megan of Dwyrain?"

Her throat went dry as her fingers clasped upon the hilt of her dagger. "I—I went riding."

"Ahh. Because of a tiff with your sister Cayley, aye?"

Her heart pounded. "But how did you know? Were you in the keep standing with your ear to the door? Who are you?" she demanded, tossing her wet hair from her face and lifting her chin proudly, mimicking her older brother Bevan. Rain dripped off her nose and chin ignobly and dirt was probably smudged on her face, but she stood her ground, refusing to appear frightened.

"I . . . feel things," he said, looking suddenly vexed, as if he would like to come up with a better explanation, but could not. "Now, let's have a look at your mount."

"She'll shy."

He ignored Megan and spoke softly to the horse. His words were nearly hypnotic, a chant of sorts at which Shalimar, snorting nervously, didn't flinch; not even when he lifted her pained leg and examined it with long fingers that protruded from gloves that covered only his palms. What kind of man was he? The mare, anxious only seconds before, quieted under his hands, and when he reached beneath his cape and withdrew a fat leather pouch, she didn't so much as nicker.

"What're you doing?" Megan asked.

"Shh!" His command was sharp. "You'll scare her." Gently, holding his gloves in his teeth, he applied the jelly-like salve, speaking nearly inaudibly to the horse, closing his eyes for a second as he wrapped his fingers around Shalimar's foreleg. The bay didn't move and appeared in a trance.

Rain pelted the ground, creating pools and splashing in icy droplets against Megan's face and cloak. Shuddering, she stepped away from the mystical man. Though she believed that there were powers on this earth that she didn't understand, powers greater than those given to men and accompanied by crown and scepter, powers that were invisible to most and granted to only a few, she felt a jab of fear.

"There now, you may go," the man said, turning toward her. His face was shadowed by his hood, but she saw that his eyes were blue as the sky in summer.

"Who are you?"

He slid his fingers through the holes in his gloves. " 'Tis of no consequence."

"A sorcerer?"

His smile was humble. "Would you want to think of me as such, so be it."

Shalimar ambled forward, no hint of her injury visible in her gait. "The horse is healed."

"Aye, but be careful. She's not meant to run on slick trails that are weakened by the burrows of moles and rabbits and badgers. Race her only where the earth is firm."

Megan, always impetuous, couldn't help her wayward tongue. "But you limp, sir," she said, motioning to his bad leg. "Why do you not heal yourself as you have the mare?"

"Ah yes, that." He thought for a second, those intense eyes studying her as if she were a mystery. "My injury is old. From my youth, before I knew how to heal. And it matters not. 'Tis a reminder to me that I am mortal and that there is suffering in the world."

"So you choose to be a cripple?" she asked aghast.

" 'Tis my fate." He threw her a crooked grin. "Now, be off. 'Tis nearly dark and the baron is not pleased."

She wanted to know more of this man, this would-be magician. "Please, come with me," she begged. "My father would want to thank you for helping me and my horse. He'd surely offer you a hot trencher of brawn or eel and a cup of wine along with the safety of the castle for the night."

The man's smile was odd. "Nay, child. I prefer the solitude of the forest." At that moment, the owl hooted again and the wizard—for that's what she believed him to be—glanced skyward. Rain ran down his face, but he didn't notice. "Hush, Owain, be patient," he said. The owl ignored him, letting loose another soft call, and the man grinned widely, showing off white teeth beneath a nose that wasn't quite straight. "He's a stubborn fellow, that one."

"You know my name," Megan said as he handed her Shalimar's reins, "but I know not yours."

" 'Tis better if you don't."

"Are you an enemy of Dwyrain?"

He hesitated and his eyes looked over her shoulder, to a distance that was of his own making. "Nay, child—now, be gone."

As if rooted to the ground, she didn't move—just stared, fascinated, into his eyes. "You speak with animals."

"I only see into their minds."

"Can you see into mine as well?" she asked.

"Perhaps." His sigh was as soft as the wind. "Is that what you'd like?"

"Nay—aye—I know not."

"Sometimes it is best if we know not what others think."

Shivering, Megan shook her head. "Tell me."

Eyeing her but a moment, he said, "So be it." He removed

one glove and took her hand in his. She expected his fingers to be frigid as the sea, but a warmth traveled from his palm to hers. "I see not into your mind, but to the years of your life not yet lived."

"You see ahead in time—you foretell what will be?"

"Aye. 'Tis my curse. Would you like to know of your unborn years?"

She could barely breathe and a part of her wanted to flee, to be rid of this odd forest-man with his gentle voice and knowing eyes, and yet she couldn't let go, for she trusted him. The warmth of his hand, his soothing voice, his trustworthy eyes. Nodding, she braced herself and wished she could stop her quaking, for surely he could feel the trembling that had suddenly afflicted her. "Tell me," she said, her words rushed.

"Aye, then." Closing his eyes, he held her fingers between his two hands. "There will be trouble at Dwyrain," he said, his voice sounding as if it had traveled a great distance through a long, narrow cavern. "Sickness. Deceit. Betrayal."

"No."

"The blame will be placed on you."

She recoiled, but he held her hand firmly.

"You will marry in the next few years at the bidding of your father, but the marriage will be cursed—"

"No, I'll not listen—" she said, but stood transfixed, unable to move.

"Your family and castle will be destroyed."

"Nay, sorcerer, I'll not believe—"

"Only true love will restore Dwyrain and your honor," he continued, his eyes squeezed shut, his head moving slowly, as if he were listening to some higher order.

"Love?" So there was hope. If she allowed herself to believe in this foolishness.

"Aye, but the faces of love are many. Some treacherous. Some deceitful. Some as shadowy as candlelight. True love must be tested, Megan, and yours will come from an unlikely source."

Her insides turned to ice. "How will I know—?"

"The man will be dark-haired, fierce of countenance, unforgiving by nature."

"He sounds like a fiend."

"Beneath his mantle of hatred, he has a true heart."

Megan yanked back her hand. "I believe you not," she said, though a part of her trusted the horrid words. "You are the voice of the Devil."

"I speak only the truth, child," he said solemnly, and a blade of dread sliced through her heart. She wanted to laugh at him, to tell him he was addled, call him a fool, but she held her tongue. Did he not know who she was, who her father was? Did he not heal her lame horse?

Before she said another word, he slipped away, as if in his own mist, through the curtain of rain. Overhead, the wings of a great owl flapped wildly.

"Wait," she cried, but before the word was uttered, she knew he was gone.

Swallowing hard, she clucked softly to the horse, pulling on the reins as she led the beast back to the great gates of Dwyrain. The man was mad, she told herself, not to be trusted—an imposter who performed some sort of trickery. But no matter how desperately she argued with herself, she couldn't cast off the premonition of doom that trailed after her, as unshakable as her own shadow, as dark as the deep waters of Hag's End Lake.

One

Tower Dwyrain
Winter 1297

"Come now, smile, Megan. 'Tis your wedding day," Ewan cajoled, lying on the bed in his chamber. He patted the white fur coverlet and smiled up at his daughter.

Even in the flickering light from the candles, Megan saw the spots of age on his thin skin and noticed that his once-fleshy face had hollowed. In his youth, his eyes had been as clear and blue as a mountain lake, but now they had clouded, leaving him half blind.

"You'll not have to look after me much longer, child," he told her. "My time here is short."

"Nay, Father—" she said, closing the door behind her and hurrying to his bedside. She sat on the edge of the feather mattress and took his cold fingers in her own.

"Aye, and I'll be expecting to see a grandson before I go, a strong, strapping lad as Bevan was," he said. Tears welled in Megan's eyes when she thought of her brother, a year older than she but now in his grave, the victim of the sickness that had taken so many in the castle, including her mother and tiny sister. Megan swallowed against a thick lump that had formed in her throat. She'd heard the gossip, knew that most of the servants and a few of the knights blamed her for the death and destruction that had befallen Dwyrain ever since she'd seen the lame prophet in the forest, and he'd cursed her as well as the castle.

Her father sighed sadly. "But ye'd best not wait too long with that grandson."

"Don't talk such madness," she chided, refusing to believe that her beloved father would soon die.

But 'twas as if he were deaf. "Holt, he will be a good husband to you," he said, patting her hands and smiling without reason, as if he had no mind left. There was hushed talk between his men that he was addled, that the loss of his wife and two children, coupled with his age, had finally caught up to him, that he'd taken one too many blows to the head in the heat of battle in his younger years. "A lucky lass ye be to marry a knight as brave as Sir Holt."

Despair raked sharp claws down her heart. "Nay, Father," she said boldly, knowing this was her last chance to change his mind.

"Do not argue with me."

Grasping his hand more urgently, she whispered, "But Father, I need not a husband—"

"Shh," he said, then coughed loudly, his chest rattling, his body clenching against the pain. "God in heaven," he growled, once the attack had passed. He reached for a mazer of wine on a bedside table. His hounds, two gray hunters, lifted their heads and glared at Megan menacingly, as if she were the reason their master no longer rode wildly through the forests and underbrush, drinking mead, whooping loudly, and flushing out deer, boars, and pheasant for them to chase.

Beneath the dogs' yellow-eyed glare, Megan inched up

her chin. Even the snarling beasts appeared to blame her for the ills that had plagued Dwyrain ever since that crippled old sorcerer had sealed her doom with his prophecy and Cayley, whom Megan had trusted with her secret, had told the story of the curse.

"But Father," she pressed on, "remember, the magician said that should I marry this man of your choosing, the marriage would be cursed, and—"

"Shh, child! I believe not in such devilment!" Ewan grumbled, bellowing as he once had, only to end up in a deep, bone-jarring hack. " 'Tis against the teachings of the church. Father Timothy said 'twas a trick the cripple played upon you, a trick that toyed with your weak mind."

"My mind is far from weak," Megan said quickly, and silently cursed the priest for his false piety. The man was too swift to point to the fault in others, too hasty to give a tongue-lashing, too eager to see punishment meted out when none was needed. Unlike Father Andrew, a kind and wise man who, during his 12 years as chapel priest at Dwyrain, had always seen both sides of a disagreement, Father Timothy was young and all-knowing, with a glint of pleasure in his eye when anyone was caught in a sin. 'Twas as if he enjoyed watching others explain their sins and beg forgiveness.

"Aye, I know you not to be thick-skulled as Father Timothy proclaims, but I cannot believe in witchcraft and the dark arts. What would your mother, rest her soul, think?" With a deft movement, he crossed himself, as he sometimes did when his thoughts turned to Violet and her early death. Then there were other times when he acted as if he'd forgotten she'd left this earth.

"I know not."

"Well, I'll ask her, the next time she comes to visit," he said, and she looked for a hint of humor in his cloudy eyes, but found none. Nay, he believed that his wife, though dead, walked these halls and that she often carried baby Rosalind with her or spoke of Bevan.

"You trust not the sorcerer's prediction but you speak with Mother's ghost."

"Her spirit," he said, correcting her as he scooted upward on the bed and cleared his throat. The effort caused even more strain on his tired face. "You think I'm addled," he said, glaring at her through foggy eyes.

"Nay—"

"It is my curse these days. The servants act as if I'm not only blind, but deaf as well, and that I have no mind left. The truth is that I do talk to your mother, Megan, and she asks about you. Aye, I know that she is dead, but believe it or not, at times her spirit glides down from heaven to be with me." He clapped a broad hand over his heart. "She was and always will be an angel. My angel."

Megan didn't know what to say; to argue against something he wanted so feverishly to cling to would be unwise. Why cause him any more pain? If he thought he could speak with his dead wife and children, what did it hurt? "Aye, Father. An angel she is."

He smiled beneath his snowy beard. "I'm glad you believe me, child, because your mother, she wants you to marry Holt!"

Megan jumped off the bed as if she'd been sitting on the red-hot embers of Cook's fires. "You tricked me!"

He laughed and the sound echoed in her heart. "No more than that silly prophet did a few years ago. Now, go on, get dressed and, please, daughter, be happy." Yawning broadly, he waved her away.

"I love Holt not," she said, and her father grimaced at the words.

" 'Twas the same for your mother and me." At the sharp lift of her head, he motioned awkwardly, as if scattering flies. "I know, I know, you thought differently, but love does not grow easily at times, even with your mother and me. Over the years I became devoted to her and she to me. Love sometimes comes with time, daughter, and you have long to live."

Too long, she thought, *if I am to be Holt's wife.* Shuddering inside, she watched as Ewan closed his eyes to rest. Within mere seconds, he was snoring gently, blissfully unaware of the treachery that was mounting against him, the treason she could feel in the hallways. Like rats scurrying through the rushes, the whispers of betrayal darted through the thick walls of Dwyrain.

"The baron, bless him, is not himself these days," Father Timothy had whispered to the steward months ago as the two men stood beside the miller's cart in the inner bailey beneath the open window where Megan had sat on the ledge. Their voices had risen up to her like smoke from a fire.

"Aye, and it's a sad day," Quinn had responded, shaking his head, his bald pate shining in the autumn sunlight.

"And without Bevan to become the baron . . . Ahh, I fear the worst and pray that a man like Sir Holt will step forward and marry the baron's daughter, Lady Megan, so that the castle will once again be secure."

"Aye. Holt would be a good choice."

Megan's heart had frozen for a second, but she had not believed that her father would insist upon the marriage.

Another time, she'd heard one of her father's most trusted soldiers, Cawfield, confide in the sheriff, " 'Tis a pity, that's what I say, when a man's mind goes. There was a time when Ewan of Dwyrain was a fierce warrior. Who would have thought?" Cawfield had been standing guard and his voice had drifted toward the bakery, where Megan was checking that Llyle was not wasting the flour that he was allotted and that there would be plenty of good-sized loaves of wastel, as Gwayne of Cysgod was visiting. But she'd stopped at the sound of the men and tarried in the rose garden, where Cawfield's voice could be heard clearly over the honks of geese and ducks waddling near the eel pond and the creak of the chain and bucket at the well. "Ewan was a strong leader," Cawfield continued. "I pray that he heals soon."

Others hadn't been so kind. The mason had grumbled, "Who can rely on an old relic with half a brain to protect us?" and Ellen, a woman who tended to the geese, had crossed herself and asked to be delivered from Satan as well as the protection of so weak a lord. Ellen, too, believed that Holt alone could rule Dwyrain as a strong, fair lord.

Was Megan the only one who doubted him?

Aye, Holt was a handsome man, tall and strong, with shoulders as broad as the handle of an ax and sharp features that had caused many a scullery maid to sigh and swoon. He was quick with his wit as well as his sword and had, in the past few years, wormed his way into her father's empty heart. From the beginning, he'd noticed Megan, even when she was but a lass, his dark eyes slitting a little as he stared at her, and Megan had always shivered inwardly, sensing that he was trying to imagine what she looked like without her clothes.

She'd overheard him tell ribald jokes to his men and had commented about one of the milking girls—that he would like to drink from her big tits and do his own kind of milking. The men had laughed uproariously and Megan had thought Holt crude.

And now she would be his bride. A sour taste rose in the back of her throat.

Realizing there was no escape, she closed the door to her father's chamber behind her and swept down the hall, her footsteps muted by the new rushes laid upon the stone floor.

Despite the fires burning brightly in the great hall and the tapestries hung on the walls and doorways, the keep was drafty. Megan felt cold as death. In but a few weeks the Christmas revels would be upon them and she, God help her, would be Sir Holt's wife.

Not for the first time, she considered defying her father and fleeing. Once upon Shalimar's broad back, she could ride swiftly through the gatehouse before the portcullis could be lowered! She would race the mare deep into the forest, where she knew of hiding places where no one, not any of her father's soldiers or even the band of outlaws that resided in the wooded hills surrounding the castle, would find her. Yes, she could ride to freedom . . . ahh, would it were so!

She nearly bumped into one of the seamstresses, who was hastening down the hall with another young woman, but Megan ducked into an alcove before being seen.

". . . doesn't know how lucky she is to be marrying the most handsome man in all of Dwyrain. I would gladly lift my skirts for that one and, oh, to be his wife . . ."

Megan's stomach clenched and she slid deeper into the shadows while the seamstress, a silly, freckled-skinned girl named Nell, paused to lean against the wall. Nell was carrying a white silk tunic with gold brocade and rabbit trim. Megan's heart dropped to the floor, for this was her best tunic, the one in which she was to be married.

". . . if I were Lady Megan, I would lick my fingers to be Holt's bride."

"And what else would ye lick?" Grace, one of the cook's daughters who often worked in the kitchen, asked with a suggestive giggle.

Megan's stomach turned over, and she realized she should step forward and scold the girl for gossiping idly, but she wanted to overhear what the maid would say next.

"Shh, Grace—such a tart ye be!"

A big girl with ample breasts and a gap between her front teeth, Grace flirted often with the soldiers.

Nell rambled on, " 'Tis true, the lady loves him not, and all the pain she's brought to this castle is but proof she has not a pure heart. Did ye not hear about the curse that prophet, the lame one Lady Megan met in the forest, laid on this castle?"

"Aye. Everyone in the castle and the villages heard, but I don't believe in prophets or curses of the pagan ones," Grace said, crossing her chest hastily, as if in fear that the very Devil himself might swoop down upon her.

"Well, ye'd better change yer way of thinkin', because since that time there have been strange deaths and evil within the walls of Dwyrain." Her voice dropped and Megan strained to hear. " 'Tis all because of her. Had Lady Megan not been out riding that day against the baron's wishes, she'd not have met the sorcerer and he'd not have laid the curse on this castle."

" 'Tis not true," Grace said, though there was little conviction in her words.

"Aye, ye can say as much because ye did not lose a brother to the sickness that crept through Dwyrain like a thief and took the lives of many, including the baron's wife, his wee babe, and his only son. Ye remember Sir Bevan, Grace, and don't be lyin' to me and sayin' ye dinna. If ever there was one who could turn a lass's head, he was one." She sighed dreamily, clutching the tunic to her.

"Another one ye would lift yer soiled skirts for?" Grace asked, raising her eyebrow.

"Aye, quick as a cat jumping for spilt cream," Nell said with a laugh as they continued, making their way past the smoldering rush lights.

Megan didn't move. Her eyes were moist, her stomach tied in painful knots when she thought of her mother, tall, stately, prideful but loving, a woman whom everyone in the castle trusted. Violet of Dwyrain. Dead. "God be with you, Mama," Megan said with a sniff, then thought of her brother Bevan, one year older than she and a devil of a boy who loved mischief. He had not been felled by the sickness that claimed so many but had drowned in the creek near Hag's End Lake.

Bevan and Megan had been fast friends, always getting into trouble, forever telling secrets. As he'd grown, he'd been groomed to become baron. " 'Tis silly, really," Bevan had told her when they were riding far from the castle one day and they paused to let their mounts sip from a stream. Over the tops of the trees, the towering walls of Dwyrain were visible and Bevan squinted as he stared at them. "Ye'd be a much better lord than I. Too bad ye be younger and a girl."

"You'll be a great baron," she'd predicted and he'd grinned.

"Ye're right, sister. I'll be the best!" Then, yanking on the reins, he'd given a loud hoot, kicked his gray palfrey in the flanks, and raced off across the creek, splashing noisily through the water.

Aye, she missed her brother and tiny, giggling Rosalind as well. Not even 2 years old, with only a few teeth and a silly, bright smile, the baby had succumbed to the dark death that had stolen through the corridors of Dwyrain.

Losing his wife and Baby Roz had been the start of Ewan's ruin, Megan thought sadly, squeezing her eyes shut, remembering her father, strong then, kneeling in the mud and laying roses on the grave of his beloved Violet. He'd wept openly, and Holt had been with him, helping him up, whispering condolences, his hands steady.

Then, only weeks later, the tragedy of Bevan's drowning. Megan had heard her father's hoarse wails when he'd been told the news, then watched his stoic decline as his son had never again opened his eyes.

Before the deaths of family, friends, and servants, Ewan of Dwyrain had been a powerful ruler, one of the most envied of King Edward's barons, a fair man known for his good sense and coarse humor. Now, he was but a shell of the man he'd once been, a husk of that courageous soldier who had ridden into battle against the Scots.

There was a time when no one in the castle had dared defy him, no one questioned his judgment, no one considered going against him. At present, there was malcontent, and the soldiers guarding the gates of the tower were new men, unfamiliar faces who looked to Holt for leadership, or old, tired friends who whispered between themselves that Ewan was addled and ill fit to rule.

Megan leaned the back of her head against the cool stone walls of the alcove and remembered the prophet's words. *You will marry in the next few years at the bidding of your father, but the marriage will be cursed—*

"Dear God, no."

Sickness. Deceit. Betrayal.

The sorcerer's words rang in her head as they had been whispered through the keep. True, they'd all come to pass. *The blame will be placed on you.*

Had it not? Most of the servants would no longer look her in the eye. Even some of the peasants avoided her. 'Twas as if she were a leper or worse. She'd been blamed for the armorer's son falling off the north tower, and for the baker's wife delivering stillborn twins—even Bevan's death, from drowning in the creek, was said to have been her fault. It mattered not that he'd been brought back to the castle barely alive and she and the doctor had tried to nurse him back to health, nor that she'd spent hours in the chapel under Father Timothy's watchful eye, praying for her brother's life.

Yet, despite all the horrors blamed on her, Holt wanted her.

Guilt chased after her as she hurried onward, toward her chamber and the cold, brittle fact that she was to become Holt's bride.

"Oh, would I were you!" Cayley eyed her sister with envy and Megan squirmed, uncomfortable in the long silk tunic that had been altered for her wedding.

She wanted nothing more than to shed this finery and ride Shalimar as fast and far away from the castle as she could. "If you want to be me so badly, then you marry Sir Holt," she said, mindful of Rue, the old nursemaid who was fidgeting with the hem of the tunic, her needle and thread working steadily.

"Shame on ye, lass," Rue muttered, but when her gaze met Megan's, there was no gladness in her tired eyes, and she quickly glanced away again, turning her attention and the conversation back to her work. "I know not why Nell could not mend this hem. Look at the way it droops! Sometimes methinks that girl has her head elsewhere!" Clucking her tongue, she worked swiftly.

Cayley pushed aside the window covering. A shaft of pale winter light slipped through the tanned hides and the noisy honks of geese rose up from the yard. There were shouts and the creak of wagon wheels and Megan bit her tongue, knowing that the few straggling guests who hadn't arrived the day before were now filing into the keep.

"Aye, Holt's a handsome one," Cayley persisted as she hoisted herself up to the window ledge. Tucking her knees beneath her chin, she stared down at the inner bailey and eyed the new visitors anxiously, searching, no doubt, for Gwayne of Cysgod.

"A handsome man does not a fine husband make."

"Oh, but it helps! Why not marry someone who is pleasing to the eye rather than an ugly old toad like Sir Oswald?"

"At least Oswald is kind." Megan finger-combed her hair and Rue squawked loudly.

"I spent hours on those plaits! Don't you be undoing them now; all the flowers will fall out!"

Megan cared not. Her worries about Holt were too deep for her to be concerned about the braids that were wound around her head.

Cayley was right, he was a handsome man with his thick brown hair, eyes as dark as midnight, and a quick, cold smile. Strong and able, Holt was considered her father's most trusted knight. He had courted Megan for nearly a year, and in that time, he'd done nothing but swear his undying affection for her and his loyalty to all that was Dwyrain. Yet she doubted him and didn't trust the glint in his eyes when he looked at her.

You will marry . . . at the bidding of your father . . . marriage will be cursed— The cripple's words rang in circles in her head, round and round, spinning ever faster on this, the day of her wedding. *There will be trouble at Dwyrain. Sickness. Deceit. Betrayal. The blame will be placed on you.*

"Your Holt will make you happy, as Gwayne will me," Cayley said dreamily. Always a romantic, Cayley had envisioned herself as the lady of Castle Cysgod from the moment she'd met Gwayne when she was but 4 years old and he a boy of 8.

"Holt is Father's choice, not mine!"

"Shh, child!" Rue hissed, shaking her graying head as she straightened and rubbed the small of her back. "I would be careful were I ye," she said, giving advice as she always had. "The castle walls sometimes have ears, do they not? Holt would not be pleased were he to hear your thoughts."

"He will hear them soon enough," Megan said, for if she was to wed this man, he would find she had her own mind, her own plans, her own life . . . or did she? Her heart sank. Whereas Cayley had forever wanted to marry, Megan had longed for something other than being a soldier's or a baron's wife.

"Here, slip your arms through," Rue instructed as she held up a wine-red quilted surcoat with threads of gold. Megan did as she was bid, including donning a mantle of forest green that was trimmed with gold lace. The old nursemaid trained a practiced eye on her handiwork. " 'Tis lovely ye are, Megan girl."

"Aye," Cayley said, frowning slightly, twin little furrows growing in the skin between her honey-colored brows. "You are prettier than I thought you'd ever be."

Megan should have been pleased, but she was not. She'd looked forward to this day as if it were the beginning of her death sentence. She would no longer have this bedchamber to herself. Holt had been given Bevan's room and would share it with her. He was not a wealthy man and owned no keep of his own, but he had sworn to her father that he would take care of Megan for all her life and be true to Dwyrain.

Ewan believed him.

Megan did not.

Without much grace, Cayley hopped down from the

ledge. "Think ye this keep is cursed?" she asked, biting her lower lip and running a hand along a bare, whitewashed wall.

Rue snorted. "Ye've been listening to idle gossip again."

"Well, I believe it!" Cayley said, staring at her sister with silent, unspoken accusations in her eyes. "Were it not, Mother, Bevan, and Baby Roz would yet be alive!"

"You blame me," Megan said, the knowledge as painful as a hot knife twisting in her heart. Even her sister had fallen prey to the curse.

"Nay, not you, but surely that monster of a cripple who you met in the forest. I remember that day, Megan, when you came riding into the castle, your skin the color of curdled cream, your eyes round and frightened, as if you'd just seen your own ghost!"

Megan remembered that dark day as well. She'd been scared to death and trembled inside. Late that night, she'd slipped from beneath her coverlet to kneel and whisper at Cayley's bedside. With the light of one lone candle chasing away the shadows of the night, she'd confided in her sister, telling an awestruck Cayley everything the sorcerer had said and done, including healing Shalimar's leg and predicting the dark fates that would befall the keep.

"He was the Devil!" Cayley had said, clutching her fur blanket to her chest.

"Nay, I think not."

"He's cursed us." Cayley sat bolt upright in bed and narrowed her eyes. "I wish I would have met him in the forest," she'd said, as she'd tossed her dark honey–colored curls over her shoulder, "for I would have laid a curse on his own black soul."

"Nay, Cayley, the man was true of heart."

Cayley had snorted her disbelief, and now, years later, as the sand drifted through the hourglass and 'twas nearing the time for her marriage to Holt, Megan feared her sister had been right after all. Dwyrain was cursed and she was the reason.

"Come now, child," Rue said with a sigh. "Father Timothy and Holt wait for ye in the chapel."

"I'm tellin' ye, 'tis a fool's mission we're on," Odell complained, rubbing his back and squinting through the underbrush to the castle rising in the distance. Astride a sorrel jennet he'd won in a dice game, he scowled against the surrounding gloom.

Wolf ignored the older man and stripped off his tunic. Odell was never happy lest he was grumbling. " 'Tis something I have to do." Untying the bag he'd brought with him, he reached inside and his fingers encountered the soft fabric of the clothes he'd stolen only a few hours earlier from a nobleman.

"For the love of Saint Peter, man, think. What needs we with a woman? Do ye not remember the law of our band?"

"I made the law," Wolf said through lips that barely moved. He patted his destrier's thick neck and stared at the throng of people moving along the road toward Dwyrain, the fortress he planned to plunder. Limestone walls knifed upward to thick battlements and towers; a wide moat was crossed by a single bridge spanning a river that surrounded the hill on which the castle was built. A town, hidden by walls cut from the same stone, lay to the east, with only the river separating it from the castle. Outside the walls were a few houses and fields that farmers tended, but the tilled land finally gave way to the woods Wolf now called home.

"Aye, ye made the law that there would be no women in our band, that women only cause trouble, that women—"

"I know what I said," Wolf growled, sliding his arms and head through a silky black tunic.

"And yet ye're willing to break yer own rules. For this one? Why? What d'ye want with this *cursed* woman?" Odell asked, blowing on fingers that showed through the ends of his gloves.

"She's not important." His new mantle was black as well, trimmed in the fur of a silver fox. Metal studs decorated his new belt and gloves.

"Not important? Fer the love of Saint Jude, then why take her?"

"Because she belongs to Holt of Prydd," he said, and felt a cruel smile twist his lips as he tightened his belt and thought of his quest. "In that respect, you're right, Odell. She is cursed."

"I hate to be the one givin' ye the news, but in case ye havna noticed, this isna Prydd we're plannin' to enter—"

"Not us. Only me," Wolf reminded him. "You're to wait for my signal then take Sir Kelvin's fine horse"—he motioned to the tawny destrier they'd recently stolen—"and ride back to camp."

"Aye, aye. Wait fer the signal. I know. But I'm tellin' ye, Wolf. This woman—this daughter of the baron—will only bring us trouble."

Wolf didn't bother answering, just stared across the great distance that separated them from the castle. His eyes were trained on the crenels of the north watch turret. Baron Ewan of Dwyrain's standard snapped in the wind, the colors red and gold bright against an ominous slate-colored sky. If ever there was a day for an omen, this was one. But Wolf trusted not in too much sorcery. Aye, he'd watched Morgana of Wenlock talk to the wind and see through a window into the future, and he'd witnessed great healing when Sorcha of Prydd had brought the near-dead back to life again, but he trusted not the dark arts. Nor did he trust God.

Mist was beginning to gather in the woods and would soon shroud his view. Then he'd have to rely on instincts rather than the help of spies within the castle. Somewhere in the surrounding trees, an owl hooted softly.

"There it is," Wolf said squinting hard. One of Dwyrain's sentries, a watchman in the north tower, paused, closed the shutters of the crenel, then opened them again. " 'Tis time."

Odell scratched his head. "Time fer what—to open the gates of hell?"

Wolf chuckled and checked the knife he'd slid into his boot. "The marriage ceremony is about to begin." A hard smile crept over his lips as the sound of church bells peeled throughout the valley. "I wouldn't want to be late."

"For the wedding?" Odell asked, rolling his eyes as if he was certain his leader was daft. " 'Twill be hours before ye get there."

"I care not for the wedding." Wolf's smile faded and determination clenched his jaw. "But the kidnapping can't start without me."

Wolf entered the gates of Dwyrain easily. No one questioned a well-dressed nobleman on a swift mud-spattered destrier. He appeared tired, as if from a long journey, and rode across the drawbridge and beneath the great portcullis that was raised in the gatehouse. Through the outer bailey without so much as a question from the sentries, he followed others and trailed behind a lumbering team of horses pulling a hay cart. A boy he recognized as Jack, a young hunter for the castle, glanced his way, then went back to sharpening the blade of his knife. Though neither acknowledged the other,

Wolf and Jack had met before when poachers had tried to steal from Dwyrain's forests and had nearly killed Jack to silence him. It had been Wolf's sword that had convinced them to take their dead stag and leave the boy alone.

Now, three years later, Jack sheathed his knife, met Wolf's gaze again briefly, then grabbed the reins of Wolf's mount before leading the stallion away.

The chapel bells had rung hours before, announcing that the marriage ceremony itself and the nuptial Mass following the ceremony had ended. Good. 'Twas important that Holt be married. Wolf only hoped Holt loved Ewan's daughter with all his black heart. She was the older of the baron's daughters, and some, including his allies within the castle walls, blamed her for their troubles, claiming she'd brought a curse upon the keep. They were only too eager to help him with his plot and be rid of Megan.

As if he had every right to enter, he half ran up the steps of the great hall and ignored a guard posted at the door, but he was stopped by a tall, lanky soldier with a scraggly red beard and a scar running down one side of his face.

"Excuse me, sir, but have you an invitation?"

Wolf paused and let a small, amused smile play upon his lips, the kind of knowing grin that one of superior birth rains on an underling. "Pardon me?"

The man's Adam's apple bobbed. "An invite, sir."

The knife in his boot rubbed against his leg and he wondered if he'd have to use the weapon. "Aye, from the baron himself."

"Yer name, sir?" the sentry persisted, glancing nervously about. No doubt he didn't want to offend any of Baron Ewan's friends.

"Do you not recognize Kelvin of Castle Hawarth?" another soldier, Sir Reginald, a man who owed Wolf his life, asked. Reginald, big and burly, looked Wolf straight in the eye and lowered his head a bit. "How be ye, sir?"

"Hawarth?" the sentry repeated, dully.

Wolf's gut tightened. "Aye."

"That's right, Wendall, Hawarth. Are you dense as a stone?"

Scarface's eyebrows drew into one thick line of concentration. "But I thought the baron was Osric."

"Aye, 'tis so. And his younger brother—?" Reginald prompted while he sent Wolf a glance that silently told him he'd gladly run scarface through with his sword if needs be.

"Lord Osric sends his best to Sir Holt and Lady Megan," Wolf said, though he nearly choked on the words.

Wendall scowled for a second and then, as if some dim thoughts appeared in his cloudy mind, he nodded slowly. "Kelvin of Hawarth," he repeated, "kindly pass. I'm afraid ye've missed the ceremony and the feast."

" 'Tis of no matter—just as long as I can give Sir Holt and his bride my gift."

Reginald's smile was as stiff as a dead dog's leg. Wolf slipped inside to mingle with the invited guests. The smells from the meal lingered, rising above the smoke and chatter, and Wolf's stomach growled at the scents of cooked salmon, venison, and pheasant. It had been years since he'd lived in a castle and the feasts he'd taken for granted as a youth were far distant.

Servants had cleared the room of tables and musicians tuned their lyres, viols, and lutes. Guests in silk, velvet, and fur gathered in groups filled with good wishes for the bride and groom.

Wolf's heart burned with a silent fury and he climbed the stairs to the second-floor landing for a better view of the newlyweds. A loud tapping interrupted the noise. Instruments stopped. Laughter and voices stilled.

On the dais, an old man pounded his cane. He was a tall man, now stooped, with a white beard and hair that had once been red. He smiled widely, though with effort, it appeared. "Please, please . . ." he said, his voice raspy. "Thank you all for coming to this, the celebration of my daughter's wedding. Please welcome Sir Holt, who has been like a son to me and now is truly part of my family." Leaning heavily on his cane, he added, "I only hope their union is blessed with many children and I live to see them. After I am gone, Holt will become the baron of Dwyrain!"

A bad taste rose in the back of Wolf's throat while everyone else in attendance clapped, laughed, and shouted congratulations. Holt beamed and his wife lost some of her color. As she held her husband's hand, no smile curved her lips, despair rounded her eyes, and Wolf was struck by her as he'd been when he'd seen her before. Though she was not as beautiful as the golden-haired one who was her sister, there was a spark to this woman that none other in the great hall held. So why did she appear unhappy? Was she already regretting her marriage vows?

"Now, musicians, play!" the old man commanded.

Immediately, music filled the great hall and the crowd parted. In the middle of the floor, Holt bowed to his bride, his eyes never leaving her face as he began to dance.

She was smaller than Wolf remembered, dressed in white, her dark hair braided with flowers and covered with a fine veil captured about her head with a thin gold band. Her eyes, when she looked at her groom, were filled with a quiet, seething fire that Wolf guessed was more than a hint of her spirit.

So this was the woman who was supposed to love Holt.

Wolf had caught glimpses of her riding on horseback either coming or going to the castle these past few months, but never had he stared at her full in the face and never had he guessed her so prideful and gloriously beautiful. Her skin was pale but smooth, her eyes wide and warm gold with thick curling lashes and finely arched brows. White and gold ribbons were wound in her hair and small flowers framed a face far too lovely for the wife of Holt.

Wolf's fists clenched.

Holt was with his new bride. His gaze never left her face, his smile seductive and full of promise.

In his mind's eye, Wolf saw them coupling, Holt naked and dark, mounting this small, white-skinned lady . . .

For the love of Christ, what was he thinking? Cursing under his breath, he stared at the woman. What did it matter how Holt bedded this woman—his wife? As long as the mating didn't happen before Wolf had kidnapped and ransomed her, it was none of Wolf's concern. Slowly, he opened his hands and started down to the dance floor. 'Twas time to meet Megan of Dwyrain.

It's over. I am Holt's wife. For now until eternity. Megan danced on leaden legs, allowing her new husband to twirl her around the great hall. He laughed and whispered into her ear, reminding her of everything he intended to do to her later that night. She shivered, not in eager anticipation, but in disgust.

"Ah, yes, my love," he said, his breath tickling her ear. "You will dance with me alone tonight and show me what kind of woman you are."

She didn't answer, couldn't think of lying with him, of having his hands touch her skin, of letting him pierce her maidenhead to spill his seed into her body. Her stomach clenched and she nearly retched as the musicians played on, the notes of their songs rising like the mist in the morning. *Dear God, help me.*

There was ever the chance of escape. Should she decide that she could not lie with this cur, she could run away, humiliate her father, and . . . and go where?

She felt Holt's lips on her neck, and her skin crawled. "Come, love, at least pretend you're having a good time," he cajoled. "I wouldn't want to get angry," he said, his eyes locking with hers, his fingers gripping her more tightly. "I have a nasty temper when I'm crossed, or don't you know?"

"I remember," she said, tilting up her chin. "I saw you kill the bear cub."

The corners of Holt's mouth cinched tight. "We needed his mother for the entertainment."

Megan had never considered bear-baiting entertainment.

"The cub didn't need to die."

"Of course he did, my sweet. He was distracting his mother. And he suffered not."

Megan closed her eyes, remembering Holt's orders and the mace that came down fast and hard, crushing the mewling, frightened animal's skull. She also remembered the furious roar of the mother bear, how the enraged beast had lunged despite the shackles on her back legs. The chains had slipped and the bear swept forward through the crowd in the outer bailey, swiping her powerful claws and leaving one soldier with deep gashes on the side of his face and severing the arm of the miller's son just below his elbow.

"Now, now, you hunt," Holt reminded her. "I've seen you with the carcasses of pheasant, stag, and boar."

She lifted her chin. "I kill not the young, nor the mothers of the young."

"So noble," he mocked. His chuckle was deep and throaty. "I'm going to enjoy you, Megan," he said, his eyes sliding down her body. "In every way."

"And I will detest you forever."

"Ah, ah, ah. Be careful what you say," he said, his eyes gleaming malevolently. "I wouldn't want to have to punish you tonight, on our wedding night." But the smile that curved his lips suggested otherwise, as if the anticipation of hurting her was somehow exciting and pleasured him.

A shiver of fear slid down her spine and she saw her father, smiling proudly, lifting his hands, asking the guests to join them in their wedding dance. Within minutes, the hall was filled with other couples who jostled and swayed, some laughing, others more serious—men and women dressed in finery, celebrating what should have been the happiest day of her life.

Several men cut in on her dance with Holt and Megan was relieved. Holt, enjoying himself, danced with other ladies, and Megan endured the smiles, congratulations, and sweaty hands of new partners. She was about to make good her escape upstairs to her room when a deep voice asked, "May I?" to her partner, and before she could think twice, she was being swept around the chamber by a handsome stranger she didn't recognize.

Taller than Holt by an inch or two, he was built strong, with wide shoulders and trim waist. His movements were quick and sure. When his gaze touched hers, the breath in the back of her throat caught, for his eyes were an intense shade of blue that cut to her very soul.

"Lady Megan," he drawled lazily.

"And you are—?"

"A friend of Holt's," was his reply, and she noticed that his hands were not soft, but callused, and in the cleft of his eyebrow was a battle scar. He was handsome in a rugged, dangerous way that surprised her, and his smile, when he showed it, was crooked and secretive and scared her more than a little.

"Have you no name?" she asked, and he laughed, holding her closer than she thought was necessary. Yet she didn't draw away—the heat of his body was distracting in a wicked way.

"None that you'd know."

"But if you're a friend of my . . . my . . . Sir Holt's—" she couldn't say it. Holt was her husband but she could not speak the word, would not let it trip from her tongue.

"Come," he whispered into her ear so softly she wasn't certain she heard it correctly. "I have a wedding gift for you and your husband." He guided her to a spot near the door where a bit of a draft moved the tapestries.

"Now—?" She glanced around, eager for a chance to leave, though uncertain.

He pulled her behind the curtain.

"Now," he said against her ear and she tingled inside. What was she doing letting this man, this stranger, touch her so familiarly? He leaned forward as if to kiss her and she told herself to step away, to slap him for being so bold, but she couldn't. To her surprise he clamped a hand over her mouth.

Her body convulsed.

She tried to scream. What was happening? She fought, struggling, but he had one arm, strong as an oak log, wedged under her breasts, the other hand pressed over her mouth.

"Do not struggle, m'lady," he said with a sneer in his voice, "and your family will not be hurt."

She bit down hard on the callused hands, but they didn't shift one little bit.

"If you fight me," he growled, "you seal their fates and

your precious husband, sister, and father will be killed. Slowly and painfully."

She went limp in his hands and Wolf felt not only a stab of regret for scaring her and lying to her, but a new emotion as well—jealousy that this woman could love a bastard such as Holt of Prydd. With the cord tucked around his wrist, he quickly bound her hands. She cried out at the injustice of it, but he didn't have time to argue with her.

As he dragged her down the steps, smiling when he noticed the sentries missing from their posts, just as he'd planned, he heard the first shouts from the great hall. No more time.

Not only his horse, but hers as well, was waiting near the cistern. "Climb into the saddle and say not a word. As you can see, I have friends here, friends who have dispensed with the guards and stolen your horse. If you breathe too loudly, I swear, I will have them destroy all that you love!"

He removed his hand from her mouth and she opened hers, only to shut it again. He helped her into the saddle, then climbed onto his own steed while holding fast to her mare's reins.

As the doors of the great hall burst open, Wolf dug his heels into his mount's sides and the stallion took off, racing like the wind through the outer bailey, hooves clattering on the drawbridge.

The feisty mare kept up, her nose at the stallion's flank, her legs a blur. Wolf slid a glance at his prize and her eyes met his for an instant. He expected hatred, or fear, but saw neither. Instead, in that heartbeat, he noticed a glint of triumph in her gaze.

Almost as if she'd been expecting him.

Two

Dear Lord, did you have to deliver me into the hands of an outlaw? The wind tore at her hair, yanking off her veil and pulling free the plaits and flowers. Tears stung her eyes as Shalimar galloped furiously to keep up with the stallion. Mayhap she should have been more precise when she'd sent up prayer after prayer asking for deliverance from her marriage, seeking a way to escape the horror of being Holt's wife. But was this man—this savage scoundrel dressed in black—the answer to her pleas? Would God play so cruel a trick upon her? Surely not!

"Halt!" Holt roared from the steps of the keep; his furious voice carried on the wind and followed them. Megan's blood turned to ice. "Guards!" he yelled. "Where the hell are the bloody guards?"

Megan hung on for her life.

"For the love of Christ," Holt thundered, his voice fading in the distance. "Stop that man! Kill him if you must. He's stealing my wife!"

The horse turned and Megan's hands, tied as they were,

tightened over the pommel of Shalimar's saddle. Mud spattered upward, staining her tunic as the dark sky cracked open. Rain and sleet slid down her back and pummeled the ground. Darkness crowded over the valley as the horses raced onward, galloping madly along the road. If only she could grab the reins, twist Shalimar around, and somehow elude her captor as well as her husband's guards. Looking ahead, she saw only the outlaw's broad back and his long black mantle sailing in the wind.

Behind them, she heard the shouts of men and thundering of hooves. Hazarding a quick glance over her shoulder, she imagined she saw the flickering lights of torches as Holt's men gave chase. Her heart drummed as wildly as the horses' hooves and yet she didn't know which was a worse fate, being kidnapped by a criminal or being caught by her husband.

My husband. What a horrid, blasphemous thought. She shivered inside, thinking that if only she knew the outlaw's intentions were honorable, she would thank him for helping her escape. But what noble man steals another man's wife on his wedding day?

The demon rode on, kicking his huge mount's sides, pulling at Shalimar's reins, making the little mare gallop at a breakneck pace. They sped frantically down the road, splashing through puddles, careening around corners, sliding through wagon ruts. Faster, faster, faster! Shalimar was breathing hard, struggling to keep up with the longer-legged warhorse, and 'twas all Megan could do to stay astride the game mare.

Think, Megan, think! she told herself as the cold air tore more flowers from her hair and billowed her tunic over her jennet's rump. As thankful as she was to this criminal, she could not trust him. For all she knew he planned to rape, maim, or kill her.

For weeks she'd thought her fate—that of marriage to Holt—was her doom. She'd nearly collapsed at the altar when Holt had slid the ring on her finger and said, "In the name of the Father, and of the Son, and of the Holy Ghost, with this ring, I thee wed."

After the nuptial Mass, Holt had received the kiss of peace from Father Timothy and passed it on to her. She'd nearly been sick. She'd been certain no fate would be worse than being tied to him for life. But this . . . this could be a swift and certain death.

She had no choice but to escape the madman who had single-handedly, it seemed, stormed through the guarded gates of Dwyrain, attended the celebration uninvited, and stolen her away right from under her husband's nose.

The road forked and her captor pulled up short. Shalimar skidded to a halt and Megan nearly toppled over the mare's head. Somehow she managed to stay in the saddle.

"Where are we?" she demanded, for she'd lost her bearings in the dark.

Still holding on to the reins of her mount, he frowned at the ground. Rain dripped down his face, plastering his dark hair against his skin. His horse stomped impatiently, as if eager to be off again. "Damned flowers," he muttered under his breath, sidling his horse next to hers. Once close enough, he reached down and raked his fingers through the tangled strands of her hair.

"Ouch!"

"Be quiet!" Yanking mercilessly on the remaining braids, he stripped the blooms from her tresses.

"Stop! What're you doing?" she cried, attempting to urge her mount away from him. His grip on the mare's reins was stronger than the armorer's vise. Shalimar sidestepped and Megan ordered, "Stay away from me!"

"Hush, woman!" he ordered. "I have spies in the castle; they would slit your husband's throat if I were but to give the command."

"You have no power!" But she trembled to think that all the deceit and betrayal she'd felt within the castle walls had been because of this man, this devil with the harsh, rugged face and cruel threats. Was he the reason that Ewan's knights no longer felt honor-bound to their pledge of fealty? Had he undermined and stripped the baron of his authority? "You scare me not," she lied. If only she could wrest Shalimar's reins from his fingers and ride . . . where? Not back to Dwyrain, not as Holt's wife, so where? "My father—"

"Your father is an old, foolish man who has put his faith and command of his army in a traitor."

"A traitor—?"

"The man you call husband, the man with whom you will soon share a bed and with whom you will bring forth children," he said, his lips curling in disgust.

Megan hoisted up her chin. "You know naught about Dwyrain—"

He laughed, and the sound was wicked as it echoed through the valley. "You're as blind as Ewan!" Leaning closer to her, he said, "If I know naught of Dwyrain, how did I capture you, eh?"

"Bastard!"

"At your service, m'lady."

"Pig!"

"Curses from a woman who would marry Holt of Prydd."

"Nay, Holt is not of Prydd," she said, bristling, then wondered why she was defending a man she did not trust.

In the darkness his gaze slid down her body and she sensed that he was seeing beneath the folds of mud-spattered velvet and silk, through her mantle, tunic, and even her chemise. " 'Tis a pity that you should waste yourself on such a man."

"At least I am not a thief, a highwayman who steals and robs and pillages and . . ."

"And what?" he prodded, his voice low.

"Rapes," she whispered. "Or murders."

This time there was no bark of laughter, no sharp denial. "Think what you will, woman," he said. " 'Tis of no matter to me." His gloved hands ripped through her hair again and she yanked her head away.

"Stop it!"

"Then take the flowers from your hair," he demanded urgently. "Give them to me! Now!" His lips pressed into a thin, hard line and he glanced over his shoulder as if expecting Holt's soldiers to appear from the shadows at any second.

"My hands are bound."

"By the gods, Odell was right," he growled, and picked—more carefully now—the petals from her hair.

"Who's Odell?" she asked. "And who are you?"

His smile was evil in the darkness. "Tonight I'm Kelvin from Castle Hawarth."

"And tomorrow?"

His gaze found hers and his stare was so baldly sensual, so intense, she gasped. Even shadowed with the night, his chiseled face was cruelly handsome. His eyes, a deep shade of blue, were guarded by thick black lashes and brows. His nose was crooked, his smile wicked. "I'll be your keeper, *m'lady,*" he said in a voice so low she scarce heard it over the pounding of icy rain.

"Nay! No man keeps me!"

He laughed, the sound wicked. "Not even your husband, or so it appears." Satisfied that the dried blooms were free of her tresses, he gave a sharp order to his horse again and took the east bend in the road. His tireless destrier charged along at a furious pace, and poor Shalimar, her coat already flecked with lather, had to race to keep up with him. As they thundered down the road, the kidnapper dropped the flowers from his gloved hand, sprinkling them on the ground until there were no more, then he pulled the reins on his mount and again rounded on her.

"Well, m'lady, 'tis time to give up your mare."

"What?"

"A fine animal she is, but methinks it would be best if she were set free."

"Nay, Shalimar is a good mare and not yet spent—" But her horse was breathing hard, lathering, and was in great need of a rest. "If we could but walk—"

"And let Holt catch us? I think not." Before she could argue any further, the captor lifted her deftly from the saddle, swung her astride his own horse, dropped Shalimar's reins, and slapped the mare's rump hard with his hand. With a startled squeal, the fiery jennet bolted, hooves flying down the east path until she was swallowed in the darkness.

"Good." Her captor was pleased.

"Are you daft?" Megan cried, trying to climb out of the saddle. She kicked and fought, slapping away his hands though hers were bound, calling out for Shalimar, but the man held her fast. Her heart filled with sudden fear. Without her mare, Megan had no chance of escape. Now she was completely alone with this beast of a man, this criminal, to be forced to do his bidding. He could ransom her to Holt, sell her, or have his own way with her. She swallowed hard, refusing to be defeated, keeping her despair at bay. "My horse is worth much—"

"I care not," he said swiftly, one strong arm circling her waist, the muscles of his forearm resting hard and firm beneath her breasts, his iron grip clenched tight around her wrists as he held her tight against him.

"But the ransom—"

He clucked to his horse and headed deep into the forest, away from the road, where the darkness was so thick Megan couldn't see. Branches slapped at her face and her back was pressed hard against her abductor's chest. Along with the rain, his warm breath tickled the back of her neck, and his smell, so like the forest, enveloped her. The horse plodded on through the undergrowth and the demon said not a word.

The sound of men's voices, still far away, whispered through the gloom. Through the bare branches of oak and yew, she spied flickering lights, the torches of Holt's soldiers casting odd points of illumination as they searched for her. As if sensing she might cry out, the outlaw's hand clamped over her mouth again.

Her mind spun in wild, frightening circles, but she would not give in to the fear that threatened her. She could not trust this man. Surely her fate with him would be as bad as it would have been with Holt, but at least she was past the sentries and could find her own means of escape.

Without Shalimar, she reminded herself, and felt a great loss.

She heard a night bird call and Wolf stiffened. From his throat came a like cry.

A signal. So there were more of them! Her heart sank. Escaping one man would be far easier than fleeing a band of cutthroats and ruffians. She shivered and the man pulled her more closely to him. His muscles were solid and she felt the shape of his knee and thigh pressed intimately to the outside of hers. She sat tall, trying to keep her buttocks from pressing against his crotch, but the task proved impossible. The saddle was confining, and they were wedged together close enough that she felt the rub of his breeches against the silk covering her rump.

"You'll be caught," she warned him when the lights had faded and the sounds of the soldiers' voices no longer reached them.

He laughed.

"And tortured!"

Again the soft, amused chuckle.

"Then hanged."

"And will you watch?" he asked, his breath feather-light against her ear.

"Aye!" she lied, for in truth she could not watch a man—any man—swing from the hangman's rope. If the rogue were captured and returned to Dwyrain, she would plead for his life.

"My father will not stand for this."

"Your father has lost control of his castle."

The words were true and rang like the dull chimes of death.

"You will be hunted down like a wounded bear."

"By your husband?" he asked, and she felt her spine stiffen and her chin lift.

"Aye."

"Good. 'Tis what I want."

"Who *are* you?"

"Can you not guess?" He leaned forward, whispering into her ear, causing a naughty little thrill to slide down her spine. "I, m'lady, am the embodiment of your husband's worst fears."

"Which are?"

"That he will be forced to pay for the sins of his past." He yanked on the reins and suddenly, over the drip of rain and soft thud of hooves, she heard the sound of water rushing through the forest. A brook splashed wildly as it cut through the trees. Her abductor let his mount drink for a few seconds before pulling on the reins again and urging the big horse upstream.

"You are Holt's enemy."

"Aye."

"Are you not worried that you, too, might be forced to face your own sins?"

His laugh was without humor and the warm arm surrounding her ribs pulled her even tighter against his chest. "Worried?" he repeated, his voice soft. "Nay, m'lady. I long for that day."

Rage and humiliation burned in Holt's gut, eating at him as hungrily as new maggots on a carcass. Icy sleet poured from the sky, creating mud and muck in the inner bailey as Holt waited in the gatehouse, his ears straining for the sound of his men. He only hoped they'd caught the blackguard who had stolen Megan. When his soldiers brought the fool back, Holt would take personal pleasure in whipping the bastard until his back was raw and bleeding, then have him hanged.

Who was he? Holt wondered, and his conscience pricked with the faces of enemies he'd made during his life. Aye, they had been many, but usually weak men or meek women who had seen the dark side of his temper. None of them would follow him here. So who would dare defy him so openly? *Who?*

His teeth gritted. All his carefully laid plans had changed. Instead of bedding Megan and basking in the glory of becoming the next baron of Dwyrain, he was standing in the driving rain, trying to conjure up the face of the cur who had deceived him.

Holt had been dancing with the scandalous Lady Peony,

elderly wife of Baron Griffin, when he'd noticed the stranger in black—a tall man who caused more than one pretty female head to turn.

Within seconds, the stranger with the fierce countenance had taken Megan as his partner, twirled her about the floor, then as suddenly as he'd appeared, vanished with Holt's new wife, leaving Holt alone in the middle of his own wedding celebration.

Holt had thought at first his mind was playing tricks with him, for his greatest fear had been that Megan would refuse to marry him, but after the ceremony when the ring was securely around her finger, he'd let down his guard, actually enjoyed the feast and music. Only later, when he'd finally understood that Megan had been abducted, he'd shouted out and then he'd heard the gasps, whispers, and titters of the guests.

"Is this some kind of joke?" Lady Peony had asked, her eyebrows lifting in delight.

"I know not," Holt had grumbled and she'd thrown back her head and laughed, an ugly braying sound not unlike that of a donkey.

"What? What happened?" Ewan had searched the great hall with his pathetic blind eyes. "Where's Megan?"

"She's been stolen away," Baron Griffin had surmised.

"What?" Ewan had leaned heavily on his cane.

"Holt's bride has disappeared." Sir Mallory had eyed each guest with suspicion.

"Disappeared? You mean she left, don't you? But with whom?" another woman, whom Holt did not recognize, had asked. Her mouth had rounded in delighted horror.

"The stranger in black, did you not see him? Those eyes, so blue, and his visage . . . oh, my." Cayley had looked to the doorway as if hoping to see the cur again.

"Like the very image of Lucifer!" Father Timothy had proclaimed. "He must be brought back!"

"How thoroughly and utterly romantic!" Cayley had said with a sigh, and Holt's men had all laughed and made jokes about his first night as a husband with no wife. Speculation had run high that the man was Megan's lover, that she'd expected him, that even now they were off in a private hide-away. His blood curdled to think of how he'd run outside into the rain, hearing the fading clatter of hoofbeats as he yelled to his lazy men to give chase.

Now, hours later, he still felt the sting of humiliation on his cheeks, the hard bite of betrayal. Guests and servants alike had gossiped and laughed at his expense and his wrath was greater than he ever could have imagined.

When at last his soldiers returned, they came with the bad news that the outlaw had evaded them deep in the forest.

"So you found her not?" Holt said, cutting through the litany of excuses made by his knights—Dwyrain's *best* men—for returning to the castle without his wife or her abductor. What a pitiful lot!

"Aye, we lost them," Sir Mallory admitted, his moustache dripping with rain and mud, defeat evident in his eyes as he tried and failed to meet Holt's stare. He was holding the reins of his horse when a page came by and gathered them, leading the sweating, lathered beast away.

"How?"

"We followed their trail," the soldier admitted, opening his palm to show a few wilted and dried blooms. Another soldier handed Megan's bridal veil to Holt. "Hoofprints and flowers from m'lady's hair. They took the fork that leads to Prydd, but . . . there were many tracks because of all the guests traveling through the rain. We found only the lady's horse, grazing alone in a meadow at the edge of the forest by St. Peter's Abbey."

"Did you search the surrounding woods?"

"Aye," Mallory said, "and the abbey itself, though the abbot was not pleased. We searched until our torches failed and the fog rolled in."

"And what of the dogs?" Holt asked, barely holding on to his temper. He should have ignored his guests and taken off after his wife himself. As it was, he looked like a fool, yet again trusting these thickheaded farmers who called themselves soldiers.

Mallory shook his head. "The hounds were useless. Once they found the horse, they knew not what we wanted."

"God's blood, you're fools! The whole lot of you!" Holt's voice resounded in the gatehouse and he threw down the muddy wedding veil in disgust. This was to have been his wedding night, when finally he would not only bed the woman who had teased his mind for years and caused his cock to become stiff as granite, but, being married to Ewan's oldest daughter, he would by rights inherit all that was Dwyrain. Taking off one glove, he slapped it against his hand, thinking hard, trying to understand the way of the outlaw's mind. "Have you any thought as to who the rogue was?"

"He claimed he was Kelvin of Hawarth."

"Kelvin of Hawarth?"

"Aye, younger brother to the baron, Osric McBrayne."

Holt squeezed his eyes closed and counted slowly to 10. Ewan saw these men as dedicated, good-hearted, and loyal, but in Holt's estimation, they were lazy mental midgets and cowards. Not a brave, smart one in the lot. "The man was not McBrayne's brother. He's an outlaw, I'm certain of it." The sky opened up, and rain sliced to the ground in heavy curtains of water. Holt, already chilled to his bones, saw no reason to stand outside. "Come to my chamber," he ordered, striding swiftly away.

In the great hall, he came upon a page and ordered wine to be sent to his room, but his thoughts lingered on the man who had so baldly stolen his wife. The criminal's face had been vaguely familiar when Holt had spied the man in black dancing with his wife. Tall and dark-haired, he'd twirled Megan on her feet until she was breathless. Holt had been about to reclaim his bride's attention when he'd noticed the stranger and Megan slip into the shadows and then quickly away.

His anger burned savagely within him.

Megan might have helped hatch the plot to humiliate Holt, for she'd made it plain that she married him unwillingly. Would she go to such lengths as to plan a false abduction just to avoid his bed?

'Twas possible. Earlier in the week, Holt had come across her in the hallway after one of her visits to her father's chamber. Holt had tried to touch her and she'd shrunk away as if he were poison. "Leave me be," she'd ordered, anger flaring in her eyes.

"Ah, Megan, I cannot. Asides, we'll be wed soon and—"

"And I'll be your wife in name only," she'd said proudly, her chin mutinous, her eyes blazing with a fire that brought his damned cock to attention. He couldn't wait to tame her, to force her to open her legs and mouth to him, to make her want him as much as he wanted her. He'd make her beg for him, tie her to the bed and touch her all over with feathers, allow some of his men to watch her surrender. But no one else would have her. Nay, they could look at her long-legged body, see the pink nipples of her high breasts, lust over the thatch of curls where her legs met, watch as their bodies joined, but only he could press his skin to hers and spill his seed in her unwilling body.

"You'll want me so badly you'll beg me to bed you," he'd told her in that hallway, and she'd slapped him. Her palm had burned an imprint on his skin and he'd grabbed her arm. "Rough ye want it, lass?" he'd growled into her ear. "Then rough 'twill be."

"You'll rot in hell before you touch me!" She'd pulled her arm away and run down the hallway. He'd been so hard with wanting that he'd slid into a dark alcove and slipped his hand into his breeches to ease the ache. No one had seen him gasping there, imagining entering her body, seeing her mouth wet with desire as she kissed and touched him. He'd bit down hard at his release but he'd been unable to stop from whispering her name in a desperate voice he barely recognized as belonging to him.

No, he would not be denied.

The page brought in a pitcher of wine and several wooden mazers, which he left on a tray near the hearth. As his men shuffled in, looking like whipped pups, Holt wondered what kind of soldiers they were. He glared at the sodden lot of them, spineless men warming their backsides at the fire, causing steam to rise from their filthy clothes. "No one steals my wife," he said slowly as he unsheathed his sword and stared at the firelight gleaming against the sharp-edged blade. "No one steals my wife and lives to tell about it. Find out who the bastard is and hunt him down. Kill him if you have to, but my wife's safety and her virtue will not be compromised!"

His gaze roved from one sad soldier to the next, and he smelled their fear. They were frightened of him, which was good. He could use their trepidation to his advantage. Holt ran a finger along his blade, pressing hard enough that a drop of blood showed on his skin. He spread it slowly over the steel and saw each man swallow a sudden knot in his throat. With a smile meant to be cruel, he said, "Do not fail me, lads."

Wolf was beginning to wonder if his plan to humiliate Holt was as clever as he'd first thought. When he'd heard that his enemy was planning to wed the daughter of Baron Ewan, Wolf had finally decided that fate had smiled on him, giving him an opportunity to belittle and disgrace the man he'd hated for so long. He'd thought only of the kidnapping, and then of the ransom, giving not too much consideration to the woman herself. He had heard that she was headstrong and that she'd been blamed for much of the pain in the house of Dwyrain, but he cared not and decided she was the pampered daughter of a rich man, a woman stupid enough to marry one of the vilest snakes in all of Wales. In his estimation, Megan of Dwyrain deserved her fate.

He hadn't expected to see a beauty and pride in her that appealed to him, nor had he thought that holding her so closely to him while astride the horse would cause him any worry. As it was, he was distracted by the warm, female scents of her and the feel of her skin so close to his. Her hair tickled his nose and his arm felt the soft, supple weight of her breasts. Despite himself, that male part of him that was always giving him trouble responded, and to his disgust his member started to swell.

"We'll stop here," he said gruffly, when the evidence of his desire could no longer be hidden.

"Here? Why?" she asked as he slid to the ground, sinking into thick mud. The sleet had stopped, but the forest was chilled and shimmering in raindrops. Only a few stars dared wink behind a thick bank of clouds.

" 'Tis as good a place as any." He helped her from the saddle, then reached into his boot, withdrew his small dagger, and sliced through the ropes that bound her wrists.

She gasped at the sight of the blade flashing silver in the night, then swallowed hard. "Where are we?" she asked, rubbing her wrists and stretching her fingers.

"Not far from the camp."

"Why have we stopped?"

He eyed her in the darkness, her white tunic nearly glowing. Even with dirt smudged on the fine fabric, she was beautiful, too beautiful. " 'Tis a wonder we weren't seen," he said, gruffly, noticing the long column of her throat and the proud point of her little chin. Angry with himself, he motioned to her dress. "But there was no time. Now, before we get to the camp, you needs wear something more . . . more common."

"Such as?" she asked, clearly uncertain of his reasoning.

"Such as these." Reaching upward for the bag he'd tucked behind his saddle, he untied the straps that had held it securely, then tossed the sack to her.

She caught it easily and loosened the drawstring.

"The clothes will be too big, but they will have to do."

She slid one hand into the open sack and withdrew plain men's clothes, brown leather breeches and long tunic, the colors of which weren't visible in the night.

Hesitating, she lifted her curious eyes to his. "Why?"

"Your dress is like a beacon, white as the moon on a dark night!"

"But we outran the guards."

"It matters not," he said, eager to be off again. Being alone with her was dangerous. "Just be quick about it."

Stubbornly, she shook her head. "I cannot!"

"Aye, you can and you will, m'lady," he said, watching her lips purse in mulish denial. "Or I will do it myself."

"You wouldn't dare—" she said, and he took a menacing step forward.

But instead of skittering away, she stood her ground, and when he brought up a hand to untie the ribbons at her throat, she didn't flinch.

"Do not touch me," she whispered, but her breath was as ragged as the night, her pulse fluttering wildly below her ear.

His own heart beat a desperate, tremulous rhythm.

"Then undress yourself."

Silently she defied him.

"Bloody hell," he muttered and instead of loosening the ribbons, he slit them through.

The fabric gaped and Megan's hands fluttered nervously. "Leave me be."

"Put on the men's clothes."

"I won't be ordered about like some kitchen wench who—oh!" He cut the ties again, pieces of the ribbons floating to the ground, and the thick velvet fabric parted farther to expose the swell of her breasts, white in the slight moonglow, heaving in mute fury. Ah, they were beautiful, soft and round and large enough to fill his palm, but he didn't let his eyes rest on their plump, unwitting invitation too long. Instead he lay the blade of his weapon between them to the next set of ribbons. "Shall I go on?" he asked, his voice but a rasp.

"Nay!" she whispered, and when his gaze reached hers again, he saw her rage, but there was more in her indignant stare, more than ire and mutiny. Unless he was mistaken, he recognized desire, hot and wanton, steal fleetingly across her face. "You're a true bastard of the lowest order."

"Aye, m'lady. Now, at last, we understand each other."

Muttering under her breath, she snatched up his bag of clothes, stalked off to a nearby tree, and started to disappear behind its thick trunk.

"Come back here," he ordered.

"But you asked me to change."

"How am I to know you won't run off?"

"To where?"

"I'll not be spending the rest of the night chasing you down."

"I swear I won't."

"I dare not take the chance." Silently, he followed her until he could see her beneath the empty branches. She was working feverishly, quickly removing her mantle, surcoat, and tunic, stripping off the white velvet, standing in only her chemise. His gaze fastened on the cleft of her breasts, dark and dusky and deep, and his blood heated as she bent over to step into his breeches and pull them over long, supple legs. Tying the length of twine about her small waist, she was able to keep the breeches from falling to the ground, and then she struggled into his tunic, the shoulders far too wide, the sleeves and hem much too long.

"Better," he said, and her head snapped up.

"You watched me!" she cried.

"Aye."

Tossing her hair off her face, she advanced upon him. Lightning crackled in her eyes. "You have no right to do this," she accused.

"I touched you not."

"Only with your eyes."

"No harm came to you."

"Yet." Dark hair spilled over her skin, and he felt a tug on his heart, a tug that he could not afford.

"As long as you are with me, Megan of Dwyrain, you are safe." He sighed and looked into her eyes. "This I pledge you."

She nearly laughed. "So now you're the noble outlaw, are you?"

He reached forward and strong fingers curled over her tiny fist. "Make no mistake, woman, I am not noble. My intentions for you are far from pure. That you are married to Holt would not stop me from bedding you if I so wanted and you agreed."

"Agreed?" she sputtered, her breath catching. "I would never—oh, for the love of Saint Peter! When my father catches you, he will skin you alive and then lay hot coals on your bare flesh."

"And your husband, what will he do?"

She stopped suddenly and stared at him as if pondering a puzzle she had not yet considered. "He will come after you," she said finally, her voice flat, her teeth sinking into her lower lip. "And, I believe, Sir Kelvin or whoever you be, he will kill you."

Cayley's knees and back ached as she knelt on the cold stones of the chapel floor. Through the open window she heard the sound of the soldiers returning and the creak of wheels as guests left the castle.

Upon Megan's disappearance, her father had collapsed and had to be carried to his chamber. Cayley had stayed at his bedside until the doctor had arrived, then Father Timothy had asked her to join him in prayer for her father's health and her sister's safe return. Cayley, who would rather have been riding with the soldiers searching for Megan, had spent the past few hours on her knees, whispering prayer after prayer.

Candles burned around the altar, their flickering flames reflecting on the portraits of Christ and the Virgin as the priest walked softly around the chapel, his prayer book open in one hand, a rosary clicking in his pockets.

Guests came and went, stopping long enough to cross themselves and whisper their own quick requests to God, but every time Cayley climbed to her feet, Father Timothy laid a patient hand upon her shoulder and searched her face with soulful eyes. "Let us not give up so easily, my child," he'd said, and she'd resumed her position, wondering how much pain she had to endure. "God is listening." Cayley wished He'd listen a little harder.

Cold, tired, and worried, Cayley wanted desperately for her father to awaken in good health. She also needed to know what had become of her sister and why neither Holt nor his soldiers had been able to find Megan and the scoundrel who had abducted her. Cayley had caught a glimpse of the man in black, his bearing resembling that of a devil, and a handsome one at that. Biting her lip, she said another quick prayer and chastised herself for her wanton thoughts, for the truth be known, she thought the stranger far more interesting than Sir Holt or her own beloved Gwayne of Cysgod, the man she'd sworn she would marry years before.

There was something about this ruffian that suggested he could make a woman's legs go weak and her heart pound in a strange and heady cadence. Aye, the outlaw was Satan incarnate; Cayley crossed herself with renewed conviction and prayed.

"That's better," Father Timothy said, laying a hand upon her bent head. His fingers touched her hair and lingered a second too long against the back of her neck. "Surely God will answer your prayers now."

She hoped so.

Nearly an hour later, the doctor announced that Ewan had awakened.

"Never again doubt the power of prayer," Father Timothy said, thankfully relieving her of her prayer duty. On aching legs, she hurried up the stone stairs of the great hall, past guards who had been stationed throughout the keep and were ever vigilant for spies or thugs or strangers. "A bit late," old Rue had said, silently motioning to the guards. "Why close the stable door once the horse has escaped?" But Holt had ordered the men to watch over everyone in the castle, and no one was looked upon without suspicion.

Passing so quickly by the rush lights that they flickered in her wake, Cayley slid through the door of her father's chamber. Only a few candles burned near the bed. A fire was lit, but it had burned down earlier and now there were only red-gold embers glowing in the grate.

"News of your sister?" Ewan asked hopefully, his dim eyes sparking for a second.

"Nay, Father, the soldiers found her not."

He sighed wearily. "Then we must pray for her safe return."

"I have prayed all the long night," Cayley said, sick of the tiresome supplications to a God who was deaf this night. Discovering mossy chunks of dry oak in a basket near the door, she tossed two dry logs onto the fire. Sparking hungrily, greedy flames crackled and hissed over the new fuel.

"Holt believes that there are those soldiers and servants who are unfaithful to me," Ewan said as he adjusted the furs on his bed with his bony hands. "He claims that the outlaw who invaded our keep had spies within the castle, men who helped him steal your sister away."

"I know not," Cayley said, though she'd sensed a change in the castle these past few months.

Somehow, Cayley thought as she walked to the window and watched the clouds part to show a sliver of moon, the magician was responsible for her sister's abduction as well.

Frowning, she sent up one last prayer. "Keep her safe, Lord. Please, keep her safe."

* * *

The tunic was scratchy and far too large and every one of her bones ached as the first gray streaks of dawn lighted the eastern sky. They had been riding for hours and Dwyrain was miles behind them, somewhere far to the south. She'd not spoken to the outlaw since catching him watching her step into his clothes. Never had a man seen her in such a state of undress; the thought bothered her.

His mount was lagging as they climbed a steep trail that crested a ridge and then eased down to a valley near a winding stream. On the far shore of the brook was the glow of a fire.

"Your camp," she said, dread clamping over her heart.

"Aye."

Laying a hand over his, she drew up on the reins. "Why did you do this?" she asked, wanting an answer from this silent man before she had to face those who called him their leader.

His eyes were dark and the lines around them proved that he, too, felt the strain of the long ride. "I came for you," he said, and she felt the jump in her heartbeat, no doubt visible at her neck. Nervously, she licked her lips, and he watched the motion. "I stole you away because you are Holt's bride."

"Why not before the marriage?"

" 'Twould not have been the same."

"Because, in truth, this had naught to do with me."

"Aye."

"So I am but a prize with which to barter."

His jaw became hard as iron and she caught a glimmer of regret, leading her to believe that she was seeing a glimpse of another man, one he'd been long before he'd taken the life of the outlaw. She guessed from the conversation they'd had while dancing, the way he'd fit into the skin of a nobleman so easily, the few words they'd exchanged in the forest, that hidden beneath his ill manners and roguish ways was an educated man, one who might be able to read as well as command, one who was shrewd in the ways of the forest as well as in the running of a castle.

Again she asked, "Who are you?"

His smile was positively wicked. "Wolf."

"You took the name of a beast."

He lifted a shoulder.

"And why do you hate Holt?"

"Because he once rode with Tadd of Prydd."

"Tadd of Prydd is dead," she said and felt a tremor of fear.

"Aye."

Her mouth was suddenly dry as sand and her fingers curled into nervous fists. "You killed him."

Wolf's eyes flashed. "I sent him to hell where he belonged."

So he was a murdering rogue. God in heaven, why did she feel safe in his arms? Why had she no fear for her life or her virtue? Why did she feel that she could trust him? Though she'd never met Tadd of Prydd, she'd heard from her father that Tadd had been a cruel leader who met with a well-deserved and painful end. At Wolf's hand.

"I have no argument with you, Megan. Nor with your father. Only Holt, your husband, is my sworn enemy." He eyed her and frowned. "What know you of him?"

"Only that he had been in my father's service for years."

"And before that?"

She shook her head. " 'Tis as if he has no past."

"That's where you're wrong, m'lady," Wolf said, tilting up her chin so she was forced to look into his eyes. "What he doesn't have is a future."

"Because of you?"

"Aye." A muscle jumped in his jaw. "Now, before we meet

my men, I think you should know that we have a rule that there are to be no women in the camp."

"Then what of me?" she asked, eyes narrowing.

"You will dress, think, and act like a man. You will do nothing to distract them. They are to think of you as one of them."

She tossed her glorious mane of hair. "Well, I certainly have the clothes for the part."

"But 'tis not enough." Was there regret in his voice?

She turned to look ahead. "What more could you want from me?"

"Only this, m'lady," he said. "Forgive me." She felt him grab her hair in one hand and then, quick as a starving dog on a shank of meat, he withdrew his knife as if intending to slice the long tresses in one swift swipe.

"Nay!" she cried, her hands flying to her head. He hesitated, his weapon upraised. "You black-hearted beast!" she cried, trying to slide out of the saddle while his arms, strong as new steel, held her against him. Tears of fury burned behind her eyes but she would not give him the satisfaction of letting them spill. "You have no right to treat me this way. No right!"

" 'Tis only hair," he said.

"*My* hair. You have no right. . . . Please do not cut it."

"But 'twill grow."

True, it would grow, but the humiliation, the idea of him taking a part of her without so much as asking, burned hot in her soul. "If you do this, I hope you roast in hell!"

"No doubt I will, m'lady," he said, sheathing his weapon and sighing as he let her long hair fall free. Clucking the horse forward, his eyes dark with self-loathing as they approached the camp, he said again, "No doubt I will."

Three

Megan bit her tongue. She wanted to rant and rave at the devil who'd captured her, to kick and scream at him, but she didn't say a word as they rode into the camp. 'Twas better if he thought she was meek and frightened.

A sharp whistle broke the morning stillness as Wolf's horse emerged from the forest. The outlaw's camp was little more than a clearing by a small stream with several dirty tents and a few wagons scattered around a fire pit.

"I was beginnin' to think ye'd been caught," a thin, short man with a shock of gray hair grumbled. "About time ye decided to return."

"Were ye worried for me, Odell?" Wolf said with a mocking grin that caused the shorter man to blush.

"Me? Worry?" Odell spit on the ground as Wolf swung from the saddle. Before he could help Megan to the ground, she hopped off the stallion's back and stood a distance away from him, her hands still bound, her hair wild about her face. " 'ell's bells, I never worry!"

"Then why were ye askin' about him every time there

was a noise in the woods?" another man, with only one good eye and a patch over the other, teased.

"For the love of—" The thin little man eyed Megan curiously as he changed the subject and said to Wolf, "So this is yer prize," narrowing his eyes as he scratched his head and studied her with a frown of distaste. "Ye gods, what are we going to do with 'er?"

Most of the men edged closer, forming a half-ring about them, and Megan managed to meet each set of curious eyes with her own stare. A sorrier group of outlaws she never wished to see!

"This is Megan of Dwyrain," he said as the men gaped at her. "She is our guest and—"

"Guest?" she repeated, stung and unable to quiet her tongue. "You call me a guest? Was I invited? Did I have a choice of whether I would come with you?"

"Shh—" he said, his blue eyes glinting as the morning mist began to rise.

"Was I treated as a *guest* or as a prisoner? Were my clothes not taken from me? Was I not forced to ride into the forest?" Rage seethed through her and though she knew she should clamp her lips together to appear meek and frightened, she couldn't stop the tirade that came from deep in her soul. "Were not my hands bound and my horse whipped so that it would run off?"

"Ye let a good 'orse get away?" Odell asked, his voice edged with concern.

"I had no choice."

Again Odell spit, this time in disgust, and Megan, though she knew she shouldn't say another word, couldn't keep her jaws clamped together. "If this is how your leader treats a guest, I would hate to think what he does with a prisoner!"

By the time she was finished, Wolf's expression was

deadly, his hands clenched in tight fists, and his bold jaw was jutted and rock hard. "I promised I would not hurt you, Megan," he said with slow measure, each word pronounced as if it was to be the last she would hear in this lifetime, "and I always keep my word. I ask that you do the same."

"You have ripped me away from my home, dragged me away from my marriage feast, and forced me to ride with you here, wherever we are."

"Have you been whipped?" he asked through lips that barely moved.

"Nay." She shook her head and her wild curls brushed her shoulders.

"Beaten?"

"No, but—"

"Raped?"

Her breath caught for a second. "Nay," she whispered.

"Bound except for your hands, which were set free when I knew I could trust you?"

When she didn't answer, he lifted a dark brow. "Nor were you gagged, hauled about like a sack of grain, or touched in a familiar manner. You, m'lady, have been treated as my guest. However, should you disobey me or make trouble with my men, then you will be treated as a prisoner." He pressed his face close to hers, near enough that she could see the angry streaks of gray in his blue eyes. "I mean you no harm, Megan of Dwyrain, but you will do as I say or suffer the consequences."

"You have no right—"

"And as for your husband, if you love him, then you must know that I will do anything in my power to destroy him."

"But why?" Megan asked, her eyes searching his face. What a puzzle he was—gentle one moment, cruel the next.

"Because he did the same to me. Now—" He looked up and found his men, quiet for once, staring openmouthed at the two of them. "Is there nothing to eat? We've been riding all night and our *guest* must be starved."

"Robin caught us some rabbits," Odell ventured. "And there's pike from the stream and bread we stole from . . ." His voice drifted off and he cleared his throat. "Let me get the fires going."

"But first, introductions," Wolf insisted, naming them each to Megan. Odell, the older scamp who wondered about Wolf giving up her house and was tossing dry leaves and twigs onto the warm coals, looked harmless enough, though she wouldn't trust him with the truth. The others—Jagger, who appeared tough and mean-tempered; Peter, with only one eye; Bjorn, blond and muscular; as well as several others. Last in the group was Robin, a boy of no more than 12 who could only stare at her and swallow hard, his Adam's apple bobbing like a leaf upon a rippling stream. His face, beneath a thatch of dark hair, turned three shades of red when at last he spoke, and upon saying her name, his voice cracked. The rest of the men laughed and made great sport, but the poor lad ducked away hurriedly, finding an excuse to slip into the privacy of the forest.

Odell had already constructed a spit over the glowing coals, and soon two rabbits were roasting, sending the scent of sizzling meat through the naked trees and bracken. Megan's stomach growled and she heard a great flapping of wings in the branches of an oak tree overhead. Looking up, she spied an owl seated near the trunk, its neck twisted so that he could view her.

"Well, I'll be buggered," Odell muttered. "Look who's back!"

"He's been here before?" Megan asked.

"Aye, lately." Odell raised his eyes up at the huge bird. " 'E's a bother, if you ask me. Bad luck."

"That's an old wives' tale," Peter put in, but he, too, glanced up at the bird in vexation. "All he wants is our breakfast."

"Sorry, 'e'll 'ave to be cookin' 'is own. I'm not wastin' my time sweatin' over an open fire for some bloody damned bird. Go on," Odell yelled, raising his hands and flapping them wildly. "Shoo away, ye overgrown pigeon. Off with ye!"

The owl only blinked and settled his head into his neck feathers.

"Ah, who cares about ye anyway," Odell complained, turning back to the charring meat, frowning as the grease drizzled onto the coals.

"Come," Wolf said, once the men had gone back to their tasks. Some hunted, some whittled, some sharpened weapons, others gathered wood or tended to the horses. One man was carefully cleaning the blades of daggers and swords, and the boy, Robin, cast several nets into the stream.

"Come with me," Wolf ordered, then led her to the largest tent situated near the forest's edge. "This is where you'll be sleeping," he said and Megan heard Odell, from the fire pit, give a snort of laughter.

"Whose tent is it?" she asked, but she knew the answer.

"Mine."

Her silly heart fluttered. "And where will you be?" she asked, lifting a dark brow and crossing her arms under her breasts.

His smile was that of a rake and her pulse thundered as he said, "I'll be outside, m'lady, guarding the door, but if you try to escape, then I'll be forced to sleep inside with you to make sure you stay until your husband comes for you." His gaze touched hers and she lost her breath. "Where I sleep—how close to you—'tis all up to you."

"Who was the outlaw?" Holt demanded of the commander of Ewan's troops, a tall gaunt-looking soldier who never smiled. Connor was his name, and he had no family and no friends; he was a solitary sort who kept to himself. He gave a few of the men the willies. But the tall man was smarter than the rest of the lazy scum that were supposed to guard Dwyrain, and Holt needed his help. Now, Connor was checking the chain mail that had been cleaned and was hanging on pegs in the armory. "And don't tell me the rogue's name was Kelvin McBrayne, for I know better."

"Nay, he was not McBrayne," the guard said, fingering the tiny links, the metal clinking softly. "He looked more like . . . well . . . 'tis not possible."

"What?"

"Years ago, I rode with Strahan Hazelwood at Abergwynn, and the younger brother to Baron Garrick was a hotheaded lad who was eager for battle." Lost in private thoughts, Connor moved from the mail to a wall of swords, the finest in all of Dwyrain. Old Ebert, sitting on a cask near the door and fixing links on another mail tunic, watched as Connor picked up a sword and tested its blade. "This boy, Ware, disappeared in one of the many battles at that time. Rode his horse over the cliff and into the sea. Never heard from again. Thought to be dead."

"And now resurrected?" Holt sneered.

Connor lifted a shoulder. "I know not, but the outlaw who came so boldly here knew how to act the part of a nobleman. His bearing, 'twas much like Garrick of Abergwynn."

Holt turned this information over in his mind. A rogue

nobleman, but why would Ware of Abergwynn have any grudge against him? They'd never met, and Holt was certain Megan's abduction was aimed at him rather than Ewan—elsewise why do it on the wedding day? "This man—this outlaw—Ware or whoever else he may be, has spies within the castle walls."

Connor's head snapped. His fingers tightened over the hilt of the sword. "Spies?" he said, but Holt guessed it was not the first time that particular thought had crossed Connor's fertile mind.

"Elsewise how could he have got in alone?" Holt lifted a small sleek dagger with a bone handle, testing its weight. It fit well into his palm. " 'Tis your job, Connor, to ferret out the spies, find who they be, how they know the outlaw, and bring them to me."

"What if I fail?"

"Do not."

"What if I discover them, but their tongues will not be loosened?"

Holt turned slowly and faced the thin man. "There are ways to convince a man to talk. Some men do not do well with pain, others are more likely to speak if they think a loved one may be seriously maimed, still others can be convinced by bribery or by desire for a woman. I care not how you find the truth," he said. "Do whatever it takes and you will be rewarded."

"With what?"

"What is it you want?" Holt asked, expecting to hear an exorbitant sum.

"A woman."

"Is that all?" Holt was relieved. Women were easier to part with than gold.

"Not just any woman, Sir Holt," Connor said, his eyes

slitting in eager anticipation. "I want the daughter of Ewan."

Holt's temper flared and he grabbed the soldier by his throat. Shoving him hard against the wall, knocking over a cask of sand, he growled, "Do not test me. Megan is mine."

" 'Tis not Megan I want," Connor said, laughing despite the strong fingers at his throat. "Nay, 'tis the second daughter, the one with hair of gold."

"Cayley."

"Aye. If I find the spies in Dwyrain and they lead to the return of your wife, then I want the lady Cayley."

"As your wife."

Connor's nostrils flared. "Nay, m'lord, I want her for my whore."

". . . to be robbed of yer wife on yer weddin' day." Red, one of the guards stationed at the door of the keep, was eyeing the peddlers, farmers, and hunters riding into the castle while observing some of the late-staying guests who were leaving at last. Red had always had an ear for gossip, so Cayley, on her way to her father's chamber, tarried in the hallway, listening to what the men were saying behind Ewan's back. " 'Tis a shame, say what?" Red continued, speaking to a tall soldier with eyes as flat as the stones on the keep's smooth floor. "To be thinkin' all day that you'll be weddin' your wife and then to have her snatched away so some outlaw can 'ave his way with 'er, and don't try and tell me that the lady's virtue will be intact when she returns. She's a pretty one, eh, and what man with blood flowing through his veins wouldn't want a go at 'er?"

"You think she was stolen to become an outlaw's whore?" the tall man said in a raspy voice that caused Cayley's skin to crawl.

"I'm not sayin' that was the reason she was taken, but I'll

be bettin' my last piece o' gold that someone besides Holt bedded her last night."

"If so, that someone will pay and pay dearly," the taller soldier replied. "Holt will not stand for it."

"Aye, Connor," Red agreed. "And methinks 'e might blame 'is wife as well. Even if she put up a fight and the man raped her, Sir 'Olt's not a forgiving man."

Cayley's stomach turned over, and she again prayed that her sister was safe.

Shouts filled the air.

"Who's at the gate?" Red asked.

"Maybe the outlaw's been caught."

Cayley's heart beat like a madman's drum.

There was a loud cry from the sentry and both soldiers rushed down the steps. Cayley, her blood cold as the bottom of the moat, slid out from the shadows and hurried through the open door and down the wet steps. Her boots sank into the mud of the inner bailey, but still she ran forward. Soldiers were dragging a half-dressed man up the path leading to the great hall.

"Call for Sir Holt!" one of the knights ordered Red. "We've got a man who claimed he was attacked by the outlaw!

"So you're Kelvin of Hawarth," Holt said, tearing off a piece of bread and handing it to the blond man his men had found wandering through the forest not far from the castle. Nearly naked, half frozen, his lips blue as midnight, he'd been discovered by two of Holt's men who were looking for the outlaw.

"Aye, my older brother is Osric, the baron, and Sheena is my niece," he said, shivering in the great hall. He sat on a bench near the fire, warming his back through the blanket that was wrapped around him. A proud man, and impetuous, he was embarrassed as he told his tale. "I was on my way to the wedding when a bastard jumped me, put a knife to my throat, gagged and stripped me, then tied me to a tree. All the while he's doin' this, he's thankin' me for the fine clothes and invitation to the wedding. Jesus God, I thought my life was over!"

He paused to chew the crusty bread. "Hours later, in the black of the night, an old man comes up to me, tells me I'm lucky not to be dead, and steals my horse, leavin' me in the freezin' rain. I started walking, probably in circles mostly, and didn't find the road until this morning."

Holt scowled as he cut a piece of cheese with the cruel little dagger he'd taken from the armory earlier. "You knew this man not?"

"Nay, never seen 'im before in my life, but before I left Hawarth, the sheriff warned me of bands of thugs raiding the roads. There's a man they call Wolf, dark of hair, with a split eyebrow, who is the leader of a group of cast-outs. They say the men know each other only by a name they chose and no women or children are allowed in the group. The men are fiercely loyal to Wolf, the only one of the lot who can read, a man who some claim was of noble birth but was cast out for some past sin."

"Think you that you were the victim of this Wolf?"

Kelvin took a bite of the cheese, then washed it down with a long swallow of wine. "Aye," he said with a crisp nod. Wiping his mouth with the back of his hand, he scowled. "Shamed me, he did. Left me to rot, though the other member of his band—at least I think the old bugger was one of the thief's men—did release me and only steal my horse. A wicked one, that, with an evil cackle that sounded like it came from the bowels of hell." Shuddering, he looked Holt square in the eye. "I scare not easily. My brother claims I'm too bold and reckless for my own good, but that night alone, strapped to the base of a tree wearing naught but my braies, hearing bats and owls and all sorts of creatures scuttling through the brush, I was scared, let me tell you. What if some beast had come by, or another murdering thug? I had not my sword or hands that I could use. Helpless, I was, and 'tis a feeling I'll not want to have again any too soon. Even after the old one cut me loose, I was near naked. If I ever come across the black-heart who did this to me, I swear I'll run him through and take God's punishment."

Holt believed him. The man felt as humiliated as he did. So Holt gained another ally in his fight against the outlaw. "This time I will go after him myself," Holt said. "You may ride with me if you like, but make no mistake, we will not return empty-handed."

Kelvin grinned. "Aye," he said. "If you can spare some clothes and weapons, I'll gladly hunt down the bastard."

"Are ye hungry?" the lad, Robin, asked her. He was fair of skin with freckles all about his face, round blue eyes, and teeth that were far from straight, but his smile was true and the blush that stained his cheeks caused Megan to return his grin.

"Aye, a bit."

In truth, she was starved. 'Twas evening. Darkness had collected over the land, bringing with it a soft mist and quiet fog that hung close to the ground. Though she'd done little but explore the camp while thinking of ways to escape, she was hungry again. The charred rabbit and fish had been hours ago and though she'd been offered a goodly portion, she'd barely touched the burned, tasteless food. Odell lacked Cook's spices and sense of timing, though no one else acted as if it mattered. The men had devoured the tough meat as if the food were a great feast, and Wolf, while he'd sliced off a shank of rabbit and eaten it with his knife, had watched her, apparently amused at her distaste for the meal.

Since then, she'd barely seen him. He'd been in one tent or the other, off riding or talking by the stream with his men. There were many questions asked of him, along with sidelong looks cast her way from each of the men. 'Twas more than obvious that many of the band resented her. Others, like charming Robin, were eager to make her acquaintance.

Wolf had not insisted she be bound. All he had asked was that she stay in the camp in his sight. When the time had come for her to relieve herself, he'd walked with her into the woods and waited on the other side of a copse of trees until she was finished. 'Twas awkward and embarrassing, but better than having her wrists or ankles tied.

The men in the camp were an odd lot, solitary sorts whom she suspected were outcasts either by their own choice or the choosing of their loved ones. Cutthroats, pickpockets, robbers, or murderers, she knew not. No one, as far as she could tell, discussed his crimes. Past lives were never mentioned, another rule of the band. Just as there were to be no women in the group, there were also no secrets shared about crimes, homes, or loves.

"Tell me about your leader," she said to Robin after he'd brought her a trencher of beans and fish that again was burned. Wolf caught her eye as he spoke to the tall blond one—Bjorn—then turned back to his conversation.

The men ate at will. Whenever their job was finished, they stopped by the fire where Odell offered up his pitiful fare. Wolf had barely eaten but he was unable or unwilling to stop long enough for a meal. There were no prayers of thanks sent to God, no formality whatsoever.

Robin sat on a stone next to hers by the stream. "Wolf took me in."

"You mean stole you away from your mother," she said, eating with her fingers as Robin did.

"Nay, I have no ma," Robin said. "She died birthin' me."

"Oh . . . I'm sorry."

He lifted a bony shoulder. " 'Tis no matter. I lived with me uncle and aunt until they died of the sickness and then Brother Anthony, he wanted me to work with the monks at the abbey, but . . . well, I took to stealin' and the sheriff caught up with me. If not fer Wolf, I woulda been cast into the prison at Hawarth."

"But Wolf found you."

"Aye. I know not how, or why, but he kidnapped me right from under the jailer's nose." Chuckling at the thought, Robin ate hungrily.

"Have you no family?"

"Not since me auntie died." He had the reverence to cross himself, then polished off the remains of his trencher. When she paused after a bite, he pointed at her uneaten portion of beans. "Will ya be eatin' that, m'lady?"

Megan shook her head. Though she wasn't finished, she could see that the lad was still ravenous and she remembered Bevan when he was but 12 or 13. It made no matter how much he ate at mealtimes or that he stuffed himself until he belched loudly, her brother could not get enough food to last him from one meal to the next. "Please, if you would finish it for me," she said, handing him the remains of her trencher. "I would not want to offend Odell."

He grinned widely and within seconds, beans and stale bread had disappeared. As he licked his fingers, smacking his lips, she tried to ask him a few more questions about Wolf, but the boy had nothing further to add and went off in search of more scraps. 'Twas obvious that this ragged band's leader was as much a mystery to his men as he was to her.

She should hate the outlaw, despise him, loathe him. For the injustices she'd been made to suffer at his hand, she should be plotting to turn him in to the sheriff herself.

Washing her hands in the icy depths of the stream, she glanced over her shoulder and watched as he walked between the tents, the light from the campfire casting gold shadows upon a hard face that was rigid and unforgiving and battle-scarred.

She had to remind herself that he was a black-heart, a man who should be flogged for snatching her away from her father. But a part of her wasn't convinced, the small, feminine part of her that found the rogue attractive and appealing. That traitorous female part reminded her that were it not for Wolf, she would today be a virgin no longer, in more than name the wife of Holt, perhaps already carrying his child. The thought revolted her and her stomach, laden with Odell's tasteless fare, threatened to purge itself.

For saving her from her marriage, she was grateful to the demon, although she had to make good her escape; if not, he would ransom her back to her husband and she would be worse off than before she was kidnapped.

She'd steal a horse. Wolf owed her one for setting Shalimar free, so she'd take his best steed as well as some food and these clothes he'd given her, tattered and large though they be.

Plotting her escape, she stared into the water's inky depths. She tried to see her image in the black ripples, but the campfire's light barely gave her enough illumination to view her pale face surrounded by wild, untamed red-brown hair. She'd hardly pass for a boy, but then she didn't have the bearing of a woman of noble birth. She pushed a shank of unruly curls behind her ear and turned her head to the side.

"So here ye be."

Wolf's voice startled her and she jumped, losing her balance and half falling into the brook. She caught herself with her hands, but created ripples that distorted her image. He was on the far side of the creek, one boot propped against an exposed root of a willow tree, his back resting against the trunk, arms folded over his chest, his dark clothes blending into the night.

"You scared me."

"Because you wandered too far from camp. 'Tis dark and not safe for you alone."

"Oh, don't tell me," she mocked, rising to her feet and wiping her hands on the long hem of the tunic. "You fear I might be abducted by some outlaw who would steal me away and demand ransom for my safe return?"

His laugh was cold as the night. "You're a sassy one. 'Tis no wonder your father wanted you married off."

"Back to that, are we?" she said, frowning as she wondered what demons plagued this man who had so boldly stolen her from her father's castle. "Tell me—why do you hate Sir Holt?"

"What know you of him?"

"Very little."

"But you agreed to marry him and plan to live the rest of your life as his wife." He made a sound of disgust in the back of his throat.

"He has been loyal to my father—"

"He would cut out your father's heart like that," he said, snapping his fingers.

Genuine fear gripped her insides. "Nay—" she said, but her protest was weak.

"Fear not, m'lady, I'll have you back safely in his arms before a fortnight passes—"

"No!" The word slipped out before she could think, and she had to bite her tongue to keep from speaking her true thoughts, which, she was sure, this outlaw would turn against her.

"Want you not to return to Dwyrain?" he asked, and the wind picked up, riding on the current of the stream.

"Aye, but—"

He waded across the creek, mindless of the depths of the icy water that swirled and splashed about his boots, his gaze fastened to hers as if her eyes opened deep into her soul. Oh, what a fool she was. She should not let this man have the tiniest glimmer of what she thought. 'Twould be dangerous for him to know too much about her, to give him that power.

"Why did you agree to marry Holt?" he asked, his voice low.

" 'Tis no concern of yours."

"Why?" he said, climbing up the short bank to stand in front of her. He was nearly a head taller than she and he craned his neck downward to stare deep into her eyes. "Do you love him?"

Her throat closed in on itself.

With one clenched fist, he propped up her chin, forcing her to look into his blue, blue eyes. Shadowed in the dark, they glimmered for a second with some deep and strange emotion that touched her before it disappeared. "Tell me."

A new emotion, one she couldn't name, started deep in her chest, causing her heart to drum and her pulse to pound and her breath to catch. Though she knew she was making a mistake by confiding in him, she admitted the truth. "Nay, I . . . I love him not. 'Twas my father's wish that I marry Holt."

"And you agreed?"

"I had no say."

His eyes narrowed thoughtfully, as if he didn't believe her. "I've heard of you, Megan of Dwyrain," he admitted, his face so close to hers she saw red-gold pinpoints of light—reflections from the campfire—in his eyes. She stood as if rooted to the earth, unable to move, unwilling to protest. " 'Tis said you have a mind of your own, that you do as you choose, that you ride in and out of the castle gates without a guard whenever you so desire."

"Not always."

"I've seen you myself, while I was waiting for my chance to steal you away."

"You were watching me?" she asked, thunderstruck. How long had he sought and plotted his revenge?

"Aye."

Anger took control of her tongue. "You are a fiend!"

His smile was touched with self-condemnation. "So I've been told." He studied her again and she wanted to squirm from beneath his scrutinizing eyes. "Your father gives you much freedom, many choices, pampers you and lets you hunt in the forests and ride far from the castle gates. Yet you say he chose the man for you."

"What concern is it of yours?" she snapped, unable to stop seething. But what reason did she have to hide the truth? If his revenge was against Holt, mayhap 'twas better if she admitted that she, too, trusted not the man she'd taken as her husband.

"Yea, 'tis true," she said, pursing her lips. "But my father is no longer young, nor well. He talks of dying and meeting my mother and brother and sister soon in heaven. He fears that my other sister and I will be able not to care for ourselves, that we need men to protect us."

He snorted as if the thought were that of a simpleton. "Thinks he that you are weak?"

"Nay, not just me. All women."

Wolf laughed. "Not always and surely not you."

She favored him with the hint of a smile as he rubbed his cheek where she'd slapped him earlier that evening.

"Father wants a grandson. He decided that because I had no suitors that pleased me and was not hasty to accept a proposal, he would pick a husband for me."

"So he chose Holt."

"Aye," she said, sliding him a glance. "He chose Sir Holt because of his bravery and loyalty and courage."

"Then Ewan must be deaf, mute, and blind as well as stupid," Wolf said. "Your husband is a weak coward whose only loyalty is to himself."

"He is not my husband," she blurted, then bit her tongue.

"Nay?" Wolf mocked. "Did you not stand up at the altar and pledge yourself to him?"

"Aye," she admitted, feeling weak. Squeezing her eyes shut, she gritted her back teeth, remembering how soft her voice had sounded, how difficult it was to say two simple words. "I do" had come after tense, silent moments when Holt's nostrils had quivered in rage and her father had pleaded with her mutely, his cloudy eyes beseeching hers.

"Then are you not his wife?"

"Yes!" The horrid word echoed through the forest.

Instead of being pleased, Wolf was vexed, his mouth blade-thin, his lips flat against his teeth. " 'Tis a pity," he said, "for this husband of yours will do naught but give you pain."

"You know not," she accused, but his eyes were dark as

the black waters at the bottom of a well. "Tell me," she whispered. "What is it you know of him?"

Wolf stared at her as if about to say more, then changed his mind. He glanced at the sky, black and starless. "Come," he said gruffly. " 'Tis time for sleep."

"You know something of my husband."

"Many things."

"Yet you will not tell me."

"Ask Holt," Wolf said angrily, "about Tadd of Prydd and the fisherman's daughter."

"I'm asking you."

"Oh, for the love of Saint Peter. Come, woman, you tire me." His skin was stretched so tightly over his face that his jawbone showed white and his eyes had darkened to an evil, murky color that warned her she was wading too far into treacherous waters.

Even so, she could not hold her wayward tongue. "But I needs know—"

"When the time is right," he bit out, fury rolling from him in waves.

She begged him to tell her more, but he refused and took hold of her hand, pulling her behind him, dragging her toward his tent. Several men working around the campsite sent curious glances her way as she argued with him. There were whispers and laughter and she imagined she was the subject of their ribald jokes and meaningful knowing glances. Her cheeks burned with color as he pushed her into his tent then closed the flap behind them.

The space was small, but in the light from the campfire she saw not only the pallet in the center, but also a chest and two sacks, one she recognized as holding her wedding dress. Several tools were stacked near the doorway and she spied a hand ax and a coil of thick rope.

Whirling upon her, he planted his hands firmly on his hips and stood between her and the doorway. "Never!" he said, his voice without compromise, his nostrils flared. "Never again defy me in front of my men."

"Why not?"

"It shows a lack of respect."

"But stealing a bride on her wedding day does not?"

Muttering a curse, he yanked on her hand and twirled her against him. Before she could break free, both of his arms held her in a grip that threatened the air in her lungs. "Do not challenge me, Megan." His voice was low, his lips nearly brushing her temple as he gave her a tiny shake. She could barely breathe, and as the light from the campfire seeped through the walls, she met his hard glare with a mutinous stare of her own.

"Do not order me about like some addled scullery maid."

"I have treated you well."

"You—you have treated me with only contempt."

His eyes drifted to her lips and she quivered in anticipation. They were alone in the dark, standing near the edge of a single pallet covered with thick furs. Megan counted her heartbeats and watched as his throat moved.

"You—you promised that I would sleep alone," she said, suddenly mindful of her virtue.

"Aye, and I keep my word," he said as her breasts rose and fell against the hard wall of his chest.

Her pulse was pounding in her head and when she licked her dry lips, he groaned then dropped his arms from her quickly, stepping back. "Mother of God," he whispered, running both his hands through his black hair. "What kind of woman are ye?"

"A captive," she said, her voice breathless.

"If I'm not here with you, what's to prevent you from sneaking away?"

"I would not—"

"Do not lie, Megan. You've been planning to escape since you first arrived. I saw you eyeing the horses and searching the woods. You've watched the men in the camp all day and even this night, hoping you'll discover where the sentries are posted and who they be."

Swallowing hard, she mentally kicked herself. How had she been so obvious?

He reached into a bag on the floor and withdrew a length of soft cord. "Give me your hands."

"Nay."

A muscle worked at the edge of his jaw. "Would you rather I force you?"

"Please, Wolf, do not bind me," she pleaded, and he hesitated, his eyes searching hers, his lips folding in on themselves.

"And I would have your word that you will not try to escape?"

"As God is my witness," she said, hoping the Lord didn't strike her dead for the lie.

He looped the cord through both his hands, stretching it tight. "Then I'll give you a choice, Megan of Dwyrain," he said slowly. "You can sleep alone with your wrists bound. Or—"

"Or?" she repeated, her heart knocking crazily, the air in the tent suddenly too heavy to breathe.

"Or I will make my bed in here with you and you can sleep unbound." One of his dark eyebrows lifted insolently and she quivered inside at the eager gleam in his deep blue eyes. "So tell me, m'lady," he urged, snapping the cord again, "what will it be?"

Four

Blankets tossed over his legs, Wolf leaned against the trunk of a tree and stared at his tent. His men were scattered about the fire, some in temporary shelters of their own, while others, the few who could stand no walls, were curled up as he was, beneath the shelter of a tree, the hilts of their swords and knives in their closed fists. Heath, Cormick, and Dominic slept fitfully, as if they'd spent too many years in closed dungeons behind iron bars. Guards were posted, their eyes searching the darkness as, ever vigilant, they tended the fire and walked around the edge of the camp.

Wolf was certain Megan would try to escape. Would he not attempt the same if he were the one who had been abducted? No small cord around his wrists would stop him. Nay, he didn't blame her for wanting to return to her home, even if it were to share a bed with Holt of Prydd. His stomach turned at the thought and a new emotion, one akin to hot jealousy, crept through his blood. He didn't like the feeling, for he prided himself on his solitude, for his need for no one else, especially a woman.

So she would try to escape and he would catch her and then he would end up sleeping in the tent with her, on the same pallet, under the same furs and blankets with her breathing softly in his ear, her body warm and comforting.

'Twould be hell. Even at the thought of it, his lust stirred. He'd been long without a woman, and none had touched him as had this one with her condemning golden eyes and tongue as sharp as a fine dagger's blade, this woman Holt had chosen for his bride. Saints in heaven, 'twas his curse to lust after his enemy's woman.

He'd planned to cut her hair, hoping to make her appear more manlike, to disguise her if they were accosted by Holt's men and also so that she would be less attractive, less feminine, so as not to distract his men or himself. But he had not been able to go through with it, and 'twould not have mattered, for hers was a beauty that was not bits and pieces—eyes, hair, lips—but all-encompassing. He attempted to force his thoughts to a different path, but his wayward mind would have none of it. He could not concentrate on plans for moving the camp, or hunting for the next meal, or training Robin with a sword; no, his mind was determined to settle on Megan, with her wide eyes the color of honey and red-brown hair spread out around her face. The curls were thick and rich and he wanted to bury his face in their scented strands and lose himself in the wonder that was this woman.

Yea, the thought of sleeping with her held more than a little appeal. He dug the heel of his boot into the ground as he remembered the few glimpses he'd caught of her breasts, pale and full, her nipples dark, ripe spheres beckoning his touch. He'd seen the length of her spine as she'd shed her wedding dress, the gentle valley that curved to split her small, round rump.

Stifling a groan, he shifted, damning his manhood that had sprung to life at the thought of coupling with her. How glorious 'twould be to join his body to hers, to thrust deep into the warm well of her womanhood, to collapse on those soft, welcoming breasts.

Aside from the pure physical comfort he would receive, Wolf considered there to be no greater humiliation for his old enemy than for Wolf to steal Holt's wife's virginity. Even if she were not a virgin, 'twould be an insult of the highest order for a hated adversary to take her before she could lie with her husband.

Smiling in the darkness, Wolf savored that particular thought, but an old, unwanted streak of nobility, one he hadn't been able to discard no matter how hard he'd tried, wouldn't allow him to attempt to seduce the woman. Though she was a fool for marrying Holt, his intent was not to hurt her. His grin faded. Such a simple plan was suddenly complicated. He should ransom her now rather than wait. For though he enjoyed the thought of Holt twisting in the wind, not knowing where his bride was—whether she was alive or dead—keeping her was dangerous, not only because of the threat of Holt's men finding them, but for other reasons as well—reasons that touched his heart and frightened him. In a few days . . . then he'd contact his old enemy and ransom the feisty woman.

He picked up a stick on the ground and idly shredded the bark from the softer white wood. Robin had offered to stand guard at Megan's door and now, seated near the flap, his arms crossed over his knees, his head lolling, he was falling asleep. With a snort, the boy shook his head to awaken, but within seconds his head was falling forward again.

Robin wanted so much to be a man; he was eager to

prove himself and would someday make a challenge for the leadership of their outlaw band.

Wolf understood a boy's need to be considered an adult far better than anyone, including Robin, could know. He, too, had been a young eager pup, ever ready to take command of Abergwynn, the castle he'd left long ago in the life he'd shed.

Now, obviously, Robin was fascinated with Megan, the first woman the lad had seen and spoken with since Wolf had saved him from the jailer. Wolf knew the emotion. 'Twas all he could do to keep his hands off her and see that his men, a randy, vicious lot, did, as well.

One of his men, Simon, had once bragged of taking a woman by force and Wolf's justice had been swift. Within seconds he'd knocked away Simon's weapon and pressed the blade of his sword to Simon's long, skinny neck. Simon had been tall and strong, his face pockmarked, his eyes never warm. He'd had arguments and fights with some of the men, and so it was with no regret that Wolf had stripped him of his clothes, horse, and weapons; banished him from the band; and left him, tied and bound, naked as the day he was born, screaming obscenities in the middle of a town to the east of Erbyn.

Simon had sworn vengeance, spitting and kicking and vowing to slice Wolf to ribbons, but Wolf had not worried. Simon was a coward, a bully who loved to prove he was stronger than those weaker—especially women.

Wolf had no stomach for rape and he would not let any of his men near Megan for fear that they might not be able to control themselves around a woman. There would be brawls and harsh words, all because they would want her attention. 'Twas the way of men—the curse of being born male. Even young Robin was already smitten.

This was one plan he hadn't thought through well enough. Was he not as bad as his men—mayhap worse? Though he would defend her honor to the death rather than see her taken by force, was he not, even now, planning her seduction? The thought of making love to Megan over and over again was a welcome balm, and he felt that if given enough time, he could seduce her. But seduction thought out so carefully, planned without her knowledge, was probably not so much better than forcing her. Even though stealing Holt's wife's virtue would be great revenge, a way to further humiliate his enemy, and it appealed to Wolf's sense of justice for the rape of Mary, he couldn't, *wouldn't*, abuse Megan thus.

Disgusted, he tossed the shredded stick aside and wiped his hands. Force and rape were what had driven him to become an outlaw in the first place, though Megan knew nothing of his past. 'Twas years before when he was just beginning to be a man, during the time when Strahan of Hazelwood, his cousin, had nearly succeeded in stealing Abergwynn from Wolf's older brother, Garrick. It had been Wolf, known as Ware in that other lifetime, who had been left in charge of the castle while Garrick was away. Ware had never doubted his ability to command and his own pride and foolishness had been his downfall. He'd lost control of Abergwynn to the enemy and then, while he and his best friend Cadell were fleeing for their lives, they had been chased to the cliffs rising high over the sea. Rather than surrender, Ware had chosen death, urging his mount over the edge of those sharp bluffs and hurtling into the blackness wherein Cadell had already fallen.

He'd thought he was dead when he awoke in a fisherman's hut and the sweetest woman in the world, the man's daughter, Mary, pressed cool cloths to his head. Her hands were soft, her eyes trusting, her lips pink and always turned into a kind smile. She whispered words of encouragement and told him that she'd never lost faith, that she was certain with enough kindness and prayer he would awaken.

He was in love with her from the moment she'd asked him how he felt. He'd blinked his eyes open and even in his fuzzy vision her image had smiled down on him. "I knew you'd wake up," she said in a voice as soft and pure as the first light of dawn. "God would not take one so young and handsome."

She'd tended to him and he'd strengthened, living with her and her father, Alan, learning how to sail and fish, how to read the storms gathering in the distance, becoming accustomed to the gentle swaying of the boat. 'Twas easy to shed his other life, to leave his past and his shame on the rocky shoals beneath the cliffs of Abergwynn. Though his memory returned, he hadn't been able to face his brother. Aside from the guilt of allowing his family to think him dead, he was content and in love—so innocently and completely in love.

He had planned to wed Mary, but before he was able, Tadd of Prydd, cruel firstborn son of Baron Eaton, had ridden through their village and altered the course of their lives forever. Mary, while selling fish in the market, had unwittingly caused Tadd to notice her, and after only one glimpse of her, he'd decided that he would claim her—not for a wife, nay, but for a night's sport and pleasure.

That evening, Tadd and a few cruel-faced soldiers burst into their tiny hut. Swords drawn, expressions murderous, they slammed the door shut behind them and waited for their leader's command. Tadd's face was red from ale. He drew up a stool, smiled evilly, and announced that he wanted only a few hours with Mary, then he and his men would be on their way. He'd pay the fisherman for his trouble, but Mary's father, a man of uncommon strength of character and faith in deliverance from the Lord, had refused, placing himself squarely between the soldiers and his daughter.

"You're being foolish," Tadd warned him, as Ware, too, tried to intervene.

"Leave here," Ware had ordered, but Tadd was quick and armed. His sword struck swiftly, cleaving Ware's eyebrow and knocking him into a watery darkness where he couldn't move.

Tears streaming down his leathery face, Mary's father tried to rescue her, and for his efforts his arm was severed at the elbow by Tadd's sword, in a swift blow that left him howling in blind pain. He fell to the floor and Ware, barely conscious and lying in his own blood, thought Alan dead.

With all his strength, Ware struggled to his feet, but the blackness overcame him and he fell again. No amount of prodding could urge his pained muscles to support him.

Mary's horrified screams rang in his ears, and through damaged eyes, he saw murky images of Tadd moving toward her. Ware screamed but no sound came from his' mouth. He tried to climb to his knees, but his legs were no longer under his control. The darkness was like a warm cloak, offering to blind him from the pain, but he fought the urge to give up the battle. Desperate, his own ragged breathing filling his head, he scrabbled for Tadd's sword, which the bastard had discarded as he'd untied his breeches. Eyes gleaming, Tadd stalked Mary, who was on the floor, trying to back away, her hands and feet failing her as they slipped in her father's blood.

"Please, m'lord," Mary had pleaded, tears streaming from her eyes, her body quaking. "Do not do this."

" 'Twill be pleasant, girl. You will enjoy it."

"Nay, I cannot—"

"Ah, but you will," Tadd said smoothly, then turned to Holt. "Hold her!"

"No!"

Ware grasped for the sword but his muscles would not move. The shadowy fog threatened him again.

Tadd's breeches fell to his ankles as Holt wrested Mary to Alan's bed.

No! No! No! Ware's mind screamed, but no words passed his lips. *Merciful God, help her! Let me save her! Do not let this happen!*

The floor was sticky with his blood and Ware stretched, only to be swept away again, but he wasn't so far gone that he couldn't hear her horrifying, bloodcurdling screams or the smack of flesh on skin as Tadd slapped her.

I'll kill you, I swear on my life that I'll kill you!

Holt held her arms over her head while Tadd, undeterred by her kicks or screams, mounted her, grunting in pleasure, his fat white rump jiggling as he rutted hard and fast, undeterred as she screamed in pain. Ware was powerless. He swam in and out of the darkness that was his mind while a leering Holt pinned Mary to her father's bed.

Gritting his teeth, he climbed to his knees, crying a hoarse, "Get off her, you sick bastard," and received a sharp kick to the face from one of the soldiers.

With a cry, he finally lost all consciousness. When he awakened, he realized that again he had failed, just as he'd failed when he'd lost Abergwynn to Strahan. But this was worse—this was not a castle; not a moat, and walls, and locked gates. This was a woman's very soul, her heart. His shame was immense.

When finally he could pull himself to his feet and stagger

over to her, he found his Mary, his beautiful, sweet, loving Mary, cowering in a corner, holding a bloodied blanket over her bruised body and allowing no one to come close or touch her. Trembling, spittle and blood collecting at the corner of her mouth, her eyes round, her face bruised, she mewed like a helpless, frightened kitten, then hissed and scooted away when he'd tried to touch her.

He'd found more blankets to cover her ripped clothes and her battered body, but though he'd tried only to help her, she'd been afraid to look at him, nor would she ever speak to him again. That day Tadd and Holt had robbed her of more than her virtue; they'd stolen her mind as well. Her father survived long enough to take one last voyage with his daughter. Alan had refused to let Ware join them, and they didn't return. A storm as savage as the wrath of God swept into the town, and Ware waited. With each day that passed, his transformation continued, and when he hadn't seen Mary for over a month, he knew she was gone from him forever.

That was the day that Ware, no longer of Abergwynn, became Wolf the outlaw, a rogue who trusted no man and asked no questions of those who chose to follow him. Having lost all his faith in God as well as trust in his fellow man, he'd given up what few possessions he had acquired and had stolen away to the forests, where he could live life alone and would make no friends.

Eventually, he'd met up with a few tattered wanderers who, like himself, had pasts they could not face, and as their numbers grew, Wolf became the leader. He alone could read, and he, though not as large as some of the men, was more agile and quick and ruthless with his sword. No one challenged him. And no one ever admitted to rape unless they wanted to incur Wolf's legendary and excruciating vengeance.

For the past few years he'd been satisfied with his vagabond, criminal life.

Until now.

Until Megan of Dwyrain had disrupted all his carefully laid plans. He'd had the satisfaction of destroying Tadd of Prydd and he'd thought that ruining Holt would only add to his vindictive fulfillment, but he hadn't considered that he might be attracted to the woman whom Holt had wed.

"Mother of Moses," he grumbled as the damp fog laid in closer about the camp. He should have killed Holt and been done with it, but he'd wanted to wound his old enemy in other, deeper ways. Death was too easy; he wanted Holt to suffer not only the indignity of losing his bride on his wedding day, but of having to search for her and appear the fool when he couldn't find her. Holt would be the laughingstock of everyone at Dwyrain, servants, guests, freemen, and soldiers alike. The news would travel to other castles and baronies as well and Holt's name would command no respect.

Then Wolf would kill him. But not before.

So what of Lady Megan? What was Wolf to do with her? He'd thought that ransoming her would solve his problem, but the very idea of returning her to Holt was unthinkable. There was not enough money in all of Dwyrain's treasury to change his mind. So he was stuck with her.

That particular thought brought an unlikely smile to his lips.

Jovan the apothecary was a short, stooped man who liked gold. Where he squirreled all his money away, Holt could only guess. Jovan wore tattered rags, his hut was a hovel, his horse, barely skin and bones, was a sorry hack with a back so swayed it appeared broken. Whereas some men liked money for what it could buy and spent their gold on fine clothes, jewelry, or women, Jovan hoarded his gold pieces jealously. He found pleasure in owning gold, not in considering what he could buy.

But it mattered not. All Holt cared about was that Jovan was greedy and knew how to keep his mouth shut.

"So we do business again," he said as Holt entered his shop. He hunched over a dirty bench, with a mortar and pestle, his knobby fingers working steadily as he ground some bitter-smelling leaves into a paste. Only one candle burned near him; Jovan would not waste precious wax just to save his eyes.

"Aye." Holt dropped a small leather pouch on the bench. The flame of the candle flickered and Jovan could barely take his eyes off the tiny parcel. His tongue rimmed dry lips and his hands faltered in their work. With a cough, he set the mortar aside.

"And you want the same herbs?" Jovan asked, his eyes gleaming with the thought of a nice, fat payment.

"Yes, the same."

"The price has gone up."

"Not much, old friend," Holt said, eyeing the dusty jars of roots, berries, and leaves.

Jovan reached for the leather pouch, but Holt grabbed hold of his bony wrist. "We understand each other, do we not?"

"No one will know, Sir Holt," Jovan said.

"I was not here."

The apothecary smiled, showing off spaces where there once had been teeth. "I know you only as a knight of Dwyrain, now husband of the baron's daughter. Soon to be baron." Was there the tiniest bit of amusement in his tired old eyes? "I will say that you have never visited my shop."

Holt allowed himself a smile and let go of the old man's

arm. “Take it,” he said of the pouch. “Just make sure your blend is stronger than the last. I have not much time.”

Jovan snorted as he unwrapped the pouch and saw the gold. Quickly, he snatched the purse in a clawlike hand and stowed his prize deep in the folds of his dusty tunic. Surprisingly agile, the old man climbed onto a ladder to reach a high shelf with a hidden door. From the cupboard, he withdrew a clean jar. “I thought ye might be needin’ this,” he admitted, smiling as if he thought he was clever. “It has no taste and will go unnoticed if dropped into food or ale.” He handed Holt the bottle and their gazes collided, each sharing his part of a private secret, each knowing that he couldn’t trust the other.

“Two drops, no more than three, at each meal,” Jovan cautioned. “Elsewise ye’ll bring suspicion on the cook.”

“The man is old already and dying.”

“Aye, but he’s the baron. He will be watched.”

Holt felt an evil grin slide over his face. “I know,” he said. “ ’Tis I who will see that Ewan of Dwyrain is cared for.”

Jovan chuckled and the sound was cold and without any soul. “Then his fate is sealed, and you, sir, will soon be the new baron.”

“That,” Holt said, “is the idea.”

Again Jovan laughed. He rubbed his hands together. “I only hope that I will be rewarded.”

“ ’Twill be done,” Holt said, thinking how easily it would be to get rid of the old man and find his stash of gold and silver. But he could not kill off the apothecary for a while, not until he was certain he didn’t need Jovan’s help in murdering his enemies.

Megan knew he would be waiting for her. As surely as the sun would rise in the east in the morn, Wolf would expect for her to attempt to flee. She had no choice but to try. Silly as it sounded, she was afraid that if she were to stay she might lose her foolish heart to the handsome criminal with the rough edges and hidden nobility. Worse yet, he would ransom her, not to her father, but to Holt, her new husband. Spittle collected in her mouth at the thought of her husband, and she knew she could never return to him.

The cords binding her wrists were not tight, and it was a simple matter to scoot off the pallet and slide over to the side of the tent where she'd seen the tools and the small ax. Silently she slid the cord over the blade, sawing until the twine broke free and she was able to use her hands again.

She wondered where Wolf had positioned himself and decided that he was probably sleeping near the door, so her best chance of avoiding him was to slip out the back. Carefully, she felt around the bottom of the tent, where the cloth walls were stretched tight. There was no room for a snake or mouse to slide through, but with her ax, she could cut a slit in the tent and . . .

She felt him before she saw him. Though she'd not heard the flap move, she sensed his presence.

"I wouldn't," he said.

"Wouldn't what?"

"Come, Megan, act not like I'm a fool. You are not the first prisoner I've kept."

"And I thought I was a guest," she mocked, turning to face him in the blackness that was the tent. Could the man see in the dark? Did he have the hearing of her father's dogs?

" 'Tis time to sleep." His voice was soft and patient and she wanted to crumple into a heap rather than think him kind. His hand reached for hers and she wanted to yank her fingers away.

"Do not touch me," she said, walking the short distance to the pallet. "Leave me alone."

"Nay, Megan, I stay."

"But you can't!"

" 'Tis my tent."

"But—"

"My camp, my rules. Lie down, woman, and argue not. I'm tired and have no patience left." He dropped her hand, snagged a rug from the bed, and sat on the ground, propping himself against the bags.

"The men, they will think that we . . . you and I—"

"What matters what they think?" he said around a yawn. "They are not gossiping old hags who will tattle to your husband."

She tried a new tack. "I won't be able to sleep with you in here."

"You weren't sleeping before."

"But I'll . . . I'll be restless."

"Not I," he said, stretching one arm over his head. "Now, either you lie down alone right now, or I'll come over to the bed and lie with you."

Her throat turned to dust at the thought of him sleeping next to her, his arms holding her against the hard contours of his body, his breath warm as summer wind against the back of her neck.

" 'Twould be pleasant," he said.

"Nay."

"Once again, Megan, you have a choice."

Reluctantly she lay down, thinking she couldn't sleep a wink with him so close. Her thoughts would run wild, her mind spin in restless circles, her heart pound with fear. She dragged a fur around her body and within minutes her muscles turned liquid and she closed her eyes, not to open them again until the first light of dawn had broken over the hills to the east and the inside of the tent was filled with a gray light.

He was already awake and watching her, his blue eyes trained on her face, his expression less harsh than before. If anything, she saw puzzlement in his gaze rather than hatred. She blinked and the ghost of a smile played upon his thin lips. "Aye," he said, rubbing his beard-stubbled jaw. "You slept nary a wink."

Feeling foolish, she sat upright and held a fur blanket to her chest as if to cover herself, though she was fully dressed in his clothes.

"Everyone here in the camp earns his keep," he said, rocking to his feet and standing. She'd forgotten how imposing he was, how his mere presence filled the tent.

"Aye."

"Peter looks after the horses, Jagger tends to the weapons, even young Robin hunts and fishes."

"And what do you do?" she threw out.

"Capture fair maidens." His eyes found hers and she caught a tiny glimpse of his inner fire, a passion that he deliberately hid. "When I've caught all I need, I lead these men and also work with them. Whatever needs be done, whether it's gather supplies, bind a wound, fix a ripped tent"—his gaze slid away to the spot where he'd found her standing, ax ready to slice through the walls—"or tend to the horses."

"You have something you want me to do."

"Aye. Do you cook?" he asked. "Some of the men have complained about Odell's fare."

She nearly laughed. "Is that so?"

"Aye, but Odell, he's touchy about it. I thought I'd ask him to let you help out."

"I know not if I could do much better."

Wolf snorted and a smile danced through his eyes. "Surely you could do no worse."

The next four days were much the same, though Odell grumbled about having a woman help him with the meals. At first she was allowed only to gut the rabbits and squirrels or pluck feathers from the birds that were killed, but once Odell discovered that she worked well and hard, she was allowed to help cook. They had only a few spices to work with and there were few herbs that grew in the woods in winter, but with a pinch of salt and pepper, purloined from a peddler who was riding near Erbyn, Megan was able to add some flavor to the meals.

The men, except for Robin, who ate anything offered him, appreciated her efforts, and some of the wary and suspicious glances she'd caught before became kind looks of appreciation.

She was allowed to go on a hunt and surprised the men, including Wolf, with her aim. Jagger, usually tough and mean-tempered, grudgingly nodded his approval when she felled a small boar.

"I knew not ladies could shoot," he said, sliding her a confused glance.

She smiled and handed him his bow, for she was not allowed to carry her own quiver or arrows. "I knew not outlaws had a sense of humor."

Even crusty Odell accepted her, though he was worried about Holt's soldiers finding their camp. But Wolf was not so foolish. He had spies throughout the forests and nearby towns who tracked Holt's whereabouts.

"He's with his men near St. Peter's," Jagger announced one day. "And an unhappy lad he is." Smiling as he tore apart a moist piece of dove, he sighed contentedly and sat on his heels. "There are two soldiers who ride with him who are as intent on hunting you down as is Holt," Jagger went on. "One I know not, a thin knight with lifeless eyes and brown hair that kinks. Goes by the name of Conroy—nay—"

"Connor," Megan said, a rock settling in her stomach. Connor was a lone man who watched everything and kept quiet. His eyes were empty, but he stared at her often, as if not seeing her.

"Aye, that's it, and the other is Kelvin McBrayne. 'Tis said he took offense to being tied nearly naked to a tree, then having his horse stolen."

"And a fine destrier he is," Odell said with a cackle. " 'ell's bells. Kelvin, 'e shoulda been 'appy we left 'im with 'is pitiful life."

"How so you know so much about who's with Holt?" Megan asked, wiping the grease from her fingers.

"I get close. Hide with the horses or in a nearby tree, just out of the campfire's light."

"He's foolish," Wolf said. "Takes chances."

"Ye get the information ye want," Jagger pointed out and helped himself to another thick breast of dove. "Odell, 'tis a fine meal ye're servin' tonight."

"Be thankin' the lady," Odell said, but smiled just the same.

There were no prayers offered up, no hint of Mass, no mention of God, though some of the men carried charms for good luck and spoke under their breaths of omens. Brave souls when faced with an enemy, they feared that which they could not see.

"I heard from Odell that some old lame witch put a curse on ye," Robin said one day. "Odell, he listens to all of the gossip in every town we pass through." Robin was at the creek, frowning, as his net had unwoven and a particularly large pike had swum away. The past few days, he'd been moody and had avoided Megan, sending her dark looks when he thought she could see him not. Now, at her arrival on the shores of the creek, he scowled. With agile fingers, he attempted to repair the damaged net.

"No witch—a prophet, mayhap, or a sorcerer. He healed my mare's leg."

"And cursed ye and yer castle, too. That's what 'tis said."

"So it would appear," Megan said, motioning with her fingers for him to hand her the net. "Dwyrain suffered in the past two years, and aye, everyone blamed me." She worked with the string, but it was frayed badly and would not hold together. "Have you more?" she asked, fingering one of the dirty, ragged lengths.

"Aye."

"Run and get it and I'll fix this."

He did as he was bid and was soon back, sullenly watching her weave the string into a simple net.

"Ye sleep in Wolf's tent," he finally said.

"Aye." So that was what was bothering him.

"Yet ye are not his wife."

His wife. How strange to think of Wolf married and yet . . . a part of her saw some woman reaching past his hard skin, finding the inner man, the kind man behind his mask of hate. "Nay, Robin, I'm not his wife, nor do I sleep with him."

Grunting in disbelief, he took the net from her hands.

"Believe what ye will, Robin, but Wolf and I, we touch each other not."

His eyes narrowed on the net, but his mind was on other things. Wiping her hands on her tunic, Megan rocked back on her heels to meet the boy's concerned gaze. "What is it?"

"Are you not married?" he asked, staring pointedly at the ring on her finger. "To another man—this Holt of Prydd?"

She nodded. " 'Tis my misfortune, I'm afraid." In haste, she worked the horrid gold band from her finger. It had been uncomfortable from the moment Holt had placed it there, a constant reminder of her mockery of a marriage, yet she'd not removed it, feeling duty-bound to wear the cursed thing. Now, however, she felt no such need and deftly tossed the tiny band into the stream. It sparkled in the sunlight before dropping into the clear water and settling between two rocks.

Robin stared at her as if she were mad. " 'Tis worth something," he cried. " 'Tis gold."

"I want it not. If you find some value to it, you may have it. 'Tis yours, Robin, all you needs do is go and fetch it, but I will never again wear it. Nor do I ever want to see it again."

He swallowed hard and stared at her, as if she were some creature he couldn't possibly understand.

"Now, let's see about your net, shall we?"

"The net . . . oh . . ." Once the string was tied and the net strong again, they dipped it into the stream where the water pooled and promptly caught a frog swimming just under the water's surface. Robin grabbed him from the net, but the slippery creature croaked in protest and struggled away, leaving the boy and Megan to laugh at his quick, ungainly escape.

They didn't notice Wolf standing behind them, watching their antics from a thicket of oak. "Robin," he said, and the boy nearly jumped from his own skin.

"Aye?" The boy's flush was hot and red.

"Help Peter with the horses. We're moving the camp."

"Tonight?" the boy grumbled, holding the dripping net against his tunic.

"Aye. Holt's soldiers are headed this way and we want not to be surprised."

Megan's heart dove. The thought of seeing Holt again struck hard, but then she'd found a happiness here as Wolf's captive. The men treated her with respect and she was beginning to know each of them, from Odell, the sharp-tongued liar, to mean-tempered and daring Jagger. Peter, with his one eye and level head, was a kind soul who trusted horses more than he did his fellow man. Bjorn, strong and handsome, was rumored to be some kind of bastard prince, and young Robin reminded her of her brother Bevan when he was young. Then there was Wolf, the leader, a man outwardly cruel and arrogant who willingly defied the law, yet who was blessed with a kinder side he kept hidden. Wolf, who saved a young boy from the jailer; Wolf, who swept her away from a husband she hated; Wolf, who carried a secret that weighed heavily on his heart; Wolf, the man who guarded her each night, sleeping near her but not touching her, holding her prisoner and yet protecting her as well. Aye, he was an appealing man, and it crossed her mind that if she gave in to the desire that awakened whenever he was near, that if she dared kiss him or touch him or make love to him, she would have cause to have her marriage to Holt annulled. But as much as she wanted her freedom from her husband, the thought of actually lying with Wolf frightened her. 'Twas dangerous to become emotionally entangled with a criminal.

Megan helped break camp by folding tents and lashing them to poles to be pulled by some of the horses. There was but one wagon and another small cart for supplies and weapons.

Wolf insisted that they travel at night, avoiding those who traveled by day.

She packed the rugs and fur blankets, lashing them to the pallet. Would she ever see her beloved father again? Or Cayley—would she be able to laugh and argue with her sister? Or ride in the fields surrounding the castle?

That part of her life was over, for even if she did return to the keep, she would have to face Holt as his bride, unless she could persuade her father and Father Timothy or the abbot that the marriage should be annulled, that she could not possibly remain Holt's wife.

She grabbed the bag holding her clothes, the white tunic, red surcoat, and green mantle, then bit down hard on her lower lip as she drew the string that would secure her bag. Surely Holt would want her not if she were no longer a virgin. Would he not cast her out as his wife if she'd lain with another man? And would coupling with another be worse than being married to him for the rest of her life?

Her gaze strayed to Wolf kicking dust into the campfire. Her pulse pounded in her temple. Could she give herself to this man, this black-heart, if only for a night? Her mouth turned to dust at the thought of his touch, warm against her skin, the pressure of his lips as they claimed hers. Her blood heated and she looked away.

Losing her virtue to him would not ease her burden. The clouds shifted, blocking out the moon, and she remembered the crippled prophet's words. Could this man Wolf, leader of this band, be the destruction of Dwyrain as was prophesied, and if so, would she really lose her heart to him?

Five

"Aye, they were here," Connor said, eyeing the soggy remains of a campfire and deep ruts from a heavy wagon. Bootprints and hoofprints were visible in the mud by the stream. "If not the outlaw Wolf and his miserable band of cutthroats, then someone like them." Bending down, he examined the crushed grass and rubbed a few wet blades between his fingers.

"How long?" Holt asked from astride his muddy destrier.

"Less than a week since they left. The fire is cold, but it looks only a few days old." Connor glanced up at the sky, where the clouds were beginning to part, and a few weak rays of sun shone on the glen tucked in the woods. "My guess is that they stayed here for some time—see how some of the grass is yellow there where it was covered for days, maybe weeks, with a tent? This camp was left only because we approached."

"Then we are close?"

Connor rubbed his jaw, scratching the short whiskers that covered his chin. "I think not, but I'll send men to inquire. They can ride from house to house and see if anyone saw a group of men and horses and one woman traveling."

Kelvin of Hawarth climbed down from his steed and stretched his muscles. His complaints, as the days and nights had stretched into nearly a week, had become louder and more annoying. " 'Tis a wild goose chase," he said now, walking stiffly to the stream and splashing water over his face. "This may not have been Wolf's camp." Giving a short, humorless laugh, he added, " 'Twould not surprise me if the cur had this place and others like it made to look like the men were here."

What a fool, Holt thought. Kelvin, so anxious to do battle with Wolf when he'd been brought to the castle, now was more than ready to return to the warm fires and fine food of Hawarth. "Wolf is clever but has neither the means nor the men to carry out such a plan."

"Has he not? What about his spies at Dwyrain? Do ye know who they be or how great their number?"

Holt's fingers clenched over the reins of his mount. "I will find them all, flush them out, and punish them. Doubt me not—before I get through with them, they will tell me everything they know of Wolf."

"If the castle is still under the baron's rule." Kelvin threw out his hands. "Mayhap the kidnapping of the lady was but a ruse to lure you and your best soldiers away from Dwyrain so that either Wolf or someone he conspires with can overtake the keep."

"Nay, I think not—" Holt said, then bit his tongue when he saw Connor's reaction. The man's blank eyes darkened just enough to worry Holt.

"What he says has merit." Connor walked slowly along the bank, his eyes searching the shallows. "Why not?"

"What would an outlaw want with a castle?"

"What would he want with a man's wife?"

Holt knew a moment of fear. 'Twas true. Wolf could have enticed him away from Dwyrain only to capture the castle for his own use when Holt and his best soldiers were searching through the woods. Though Wolf had but a small band of men, there were spies within the castle walls, spies who could turn against the guards in the keep. Even those sentries could not be trusted, not fully, for their first allegiance was to Ewan, and as long as the old man lingered, there was the chance that his mind could be turned against his new son-in-law.

"Aha," Connor said and waded into the stream. He reached into the water as if he planned on catching a fish with his bare hands, but instead plucked a piece of gold from the streambed. With a cold smile, he turned and plowed his way out of the water. "Methinks, Sir Holt," he said, grinning evilly as he extended his fist, slowly opened his fingers, and showed the tiny gold band in his wet palm, "your wife is not honoring her wedding vows."

They traveled three nights, stopping in the forest during the day only to rest, always moving to the north. Megan was beginning to wonder if they would ever stop for more than a few hours so that she would have enough time to sneak away from Wolf and his band of loudmouthed, bad-mannered, yet good-hearted men. They were a sorry lot, though happily so, and Wolf, the black-heart, was a hard, dangerous man she wished she'd never met. She was always nervous and wary around him, but fascinated as well. His smile was captivating, his wits were sharp, and his gaze, ever restless, never moved too far from her, as if he expected her to bolt at any minute.

Though it had been nearly a week since she'd been abducted, he refused to trust her, insisting on sleeping near her, never letting her out of his sight except for the nightly meetings around the campfire when the men gathered together, whispering among themselves. Megan couldn't hear what they were saying, but knew that it involved her and her fate, for often one of the men would frown, cast a glance in her direction, and argue under his breath.

'Twas unfair to be treated so; she could do nothing but plan her escape.

The best time would be during the day, when the men were resting and Wolf, as was his custom, took one man, usually Bjorn, and rode ahead, searching the countryside, looking for a new hiding spot. Often Robin and Jagger went hunting and Odell was busy tending the fire and spit, but he always found jobs to keep her busy. She hauled water, washed the few pots they had, cleaned fowl and fish, or helped sharpen the cooking knives. She considered stealing one of the sharp blades, but Odell knew his few weapons and pieces of cutlery. Before she could find a way to sneak away from the camp, Wolf always returned and trained his suspicious eyes upon her once again.

On the fourth night, they veered from the road and continued on what appeared to be an old deer trail, slogging through muck, easing the wagon through the trees with torches as their only light. The horses shied, and Megan shivered in the wind as she rode upon a gray jennet and held on to the saddle pommel. Her hands were free, but the reins of her horse were firmly in Wolf's hands as he drove to the remains of an old chapel tucked near the bend of a river. The water moved swiftly, a dark, wide ribbon that tumbled over steep cliffs, creating a waterfall not 20 yards from the back door of the ancient church.

" 'Ere?" Odell grumbled. "Ye expect us to make camp 'ere?"

Wolf's smile was a slash of white in the darkness. "And what's wrong with it?"

"It's falling down around us. We'll be lucky if the roof don't give way and crush us!"

"Here we have a choice. At the last camp, we did not. Those who want to sleep inside may; those who favor tents or the bare ground can do as they wish."

Odell, upon the destrier he'd stolen from Kelvin of Hawarth, edged his mount forward and raised his torch high so that a pool of flickering light fell upon mossy stone walls. Ivy climbed up what had once been a great fireplace but now was a pile of rubble, and beams, charred from a great fire, held up only a portion of the roof.

"Looks like the Devil himself was 'ere," Odell said and crossed himself swiftly, one of the first signs Megan had ever seen that some of the men concerned themselves with God.

"We make camp here," Wolf said, and though a few of his men grumbled under their breaths, most climbed off their tired mounts, stretched, and hurriedly went about constructing the tents and a fire.

"We'll be inside," Wolf said as he slid from his saddle, and Megan hopped to the ground. Her muscles ached from hours in the saddle and she saw no point in arguing. "Odell's right—part of the old chapel is unsafe, but there are rooms where the roof is intact and the walls strong, and 'tis warmer than outside."

"You know this place well?" she asked, eyeing the blackened rafters that creaked in the wind.

"Well enough," he said gruffly, then ordered his men to bring his pallet, rugs, and bags to a corner room with a small window and a spot where another fire had been lit.

The floor was stone, the walls solid, the ceiling appearing steady.

Through the window, she saw sparks from the fire drifting toward the sky and she realized how alone she was with this man. Oh, she'd been in his tent with him each night, but the walls were only thin cloth and she'd not felt so distant from the rest of the men. But here, in a chamber, they were more removed from the outlaws who gathered in their tents around the fire.

"You're not pleased."

"I hate being a prisoner."

"Is it so bad? Have you been mistreated?" She heard him stake out a place near the door. " 'Twill not be forever," he said, and she thought she heard a smidgen of regret in his voice, but it could have been her mind playing tricks on her. "Soon enough I will return you to the arms of your beloved Holt."

"When?"

"Shortly I will send a note for your ransom, then you will be returned safely to Dwyrain."

Her stomach clenched at the thought of facing Holt, but she held her tongue and slid out of her boots.

A yawn escaped him, and in the darkness she saw him wrap a fur rug around himself and prop his head against the bag holding her clothes. "Now that he has tasted of bitter disappointment, I'll only too gladly give him back his wife in exchange for gold."

Her insides froze. "Gold? So that's what this is about. Money." She said the word as if it tasted bad. "You're nothing more than a common thief."

"Not so common, m'lady," he retorted sarcastically, his hooded eyes trained on her, his smile as dangerous as the predatory beast for which he named himself. "But, aye, I am a thief."

* * *

Holt took aim at the stag's chest and the great heart beating within, pulled back on his bow, and watched as his arrow, usually true, veered away from its target, thwacking hard as it landed in the soft white bark of a birch. The startled buck fled, leaping high over a hedge of brush and disappearing through the forest.

None of his men said a word. What they thought didn't spring to their lips. As the best archer in all of Dwyrain, Holt should not have missed so clear a shot, but he was bothered, his mind elsewhere than on game. He'd sworn he wouldn't return to the castle empty-handed, but he had no choice. Out of supplies and without new information as to where the rogues had fled, spending more time in the forest was useless. And he had to return to the castle for fear Wolf's intentions were to take over the keep.

"Bloody hell," he growled, seething inside to think he'd been bested by a cunning criminal who had stolen his wife and no doubt bedded her as well. As a painful reminder of her faithlessness, he wore her wedding ring on his fifth finger.

Kelvin and Connor had convinced him to return to Dwyrain and wait for word of ransom. The winter air was tinged with ice, frost lay on the ground, and the outlaws' trail was as cold as death. The Christmas revels were soon upon them, and Connor believed that each day away from Dwyrain was another day for the outlaw to take over the castle. Connor . . . an odd one. Deadly. A man who would be brutal to Cayley.

As the stag disappeared into a thicket, Holt motioned for his men to move on. He'd leave Connor with a few men to keep looking in the forests and towns, ever searching for the elusive outlaw and stolen bride. Holt would return to

Dwyrain and become baron, for certainly the poison he'd had Nell slip into Ewan's wine would be taking its toll, and the old man, already ill, would be perilously near death, if not dead already.

Half the men continued on their quest. The other half, some of whom would later return to the search party with more supplies, returned to Dwyrain with Holt, but as the horses drew nearer to the castle, Holt's fury mounted.

Megan's ring burned against the skin of his finger and he argued with himself. Whether she was with him or not, he would inherit the castle. He was her husband, and though he suffered a few insults and raised eyebrows and unkind jokes, he would still be baron. Those who opposed him would be silenced forever. If he never saw Megan again, 'twould not matter.

Except that she had escaped him. He'd waited for months to have her serve him, to see her naked on her knees, to force her to do his bidding. He'd savored thoughts of the wedding night and dreamed of how it would feel not just to mount her but see her surrender to his power. For nearly a year she had avoided him, argued with her father about his courtship, defied him at every turn, and he'd waited, somewhat impatiently, because he'd known in the end he would win.

And he'd been thwarted. By a scar-faced outlaw who acted as if he delighted in Holt's humiliation. Why else had there been no demand of ransom?

They plodded on for hours, and at the final bend in the road, the trees parted and Holt caught his first view of Dwyrain in nearly a week. Tall and proud, a giant that swelled from the very earth on which it was built, the castle was one of the finest Holt had ever seen. When he'd left Prydd years ago and come into Ewan's service, he'd silently vowed that someday the keep would be his. He'd started by being of service to the old man, proving himself worthy, using his brains, brawn, and skill to gain Ewan's trust.

And then there was Megan, beautiful, haughty first daughter of the baron, second in line to inherit the castle. Only Bevan stood in Megan's way of inheriting all that was Dwyrain. Fate had cast Holt a great favor in the form of the sorcerer's prediction. Even now as he rode through the brittle-cold afternoon to the gates of Dwyrain, Holt smiled. The prophet's words, foretelling that so many would die, that there would be great pain and loss, destruction and deceit within the castle walls, that Megan would be blamed, had all been too good to be true. Aye, the prophecy had come to pass, but Holt had felt no qualms about hurrying it along a bit.

Bevan's reckless nature had given Holt an opportunity to poison the lad while he was recuperating from a nasty spill off his mount and near-drowning. By killing Bevan, Holt had removed Ewan's son as the final obstacle to Megan's inheritance, and from there it was only a matter of convincing the old man that no one would want to marry her. By the gods, it looked as if that pathetic cripple had been right, and had cursed her.

It took little to persuade some of the servants and a few of the more superstitious knights that she was the reason for the illness that swept through the castle. Had not it been foretold? And when any misfortune befell the castle or those who worked there, it was a simple matter to remind the victim or his family that there was a curse on the keep.

The only part of the prediction that worried him was the piece concerning the marriage being cursed and something about restoring Megan's honor only through true love or some such pig dung. Not that Holt believed in the prophecy; it was just a convenient ploy to use against the simple minds in the castle.

He heard the sentry's shout and the blast of a trumpet announcing his return. Soldiers scurried over the wall walks and Holt smiled to himself. Let the little people hurry to serve him. 'Twas his destiny.

First, he'd show his respect, visit Ewan, eat a hot meal, drink wine, and then find himself a willing wench who would take his mind off Megan. At least for the night.

"You found her not?" the old man asked from his bed. Unable to rise, he hardly moved, but sighed loudly, disappointment etched across his brow. He was ill; the herbs were working their magic and Holt could barely suppress a smile. He was so close to becoming baron, he could feel it; the promise of death hung heavy in the air.

"Nay, the outlaw eluded me." Holt crossed the room and sat on a bench near the fire, warming his backside as he silently willed Ewan of Dwyrain to die. "I left Connor with some men and will send others with supplies to join them soon. But I did not want to stay away from the castle too long in case there was a demand for ransom or . . ." He let his voice drift away.

"Or what?"

"Well, or news of Megan."

"News?" Ewan said and his lips compressed. His washed-out gray color paled even more. "What kind of news?"

Holt sighed and plowed his hands through his hair. " 'Tis possible that this outlaw, the one they call Wolf, is an enemy of yours or mine. It might not be money he's after."

"What then?"

"Perhaps her virtue."

Ewan closed his old eyes and shook his head in vehement denial. "I think not."

"Or her life," Holt added, and his father-in-law physically jerked, as if his ancient heart had stopped beating for a moment before jolting into rhythm again.

"Nay, she's alive," Ewan gasped. "I cannot lose Megan, too, not after the others . . ." His old voice faded.

"I pray she's safe," Holt said, but his voice sounded full of doubt.

"You must find her!"

Holt's eyes slid away. "I'll do what I can, m'lord, but I cannot promise."

"You must!"

" 'Tis not that easy. There are spies within the castle walls—those who would betray you and follow the criminal."

Jaw clenching beneath his beard, Ewan said, "Then flush them out, Holt. Find out what they know. Mayhap they can tell you where the cur is holding my daughter!"

"As you wish," Holt agreed, then walked back to the bed and offered Ewan his cup of wine. Smiling inwardly, he watched as the old fool drank a long sip, then slid back between the linen sheets. Ewan's eyes closed and Holt wished him dead. It would be so easy to smother the man, as he was already weak, but as that thought chased through his mind, the door opened and Cayley entered.

"You found Megan not?" she asked, casting a worried look at her father's sleeping form.

"Nay, the blackguard eluded us."

"A pity," Cayley murmured, crossing herself.

"Aye, that it is," Holt said as Cayley walked to her father's bedside and laid cool fingertips to his forehead. He didn't move.

"He gets worse with each day. I thought that if Megan were to return he might recover a bit . . ." Sighing, she brushed a strand of white hair from his forehead.

"He is near death's door," Holt whispered, wishing he could find a way to push the baron through that black portal just a bit sooner.

The moon was high, the campfire mere embers, and Megan knew she had no choice. If she were to escape, she had to leave now while Wolf slept peacefully near the door. Quietly, she slipped from his pallet and across the room to the window, where, with one final glance over her shoulder to see that he had not moved, she hoisted herself up and slid through the opening. She landed with a soft thud on the frozen ground and slowly edged her way around the old chapel. Two sentries, shoulders propped against trees, stood near the clearing where the horses were tethered. Though their backs were to her, she could not get past them and steal a horse as she'd hoped. No, she would have to make her way on foot and hope that by the morning's light she had put enough distance between herself and the camp to elude Wolf.

Her heart squeezed at the thought. There was a foolish part of her that longed to stay with him, to trust him. *You are addled,* she told herself. What would she want with a criminal, a man always on the run, a man who lived by his own rules? Rather than dwell on the dark turn of her thoughts, she crept to the river's edge and decided to follow it upstream, keeping to the banks until she came to a crossing, either a shallow spot where a road splashed across the current, or, if she was lucky, to a bridge. Sooner or later she would come across a village or a traveler who could direct her toward Dwyrain.

And what then? Give up? Live as Holt's wife? Nay! She'd plead with her father and Father Timothy or the local abbot to have her marriage annulled. *Why?* So that her father could insist she marry another man, one no better than Holt? What other options did she have? Life in a nunnery? Or could she find a hut where she could grow and sell herbs and mix potions as she'd watched Rue do?

"Oh, bother," she muttered under her breath as a cloud passed over the moon and the night grew dark. She picked her way carefully, slipping on rocks, holding on to branches and roots that grew out of the bank, and telling herself she was glad to be rid of that wild group of cutthroats and thugs. She was better off away from them, including grumpy Odell and sweet Robin. Now she wouldn't have to feel Wolf's intense eyes on her, nor would she have to train hers away from the unforgiving lines of his face—masculine, rugged, and sensual. When his eyes sought hers, she felt as if hundreds of butterflies filled her stomach. Her heart pounded so loudly that she was certain the entire camp could hear it. When she felt his gaze on the back of her head she had to force herself not to turn around and search his face for just a tiny bit of nobility that she was certain was visible in his unforgiving countenance if only she knew just where to look.

As if it mattered. Now she had to walk to the nearest town, steal a horse if needs be, and hurry to Dwyrain before either Holt or Wolf found her.

The clouds parted again and the river glimmered silver in the wavering moonlight.

"Did you really think you could escape so easily?" Wolf's voice, the merest of whispers, reverberated through the canyon as well as her heart.

Whirling, she saw his dark form sitting insolently on a

mossy boulder not 10 feet from her. "I . . . I was thirsty and wanted a drink . . ."

He laughed so loudly she jumped. "A drink?"

"Aye."

Clucking his tongue, he shook his head. "Is the water better here than down at the chapel?"

"I thought—"

"You thought you could escape, that you could elude me and . . . what? Walk the entire distance back to Dwyrain this night?" When she didn't answer, he stretched to his feet, a tall man looming in the darkness. Slowly he advanced on her. "Come, Megan," he said gently. " 'Tis cold out here."

"As if you care for my comfort."

"I do," he said, though his tone was tinged with mockery.

"Then return me to Dwyrain."

"All in good time."

"For the right amount of gold."

"Aye," he said, and the smile left his voice. She felt his gaze move to her lips. "Why else?"

"I know not." She was quivering inside and was afraid it wasn't from the wind that cut through her clothes as it tore down the valley. No, her trembling was because he was close to her, so close that the toes of his boots touched hers.

"Come inside."

"Nay."

"You would defy me?" There was a hard edge to his voice.

"I will not be ordered about like a slave!"

"Mother of God," he growled under his breath and one hand reached forward to clasp her upper arm. "If you haven't yet noticed, Megan, I'm not a patient man!"

"Nor I a patient woman."

"Get back to the chapel and be thankful that I don't put you in chains—"

She gasped and tried to draw her arm away. "What kind of beast are you?" she said, fury spurting through her veins. "You drag me away from the castle against my will—"

"Liar." The word was spoken so softly she barely heard it, and yet it echoed through her heart over and over again, repeating itself and mocking her. He dragged her closer to him, so close that even in the night she saw the breeze move through his hair and the reflection of the moon in his eyes. Her traitorous heart beat faster. "You wanted to be free of the castle," he guessed, his breath caressing her face as he stopped in front of her. "There was a part of you that longed to soar away from all the thick walls and responsibilities."

"Nay," but the lie tripped on her tongue.

"And freedom isn't all that you want," he said, fingers nearly punishing in their grip, moonlight splashing over the ruthless planes of his face. "There is more, much more," he said, and a cold sweat beaded beneath her hair at the suggestion in his words.

"More?"

" 'Tis the reason you flee now." His fingers became more gentle and she saw his throat work.

"Which is?"

"Me. You're afraid of me and what your heart is telling you."

"I know not what you say—"

"Liar." Again that damning word. "You feel it, too, Megan," he said.

"What?"

He was so close she smelled the lingering scents of smoke, leather, and the earth all mingling together and causing her pulse to pound. "The wanting."

"Wanting?" she repeated, feeling silly.

"The wanting between a man and woman." His breath

fanned her face and she felt his heat through his fingers—hot, hungry, pounding.

Her skin prickled in anticipation, though she could not give in to the wanton thoughts that heated her blood. True, she'd thought fleetingly of seducing him, of finding a way, any way, to have her marriage annulled, but she couldn't so callously cast away her virtue to this . . . this criminal. "I want you not," she lied, trying to deny that which had caused her so much pain. "I'm married—"

"Aye, to mine enemy." His eyes were a dark blue, the color of the sea at midnight, and his face, handsome though it had once been, showed the ravages of battle, a scar that cleaved one eyebrow, a nick on his ear that was visible when the wind tossed the hair from his face. The Wolf, they called him, and so like that frightening beast he was.

"I—I cannot."

"But you will," he said, as if the knowledge had been with him since her capture, as if he'd planned to bed her before she could even lie with her husband. She swallowed hard and his gaze drifted to the circle of bones at the base of her throat. "You're a sweet liar, Megan of Dwyrain, but your eyes give you away." One callused hand reached forward, twining in the thick strands of her hair to brush her nape. "You need the wind in your hair, the song of the falcon in your ears, the power of a steed beneath you." His hand slid lower to surround her throat in a grip that was as powerful as it was gentle. "You need a man who can tame your wild spirit, a man whose black heart is a match for your own."

"Nay," she whispered, but her lips trembled and her skin, where he touched her throat, throbbed. "Please," she said, then cleared her throat. "Unhand me."

"Oh, I will, little one, but not before you admit it. Say the words."

"I cannot."

"You want me."

"Nay," she cried again as he drew her near. His lips were close enough to hers that she could fairly taste him.

His smile was that of a devil. "Then prove me a liar," he ordered before drawing her body to his and claiming her mouth with a hard, savage kiss that seared through her blood and pierced her very soul.

She wilted against him, her body having a will all its own. His hands splayed over her back and beneath her clothes, her skin tingled, ready and anxious. She didn't cry out when he pushed her against the trunk of a tree and fit his body intimately to hers. She felt his heat, his need, the soft throb of desire that ran from his veins to hers.

His tongue tickled the seam of her mouth and she opened to him, thrilling as he groaned and rubbed against her. Wild, hot, and decidedly sinful thoughts ran through her mind as his fingers slid lower to cup her buttocks and hook around her leg, jerking forward so that her thigh surrounded his.

"Megan," he growled as he lifted his head and let out a long, quivering breath. "God in heaven, you are a temptress." His eyes glazed as he dropped her leg and gasped for breath. She nearly stumbled, but he caught her. "Come, this is madness!"

"I cannot, will not—"

"I'll not hurt you, little one, if that's what you fear."

"But—"

"Trust me," he whispered, and she wanted to—oh, how she wanted to believe. In her mind's eye, she saw herself staying here with this man, envisioned what life would be without the comforts of the castle, the warmth of her family. He kissed her again, so soundly she could barely breathe.

When he lifted his head, he stared at her long and hard. "Mother of Moses," he whispered.

She expected him to take her in his arms again, but he stepped away, holding only her hand. Disappointment welled in her heart, and her legs were as strong as Cook's pudding when she tried to walk. He half dragged her back to the chapel and she couldn't stop her heart from racing at the thought of the night alone with him, the night stretching ahead. Not that she could kiss him again, not that she would let him touch her, not that she would . . . At the bend of her thoughts, she bit her lip and followed him through the door, across the cold stones, and then gasped as he pulled her down on the pallet with him.

"I'll not sleep with you—"

"You have no choice."

"Nay. I'm married—"

"An excuse, m'lady."

"Wolf, I cannot—" But her protests were silenced by a kiss that burned through her body.

When he lifted his head, she felt him shudder. "Sweet Jesus," he said, as much a prayer as a blasphemy. "Now, Megan, do not move. Just lie in one spot. I will lie here with you and I will hold you close so that you do not escape, but I will not touch you in a way you do not wish, and we will sleep. Within days I will send a messenger with a ransom demand and soon you will be home to face your father or your husband."

She swallowed back the urge to cry out that she'd never return to Holt.

As he climbed beneath the covers, he kept his fingers around her wrists, and turned his body so that it was behind hers, fitting intimately against her curves. Her back was pressed against the wall of his chest, her calves brushed his shins, and her buttocks fit in the crook of his waist and crotch. Closing her eyes, she felt his manhood, hard, wanting, nearly quivering as it was pressed against her buttocks, but he didn't move, just held her close and tried to sleep. She didn't dare even twitch, afraid of what one small movement might cause, certain the simmering heat in her blood would spark to life. Never before had she experienced true wanting—the hunger between a man and woman—but right now she understood that desire all too well.

Holding Megan against him, Wolf gritted his teeth. Her body was warm and fragrant and he wanted to bury his face in her locks and make love to her until dawn.

Sleep eluded him and images of her, naked and willing, filled his wayward mind and caused his eager member to harden and swell. He'd been a fool, dallying with the woman, teasing Holt, keeping her rather than ransoming her right away. But the money had been of no consequence; Holt's humiliation had been the prize.

Now the situation had changed. Keeping Megan with him was not so much punishment for Holt, but sweet torment for Wolf. He couldn't look at her without wanting, couldn't speak to her without wondering what it would feel like to lie with her, couldn't hear her footsteps without his heart tripping a little more quickly.

He must be mad. What would he want with a beautiful, feisty tart with a tongue like the sting of the whip? Why did the woman fascinate both him and his men? He saw how easily she flirted and how half his soldiers were willing to do her bidding. Even mean-tempered Jagger smiled when she was around, and Robin—the boy was smitten.

'Twas strange how most of the men accepted her, though they had a solid unwritten law that no woman could be a part of their band. Some of them appeared half in love with her, others amused by her, still others restless and prone to fighting, like bucks interested in a single doe.

The sooner he was rid of her, the better for all—and Holt's money could be put to good use. But the thought of returning her to his enemy, the idea that Holt might take some of his fury out on her, the merest inkling that Megan would lie with him, caused a burning in Wolf's guts, a painful jealous heat that kept him awake as he held her small wrists in his hands and felt the rise and fall of her chest against his knuckles.

Why not bed her? Why not seize his ultimate revenge against Holt and strip her of her virginity, not brutally as Holt had allowed Tadd to rape Mary, but slow and with care, making her quake with wanting, feeling her go limp and hot with desire? She would be supple and willing, and oh, the sweet rapture of it.

He squeezed his eyes shut and clenched his body against the vision of her lying naked and pure beneath him. No, he could not soil her, could not defile her, could never make love to her, as she was another man's wife. And yet he wanted her, with an aching lust that stormed through his blood and clamored in his brain. Her rump brushed his cock and he thought of the sweetness of entering her, of hearing her pant against his ear, of listening to the sweet moans from her lips.

She wasn't what he expected. She claimed she loved not Holt, and Wolf clung to that thought, though he damned himself for caring. *Oh, Megan. What am I to do with you?* She touched a dangerous, rebellious part of him, a part that caused him to second-guess his plan. Strong and determined, she claimed to want to return to Dwyrain, yet he sensed the hesitation in her voice, that a part of her would like to remain free of castle life, away from her responsibilities.

Though she was a prisoner with the outlaws, she had no castle walls that bound her, no duties to perform as Ewan's eldest daughter, no Mass to attend. She had found a new kind of freedom, and she embraced the nomadic life as Wolf once had before he'd become jaded and tired of moving from one spot to the next, forever looking over his shoulder while outrunning the law.

There was a time only a few months back when Wolf had been offered his freedom, when he'd met his family at Abergwynn, but he had yet unfinished business with Holt. Once through with this, he silently swore to himself, he'd give up his black-hearted ways and return to Abergwynn, which was all well and good, but what would he do with Megan? Could he really ransom her back to a husband he knew to be cruel and ruthless?

She sighed softly and he felt his cold heart of stone begin to crack.

Six

Holt's hands curled into fists. He wanted to bash the sheriff's thick skull against the wall in the great hall. Servants cast worried glances his way and shuffled hurriedly from the room, hiding behind tapestries, as they wanted no part of his wrath. The two men who'd come with the sheriff stood near the door like trained dogs, not saying a word, not accepting the wine that Holt had offered.

"The man is an outlaw," Holt said slowly, as if the dolt hadn't heard correctly. "And he stole my wife. I want him and his pack of criminals found and brought back here, and justice served."

"I know, I know," the sheriff, a doddering old fool named Herbert, agreed. He belched into his cup of wine, then took a long gulp. Holt wanted to strangle him for sitting on his fat rump when he should be off chasing thieves and kidnappers. "Wolf's been a pain in my arse for a long time as well. I've got my best men tracking him down."

"Do they know where he is?"

Herbert scratched his head and scowled. "Nay, but he's a

slippery one, that Wolf is." He finished his cup and eyed the wine jug longingly. "How's the baron? Heard he collapsed at the wedding celebration."

" 'Tis true. Losing Megan has nearly killed him," Holt said, gladly shoving some more guilt onto the corrupt sheriff's conscience.

Herbert turned his eyes away from the wine. "And where does that leave ye? If the baron dies, will ye, as Lady Megan's husband, become the new lord?" He rubbed his palms on the front of his dirty breeches. "A sticky problem, eh? Since your wife was stolen away before ye bedded her." Struggling to his feet, he cast one last baleful glance at the wine, then snapped his fingers to the two guards he'd brought with him. "Worry not, Sir Holt. We'll find the rotter." He marched out of the hall with surprising speed for one so heavy. His two soldiers followed without a word, treading after the old fool blindly. For a second Holt experienced the sharp pang of jealousy. Would any of the soldiers guarding Dwyrain obey him without question? Fight to the death?

As Herbert had so pointedly reminded him, the castle was not quite his. Should Ewan die, Dwyrain by rights would fall to Megan, and, as her husband, Holt would inherit the castle, but since the marriage had never been consummated, it could be easily annulled. If Megan were found dead before the old man gave up his ghost, the castle and lands would revert to Cayley, and then Holt would be left with nothing. All his plotting—years of scheming and allying himself with Ewan—would be for naught.

Snarling at a page to bring him more wine, Holt refused to be thwarted. There was blood on his hands already, and the poison he was slipping into the old man's cup was slowly working.

He didn't mind hurrying Ewan to his grave more rapidly

than nature intended. But he couldn't be foolish enough not to make sure that he inherited the castle. If it fell to Cayley and she married Gwayne of Cysgod . . . By the gods, it looked as if he might have to find a way for Megan's younger sister to meet with an accident.

That particular thought wasn't pleasing. Killing women was difficult because of the joy they could give a man. Fingering the hilt of his knife, he frowned. Nay, the answer was not to take Cayley's life. He had promised her to Connor, but there might be a more permanent solution. Why not double-cross Connor and marry her off? This thought appealed to him. However, right now he had to find Megan and that damned outlaw.

Near the morning fire, Wolf talked in low tones to his men, pointing emphatically to Bjorn before spying Megan as she carried a basket of herbs she'd collected near the creek. Several heads swiveled her way and ears burned a bright red at her approach. She'd never before intruded on one of their meetings, meekly allowing them to discuss her and her fate, but she was tired of being treated as if she had no say in what was to happen. She dropped the basket with a thud and it landed at Odell's feet.

"What's this?" she asked, plopping down on the cold ground where the men squatted. Several had knives and were drawing in the dirt, as if making maps.

"We're discussing what to do with you," Wolf said, his eyes burning with fury at her indignation.

"Without talking to me?" She let her eyes rove to each man.

Jagger cleared his throat and sheathed his knife. Bjorn's smile widened, but he found interest in cleaning his fingernails with his blade. Odell muttered under his breath and stoked the fire with a long stick, and Robin's eyes slid away. Only Wolf held her stare with an intense glare that nearly made her flinch.

"So what plan have you chosen, hmm?" she asked, defying the leader of these men.

"Ransom." Wolf rocked back on his heels. "We just haven't decided how much."

"No? I think 'twould be easy."

He raised his split brow, inviting her to continue.

"How about thirty pieces of silver?" she asked, then dusted her hands, stood, and whirled, storming away from the fire toward the chapel.

"Ouch," Odell muttered. "That stings a mite, don't it?"

Bjorn had the nerve to laugh and Wolf, seething, couldn't resist rising to the bait. He followed after her, catching up with her at the ruins and dragging her inside. "I thought you'd want to return to your castle."

"Did you? And what of my husband? Did you think I wanted to see him again? Did I not tell you that I married for duty? You know I love Holt not!"

His jaw clenched so hard it ached. Her face, fresh-scrubbed with water from the river, turned up and her tangled hair fell around cheeks flushed with color. Her fists were curled as if she'd like nothing better than to batter his chest and her eyes, the color of light ale, snapped fire.

"My father will find you, Wolf," she said. "And when he does, he will have no mercy on your black soul. 'Twill be as if hell itself were unleashed on you!"

"Your father is not the man he once was," Wolf said, refraining from telling her that he'd learned only this morning that Ewan of Dwyrain was gravely ill. Jagger had ridden late last night to meet with spies in the castle, and the word was not good. Ewan, after collapsing just after

Megan's kidnapping, had become inattentive and confined to his quarters. The priest and Cayley visited him often and he was bedridden, surely dying. By rights, Megan should be with him, to ease his suffering and to be within the castle when he died, so that she, or Holt as her husband, could rule the keep.

"My father will not rest until I am safely returned."

"And your husband?"

She shuddered visibly, her skin turning pale. "I will talk to Holt," she said.

"And say what? That you changed your mind? That you were marrying him only as an obligation and now you feel no need? What?" he asked, unable to resist moving closer to her and watching her lips. They trembled slightly and her pulse, so visible at the open throat of his old tunic, fluttered.

"I have not decided."

"Time is running out," he said, and the irony of his words reflected in her eyes. Their time together was fleeting as well.

She was the first to look away. "So that's it, then. You'll send a messenger to Holt."

"Have I not promised as much?" Guilt sliced through his heart at the tightening of her mouth. What would her fate be with the man who had held down a sweet maiden while another raped and used her? How could he ever release Megan to such a beast? He'd once thought that Holt's humiliation would be enough to satisfy him, but he'd been wrong. Now, because of Megan and his fear for her, Wolf wouldn't be satisfied with less than the bastard's death.

He reached forward, tracing the slope of her cheek with the tip of his finger. "I meant not to hurt you, Megan."

"Ha!" But she quivered beneath his touch.

"I wanted only to wound Holt."

"Nay, Wolf. 'Tis more than that. 'Tis not only the wounding you wanted, but also the savoring of your vengeance." She stepped away from him and shook her head, her red-brown curls brushing her shoulders. "Whatever it is that makes you hate Holt so, you nourish it, feed it, keep it alive. You delight to think that you thwarted him, that he is vexed because you are cleverer than he, but you will not be satisfied to return me to him. Whatever this rift is between you two, 'twill not be mended by gold coins." She shoved aside his hand and looked up at him with disdain. "Money will not ease your pain, nor will causing Holt a smidgen of humiliation. Nay, this—whatever it is—that festers in you will be cleansed only by your death or his."

The truth of her words cleaved all hope he bore of purging himself of his burden of hate. Had she not voiced what he had already considered? She turned away from him, but he grabbed her arm, spun her to face him. Without another thought, he held her fast, as if afraid she would disappear, then captured her mouth in his.

"No," she whispered, but opened her mouth to the pressure of his tongue. Small and yielding, her body fit against the harder contours of his. Her mouth was sweet, and Wolf's mind swam with hot images of making love to her. He pressed harder, shoving her back against the wall, one hand reaching upward to feel the weight of her breast. Even through the coarse fabric, he noticed her nipple harden, and a part of him lost all control. He reached beneath the hem of her tunic and soft chemise to her warm, waiting flesh.

"Wolf," she cried as his fingers scaled her ribs slowly, laying siege steadily. Her breathing was rapid and shallow, her mouth an open invitation as he kissed her.

The swelling between his legs was hard and hot and

needing release. He skimmed her nipple with his fingers and she sighed into his open mouth.

Lord help me, he silently prayed, but he couldn't resist her sweet temptation and he lifted the coarse tunic over her head. Then, through the thin fabric of her chemise, he touched her with urgent fingers. Moaning, she leaned closer as he kissed her eyes, her neck, her throat. His blood thundered in his ears. Surely he was crossing some forbidden line, and in so doing, damning them both, but he couldn't stop.

"I . . . I cannot," she insisted, trying to push away, but he was strong, and as she twisted from him, he slid his arms around her, his hands cupping both her breasts as he held her close to him, and he kissed the back of her neck, leaving a trail with his tongue. Through his breeches his hard, stiff member was pressed against the valley of her rump. "Wolf, please—" she murmured, and he turned her again, looking into her eyes, searching her face before he kissed her with all the passion that seared through his blood. Her resistance was without conviction, and soon her arms wrapped around his neck and she was clinging to him, her breasts rising and falling beneath the chemise, her mouth such soft, sweet wonder.

He dragged them both to his pallet, and there, nestled in the furs, she gazed up at him, her eyes filled with surrender as his heart beat a wild, primal cadence. Slowly, he untied the ribbons of her chemise, parting the light cloth, exposing exquisite white flesh.

With a finger, he rolled the fabric back until both her breasts were visible, straining upward, a slight image of tiny veins beneath her skin, her glorious pink tips hard and wanting. He thought she would blush or turn away, but she stared straight into his eyes, and when he lowered his head and brushed a feather-light kiss across one sweet bud, she sighed deep in her throat. "This is wrong," he growled, and again the dark nipple puckered expectantly.

"Aye, we cannot."

"We mustn't," he agreed, but lowered his mouth around the sweetness of her skin and touched his teeth and tongue to the ripe, willing mound.

With a cry, she arched her back and he caught her, big hands splaying over the curve of her spine, holding her tight as he suckled, like a hungry babe, wanting so much more, feeling her tremble with her own desire.

"Wolf," she cried, and it was more a plea than protest. His groin was tight and he thought only of lying with her, of thrusting into the warm, moist haven that was hidden between her legs, of coupling with her far into the night. Still kissing her, he moved, rolling atop her, spreading her legs with his knees, gazing down at her naked breasts and beautiful flushed face. It would be so easy to love her . . .

And then what? She was married to Holt, a woman pledged to another. In that instant, that small flame of nobility, the one he'd tried so desperately to extinguish, sparked in his brain and he knew that he could never have this woman; no matter what, she was married to another man. No matter that Holt was his sworn enemy, no matter that she'd never loved him, no matter that she'd never lain with him, 'twas a sacrament he couldn't break. With all the effort he could gather, he rolled off her and away, landing on his feet and swearing roundly.

"For the love of Christ, what am I to do with you?" he asked, breathing hard, squeezing his eyes shut, pinching the bridge of his nose as he willed the wild heat roaring through his blood to cool.

"I thought you were going to ransom me," she said

saucily, though she was dying inside. What had she just done? Nearly given herself to this man—this criminal who had told her that he was sending her back to her husband for a few coins?

Shame colored her cheeks, but she stiffened her spine as she tossed on the old tunic and shook her hair off her face. "If you're going to sell me, Wolf, be done with it!"

"I told you, 'tis not the money."

She tied the strings at her neck and said, "I believe not a word you say." A tic developed under his eye, and she should have felt some sort of satisfaction for vexing him, but the truth of the matter was that she was wounded inside. She'd never felt such longing, such craving for a man, and the way she'd acted like a hot-blooded wench, writhing and wanting him to lie with her, brought fear deep to her heart. 'Twas not wise to give a man such power. 'Twas not wise at all.

"Father . . . please, wake up," Cayley said softly as she took Ewan's hand in her own. She knelt in the rushes by his bed. His two hounds lay next to him, their ears perked, their suspicious eyes trained on her. Each day, Ewan appeared weaker. His skin was cool and paper thin, his eyes mere slits.

"Has . . . has Megan returned?" His voice was but a rasp, far from the loud bellow that used to announce his arrival. It had been long since she'd seen him stand without a cane or heard him tell a ribald joke, which had always earned him an elbow in the ribs from his wife.

"Nay, there is no word of Megan, but Rue told me that you refused your dinner."

"I have no hunger."

"Please," she pleaded, but his eyelids closed again and he drifted off, as he did often when she visited. His breath was so shallow it barely ruffled the soft hairs of his moustache.

She couldn't imagine life in the castle without him. Who would she turn to? Who would perform the duties of the lord? So many people depended upon him, and she loved him with all her young, willful heart. *Please, Father, do not die. Stay with me here at Dwyrain. I have no one else. . . .* And that was the sad truth. If Ewan died, then her only family was Megan, the sister with whom she'd spent so much time arguing and fighting. Even the love of her life, Gwayne of Cysgod, no longer visited. There were ugly rumors that he was betrothed to someone else and Cayley felt disappointed, but not the great heartrending sorrow she had expected.

With all the trouble in the castle, she felt as if the very walls of Dwyrain were tumbling in upon themselves, just as it had been foretold by that snake of a prophet. If only she could have one chance at that pathetic worm of a man, she'd spit in his face and curse him to hell. He was the reason for all of the trouble at the castle, not Megan.

Please, Lord, see her safely home.

The terrifying thought that Megan might already be dead crossed her mind, but she pushed the idea firmly aside. Megan was too strong, too stubborn, too cursedly defiant to die. And surely the outlaw did not steal her from within the castle walls just to kill her. Or did he?

Nay, she wouldn't believe it. When she conjured up the face of Wolf, for he was now blamed for the kidnapping, she envisioned strong, forceful features, a countenance set by fierce determination, a powerful enemy, but she did not consider him a murderer. And soon he would be found. Holt wouldn't rest until he was flushed out and captured.

She should have felt a flicker of hope in those thoughts, for she had once trusted Holt, believed in him as her father did, thought him a capable leader and honest man. But lately, she had discovered her first misgivings. He surrounded himself with men she did not trust. Connor, a knight who kept Holt's counsel, was a hard-hearted man with eyes that missed nothing, and Kelvin of Hawarth was a simpleton who appeared to enjoy other people's suffering. Jovan, the apothecary, was reputed to be a miser who would sell his own daughter's virtue for the right price, and Cayley had seen him once in Holt's company.

Holt himself was more than troubled and worried over Megan's disappearance. In his agitation, he showed another side to himself.

"Oh, Father, you must wake up and take your place as baron," she said, desperation and fear clutching her throat. For the first time in her life, Cayley felt as if she could rely on no one but herself, and that feeling scared her half to death. Were the situation reversed and she the one captured, Megan would have known what to do. Megan had always called her weak, and now, finally, Cayley understood why. She didn't have the first notion how to help her sister.

There was a soft knock on the door and one of the dogs growled low in his throat. The other lifted her nose aloft, sniffed the air, and snarled. Cayley, who had been kneeling at her father's bedside, climbed quickly to her feet just as Father Timothy entered. One look at the bed and he sighed, crossing himself as he said a quick prayer for the baron's recovery, keeping a wary distance between himself and the sharp teeth of the hounds.

"He is no better?"

Cayley shook her head. "Nay."

"Mayhap 'tis his time," the priest said as he moved closer, and one dog leaped to his feet. With lowered head, the fur on the back of his neck bristling, the male growled a low warning. His mate, a bitch with dark spots, pulled back black lips to expose her wicked fangs. Her eyes never left the priest's soft throat.

He swallowed and his tongue rimmed his lips nervously. "Must the dogs be kept in here?"

" 'Tis what Father wants."

"But they are dangerous and should be chained outside near the gate."

Cayley never had much cared for Timothy. "Mayhap you would like to take them to the gatekeeper."

The priest's thin lips drew tight, as if a drawstring had pursed them. "Mayhap one of the guards should slay them both."

"My father would not be pleased."

Father Timothy offered her a patient, tenuous smile. "I was only joking, child. These beasts shall stay with the baron. Now, let us pray," he suggested, and though his words had a soft, even cadence, the thin man who was baron did not move beneath his blankets and the hounds who guarded him never gave up their tense, growling vigil.

The priest was in the middle of the third decade of the rosary when the door swung open and Holt strode in. He stopped near the fire, surprised to find anyone with the baron. Father Timothy, unhappy about being interrupted, motioned Holt to close the door and fall to his knees as the priest continued his litany. Cayley shot a glance at her brother-in-law and her heart turned to ice. How had she ever thought him handsome or kind?

Strong he was and possessing an authority few questioned, but there was a menacing cruelty about him she hadn't noticed before. 'Twas as if she'd been blind and some angel had touched her eyes and given her sight.

When the prayers were finished, Holt helped Cayley from her knees. "Your father, did he awaken?"

"Only long enough to ask about Megan," she said just as the sentries gave up a shout. There was a pounding on the door, which flew open, and one of the guards, breathless and smiling, snapped to attention in front of Holt. "The sheriff and some of his men have returned," he announced.

Cayley's heart knocked in anticipation.

"They've located Wolf and my wife," Holt said, his eyes flaming with triumph and vengeance.

"Nay, m'lord," the guard replied and Holt's jaw turned to granite.

Cayley bit hard on her lip.

"Why have they returned?"

The guard slid a glance to Father Timothy. "They found a man in the woods, a sorcerer lurking about the forest of Dwyrain, a man who limps."

"The crippled prophet?" the priest asked, a look of fear sliding through his eyes before he straightened his spine.

"Aye."

Holt's face grew thoughtful. "Bring him to my chamber."

"Should he not be chained and locked in a dungeon? He's nothing but a heathen," Father Timothy protested.

"There's time for that later. First, we needs discover what he knows."

Cayley started to follow the men out of the room, but Holt, hearing her footsteps, stopped at the door and turned on her. "This concerns you not, sister-in-law."

"It concerns me greatly," she argued. "He may be the man who cursed Dwyrain, and if he is, I want to be the first to condemn his soul to eternal damnation!"

Seven

"*This* is the sorcerer who cursed Dwyrain?" Holt said, eyeing the pathetic creature the guards held in the gatehouse. He was tall and thin with the coarse, tattered clothes of a beggar and a mud-colored cape with a hood that had been yanked from his head. His hair was lank and uncut, his beard a scraggly uneven growth hiding his chin. His hands were bound and shackles hobbled his gait, but he appeared calm and fearless, mayhap even a simpleton.

"Cursed?" the man said, and when he looked into Holt's eyes, the would-be baron felt certain fear. This man was no weakling as he'd first thought, and his soft-spoken voice was deceptive—the truth lay in his eyes, cold and blue as a clear winter morning. "I cursed nothing."

Cayley, who had the nerve to defy Holt, strode up to the captive. "Are you not the sorcerer who met Megan in the woods two winters past?"

The man's smile was crooked and self-deprecating, indicating the kind of humble intelligence that caused a tremor of fear to pierce Holt's heart.

"Aye, I came upon her in the forest. Her mare was lame."

"You healed the horse and cursed us all!" Cayley cried, fury twisting her face. "Mother, Bevan, even tiny Roz—" Flinging herself at him, she began to batter him with her fists and Holt didn't stop her. If this man were as powerful as was believed, then he could shield himself from her blows, untie the ropes that bound his hands and feet, and stop her, but he didn't. Instead he stood proudly, unflinching, and didn't say a word as she cursed him and flailed mercilessly at his face and chest.

"By the gods," Reginald muttered under his breath. "Has she lost all sense?"

"Cayley—" Holt finally restrained her, but not until most of the fight had left her and she was sobbing pitifully, tears running from her eyes, her throat so clogged she could barely speak, her pain raw as the wind that tore through the outer bailey. "Take her away," he said to several of the guards, and she fought them off.

"Unhand me!" she cried.

The guards stopped for a second.

Holt's fury grabbed his tongue. "I said, 'Take her away.' " Were all his men so soft they wouldn't restrain a woman? God's eyes, he was surrounded by fools. Pitiful fools. Soon, he would take care of this stubborn woman. Cayley was fast becoming a thorn in his side. The sooner he got rid of her, the better.

"Don't touch me! I'm still the baron's daughter."

The man held prisoner said in a voice as calm as deep water, "Megan is safe, Lady Cayley."

Holt's gut twisted. "Know you where my wife is?" he demanded, new rage burning through his blood.

"Nay, only that she's safe." The prisoner's face was so untroubled Holt felt another sharp jab of fear. The man should have been furious for being restrained, resentful that the hellcat of a woman had attacked him, or, if not angry, then afraid for his very life that he was to be held in the castle to which he brought such tragedy and pain. But he was serene, as tranquil as a lazy summer day.

"Where is she? Who is she with?"

" 'Tis only a feeling," the strange man explained.

"So you don't *know* she's safe? 'Tis but a *sense?*"

"Aye." The man's gaze moved to Cayley again. "Be strong."

"You lying bastard!" Cayley cried. "You know where she is! You—" Two guards clamped powerful hands around her arms.

The sorcerer stepped forward as if to help her, but he nearly tripped, his bad leg dragging a bit. A soldier yanked him back and he fell to the gatehouse floor, cracking his head against the worn stones. Cayley gasped, and Holt felt nothing but loathing and fear for this pitiful excuse of a man.

"Throw him into the dungeon," he commanded, "and when he wants to tell me more about where I can find my wife, bring him to me. Otherwise, leave him to rot. No food, no water, nothing!"

Cayley shook her head. "You cannot—"

"You're the one who condemned him to hell, m'lady," Holt sneered. "I'm just carrying out your request."

"Nay—"

"Take her to her room. Place a guard at her door."

"You cannot restrain me."

"You're not in your right mind, I'm afraid," Holt said. "Do not fret, Lady Cayley. 'Tis for your own good."

Megan watched the boiling water steam and thought longingly of a warm bath. Snow was drifting from the dark sky and a cold wind whistled through the surrounding trees, causing their dark, leafless branches to dance eerily. Feeling alone, she shivered. Wolf had left the camp. Again. There were days when he was gone for hours. Sometimes he rode alone; other times, some of his men accompanied him. She was never asked or allowed to ride with him, nor was she told what he did. But when he left, one guard was always asked to watch her closely, and no matter how she flirted with the man or complained of needing time to herself, she was never alone for a minute. No one wanted to incur Wolf's wrath should she escape.

She was surprised how the camp changed when Wolf was away. The men were more silent and brooding, and she felt as if something vital, the heart of their small group, had stopped beating. Even Cormick, the kindest of the lot, was in a foul mood.

"Fool," she muttered under her breath as she plucked the feathers of a goose unlucky enough to have been on the wrong end of one of Robin's arrows. These days, the boy was always off hunting, trying to avoid her, as if sensing that she and Wolf had grown closer.

She dipped the carcass into a pot of boiling water, soaking all the quills and pinfeathers as she'd seen some of the serving girls at Dwyrain do. Working swiftly, she plucked the wet feathers and dropped them into a bucket. Her breath fogged in the air and her fingers grew numb, but she didn't complain. Jagger and Cormick spent hours chopping wood; Peter, brushing the horses and cleaning up after them; Robin, sharpening knives; and others cooking, cleaning, shoring up tents, tanning hides, and mending or polishing weapons. Each man worked hard and complained only a bit now and again.

As the wet feathers stuck to her hands, she glanced at the

slate-colored sky. Surely the Christmas revels had begun at Dwyrain. 'Twas that time of year when the castle would be decorated with holly and ivy, and the Yule log—the trunk of a great tree—would be dragged by horses from the surrounding woods and hauled into the great hall to burn for days. Music, wine, dancing . . . she missed it, and thought often of her ailing father. And yet, would she return? If she had no threat of her marriage to Holt, would she think of Dwyrain as her home?

Surely Wolf would send a messenger soon with ransom demands, though he hadn't as yet, and he was cross most of the time, snapping at his men and ordering her about as if she were his servant. He'd taken his post at the door of the chapel, and had never kissed her again. After the day when they'd nearly made love on his pallet, he had not touched her and kept his own counsel. The men had begun to mutter behind his back, remarking on his black mood, and sliding worried glances in her direction.

The day before, Jagger had once questioned him about the ransom and Wolf had leaped to his feet, grabbed his dagger, and demanded to know if the big knight was asking for a fight. Jagger had held up his hands and backed away and Wolf, his jaw working in quiet fury, reminded everyone in the camp that he gave the orders.

Odell had been amused, Robin wide-eyed and frightened, Peter disgusted, and Bjorn ready to take on either man who became victor.

"This is your fault, ye know," Odell had whispered to her later when they were alone. She had been adding chunks of wood to the fire and trying to avoid the smoke while Odell was skewering three skinned rabbits for the spit.

"Mine?"

"Aye. Wolf's got a woman on his mind. Like as not, 'tis ye."

"How can you tell?"

" 'Tis easy. Wolf is usually a silent man who leads with a low voice and a strong fist. Of late, he's been moody, growling at the men, expecting perfection, and there's a dark look in his eyes all the time." Carefully, Odell placed the crossbar over the forked sticks that held the meat over the flames. "Anyone who stumbles across the Wolf's path is likely to get a tongue-lashing, if not more. 'E's spoilin' fer a fight, 'e is."

"I don't see how you can blame me."

Odell made a sound of disgust in the back of his throat, then spit into the fire. "Do you not see it?" Gray eyebrows lifted as flakes of snow drifted from the leaden sky. "The way 'e looks at ye, m'lady. I've been with Wolf a long time—years—and I've never seen his expression like this afore." He lifted his hood over his head. "Tell me this, why do ye think 'e's takin' so long to ransom ye, eh? He puts the whole camp in danger—not that we care, mind ye—by keeping ye here, and yet he does nothin' to change things. I'm tellin' ye, it ain't like Wolf."

Now, she finished plucking the bird, then singed its skin in order to remove a few stubborn quills. The task was nearly finished when she heard the thunder of horses' hooves resounding through the forest. Megan's heart soared and she looked up to see Wolf's steed galloping through the underbrush. But the smile on her face vanished when she realized that Wolf wasn't alone and saw the blood on his face and hands. He was holding Robin's slack body, and as the horse slid to a stop, Wolf, still carrying the lad, leaped to the ground.

"Boil more water. Hurry!" Megan ordered Odell as the men gathered around. "Find me some cloth—"

"Bring his pallet into the chapel," Wolf yelled at Peter.

"Dear Lord, what happened?" Megan asked, her eyes settling on Robin's pale face as they hurried into the old building.

"Robin nearly killed himself trying to slay a bear. The animal was wounded and had knocked Robin's quiver to the ground when I came upon them." Peter, hurrying, lay Robin's pallet near the fire and gently, Wolf placed the boy on his bed. Robin gave a soft moan, but his eyes didn't flutter open and he was white as death.

Not waiting for anyone's approval, Megan bent over the boy and lifted his bloodstained tunic to reveal a jagged, bloody rip near the boy's waist. Deep claw marks dug into the flesh but did not slice to his organs. Blood, sticky and hot, was smeared across his white skin. "Hand me that bag," she ordered Peter as she motioned toward the sack wherein her white tunic was hidden. As Peter tossed her the bag, she sent up a prayer, then catching the sack, she opened it, withdrew the tunic, and began ripping it into strips. Peter and Heath built a fire in the chapel where the roof had given way and Odell carried in a pot of near-boiling water. Smoke curled upward through the opening in the rotting thatch and snowflakes drifted into the room, only to melt as they met the heat of the fire.

Please, don't take this young one's life, Megan silently prayed, remembering all the other times her prayers had gone unanswered.

"Now, Robin," she said gently, "you just hold on. We'll tend to you and see that you get better."

Wishing she had the herbs Rue used, Megan soaked some of the strips of silk, then washed the blood away. "Find a needle and thread," she said. "Dominic was mending earlier." Within seconds, she was stitching the wound, hoping the torn flesh would hold, worrying about the blood that continued to flow. She wrapped his torso in the lengths of white silk, and prayed that they would not stain scarlet.

Wolf watched her work in silence, listening to her talk to the boy who could not hear her, noting that she tore up her wedding tunic as if it were already rags. She was efficient and calm, ordering the men as if she expected to be obeyed, stitching confidently, without qualm, offering all of herself for the boy's life—just as Mary had given him his own life back so many years before. 'Twas funny, he thought, for after Mary had disappeared, he'd told himself he never again would care for another woman, never desire one as he had her.

Now, because of Megan, all of his promises to himself seemed foolish and so easily broken.

"Why in the name of the Virgin would he go after a bear?" Odell asked, scratching his head.

Wolf's eyes trained on Megan. "Mayhap to impress someone."

"Me?" she asked, her fingers never stopping their fluid movements.

"The lad was seeking the lady's approval."

"No!" Megan shook her head. "Why would he do anything so foolish?" she asked, but blushed, as if she heard the truth in his words and felt a sense of guilt that he might well be right.

"Because he is smitten with you, *m'lady,*" Wolf said, anger causing the blood to rush from his face, and he shot a furious glance at the outlaws gathered in the decrepit chapel. "As are half the men in this band."

Several of the men visibly started at his accusation and Jagger appeared about to argue, but spying Wolf's white-lipped fury, he had the good sense to keep whatever was on his mind to himself. Jagger cleared his throat. "Methinks you bring us ill luck, Megan of Dwyrain."

"Ahh, then mayhap we're even," she shot back, though her eyes were fixed on Wolf. "You've been the curse of my existence for nearly a fortnight."

"And you'll be mine to the end of my days," he muttered under his breath.

A tiny hole ripped in her heart, but she pretended it didn't exist and went about her work as if she felt no pain, as if his words didn't have the strength to wound her.

When she was finished and the boy was resting, she glanced up at Wolf. "Now, what about you?"

"I'm fine."

"I think not. Lift your tunic."

"What? I'll not—"

"Lift your tunic, Wolf, for you are the leader of these men and they depend upon you." She motioned to the crowd of his followers, who were lingering in the room. "Yea, even I am forced to rely on you, though I detest it."

"Do you?" he said, his eyes narrowing as he lifted his tunic, and she saw his wounds, not as deep as Robin's, but nasty cuts from the swipe of a powerful paw. The slashes across his skin from the day were not his first. Scars of all sizes cut across his dark skin.

"You've been in your share of fights."

"More than my share."

"And flogged as well," she guessed.

His mouth curved into a half-grin that caused her stomach to tighten. "More than once."

"Why?"

"I'm not good at taking orders."

"And what of this?" she asked, running a finger along the cleft of his brow.

"A gift from Tadd of Prydd, so I forget him not."

" 'Twas then that you met Holt."

"Aye," he said, his voice sounding far away, as if it were in a cavern, and his face turned fierce, the way it always did whenever Holt's name was brought up.

"Sit," she ordered, and with only a slight hesitation, he did as he was bid, glaring at his men as if he expected some of them to make comments about him taking orders from a woman.

"One of you stay with Robin. Two others—Dominic and Heath—go and retrieve the bear from the other side of the river," Wolf commanded. "It lies near a small knoll in a thicket of oak and ferns. The rest of you have work, do you not?"

With a few glances cast among them, the men took their leave, and she was alone with him again, aside for the still-unconscious Robin. She cleaned his shoulders, abdomen, and back, washing each cut and scrape, sewing only a few stitches in the largest of the claw marks, trying not to notice the ripple of his muscles when he moved or the dark hair spanning his chest and arrowing down to the band of his breeches. Beneath her fingers, his skin was warm, his muscles hard as stone, and his eyes, smoky blue, watched her beneath half-lowered lids. " 'Tis true, you know," he said when she'd bitten off a length of thread.

"What?"

"Half the men are in love with you."

"They just haven't had a woman in their midst," she said, feeling her cheeks turn a hot scarlet hue.

"They want me not to ransom you."

"And you, Wolf, what do you want?" she asked, her voice breathless.

He stared at the floor, then studied his hands for a second. When his eyes found hers again, there was regret in his gaze. "I have no choice in this, Megan," he said. " 'Tis out of my hands." His lips were blade-thin. "You are wed to Holt."

She choked back a cry of desperation, for she realized then that she was beginning to care for this rogue with his tortured soul and seductive gaze. She'd known from the first time she'd seen him and he danced with her that he could be dangerous to her heart, and later admitted to herself that she was attracted to the demon, but now her feelings had deepened. "As I said, I—I love him not . . ."

"Then you should not have spoken the vows."

"And had I not, I would never have met you." Proudly she lifted her jaw and tossed her hair off her shoulder.

A sad smile touched his lips. " 'Twould have been better for all."

From his pallet, the wounded boy moaned, and Megan hurried to his side. "Robin? Can you hear me, lad?"

Groaning, he blinked his eyes and a smile lighted his face. "Is this heaven?" he asked in a rough whisper.

"Nay, just an old chapel." Tenderly, she brushed his hair from his forehead.

"Be ye not an angel?"

Megan felt tears gather in her throat. "I think not, lad."

"Ahh, but ye're prettier than any in heaven," he said before his eyes closed again, and his breathing was once more slow and steady. Adjusting the furs over his body, she glanced over her shoulder at Wolf, but instead of appearing relieved that the boy was coming around, he only glowered through the window at the snow falling to the frozen ground.

"He's right," Wolf finally said, turning to face her again. "You are an angel of mercy to most of these men." He didn't bother smiling. "And I, methinks, am the Devil."

Before she could answer, there was a commotion on the other side of the rubble that was one of the standing walls. Wolf, pulling on his tunic and mantle, walked through the door with Megan at his heels.

Dominic and Heath had returned. They were leading Robin's gray rounsey, across whose swayed back was the gutted carcass of a great bear. Thick black hair covered the beast and blood was crusted over its nostrils. Its eyes were glazed and dead, its hideous claws sharp as steel.

"Ye gods, what was the boy thinkin'?" Odell muttered as the crowd around the riders grew. Dominic dismounted swiftly, and with the help of Peter and Jagger, pulled the dead bear to the ground. "We'll be havin' 's a new warm rug, now, won't we?"

Wolf dug his fingers into the dead beast's fur. "Robin will. 'Tis his kill."

Swinging a bloody sword, Heath laughed as he hopped to the ground. "Then why was it your blade we retrieved from the animal's heart?" He tossed the weapon to Wolf, who caught it deftly.

"I would not have slain it, were it not that Robin was in trouble."

"Good thing you were nearby," Odell muttered, sizing up the dead bear. "Or the boy would be dead now, instead of the beast."

Megan's blood chilled at the thought. 'Twas true enough that Wolf, demon though he professed to be, had risked his life to save the boy. Not only were his scratches proof enough, but the fact that the great beast was felled with a sword at close hand rather than an arrow from a distance, only proved to her that Wolf was far more virtuous than he would let anyone, even his most trusted men, believe.

* * *

Holt drew back his arrow until his bowstring was tight, then let go. The slim missile sizzled through the air, hitting the target with a snap. The arrow pierced through the tarp, which was painted in the shape of a boar and covered a haystack.

"Good shot," Sir Oswald said. "Right in the bugger's heart!"

Holt snorted at the praise, for Oswald, the ugliest of all the knights, was known to lick the lord's boots for favors.

"Has the sorcerer spoken?" Holt asked, withdrawing another arrow from his quiver and wishing that the painted pig was really Wolf, his tormentor. His eyes narrowed as he focused on the target.

"Nay, well . . . aye, he's spoken, but to the walls, and through the bars to no one. The man is daft, I say."

"Or pretends to be."

"If he were a true magician, why does he not save his skin and disappear from the dungeon, eh? Or why does he limp?"

"Mayhap 'tis all for show," Holt suggested, though the same thoughts had run through his own mind.

Oswald rubbed his flat chin thoughtfully. "Nay, methinks the man's a fraud."

"He has but one more day and then, if he doesn't speak of his own accord, I'll force his tongue."

The toad's eyes gleamed. "Flog 'im, will ye?"

"At the very least." Holt shot again, and his arrow was true once more, piercing deep into the heart of the painted beast. "Or I'll turn loose the peasants who believe he is the reason they lost loved ones to illness or injury." That thought brought a smile to his face. Many would thank him for the chance to seek a bit of personal vengeance for the curse. "Now, Oswald, deliver my message and remind him that I'm not known for my kindness."

The ugly knight, eager to become Holt's pet, lumbered off past the fish pond and toward the dungeons. Holt only hoped he could convey the proper fear to the man whom most believed to be the sorcerer who had cursed the keep.

For two days the prophet had held his tongue, though he'd been given no fresh water or food and had been chained to the wall, where he'd sat in the dirty straw of his cell, his only companions being rats and fleas. But no prodding would make him speak of Megan again. Holt had reasoned with the man, threatened him, and even tried to bribe him, but received no satisfaction. 'Twas as if his newest prisoner had no idea that he was being held against his will, that he was being starved, that he was being punished.

'Twas enough to drive a sane man mad.

Worse yet, the old man wouldn't die. Though he was being given poison in his wine, Ewan lingered on, floating in and out of consciousness, asking about Megan and conversing with his dead wife as if she were lying in the bed with him instead of rotting in her grave as she had been for nearly two years. Holt had tried to visit Ewan, hoping to aid his ill health along, but each time he'd stopped at the lord's chambers, there were other guests, either the priest or the old hag Rue or sweet, young Cayley. 'Twas as if the old man had guardian angels posted and their vigilance was keeping him alive. Even the damned doctor had made it his practice to visit Ewan each day, checking his urine and telling all that the baron was not improving.

For that, Holt was thankful. Ye gods, if the man didn't die soon, Holt would begin believing in miracles. He thought of visiting old Jovan again, but seeing the apothecary was dangerous. There were too many suspicious eyes in the castle, including those of Cayley, who had once seen him with the old man. He sighed. The baron's second daughter had once trusted him, but now avoided crossing his path. Aye, if he hadn't had other plans for her, he'd bed Cayley himself.

Women, they were difficult to understand, though he tried not. Long ago he'd decided they were put on this earth for only one purpose: to pleasure him.

Wolf drew in an unsteady breath as Megan smoothed the salve over his injured muscles. Outside, the wind howled around the old chapel, but within the decrepit building, it was warm. They sat by the fire, watching the flames throw golden shadows on the stone walls and listening to Robin's even breathing. The boy had awakened but once today, eating only a few mouthfuls, moistening his lips, then drifting away again.

Megan's fingers slid across Wolf's back and over his shoulder. His body stiffened, though not from pain, but the sweet, gentle pressure of her hands. The ointment eased the burning of his wounds, but her hands created another heat, one rising up from the center of him, and he shifted as his manhood swelled against the ties of his breeches. Such sweet, sweet torment.

Grinding his back teeth together, he ignored the desire throbbing through his veins and prayed noiselessly that it would soon end.

"Tell me of Holt, why you hate him so," she said. " 'Tis only right that I should know of him, since you're planning to return me to him."

Wolf's jaw ached from clenching.

Her fingers were more persuasive. "Should I not know the man to whom I'm married?"

"You're married not to a man, but a beast from hell," Wolf said, and whether it was right or wrong, he told her all that he knew of Holt, of how Holt had ridden with Tadd of

Prydd and how, while Wolf struggled with consciousness, he had held Mary down so that Tadd could rape her.

The fingers on his back stopped their fluid movements. "Why should I believe you?" she asked. "You are a criminal."

"I only say what I know."

"I believe you not." But there was doubt in her voice.

Wolf whirled around and grabbed her hand before she could touch him any longer. "Believe what you want, woman. You asked and I told. 'Tis simple." Angry with himself, with her, with the world in general, he snatched up his tunic and tossed it over his head. When he looked down at her, he saw the fear in her eyes, knew that he'd been its source, and silently damned himself. She was the root of all his confusion and malcontent, she was the reason he wasn't thinking, she was the reason he felt the need to stay within the confines of the camp rather than to go out riding, and she was the reason he wasn't following his plan and sending her back to Dwyrain where she belonged.

With her husband! He strode outside without his mantle. The breath of winter swept over the land, causing pieces of ice to gather in the stones by the river and dusting the forest floor with snow. He should have been freezing, but his skin was still warm from her touch. Christ Jesus, he'd been such a fool to let her into his heart, for, though he denied it to himself over and over again, she'd gained purchase deep in that locked chamber of his soul. A string of curses rolled off his lips as he crossed the campsite. Some of the men warmed their hands near the fire; others worked in their tents. The bear's hide was stretched on poles, the meat cut away, the claws and teeth saved for Robin when he awakened.

What was he going to do with the woman? What? He had no choice but to send her back to Holt, but his guts ached and his mind burned with foreboding at the thought. Angrily, he spit into the ferns growing near the river. He would have to kill Holt, he decided again, and make Megan a widow. Though she professed not to love her husband and Wolf believed her, killing him would be cold-blooded murder. Despite the fact that Holt had been a part of Mary's rape, he was not wanted by the law; in fact, according to his spies, Holt might very well become the baron if Ewan were to die.

Which was another source of his irritation. Plucking his knife from its sheath, which was strapped to his waist, he squatted by the river and stared into its swiftly moving depths. The plan in which he'd found so much delight was now causing him only pain. Cleaning his fingernails with the tip of the blade, he argued with himself, but could find no solid reason, other than his own selfish lust, to keep her any longer. Her father was dying and he would not hold her prisoner when she might not see the old man again. Mayhap she could get her marriage annulled if she pleaded with Ewan of Dwyrain.

Ah, she was trouble. Sweet, tempting trouble. As Mary had, as Morgana had long ago, Megan touched his black soul.

Would he never learn? Years before, when he was known as Ware of Abergwynn, he was half in love with the woman who would become his brother's wife and lady of the keep. That alone was a curse, but later, he'd lost Garrick's castle to his enemy while left in charge.

Wolf slammed his knife into its sheath and kicked at the icy stones of the bank. He'd never forgiven himself for that mistake, and it wasn't his last, oh, no. Then there was Mary . . . sweet, trusting Mary, turned into a pitiful, withdrawn half-brained woman after Tadd of Prydd had raped her. Closing his eyes, Wolf tried to block out the memory of a panting Tadd rutting on Mary while Holt helped hold the girl down. Her screams reverberated through his brain, haunting him. Once again, he'd been useless.

And now he found his sworn enemy's wife attractive. More than attractive. If he cared not for Megan, he'd love to bed Holt's bride and laugh about it, to send her back to her husband, defiled and dirty. He would never rape her, but he would seduce her. After she lost her heart and virginity to him, he'd toss her back to the man to whom she'd vowed everlasting love and fidelity.

But he couldn't. Because of Megan and that blasted thread of nobility that bound his soul. Try as he might, he was never able to unwind it.

"Hell," he muttered, damning himself again. He had no choice but to send her back.

Injustice gnawing on his guts, he spit again. 'Twas settled. Come morning, he'd send two messengers to ride to Dwyrain with ransom demands. This woman, like every other woman he'd been cursed to care for, would soon be out of his life forever.

Eight

Oooh," Robin moaned, wincing as he levered himself onto an elbow. "Where—what—ooh!" He flopped down on the bed, and Megan felt tears of relief star her lashes. The boy was alive! He was going to live. She whispered a quick prayer of thanks before taking his rough hand in hers.

"Robin?"

"Go 'way."

" 'Tis Megan."

Eyes closed, he moved, his tongue moving over his teeth. "The lady?" he murmured.

"Aye." She squeezed his hand and one of his eyes cracked open, only to close for a second.

"Oh, Lady Megan!" His eyes flew open again, this time clear and bright. "What happened . . . ? Oh, the bear."

"Aye, you and he had a bit of a disagreement, and he got the better of you."

Robin groaned and blushed. "But how did I live?" Trying to raise himself upright, he sucked in a swift breath.

"Careful—you didn't come out of this without a wound or two."

"I feel like dog dung. Did you find me in the forest?"

"Nay. 'Twas Wolf. He came upon you and ran the beast through."

Clarity sparked in the boy's eyes as if suddenly his memory had returned. " 'Tis true," he finally said, and his pale face colored. "I should not have gone after him."

"Not alone," she said, but decided he was punishing himself enough and did not need to be told that he'd been foolish. "If you're feeling well enough, Odell has cooked part of the beast, and 'twould be justice for you to eat a piece of him."

Robin laughed and the sound touched Megan's heart, even though he winced in pain.

"Where's Wolf?" Robin asked, glancing through the dark chambers.

A fine question, Megan thought, for she'd wondered that herself. He'd left the camp hours before with Bjorn and Cormick. Somberly, they'd saddled their mounts and ridden away without so much as a word to her or any of the men. They could be hunting, she decided, though with the bear, they had meat enough for nearly a week. They could be out robbing someone traveling on the road or searching for Holt's soldiers, or they might be in the nearest town, drinking ale, playing dice, and whoring.

She scowled at the turn of her thoughts, for jealousy invaded her blood whenever she thought of Wolf lying with another woman. 'Twas an image that burned in her thoughts each time he left the camp.

"Wolf and some of the men have been gone this afternoon, but when they return, he'll be pleased to see you awake."

Robin struggled to his feet and Megan wanted to restrain

him, but didn't. The boy wasn't woozy, though he grimaced a bit as he walked outside and felt a blast of winter air rip through his thin body. She handed him a hooded cloak, which he donned, and Odell, stirring the coals beneath a boiling pot, cracked a smile at the boy. "So ye decided to stay with the livin', did ye? A fine choice, m'boy. Come and see the skin of the beast ye helped slay."

Cackling, Odell led the eager boy to the bearskin, and Megan rubbed her arms against the cold. Though she was this motley band's captive, she'd never felt more free. With no castle walls to surround her, no priest's silent scorn, no duties aside from those of surviving, she experienced a vigor she'd never enjoyed as daughter of the baron.

A sharp whistle and hoofbeats announced Wolf's return. Megan bit down hard on her lip and tried to stop the sudden clamoring of her heart. 'Twas foolish. He cared not for her. As he rode into the clearing, she couldn't keep an expectant smile from creeping over her lips. His gaze touched hers for a silent heartbeat, then landed full force on the lad. "There ye be, Robin," Wolf said, falling into the easy speech of his men. "And Odell, here, had given ye up fer dead."

"Nay, I never said—" Odell protested, but caught the twinkle of devilment in Wolf's eye. "And curse and rot yer soul, ye foul creature of the forest," he said with a grin as he realized he was being teased.

Wolf slid lightly to the ground and touched Robin gently on the shoulder. "If I had any brains, I would have your skin stretched like the bear's!"

Robin folded his lips in upon themselves and stared at the ground.

Wolf wasn't finished. "Goin' after that one"—he hitched his chin toward the glossy black hide drying beneath a tarp—"could've cost you your life."

Robin's gaze didn't falter, but his jaw jutted mutinously and the muscles in his shoulders bulged a bit.

" 'E's alive, ain't 'e? Jest a mite clawed up, and we got meat enough fer the week and a fine new robe—"

"The skin is Robin's, Odell," Wolf reminded the older man quickly.

"I know, I know." Grumbling under his breath, Odell ambled back to the fire, and Wolf, locking eyes with Megan for an instant, called a meeting together.

Megan wasn't about to be treated as an outsider any longer. Despite Wolf's hard glare, she walked to the fire and sat on a stump, warming her hands, while the rest of the band gathered together. Meat sizzled over the fire, the flames danced wildly with a breath of wind, and afternoon faded into night.

"There be no women in our midst," Odell said, though not unkindly.

"I'm here. I'm a part of this group, even if only as a 'guest.' " Defiantly, she refused to budge.

"This concerns you not," Wolf said.

"Then why should I have to leave?" Crossing her ankles, and tucking her arms under her breasts, she turned her face up saucily and smiled, silently begging him to continue.

"Megan, please," he said with a quiet calm that was more frightening than a furious rage. " 'Tis man-talk."

"Have I not cooked for you?"

The men exchanged glances, but no one argued.

"Have I not helped mend your torn breeches? And you, Peter, did I not find some softer fabric for your eye patch?"

"Aye," he agreed, though he wouldn't meet her stare.

"And Dominic, when you needed help cleaning the weaponry, did I not offer assistance?" Before he could answer, her gaze swept to Heath. "I've helped you tan hides, and Lord knows I've done my share with Odell."

Several men laughed and nodded their heads.

There was a quiet muttering in the background as Heath whispered something to Peter.

"Have I not cleaned, hunted, and helped make camp?"

"Can't argue there," Robin said, his eyes shining in awe as he looked at her.

She stood slowly, inching up her chin, standing toe to toe with the lord and master of the outlaws, the man called Wolf, the renegade to whom she'd unwillingly given her heart. "And have I not, when you were injured, stitched you together and balmed your wounds?"

A muscle in the side of his jaw tightened.

"Why then, just because I am not a man—nay, because I am your guest—would I not be allowed to listen and speak my mind? Have I not done everything I could to help you?"

"But you tried to escape."

"And failed."

"Why not let her listen in?" Dominic rolled his hands toward the darkening sky.

"Aye, but she's got no say." Jagger, sitting on a rock, hung his hands between his legs and shook his head. "The rule is 'no women—' "

"So be it!" Wolf declared. "Sit, Megan; hear what we have to say, because I lied when I told you the talk is none of your concern." He glanced around the fire to each of his men, their hooded cloaks dusted with snow and their faces illuminated by the golden flames. Megan eased back onto her stump but heard the knell of doom thundering in her ears. "Bjorn and Cormick have already been sent to Dwyrain. In Bjorn's pouch, he carries a letter from me that states that I have Holt's wife and am willing to return her in exchange for gold."

Megan felt as if the world had begun to spin.

"Just like that?" Odell wondered aloud.

"It should have been done a week ago."

"By the gods," Odell whispered.

Megan's heart pounded painfully in her chest. *No! No! No!* she inwardly cried. She could not think of leaving. Not now. Not ever! "You are sending me away?" she asked, her voice catching. Somewhere nearby, an owl hooted mournfully.

"Aye. Your father is ill, Megan," he said gently. "The day I took you from the castle, he fell and had to be carried to his bed, where he has remained."

"Nay!" she cried. She knew, of course, that her father was no longer the strong leader that he'd once been, that ofttimes he'd been confused, that he'd even thought that he talked with her dead mother and Baby Roz, but Megan refused to think Ewan would die soon and refused to believe the painful words. " 'Tis but a trick to lure me back there."

"No trick," Wolf said gently, then cast a tormented glance to the stars just starting to appear in the vast, dark sky. "Asides, you needs be with your husband."

"After what you told me of him, you would send me back?"

" 'Twas not I who married him," he reminded her. "And in my letter, I've demanded that as part of your ransom, no injury befall you. Should I hear that you are being mistreated, I've vowed to storm the castle, sneak into his bedchamber, and cut out his heart."

"You think a threat will change him?" she mocked.

"Would you rather stay here?" A challenge flamed in his eyes.

"Never!" she lied, feeling torn between two homes, the castle, with its secure walls and comforts, and the forest, where she felt free even though she was held captive.

"So be it." He searched the faces of his men as Megan's heart turned to ice. "We'll wait here for Cormick and Bjorn's return, then send Lady Megan home, break camp, and move on."

"Bring in the new log," Holt ordered, his face flushed from wine, as peasants and knights guided a huge horse into the hall and rolled the log onto the iron dogs in the fireplace, sending ash and embers flying. Sparks and laughter erupted as Holt lit the new log and watched the dry wood catch fire.

Shouts of "wassail" and "drinkhaile!" floated over the songs being played by the musicians in the gallery, an alcove cut high into the wall facing the lord's table, where Holt sat near a comely seamstress.

The Christmas revels were upon them, the great hall decorated with ivy, holly, and mistletoe, and peasants, knights, servants, and lords all rejoicing. Holt had decreed that there would be merriment in the halls of Dwyrain despite the fact that his wife was missing and the tired old baron was hovering near death.

"If only Lord Ewan could see this," Rue whispered to Cayley as she wiped her hands on her skirt and tapped her foot in time with the drummer. They stood near the stairs, where pages and servants hurried to and from the kitchen. " 'Tis a pity he can't join us." Sadness stole through her old eyes.

"Aye, I think I'll take something up to him. Cook's saved him a joint of venison and some pheasant, along with his soup."

"A good daughter ye are, Cayley girl," Rue said, slipping back to the name she'd called Cayley when she was but a child.

Not as good as you think, Cayley thought as she hurried

to the kitchen and carried a tray to her father's room. But the baron didn't move when she entered. The tempo of his breathing never wavered, and even though she spoke to him, he remained blissfully asleep, unaware that there was treachery within the castle walls, that Megan had not been found, that the outlaw roamed free. Nay, her father was probably dreaming of happier times when the family was together and his wife and all his children were alive.

"Sleep well," Cayley said, pressing a kiss to his temple and adding more heavy logs to the fire in his room. She tore off big hunks of the meat, wrapped the greasy chunks in a towel, poured wine into his cup, and took the bottle. Her heart thudding in fear at her plan, she left his tray at his bedside and knew that he would eat no more than a few spoonfuls of broth and drink even less wine. Once a robust man, he had wasted to nearly nothing. Something had to be done, and Cayley, though she cringed at the thought, was the only one to do it. Whereas Megan had always leaped at adventure, had ridden as well as Bevan and shot an arrow straight and true, Cayley had been content to be considered silly and pampered, enjoying the attention of men and pretending that she was helpless.

Ofttimes her mother had reprimanded her, telling her that she was lazy and needed to work some around the castle. Lady Violet had insisted that her daughter learn how to embroider, keep the books, and care for the poor by passing out alms—money and any uneaten food in the castle. Violet had even dragged Cayley with her to the nunnery, hoping her second daughter would take an interest in some charity, but Cayley, at that time in her life, had been interested only in herself. She'd seen no reason to do for herself when others, be they friends, relatives, or servants, were willing to do for her.

"Stupid girl," she told herself now, for she had no skills on which to rely and few friends to help her. Oh, if only Gwayne were here, but that thought was not as comforting as it had once been. She'd heard nothing more of his betrothal, but she saw him in a different light and what she had once considered clever, now she thought mean. He was vain and pompous. In all the while he'd courted her, he'd never once spoken of love or marriage.

Well, she had not the time to be thinking of him. She had much to do. Gritting her teeth and wishing she'd taken the time to learn how, if nothing else, to handle a weapon, she set her plan into motion. She'd have to rely upon her wits rather than swords, axes, and arrows. She stopped at her chamber to don her hooded cloak, ducked through the corridor, and was relieved to find no guards at their posts.

Darting down the stairs, her cloak billowing behind her, she slipped through the kitchen and out the door.

The sound of music from lutes and pipes followed Cayley as she held her skirt high and ran. Her boots sank in the mud and mire as she crossed the inner bailey to the north tower, under which were the dungeons.

"Be with me," she prayed, her voice the barest of whispers as she opened the door to the guardhouse. Curved stairs led ever downward. In the darkness, rats scurried from her path. She carried only a solitary candle, its flickering light reflecting on the cold stone walls, which always appeared wet. The smells of rotting straw, mildew, and urine rose from the dungeon, nearly choking her. The guards, too, were in the keep, their sorry charges left alone in the dank cavern, which held the enemies of Dwyrain.

Shuddering, Cayley made her way down slippery steps and past cells, where eyes gleamed at her from within the gloom.

"Who goes there?" one raspy voice asked.

" 'Tis the lady." Another, deeper, voice.

"What lady? Violet?"

"Nay, she's been dead two or three years. 'Tis her daughter."

"A comely wench, say what?"

"Sorcerer?" Cayley said, her voice thinner than usual, a tremor running through it. "Are you here?"

"So you've come." His voice was smooth as the ice that sometimes covered the lake in coldest winter.

"Aye."

She walked on, holding her candle aloft, trying to keep her wits about her when she imagined all sorts of vile creatures swooping out of the darkness at her.

"Good. I have much to say."

She followed the sound of his voice to the lowest cell, where water dripped from the ceiling and the straw on the floor was moist and fetid. The stench was unbearable, the rooms cold as death.

"I have no key," she said, shivering, "but I overheard Holt say that you've been given no food."

" 'Tis true."

"Nor water."

"I've survived."

"I don't know how." She held her candle aloft and found him chained to the far wall. "My God," she whispered, crossing herself as before her very eyes he slipped out of his shackles and limped, unbound, across the cell. "How did you—?"

" 'Tis not magic, child," he said in his soothing voice. "I found a nail in the old straw and was able to pick the locks. The guards, they know not."

"You're not afraid I will warn them?"

"I think not, though you do not trust me."

"I hated you."

His smile was cautious. "I know." Through the bars he asked, "And now?"

"Now there is trouble dark and deep within Dwyrain, but I think you are not the cause. I—I cursed you, said I wanted you to roast in hell and—"

" 'Tis forgiven. Asides, anyone who would steal venison from the lord's table and wine from his mazer would not endanger their only friend."

"You—you are my friend?" she asked as she handed him the bundle of meat and bottle. He ate hungrily and started to drink from the bottle, only to stop and spit the wine on the floor.

"What?"

" 'Tis poison you bring!" he said, coughing and gasping.

"No—"

In the candlelight, his eyes turned harsh. " 'Tis only a little, but enough, if given over time . . ."

"Dear God, no," she cried, stepping away and nearly dropping her candle. Wax slipped down the metal holder and burned her hand. " 'Twas meant for my father. No one else would dare touch wine from his cellar. I brought it to you only so no one would notice." Her throat turned as dry as milled flour and ugly thoughts began to fill her mind.

He eyed her in the darkness, then spit again. "Your father is being poisoned."

"No, I'll not believe . . ."

" 'Tis true, Cayley. Whoever is giving him wine each day is making sure that he will die."

She leaned against the wall. "Holt," she muttered, finally understanding why her sister did not trust the knight who would now inherit Dwyrain. "Holt allows no one to take my father the wine except one of his most trusted knights—or Nell. Because of the revels, 'twas forgotten . . ."

"Listen to me, Cayley," the sorcerer said, his voice low and deadly. "You must trust me."

She bit her tongue. Though she wished him no ill will, she could not forget the pain and suffering that had been with Dwyrain these two years past. "Trust you?" she repeated. "Even though you cursed the castle and—"

"I thought you understood, girl!" he said, losing the calm that had been with him each time she'd seen him. His fingers curled over the rusted bars of the cage in which he was kept. "I told Megan only what I saw. It came to pass through no fault of mine, but if you do not listen to me and help me, your father will die, Megan will return to Dwyrain only for Holt to shame her and use her to gain possession of this keep, and you and everyone you hold dear will live as his prisoners."

Wolf stayed out much of the night, but Megan sensed his presence the instant he walked through the door of their chamber in the decrepit old chapel. She'd lain for hours, not sleeping a wink, jumping at every sound.

A few embers glowed red in the fire and he paused to add another log. Lying on the pallet, Megan feigned sleep, while plotting how she would elude him. She would not let him haul her back to Dwyrain like a prisoner. Nay, if she intended to return to Dwyrain, 'twould be her own way. She wouldn't be traded for a few coins, like a sack of flour or prized horse! If this taste of freedom had proved anything to her, 'twas that she was her own woman and she needed no man to tell her what to do.

Soft snoring rippled down the roofless corridor from the chamber where Robin and Odell were sleeping near their fire, but Megan found no comfort knowing they were close by. Whenever she was alone with Wolf, 'twas as if they were the only two souls in the world and she thought of nothing save him.

For the past few nights, Wolf had taken up his vigil at the doorway, watching over her but not lying beside her beneath the furs. 'Twas better, she supposed, as when he was near her, his body molded around hers, her thoughts turned wanton and through the hours of the night, she fought the urge to turn in his arms and kiss him, to kindle the sinful flames of passion that perpetually ignited whenever his skin touched hers.

She heard his boots scrape against the floor. "I know you sleep not," he said and sighed wearily as he slid to a sitting position near enough to the fire that golden shadows were cast upon his face. "I brought you something."

She didn't move, but through slitted eyes watched as he opened his bag and removed a tunic—shimmering green silk trimmed with gold velvet.

"Something to replace the tunic you tore up to bind Robin's wounds."

Unable to ignore his kind gesture, she pushed herself to her elbow and shoved a handful of hair from her face. "Is this what you want me to wear when you return me to Holt?" she asked, unable to keep the sting from her words.

His lips flattened.

"So that he will want me? So that he will take me as his bride?" She couldn't help the hurtful words, and they tumbled out of her mouth in rapid succession, one after the other, meant to wound as she'd been injured.

Tossing the tunic to the floor, Wolf leaped to his feet, strode to the pallet, and yanked her from the covers. His fingers held her fiercely, digging through her chemise to her upper arms and dragging her to her feet. "Understand this, woman," he said in a voice that was nearly a growl. "I want you not to return to Holt, and if there was a way to keep you from him, I would. But there is none. In the eyes of the land and the church you are his wife; you pledged yourself to him and there is nothing I can do about it."

She hoisted her chin upward and narrowed her eyes at him. "Then let me go," she demanded, knowing that deep in her heart it would kill her to walk away from him. "Leave me to my freedom."

"Is that what you want?"

"Aye," she said without hesitation, though deep in the darkest recess of her heart, she knew that what she truly wanted was to stay with him, to be his wife, to become an outlaw's woman. Shame burned up her spine, but she could not lie to herself. This man touched her as no man ever had and none ever would again. She was as certain of that single damning fact as she was of her own name.

"You vex me."

"As you do me."

"You test my will."

"You try mine."

"I cannot have you here with me."

"I know. Oh, dear God in heaven, I know," she said, and her skin, beneath the tense fingers holding her in a death grip, tingled. Her flesh, where his breath brushed over it, heated; her heart, trapped deep in her ribs, hammered anxiously.

His eyes were as tortured as her own condemned soul. "God have mercy on me," he muttered roughly as his lips crashed down on hers, hard and hot, unforgiving and filled with want. Desire trumpeting through her body, Megan sighed, opening her mouth to him, feeling her bones turn to jelly as together they fell upon his pallet.

Passion turned her thoughts around. She would not listen to the doubts swiftly slipping from her mind. Though he was a murdering outlaw, she wanted him. Despite the fact that he could cause her to act like a shameless kitchen wench, she hungered for him. Even though she would be banished for the rest of her life, constantly reminded that she was a wanton harlot, she could not resist him. That she was married was of no consequence; this man, this Wolf, was her one true love.

His kiss was deep and anxious, his moan as fierce as the tide at midnight. Sliding the neckline of her chemise over her shoulder, he pressed warm lips to her bare skin. With a gasp, she quivered inside. In the firelight, his face was composed of deep angles and grooves, dark shadows and golden slopes, and he was anxious as he kicked off his boots.

"I want you," he admitted, his countenance fierce, as if in the saying of the betraying act he would have to fight. He untied the ribbon of her chemise, letting the soft fabric fall open so that he could view her breasts in the firelight. "But you are Holt's wife." He traced the rim of her nipple, that dark ready circle, with the tip of his finger.

"It matters not," she gasped when he found the hard button and rolled it between his finger and thumb.

"Yes . . . yes, it matters." But he pulled her close and clamped his mouth to her breast, kissing, teasing, tasting, laving while she writhed against him. Heat boiled through her blood, and deep in the very depths of her, where she was untouched, she felt a new tingling and warmth, a dark yearning that only he could fill.

She didn't protest when he yanked down her chemise, baring her torso to the shadowy light, looking down at her with the savage possession of one who was used to taking rather than asking.

"You are sure, m'lady?" he asked, his voice ragged as he

skimmed the hated flimsy garment down her legs. She lay naked before him, her skin flushed with desire, the nest of curls at her legs dewy with a craving she'd never before felt. She nodded.

"You want me, little one."

"As you want me."

"Aye," he admitted, taking her hand and placing it on the front of his breeches. Through the fabric, she felt his manhood, stiff and upright.

Her throat went dry and she leaned upward, kissing him and sliding his tunic over his wounded shoulders. "Show me."

His lips locked over hers and he rolled her onto her back. Pressed into the rugs, she welcomed his weight as he rubbed against her, his breeches rough upon her skin, the dark hairs that swirled over his chest tickling her breasts. Her skin was afire, her senses alive, and he dragged his mouth from her lips, past her chin, along her neck, and lower, pausing at the circle of bones at the base of her throat.

She bucked as he kissed her breasts again and slid ever lower, his tongue rimming her navel as her fingers clenched in his thick hair. She could scarcely breathe, and her heart was pounding in a wild, uneven cadence as he slid his hands down her legs, slowly and lazily, drawing them up as her mind swam in the warm whirlpool of his love. Writhing against the pallet, she caught her breath when his fingers first touched her in that most private of places and then gently probed, moving slowly at first and then faster as the heat within her grew. She cried out in lust and fear, moving with him, letting him take her on a ride she'd never felt before.

"That's it, little one, give yourself up," he said against her inner thigh, and something inside of her broke, a dam that was holding the heat at bay. Faster and faster he stroked her, sending her hips into wanton thrusting. With a cry, she lifted up, only to fall back to the fur, her skin drenched, her mind spinning. She had trouble finding her breath and her heart would not be quiet, but he was not done.

As if there was more loving to have, as if the earth hadn't splintered before her very eyes, he slid beneath her legs, lifted her rump with his hands, and kissed her more intimately than she'd ever expected.

She convulsed, but he held her tight, whispering into her that 'twould be all right, that she would fly like a falcon again, and before she could protest, he was close to her, his breath hot, his mouth wet, his tongue seeking new areas to plunder. Shuddering, she closed her eyes and bucked upward, wanting more, so much more, until it came, that wonderful hot spasm of release, and the world spun again.

As she cried out, he slid up her body, holding her to his rock-hard muscles, cradling her as the first tears—of joy or sadness, she knew not which—slid down her cheeks. She sobbed brokenly and realized that she cared for him far more than she'd ever dared admit to herself, that she was a soul lost and he was her anchor—that, curse and rot his stubborn hide, she loved him.

Nine

"He just took off. I don't know when, but I woke up needin' to relieve myself and noticed 'e was gone," Odell said, shaking his head and staring at the ground as if he expected Wolf to flog him for letting Robin slip away. A few men had awakened and gathered around though dawn had yet to send her gray light through the valley.

Megan had awakened from a particularly wanton dream when Wolf, his arms surrounding her, had started. "Something's amiss," he'd whispered into her ear, and she knew he was right, for Odell was cursing loudly and angrily. They'd hurried down the crumbling hallway and outside to find him muttering, grumbling, and swearing by the remains of last night's fire. Odell had admitted then that Robin was missing.

"Why?" Wolf asked as he rubbed his jaw and glared at the older man. "He was injured, for God's sake."

" 'Twas that he felt like a fool. Embarrassed he was about nearly being killed by the bear. He'd hoped to bag that beast and bring it to the camp so that he would look like a man rather than the boy we take him for."

"He is a boy," Wolf said.

Odell dug at the coals with a stick as Peter carried over more firewood. "Aye, but he wants to be thought of as a man." He looked over his shoulder at Megan. "Especially since the lady arrived."

So 'twas her fault the lad was missing, she thought and read the silent suspicions on the men's faces. "Where would he go?" she asked, knowing that he had no home.

"After Cormick and Bjorn." Wolf's voice was filled with conviction and he stared at the surrounding woods as if he was envisioning Robin's flight. "He asked to be sent to Dwyrain as a messenger."

"Aye," Odell said, as a pitchy log caught fire and flames popped and crackled, lighting the ground surrounding the fire pit.

Wolf, who'd been calm, kicked angrily at a stone near the bear's hide and flung Megan a dark look.

He blames me. Everyone blames me!

"I'll go after him. Jagger, come with me; Heath, go to the village, see if there's word of him. Dominic, you're in charge, and no one," he said, eyeing each and every man until his gaze landed with deadly aim upon Megan, "is to leave. As soon as Bjorn and Cormick return, we'll break camp and move, but until then, we stay here."

No one dared argue, and as the first light of morning crept across the land, he and Jagger climbed upon their horses and rode through the trees. Megan watched horses and riders disappear through the trees and she shivered, not from the frosty wind that chased down the river and knifed through her bones, but from the horrid thought that she might never see Wolf again.

* * *

They caught up with the boy in early afternoon, when they spied the gray hack he'd taken with him tied to the bare branch of an apple tree. Robin, wrapped in his mantle, was lying on the ground and didn't start when Wolf and Jagger approached, nor did he open his eyes when his name was called. Only when Wolf touched the lad's shoulder did he awaken, blinking hard as his eyebrows slammed together in confusion.

A second later his situation must've dawned upon him and he started. "Wolf! J-Jagger."

"Aye, lad," Wolf said, squatting next to the boy and rolling back onto the worn heels of his boots. " 'Tis time you came home."

Robin closed his eyes for a second. "I didn't do a very good job of runnin' away."

"Is that what you want? To be rid of the band?"

Robin looked down at his hands, as if fascinated by the dirt beneath his fingernails. "Nay, I—" He struggled to a sitting position. "I just wanted to be a part of the group, not treated like a lad." His jaw, unblemished by a beard, jutted in silent rage and Wolf remembered himself as a youth, straining to be a man, defying his older brother, thinking battles and killing for a cause were noble and glorious pursuits. How many times had Garrick said the words that echoed through his mind?

"Be patient, Ware," Garrick had advised. "Study hard, learn your skills, do not hasten off to war." Every bit of his counsel had fallen on deaf ears, for Ware of Abergwynn had been prideful, mulish, and eager to prove himself a man.

"You will come with me when I meet with Holt," Wolf said now as he clapped the boy on the back. "He will have men with him and want to kill me. You will guard me against them."

The boy's eyes widened expectantly and Jagger coughed, trying to catch Wolf's eye. "Truly?" Robin asked.

"Truly."

Again Jagger coughed, and this time he said, "Do you think it's wise, with one so young—"

" 'Twill be fine. There will be others as well, but Robin will ride with me."

A smile split Robin's stubborn jaw. "When?" he asked. "When do we ride?"

"Upon the return of Bjorn and Cormick," he said, then repeated Garrick's oft-spoken but never heard advice, "Be patient, lad; there are many years yet for battle."

With Wolf in the lead, they made their way to the camp, avoiding any of Holt's soldiers and seeing only a few carts and travelers upon the road. It was dark by the time they returned, but Megan was waiting, her beautiful face expectant when Wolf rode into the circle of light cast by the fire.

"So you're safe," she said to the boy as Robin dismounted.

"Aye."

"Well, come along. Odell's made a fine stew with some of the bear meat . . ." Wolf watched as she helped the boy to a trencher of the thick, greasy soup. Robin's eyes glowed and he couldn't keep a grin from his face as she fussed about him. Aye, he was smitten, as were several of the men. Peter's one-eyed gaze followed her about when he thought no one was watching, and even gruff Jagger managed a grin when she was near. 'Twas a problem. Wasn't he, too, enchanted by the lilt of her voice or the sparkle in her golden eyes? Didn't he think much too long about the slope of her shoulders, the sway of her rump as she walked, or the bounce of her breasts? 'Twas enough to distract a man, to cause his member to spring to attention at the most awkward of times. Already, the men, though they knew it not, were vying for her attention.

'Twould be good to be rid of her, or so he tried to convince himself, though he could not shake the memory of their lovemaking.

Cupping her hand near her mouth, she said something into Robin's ear and he threw back his head and laughed uproariously, as if she were the most clever woman on earth. Jealousy, his old enemy, slithered into Wolf's veins and caused his jaw to clench so hard it ached.

He could not let himself become too attached to her because she was the cur Holt's wife and could never be his. That painful thought brought him up short. He'd not considered marriage since Mary's death, had vowed that he'd never allow a woman close enough for him to ponder wedding her, but with Megan, he'd let his mind run wild.

"Bloody fool," he muttered low and under his breath. Somehow she'd gotten to him, and if he didn't keep some distance between them, he'd try to bed her. Hadn't he nearly done the deed just this past night?

Though he'd love to humiliate Holt further by stealing his wife's virginity, he could not dishonor her or shame her by claiming her as his own when he had nothing to offer her—no castle, nay, not even a house, no money, and no life except to run from the law.

He had to return her to her husband, or, as he'd decided more often with each passing day, kill the bastard and make her a widow.

Megan slipped from beneath the furs. Holding her breath, she pulled on her clothes and silently prayed that Wolf, wherever he was, wouldn't return before she'd escaped. He'd stood at the door of the chamber, not crossing the threshold, not allowing himself near the pallet early in the night. Once he appeared convinced that she was asleep, he waited a few more minutes, then left his post. Now was the time to escape.

Heart thudding, she walked to the sack he kept near the door and reached inside. Her fingers scraped a hatchet and a mason's tool of some kind before brushing against a small dagger with a curved blade. Her fingers curled around the smooth bone handle. Slowly she extracted the wicked knife, then searched further until she came to a length of rope, the same rope he'd used to restrain her. It was fitting somehow that she'd make good her escape with some of the very tools he'd used for her capture.

She had no choice but to leave. Knowing the depth of her feelings for Wolf and that he planned to ransom her to a cruel husband she should never have married, she wasn't about to stay here and wait like a lamb for the slaughter. Nay, she had to find a way to wrest herself free of the shackles of her marriage. Since nearly making love to Wolf, she'd known she had to come up with a plan to liberate herself.

The first step was to sneak away from the camp. Biting her lip, she crept to the window and, as she had once before, hoisted herself to the ledge and slipped through the opening. She landed without a sound on the frosty ground and silently cursed when she realized her footsteps were visible in the snow. A hunter such as Wolf would track her without much trouble, but there was naught she could do.

Then she saw him. Sitting near the fire, staring into the flames, his expression hard and faraway, as if he, too, were laying plans. Golden shadows played upon his face and a thick black cloak kept him warm. Her heart nearly broke when she realized she was leaving him forever, that this would be her last vision of him, a lonely man staring into the flames.

Just leave! Now! While he's let down his guard!

Silently she sneaked around a crumbled corner of the chapel, and praying she wouldn't snap a twig, slunk past the tethered horses. One, a bay mare, nickered before Peter, from his guard's position near the rear of one of the tents, hushed the horse with his gentle voice.

Megan nearly jumped from her skin. Quick as lightning, she ducked into the woods and watched while Peter stood with his backside to her. Leaning against a tree, he stared with his solitary eye across the river. Eventually, he took a short walk around the animals before striding to the fire. Megan didn't wait. This was her chance.

Certain he would turn and spy her in the withering moonlight, she untied a small brown horse that wouldn't easily be missed. She would have loved to steal Wolf's destrier, but he was a tall horse, a restless animal, and Peter was certain to notice he was gone.

The brown, a swift little jennet, was a calm enough beast, and Megan worked nervously, untying the tether, praying the horses wouldn't make any noise. Once the tether was unbound, she led the mare into the woods near the river. They walked close to the rushing water so their footsteps were muffled by the noise. Only when they were far enough from camp that the fire no longer glowed through the trees did Megan loop the rope around the jennet's nose and ears, then climb upon her slick back. The horse snorted and side-stepped, but 'twas no matter. No one would hear.

"Let's go, girl," Megan said, planning to reach the road, where the mare's hoofprints would blend with those of the others that had passed during the day. The snow had fallen much earlier and though a few solitary flakes drifted to the ground, most of the white powder had lain in patches since the afternoon.

As she rode, she trained her ears backward, listening for the barest of whispers or the clop of horses' hooves, half expecting a band of men to leap from the shadows at any second. Nerves strung tight, hands sweating in her gloves, she felt as if the mare were moving much too slowly, that she had to put distance between her and the camp. But Wolf was not the only enemy she feared, for, if Wolf's spies were correct, Holt's soldiers were scouring the hills and woods, searching for her.

"Come on, come on," she encouraged, though they were traveling as fast as possible through the forest and the overgrown deer trail that curved away from the river and—

"Well, well, well." Wolf's voice rang through the forest and her heart flew to her throat. Where was he? "Taking a midnight ride, m'lady?" The sound ricocheted around her and she squinted into the gloom.

"Aye, I'm leaving," she said boldly. Damn, if only she could see him! "I'll not let you sell me, Wolf." He'd have to chase her down if he wanted to catch her. She pulled on the reins, hoping to turn away from the sound. "Hiya!" she yelled at her mare, but as she started to urge the fleet horse forward, he appeared from the shadows, dark, looming, and furious atop his destrier.

"We need to talk," he said, grabbing the reins and stripping them from her fingers. Hopping from his horse to the ground, he reached upward, caught her hand, and caused her to tumble into the strength of his arms.

"Unhand me," she commanded, but he only held her tighter. She slapped at his face, tried to kick, but he laughed at her foolish attempts. "I'll not let you send me to Holt!"

"You were told not to leave camp."

"By the leader of an outlaw band! A criminal!"

"Is that what you think of me?" he asked, and in the moonlight she saw that his eyes were hooded, his jaw clenched, his lips white and thin as the blade of a new sword. Menacing and seductive he was, and her heart thudded, not with fear, but with a new, restless longing. Her mind burned with images of lying with him on the pallet, how she'd writhed and begged like a common wench. Her throat turned to sand and her pulse throbbed at the feel of him.

"You should have thought of that afore you decided to marry him."

"Just let me go. What matters it to you? You'll get your ransom, for my father will pay it, and I'll not have to be returned to a husband I detest."

"A husband who will hunt me and my men like foxes in the field for the rest of my days," he reminded her, his voice edged in anger.

"Would you not enjoy it? Giving chase, eluding your enemy, vexing him?"

He searched her face for a heart-stopping instant. "Aye, 'tis true. I'd like nothing better than to cause Holt anguish and laugh at him, but there comes a time when a man must stop running."

As his gaze touched hers, she was suddenly lost, her anger drained away, and the cold, brittle night closed around them. A rush of wind rattled the dry leaves, sending them skittering across the snow-dusted ground. "What are you running from?"

His smile gleamed white and wicked in the darkness. "I know not," he said, shaking his head. "Myself, mayhap, or the mistakes of my youth."

"You will make another if you force me to return to Holt."

"Do you not want to see Dwyrain again?"

"Yes, but—"

"And your father?"

"Aye. I miss him."

"Then you have to go to Dwyrain as Holt's bride," he said, but his lips barely moved. When she stared at them, that newly awakened beast of desire lying deep within her stretched its legs and unleashed its sharp claws. She could not trust this man, didn't dare give him her heart, but the deed was already done; nothing remained but the physical act of loving him. What would be the consequences of that one, dark, unforgivable act?

She would be condemned. For the love of Jesus, she could not, as a married woman, even consider adultery, but the strength of his arms holding her close to his chest, the thunder of his heart beating a hard cadence not unlike her own, and his eyes, hidden when a gust of wind blew his black hair before them, worked to change her mind. What would be the harm of it?

Were she to give herself to Wolf, her marriage would certainly be annulled and she would not be forced to stay with Holt. However, her father would never forgive her for bringing shame to the house of Dwyrain. Ewan would surely disown her and mayhap banish her. Then she would lose everything.

"Come," he said, carrying her to his horse.

"No!" Desperate to free herself, she pushed hard against the wall of his chest. "Let me go."

"I cannot."

"Then 'tis about money—pieces of gold and silver—nothing more!" she accused, and she felt him stiffen.

The skin over his face tightened but he didn't answer. As

he reached for his mount's reins, she felt his grip lessen. Using every ounce of her might, she twisted hard and kicked at the horse. With a surprised snort, the animal backed away. Muttering under his breath, Wolf tried to restrain the beast, but the destrier tossed his great head, let out a frightened neigh, and began to rear. Heavy hooves flailed, striking the air, causing Wolf to step away.

"By the gods—"

Megan writhed and yanked herself free, her feet touching ground as Wolf tried to soothe his horse. The mare shied and Megan took off running, heading through the bracken, her boots slipping on the snow, her face being attacked by branches and vines.

"Megan! Holy Christ, where do you think you'll go that I'll not find you?" he said, and then there was silence. Her throat tightened and she knew he was stalking her through the thin, leafless trees. She ran faster and faster, intent on getting away, not because she feared him, but because she couldn't trust herself alone with him, and if she was forced to return to the camp with him, her plan to extricate herself from her marriage would be thwarted.

Her breath was coming in short, shallow gasps, her legs beginning to ache, her mind spinning ahead when he caught her. "Little one, stop," he ordered and then, as if from the very soul of the forest, a hand reached forward and clamped over her arm.

"No!" she cried, but he tugged, spinning her against him, enfolding her in his arms.

"Shh!"

"Leave me be, you bastard!" she half screamed, her fists raining blows on his neck and shoulders.

"Ahh, my lady," he said as he held her and stared into her furious eyes. "If only I could."

She tried to step away, but could not, and when his lips, cold with the night, found hers, she gasped. Her skin was instantly alive, her heart, already drumming, beginning to beat an erratic, wild tempo. She could not trust herself to kiss him, to touch him, to feel his body against hers, but neither could she stop.

Inside, her bones melted as surely as a candle left too close to a flame, and a wild storm of yearning began to rage deep in her heart. As his tongue parted her lips, she opened to him, unable to resist, hot blood flowing through her veins. A primal throbbing started deep within, yearning and moist, and his mouth was savage, his tongue merciless in its assault.

The wind swirled around them, billowing his cloak, stirring the dry leaves clinging to the branches. Moaning, desire pulsing through her body, she closed her eyes, lost in the scents of smoke, leather, and that musky odor that was only his.

His mouth was insistent, his tongue bold, his hands possessive as the kiss deepened. Denial formed in her mind, only to skitter away like the stars fleeing the dawn. Her arms, as if they had a mind of their own, wound around his neck, and the world began to spin. She didn't protest when he lifted her from her feet and carried her to the base of a strong fir tree with its soft carpet of needles.

"Say no," he begged in a deep rasp as he untied her mantle, but no words formed in her throat. "By the gods, Megan," he insisted, his face tense, his eyes filled with a savage fire. "Stop me."

"I—I cannot."

Before the words were out, he kissed her again, his mouth warm and wet as it touched her eyes, her cheeks, her throat. He yanked the mantle over her head, and soon, her tunic as well. Her breasts, straining upward, proud nipples erect, beckoned him, and with a tortured groan of surrender, he dropped his mouth over one proud point and began to suckle.

Megan jolted, her body arching upward, her spine bowing as she held his head close. He captured her buttock with one big hand and held her close to him, letting her feel, through the rough fabric of his breeches, his hot, swollen member. He kissed and suckled, teased and tormented, until the silk fabric was wet and cool where the wind caressed it.

"This is wrong," he said with a fatalistic groan. He lifted the garment over her shoulders as if it were a bridal veil.

"Nay, 'tis right."

The breath of winter skimmed over her naked flesh, and Wolf stared down at her an instant, before reaching for the ties of his breeches. Slowly, he undid the knots, and Megan, watching him, lost her breath.

Discarding cloak, mantle, and tunic, he kicked off his boots, then, with his breeches open, he guided her hand to his crotch. "This is how much I want you," he said when she felt his hard, hot flesh. "I ache and yearn for you, and I would do anything if I could end this torment another way."

Leaning forward, he kissed her lips. "I planned this not," he said, in a voice filled with conviction, as his weight carried them to the tangle of clothes that was their bed. "I wanted to hate you."

"Aye." Reaching up, she touched the side of his face, feeling the stubble on his cheek against her palm. "And I wanted to detest and thwart you."

"Do you still?"

She couldn't hide the mischievous smile that played upon her lips. "Aye," she agreed, wrapping her fingers around his neck and drawing her face close to his. "Can you not tell how much I despise you?" Laughing, she kissed him, and he groaned.

" 'Tis serious, I am."

"Then prove it, outlaw." She held his gaze, and as he cast off his breeches, she felt only a tremor of fear. She loved this man with all her heart. 'Twould always be so. 'Twas right that they joined, as natural as the turn of the seasons.

His lips crashed down on hers again and he covered her body with his, keeping her warm as his knees pushed her legs open, and he touched her breasts with hard, eager fingers.

"You are a virgin?" he asked, his breath a warm balm against her skin.

"Aye."

"Then I will be gentle."

"Nay," she said, looking up at him, feeling wild and reckless, her skin on fire, her pulse pounding. "Take me as you would to pleasure yourself, Wolf. Let me feel what it is you want."

With only a second's hesitation, he wrapped his arms around her middle and splayed his fingers over the curve of her spine and the cleft of her buttocks. "We will pleasure each other, woman," he said slowly and lifted her hips to kiss her abdomen and the thatch of curls between her legs. His fingers and tongue were magic. The world swam again and Megan let go, losing herself in the uncharted waters of desire. He touched and kissed her in the most intimate of places, teasing her, heating her blood, bringing her to the brink so that she bucked up against him, demanding more as she cried out in sweet, sweet torment.

"In time, little one," he promised against her thigh, and she arched upward again and again, straining for a release only he could give.

"Please," she begged under the gentle, relentless assault of his tongue and fingers.

He was sweating despite the frigid air, and she saw his face, tight with restraint, as he climbed upward, spreading her legs wide. Without kissing her, he took her in one, strong swift thrust that caused her to let out a cry as raw as the night itself. A bright burst of pain knifed through her, but he held her fast, withdrawing slowly only to enter again. " 'Twill be all right," he assured her, and his lips found hers again.

Desire pounded through her brain as he began to move more swiftly. His muscles strained and her fingers dug deep into his skin as he loved her, faster and faster, easing that first tiny bit of pain until she felt nothing but that same dark, dusky yearning that she experienced when he kissed her. In that sublime second, she was swept away, and the stars flashed a brilliant hue as he convulsed against her. "Megan!" he cried fiercely. "Oh, love!"

With a triumphant yell, he fell against her, crushing her breasts, his sweat-soaked body joined with hers as she floated away on a cloud of contentment, not thinking of the morrow, not worrying about her freedom, not concerned with anything other than this one glorious man.

"Are you hurt?" he asked, when his heart had quit beating so wildly he thought it might burst.

"Nay." Her breath was feather-light upon his skin, and he wrapped them both in his cloak, holding her close to him, trying to protect her from the cold winter air. Tenderly, he kissed her forehead and wondered why this woman touched him so deeply. What was it about her that had crept so easily past the barrier he'd worked years to construct, the wall that kept him from caring too deeply for anyone?

* * *

Cayley hoped to visit the cripple again. The man, whom she'd sworn to detest, held a fascination for her. She sneaked out of her room and was halfway down the hall when she heard the laughter—a woman's laughter, soft but distinctive—chasing down the corridors. The bolt on Holt's door clicked loudly.

Cayley ducked into the shadows.

"If ye be needin' any more favors, m'lord," Nell, the freckled seamstress, said as she tossed her hair from her face, "let me know."

Holt's voice was low. "Mayhap next time you can bring your friend, Dilys, with you?"

The seamstress pouted. "Dilys? She's scrawny."

"Ah, but she has some fine qualities. I think she could learn to pleasure a man."

"She's but a lass, barely ten." Nell shook her head. "Nay, I think not—"

"Bring her with you tomorrow," Holt ordered, grabbing Nell by the neck of her tunic and running his hands familiarly over her breasts. She arched her spine and purred like a cat. "You need not Dilys, m'lord," she said, lolling her head and exposing her throat and a breast that Holt chose to bare. His fingers ran distractedly over her nipple. "I will do whatever you want."

"You're but one woman, Nell, and an amply endowed one at that. But sometimes one mouth is not enough. Bring Dilys to me tomorrow." His voice turned hard and he pinched her nipple, causing her to cry out. "And tell her not what I intend to do with her. 'Tis better when there's a bit of surprise—aye, even fear—involved."

"You intend to frighten her?" Nell asked, trying to step away, but Holt wouldn't let go.

"Just a wee bit. 'Twill be fun. Come, Nell, be a good lass."

And with that, he covered her breast and shut the door. Nell slipped down the stairs and Cayley cringed, the contents of her stomach turning sour.

Wolf's gentle snoring was soft against her nape and Megan, too, wanted nothing more than to sleep with him in the waning moonlight, to cling to him and hold him forever.

But she could not.

They'd coupled thrice already and she tingled at the memory of each savage union, when they'd used the soft fir needles and their clothes for their bed. Finally, sated and spent, he'd fallen asleep, and now Megan had to make good her escape. Though she longed to stay with him, this was her last chance to leave. She planned to ride to Castle Erbyn and speak to Lady Sorcha. If Wolf spoke the truth about Holt, then her husband was a traitor to Dwyrain. However, Ewan would not take the word of an outlaw against that of his most trusted knight. Therefore, she must uncover the truth herself by speaking with Lady Sorcha, who was Tadd of Prydd's sister.

Surely Sorcha would know of Holt, had he been in Tadd's army, thus proving Wolf to be honest or a liar of the highest order. Gently, she lifted Wolf's arm away from her waist and slid out from under his cloak, which they'd used as a coverlet. The air was chill upon her skin as she silently pulled on breeches and tunic while forgoing her mantle, which was crumpled beneath his body. Hardly daring to breathe, she edged to the horses, tethered together in a thicket of oak. Untying the reins and rope with fumbling fingers, she sent up prayer after prayer that Wolf would sleep.

Once the knots were free, she led both beasts away from the fir tree and deeper into the woods. She couldn't take a chance that he might catch up with her, for if he did, everything she'd planned would be ruined—the execution of her plan was certainly the salvation for them, each and every one.

Nervous sweat collected on her skin as she slid a bridle over Wolf's stallion's head. She didn't bother with a saddle, and shivering, she climbed onto the destrier's broad back and held on to the reins of the smaller horse's bridle. Guilt clung close to her as a shadow as she clucked her tongue and followed the lowering moon. He would awaken alone, without even a horse to carry him to camp. She found no satisfaction in the thought, but urged the horses forward and wondered why she didn't feel relieved that she'd out-tricked him.

Tears filled her eyes and she told herself their sting was from the fierce wind tearing through the hollow and had nothing to do with leaving her heart in the forest. Somewhere overhead an owl hooted, as if mocking her for her foolishness, but she stiffened her spine and refused to glance over her shoulder, didn't notice that she was being watched, that standing deep in the shadows of the forest, the outlaw called Wolf watched her leave him, making not one single sound of protest.

'Twas his punishment for bedding her. Despite the demons that had screamed in his head, despite each of his promises to himself, despite the fact that she was his enemy's wife, he'd made love to her with a passion he'd never before felt.

Never had the earth shifted beneath him, never had he joined with such a willing, loving virgin. Never had he felt such a total release of his soul.

His fists clenched as he hid in the night-shrouded forest and he sent up a prayer—the first in years—for her safety. The urge to chase her was strong, and he had to force himself to let her go. 'Twas what she wanted.

Ten

"We *lost* 'er?" Odell repeated, eyeing Wolf as if he'd finally and truly gone daft. He pushed off his hood, though the wind was bitter cold as it raced and screamed through the surrounding trees. "Two 'orses gone, too, includin' yer favorite?"

"That's what I said," Wolf grumbled, meeting the gaze of each of his men with his own brutal stare. Amusement flickered in more than one pair of eyes and smiles were held in check by quivering muscles near the corners of their mouths. Apparently, they thought it great sport that their leader had finally met his comeuppance, and by a woman, no less.

Let them think what they would. Bone-tired from a night of lovemaking and then hiking back to the camp, he wanted none of their nonsense, but understood that he would be the butt of jokes for days to come. 'Twas part and parcel to her release. At the thought of her leaving, he felt a deep emptiness, as if she'd cut a hole in his heart.

"Christ a'mighty, what about Bjorn and Cormick? They're going to look like bloody fools demandin' ransom for a woman who comes dancin' through the gatehouse with two of the finest 'orses in the land!" Odell spit disgustedly into the fire and the flames crackled and hissed. "By thunder, Wolf, sometimes I donna know what goes through that stubborn 'ead of yers!"

"Bjorn and Cormick will return before Megan reaches Dwyrain."

"You 'ope; elsewise, they might be in for the fight of their lives!" Odell made a sound of disgust deep in his throat.

"He's right about that," Peter agreed, his one good eye clouding with concern.

" 'Olt'll torture 'em, sure as I'm an honest man." He threw his hood over his head again.

Jagger snorted. "We know how honest ye be, Odell."

The older man spit again. " 'Olt, 'e'll use the rack or worse. Pokers, heated in a fire, or the press, or 'eaven only knows what else. Whatever it is, 'twill be wicked." His eyes glowed as hot as the coals in the campfire. "I've heard stories about 'im cuttin' out men's tongues or slicin' off their cocks and—"

"Enough!" Wolf commanded. He'd take a bit of ribbing—that was to be expected—but no one could accuse him of putting his men's lives in jeopardy. Striding to the fire, he warmed his hands and feet. His toes were numb, near frozen from wading across icy streams. "We ride at dawn, Jagger and me. The rest of you will stay here and guard the camp in case Cormick and Bjorn return and somehow we miss them. If no one returns in three days, move the camp to the hills behind Prydd. I'll find you."

"Nay, I'll not be left behind—"

Wolf's harsh glare stopped Odell's quick tongue. With a sheepish glance, he lifted his cowl and scratched his balding head.

Robin's chin jutted forward. "Ye said I could ride with ye," he reminded Wolf.

"When it came time to deal with Holt."

"Be ye a liar?" the boy insisted.

"Nay, but—"

"Ye promised," Robin said stubbornly.

"That ye did," Peter reminded him, and Wolf's fists clenched.

"Is yer word not good?" Robin asked, and again the men stared at him.

Knowing he was making a mistake, Wolf nodded. "Aye, you ride as well . . . but no one else," he added when he saw an eager light appear in more than one man's eyes. It had been long since they'd battled; many were thirsty for the excitement of waging war. "We'll ride straight to Dwyrain. Once there, we'll help Cormick and Bjorn if they need it."

"What of the lady?" Robin asked boldly, and the men who had been restless suddenly quieted, only the wind rushing through the leafless branches and stirring up the flames of the campfire making any sound.

"What of her?"

"Will ye not bring her with you when ye return?"

Two dozen eyes bored into him and Wolf realized then that she'd touched each of the men in special ways. Damn her. "Nay," he said gruffly as he read bitter disappointment on the boy's young face.

"But—"

"She wants not to be with us, lad."

Squatting near the fire, Wolf stared into the flames, and that hopeless idea settled as surely as lead in his heart. Why had he been so foolish, thinking she could care for a rogue like him? When had he lost his heart to the saucy tart with a tongue that could sting like a whip? 'Twas a silly notion to think that she could really care for him, and Wolf didn't appreciate being considered a fool.

Nor could he explain why he'd let her go, how he'd felt as if he were a self-serving king holding a rare, unhappy bird in a cage. She was a noblewoman by birth and could not be expected to give up everything that she had at Dwyrain—wealth, family, servants, even a husband—because an outlaw fancied her. It had taken every bit of his willpower to let her leave after making love to her, but his instincts told him he had no choice.

If she escaped and returned to Holt, the bastard might not harm her, though the fact that she wasn't a virgin would be difficult to disguise and would enrage Holt even more. Wolf's jaw tightened when he imagined his old enemy taking out his vexation, vengeance, and anger on Megan.

Holt had better not be so foolish, for if the bastard ever laid one hand on her, Wolf would gladly slit his throat. And then again, if Holt truly became Megan's husband, joining feverishly with her . . . getting her with child . . . By the gods, what a mess. Already, Megan could be carrying the first beginnings of their own babe. His throat turned as dry as seeds in the wind. What if even now there was a child growing in her womb? Would Holt claim the infant child as his own issue?

His fury became dark, his eyes narrowing with a newfound reason to hate his old enemy. Rage burned bright in his blood and his fingers curled anxiously around the hilt of his sword as he thought of it, the mating of Holt and Megan. 'Twould be a pain he would never be able to expunge, one he would bear as his own personal cross, one he would carry with him to the grave.

He felt the men's stares and scowled to himself. Life as an outlaw in the woods had lost much of the appeal that had once been strong within him. There were several men in the band who were capable of leading the others. Bjorn was strong and fierce, a levelheaded man capable of extreme savagery if 'twas necessary. Jagger, too, was strong, though somewhat dim-witted, and then there was Odell, with his mercenary heart. Nay, he'd be a bad choice.

"Make ready," he said as he turned on his heel and returned to the pallet in the empty chamber he and Megan had shared. The ashes were cold where the fire had been, a chill wind blew through the window, and the room was as dark and cold as the bottom of the sea. Gritting his teeth, he flung himself down and drew up the hides and furs, trying to ignore the scent of her, which lingered on the bed. "Damn it to hell," he growled and attempted to push aside the vivid images of making love to her, how her supple legs surrounded his waist, how she smiled up at him in the moonlight, how her skin, so white, was smooth as marble, how her blood would fire so easily.

I love Holt not, she'd said over and over again, but she'd been eager to leave. Why? Had she lied to him, and did she truly care for the man she'd pledged to love before God and country? Or was it, as she'd insisted, a marriage she couldn't avoid? Then why return to the scoundrel?

Because she thought you were going to sell her to Holt! Why would she want to stay? What choice had he given her? Tossing off the damned coverlets, he rolled to his feet and decided he had to hunt her down. Before she reached Dwyrain, he had to find her and speak with her and . . . and what? Offer her the life of an outlaw? A future running from the law? No home? No warm hearth? No servants? No real bed? What of children?

"Bloody Christ," he growled, stalking out of the room and striding to Jagger's tent, where the big man was already snoring. He placed the toe of his boot against Jagger's ribs and the man snorted, cried out, and was on his feet in an instant, a blade ready in his hand.

"For the love of Jesus, Wolf, ye scared the piss right outta me!"

Wolf had no time for explanations. "I ride tonight."

"But ye just got in."

"It matters not."

Muttering under his breath, Jagger found his mantle. "I'm beginnin' to think that Odell's right about ye, Wolf," he said, shaking his head and adjusting his hood as he stepped out of the tent and frowned at the snow beginning to drift from the dark heavens. "Ever since ye kidnapped the lady, ye've been actin' strange, like ye're not right in the head."

"I'm not," Wolf admitted. "Now, will ye ride with me or not?"

"Aye, I'm with ye, but what about the boy? He'll only slow us down."

"He comes," Wolf said, hoping that he wasn't sending Robin to an early grave.

Cayley couldn't help herself. 'Twas as if the magician had cast a spell upon her. She stealthily crossed the bailey, sending a goose squawking and nearly bumping into one of the stableboys, who was leading a gray jennet from the farrier's hut. 'Twas nearly dark, the air cool as it pressed hard against her cloak as she approached the north tower. She carried with her a bucket of Cook's bean and brawn soup and a dark loaf of bread. The smell of the soup caught the attention of some of the baron's dogs, who were being walked near the dovecote. They turned their noses upwind, let out hungry whimpers, and were reprimanded by the page whose duty it was to care for them.

Cayley clutched her cloak around her and stepped around the piles of horse dung that had not been cleaned away by the gong farmer.

The stairs leading downward were as dark as pitch. She snagged a rush light from its sconce, mounted near the door, and used the flickering light to guide her down the gritty steps. As she hurried by some of the cells, she heard hoots and whistles, but she ignored them and hurried onward.

In the dungeon, the sentries had changed, and one of the men she trusted, Sir Stephen, a gangly young knight with pockmarked skin and hair as straight and unruly as straw, was guarding the prisoners.

"Who goes there?" Stephen called out.

" 'Tis only me," Cayley replied, feeling suddenly as if she needed fresh air. How could the men stand to be held in such decay and filth? "I brought fresh food for the prisoner and for you, Sir Stephen."

"Say what? Did Holt send ye?"

"Nay, 'twas mine own idea," she said as she approached his stool and small table. "I thought some good food might jolly our prisoner into telling me more about my sister."

Stephen snorted and shook his head. "Ye're wastin' yer time, m'lady. Kind as ye be, the man's daft. Completely out of his mind." Stephen pointed a finger at his head and rotated his hand. "You'll not get a straight answer from that one."

"At least let me try. Now, about the soup." Stephen, ever hungry, tore off a thick hunk of bread, dipped heartily in the broth, and motioned for her to do the same. "Has the prisoner given us his name?"

"Naw, but I 'aven't asked. Don't care what 'e's called." He ate hungrily, chewing with a great amount of noise, grinding teeth and making contented grunts as she tore off a piece of bread and dunked it in Cook's stew.

"I'll give this to him, if you let me into his cell."

"Say wha—?" He lifted his head and greasy soup dripped into his scraggly beard. "You want inside?" he asked, hitching a thumb toward the barred alcove the sorcerer now called home.

"Yes."

"Nay, m'lady, I cannot trust 'im."

"But he's bound, is he not?"

"Aye, but 'e's supposed to be some kind of magician, say what. 'e might jest disappear if I lets ye into the cell."

"If he truly was a sorcerer, why would he not escape with the door locked? Why would the restraints hold him?"

Stephen considered as he chewed, then wiped his mouth with a grubby sleeve. "I guess they wouldn't."

"Right. So there's no reason I can't speak with him and find out what more he knows, is there?"

Stephen frowned. Even in the poor light, she saw great lines furrowing deep in the skin between his eyebrows. "I don't think that—"

"And as the baron's daughter and lady of the castle, I'm not asking you to open the cell to me, I'm ordering you to do it."

"Well, that's it, then, ain't it?" Shoving away from the table, he rattled his keys and opened the metal door, which screeched on its rusting hinges.

Cayley slipped through the opening and found the magician seated in a dark corner of his cell. Above him, there was a small hole bored into the wall to let in a bit of fresh air. The breeze was faint, but enough to make it easier to breathe. "You want to know more of your sister," he said in that calming voice of his.

"Aye." She handed him the bread, and he took it gratefully. Then in a voice so low she could barely hear him, he said, "Two men are riding to Dwyrain. They come with news of

Megan and will be treated as enemies, for they are outlaws."

"Criminals?" she gasped, her heart pounding in dread. "They know of Megan?"

"Aye, but they will not speak, for they are loyal to their leader, a man who hates Holt."

"How do you know this?" she demanded.

"I know." Again, the calm, reassuring tone that frightened her.

"Who be they?" she asked, glancing over her shoulder to the guard, but Stephen paid no attention to them as he dipped into the soup again.

"They be friends, though they will be brought to this prison and flogged. One will die. The other will help you find your sister and save the castle."

"Die?" she repeated, her throat turning to dust. "Die?"

"Aye, there is naught either of us can do."

"You speak with a devil's tongue," she hissed, frightened. "How can I trust you?"

"How can you not?"

She wanted to run, to hide, to wake up from this foul nightmare she'd been living, the one that had started when Megan had been kidnapped and her father had collapsed, leaving Holt to rule Dwyrain. If only Megan had fought her attacker, if only she'd escaped, then maybe Cayley herself wouldn't have to fight, wouldn't be forced to meet with prisoners in the dungeon or make plans to save her father and the castle. Her shoulders were just too small to carry so big a burden.

"You are stronger than you think," he said, as if reading her thoughts. "You doubt me still, but all that I have said, 'twill come to pass."

"Where is Megan?" she demanded.

"That I don't know," he admitted, his voice more ruffled

than before, as if he were irritated at the limits of his powers, "but you will need these men and must befriend them as you've befriended me."

"But they are criminals."

"Friends," he said as Stephen rattled his keys again, indicating that it was time for her to leave. Obviously, the soup was gone.

Megan's stomach grumbled loudly as she rode onward. She paused only to eat once a day, and that was usually a scant meal, as she had no money and her only weapon was a small knife. She'd fashioned a basket with willow branches and had caught fish from each creek she'd crossed, plucked winter apples from a tree she'd discovered on the first day of her journey, and stolen eggs twice from a farmer's untended chicken's nests.

Four days had passed since she'd left Wolf, and as she rode through the snow and sleet, past villages and through dank woods, her thoughts continually strayed to him and she tried to imagine what he'd done when he'd found her missing. Had he been furious and enraged, or relieved to be rid of her? Had he ranted and raged, damning her to hell, or had he smiled inwardly that she was no longer his burden? Had he returned safely to his camp, only to be the laughingstock of his men? She smiled faintly at that thought. Had he then climbed aboard another swift steed and set off after her? Would he appear at the next bend in the road? Her heart raced impatiently with that thin hope. Or would he meet with Holt and try to explain the fact that he had no wife to return for his blood money?

Not that she cared. Wolf could suffer these and every other kind of indignity for his plans to ransom her to an enemy he detested.

But she couldn't stop her heart from taking flight every time she approached another traveler, a man who sat tall upon his mount, a man with black hair and broad shoulders. Her pulse always pounded wildly for a second, only to return to its regular, even cadence when she drew close and she saw that the rider was not Wolf and bore not much resemblance to him. Oh, wayward, willful heart!

How willingly she'd given herself to him! The shame that should have been her companion, the disgrace of having lain with him, did not chase after her. Truth was, she had no regrets. If she could spend another night with him, she would gladly share his bed and suffer the consequences, for she was not married in her heart, nor had she slept with her husband.

Her plan—pray that it worked!—was to prove Holt to be the traitor she knew him to be. She'd find that proof in Erbyn, which was still several days' ride away. *God help me,* she silently prayed as the snow fell in flurries that obscured her view and chilled her deep into her bones, *and please, please be with Wolf. Give him peace and keep him safe.*

Absently, she rubbed her abdomen, heard her stomach growl again, and wrapped her shawl more tightly around her neck. She only hoped that Sorcha of Erbyn could help her.

Holt eyed his new prisoners with disgust. How easily tricked they'd been, how angry they were that when they'd shouted that they came in peace, they were set upon by half his army. Now they knelt before him, their hands and feet bound, ropes around their necks like common beasts of the field, their noses nearly pressed into the frozen mud and manure behind the stables. Sipping from a mazer of wine, he walked in front of them and felt a grain of satisfaction. Things were finally turning around. These poor, idiotic brutes, sent by Wolf the outlaw, were under his power.

"Did you think I would barter for my wife?" he asked, his long surcoat twirling behind him.

"I only bring the letter." The big blond one had the nerve to glance upward, but at a lift of his eyebrow, Holt signaled for his soldier to pull on the noose. Oswald was only too happy to wrap the heavy rope one more time around his fist, causing the kneeling cur to cough.

"Aye, you bring a letter from the Wolf." Holt read the perfect scrawl again. 'Twas true the outlaw was no common man, but educated and, no doubt, from a noble house. "But *friend,* 'tis not only a gentle missive, but a demand for ransom."

This time the yellow-haired giant didn't say a word.

"Fancy that." Holt clucked his tongue, then took a long swallow from his cup. "Nay, I think not. Instead I think you and your companion here will join my other guests in the dungeon."

"Wait!"

Holt's temper snapped as he spied Cayley striding across the outer bailey. Without being restrained by a wimple, her blond hair flew behind her like a golden banner. Her small face was set with anger, her jaw stretched forward defiantly. He'd taken her for a brainless twit, interested only in herself, but lately, since her father had fallen ill and Megan had been kidnapped, Cayley made herself a much stronger presence than she had been. 'Twas no wonder why Connor wanted to bed her, though Holt had no intention of honoring his bargain with the surly knight. Nay, he had other plans for his feisty sister-in-law. 'Twas almost as if she'd risen to new heights in the face of adversity, and it bored Holt. Now, she was bearing down on the men as if she were driven by an inner fire, her boots clicking on the hard, frozen ground.

"Who are these men?"

"Criminals," Holt replied, and she wasn't surprised or even repelled. " 'Tis no concern of yours."

"Why not? Am I not the baron's daughter, his only issue here at the castle?"

"Cayley, dear, this"—he waved toward the men groveling at his feet as if they were insignificant flies swarming over horse dung—"is to be handled by men."

"I see not why. If they are here to ransom Megan, then give them the money or whatever 'tis they demand."

So she knew about the ransom. Either she'd been hiding nearby listening to the conversation or she had a spy within his ranks of soldiers—a spy who had run to her with the news. "Nay," he said with forced patience. "I'll not pay. 'Tis what the criminals want. They won't be satisfied with the first demand, but will ask for more, again and again. 'Tis impossible to barter with them. They have no sense of honor."

"Such as yours?" Something flickered in her gaze, a hint of distrust that he hadn't seen before.

"Aye, such as mine." Holt ignored her and glanced at Oswald. "Take them both to the north tower and leave them there until I call for them."

"Nay. They are our guests. If they can tell us that Megan is well and safe—"

"She is," the blond one said.

Oh, he was a bold, rebellious one, and Holt could almost feel the snap of his whip as he cracked it over the outlaw's broad back.

"Where is she being held?"

"That I cannot say."

"Cannot or will not?"

"She is safe. Unhurt. She will be returned when the demands of the letter are—aahh!" Holt kicked the lying cur in the ribs, the toe of his shoe digging deep in the hard-muscled flesh.

"Where?"

The big man had the insolence to lift his head and glare at Holt with unyielding eyes. Though there was already a bruise forming on his skin, he didn't flinch when Holt rounded and kicked him again.

"Stop!" Cayley cried. "Do not—"

"Take her away!" Holt ordered to another guard standing near the inner gate.

The soldier hesitated. "But she's the lord's daughter—"

"Take her!" Holt was sick of excuses and whining and pathetic attempts by the men to weasel out of their assigned tasks. "Do it now. Lock her in her room."

"Nay, Holt, you cannot!" Cayley cried, frantic. "You must keep these men safe!"

"I can do anything I wish, and I will," he said, his hands curling around the stem of his mazer just as Father Timothy hurried out of the chapel. The clumsy priest nearly stumbled over the hem of his robe at the sight that met his eyes, and for a second Holt thought the priest had drunk too much of the holy wine again. Lately, Timothy had been having second thoughts about his allegiance to Holt and he, as a minion of the Almighty, was becoming a royal pain in the arse.

"You are not yet baron!" Cayley cried.

Holt turned to the immediate problem of Cayley's newfound sense of injustice. " 'Tis only a matter of time, m'lady, before the baron leaves this earth."

She gasped. "Nay!"

He couldn't help but smile. He crooked his neck, hitching his head in the direction of the keep as he ordered the nearest soldier, "Post a sentry at her door."

"I'll not be treated as a prisoner!"

Holt rolled his eyes. "Of course you will, m'lady," he drawled, "unless you do as you're told, which seems to be harder for you each day. Now, guard, take her."

He watched as a knight, a silly fool of a lad named Foster, grabbed Cayley's arm and led her toward the keep. The girl fought and argued, yanking hard against the hard manacle of the lad's grip, but Foster forced her across the snow-dusted grass of the bailey.

One of Holt's first duties as new lord would be to marry her off, and not to Connor, who wanted her so badly. Nay, Cayley, the beautiful, mule-headed daughter of Ewan of Dwyrain, would be worth much to some of the older barons whose wives had died. He would have to pay no dowry, because there was one man, Baron Rolf of Castle Henning, a tired old soldier, who was rumored to like to watch his young wives play and mate with his soldiers or servant boys while he watched. 'Twas said that Rolf had an entire chamber filled with peepholes where he could witness his wife's seduction and betrayal, then find her unfit as the lady of his castle. Four of his wives had died and two had disappeared, run away, it seemed. Yea, Rolf would be a good choice to tame Cayley.

As soon as he was baron, Holt would force her to marry.

Today, however, 'twas his mission to deal with the two traitors who dared try and sell him his wife. "Take them away," he ordered the soldiers who held the ropes surrounding their necks. He finished his wine. "I'll flog them later."

Father Timothy made the sign of the cross over his chest as he watched Cayley being dragged into the keep against her will. "In the name of our God, Holt," he said in a low, desperate voice as his gaze shifted over the few meager troops still holding the prisoners, "what are you thinking?"

"I'll have no disrespect," Holt said, tired of arguing with everyone. Cayley was supposed to be her submissive self and the priest had promised to be his ally. Now . . . since the time the sorcerer had been dragged into the dungeon, loyalty to him had begun to waver, Cayley appeared to have grown a backbone, and the priest was suddenly God-fearing.

Father Timothy eyed the two new captives, then his gaze wandered after Cayley again. She was struggling like a beast from hell against the soldier's grasp as he hauled her up the steps of the keep. From the corner of his mouth, Timothy said, "Lady Cayley cannot be treated like a common wench, and these men," he motioned to the new prisoners, "if they bring word of Lady Megan, should be taken in as guests of the baron."

"Even if they bring a note of ransom from the outlaw Wolf?" Holt asked, arching one eyebrow disdainfully. "I think not."

" 'Twould be the Christian gesture to offer them—"

"Food and shelter?" Holt cut in sarcastically as he sneered at the two captives. "Or, mayhap a cup of wine and a trencher of brawn? Or . . . wait, they might prefer a night in bed with a wench from the kitchen!"

"Nay, Holt, do not mock me. 'Tis only that if you are to become baron, you must look like a fair and even-tempered leader."

" 'Tis not a matter of 'if,' but 'when' I become baron, Timothy," Holt said, his eyes narrowing on the soldiers and prisoners. " 'Twould be a good idea to remember where your allegiance lies, for I know much about you."

The priest's face sobered and turned a sick shade of gray. 'Twas so easy to humble a prideful man whose guilt and piety constantly battled with each other. "Aye, 'tis right you are," Timothy said and crossed himself hurriedly.

Holt chuckled. "Amen." He motioned to his beaten prisoners. "Take their sorry arses into the dungeon and put them in the lowest cells, next to the sorcerer. Mayhap we'll get lucky and he'll place a curse on them so that they'll talk."

The blond one sneered and the other glared with eyes filled with hate. Well, let them rot. There would be no bartering with him about his wife, and if he ever found the outlaw rogue who had stolen her away, he'd personally see the man drawn and quartered.

Cayley paced from one end of her chamber to the other. Who would save her father now that she'd been foolish enough to get herself trapped in her room? For the past few days, ever since the sorcerer had convinced her that Ewan's wine had been poisoned, she'd poured out his mazer and filled it herself. She had no idea who was fouling his drink, though she'd tried to watch as Cook prepared Ewan's dinner. Nell sometimes carried Ewan's tray to him, as had she. There were others as well, pages and serving girls, none of whom Cayley thought would try to kill the baron. No, the poison had to have come from Holt, who was rarely in the kitchens . . . but he visited her father daily to report to Ewan about what was happening within and without the thick walls of Dwyrain, and though Ewan hardly responded, Holt considered it his responsibility to tell the old baron everything.

And doctor his drink?

Cayley's heart sank. It didn't matter that she had poured Ewan wine from a new jug before his tray was taken to him. The dark deed was done later.

How could she have been so blind? "Father, I'm sorry," she said softly, wishing there was a means of escape from her chamber and knowing there was none.

She should have confided in someone, but she'd been frightened and wasn't sure whom to trust anymore. The castle had once been a happy place where she'd grown up in the glow of her parents' love, with siblings around her. 'Twas no longer. In the past two years, Dwyrain had become dark and sinister, not the same safe haven she'd lived in all her life.

She no longer walked freely through the gardens of marigolds and fragrant roses, nor did she linger at the dovecote, watching the birds fly in and out, nor did she ever take long walks through fields strewn in wildflowers. This year, she found no joy in her favorite season—the Christmas revels, with their merriment, dancing, feasting, and general feeling of goodwill.

A soft knock sounded on the door, and the sentry opened it to allow Rue, the old nursemaid, into her room. With a cry of delight, Cayley ran across the chamber and flung herself into the old lady's arms.

With a cluck of her tongue, Rue asked, "Now what did ye do, Cayley girl, to get yourself locked away?"

"I asked that Holt hurt not the new prisoners—the messengers from Wolf."

"And he disagreed?" Rue lifted a graying eyebrow. "Ah, child, will ye never learn? As stubborn as yer sister, ye are. Well, we'll just have to find a way to get Holt to set ye free, now, won't we?"

"Aye, but first we must take care of Father." Cayley swallowed hard, hoping she could trust the nurse and knowing she had no choice. Many people, servants, knights, and freemen, had, because of the sickness and curse, been unhappy with Ewan's rule and were embracing Holt as their new leader. They apparently thought Holt could assure them of more prosperous and healthier times. Some of the baron's most trusted men had turned away from him and become followers of Holt. She only hoped Rue, who had lost her own daughter to the sickness, had not turned her allegiance away from Ewan. "You must help me, Rue," Cayley said, desperately clinging to the older woman's sleeve. "You must help me thwart Holt's plan to murder Father!"

"Worry not," the strange one in the next cell said as the rush lights burned low in the dungeons of Dwyrain.

Bjorn turned toward the sound and thought he heard the rustle of wings, as if a bat or bird was with the cripple who dared speak to him. Bjorn was not a man easily frightened. Ofttimes he was told he was much too bold and reckless, that he cared not for his own life.

'Twas true, he thought, for though he loved the freedom of living the life of an outlaw and spat upon the rules and laws of the land, there was a part of him that wanted always to defy death, to test his courage, to kill that sorrow that was buried deep within him. He longed for a chance to find out the truth of his birth. Was he, as Tadd of Prydd had insisted, just the bastard son of a whore or was he, as his mother had assured him, a prince among men, the son of German royalty? He wondered now, as he stood in a wet cell that was cold as a corpse, who his father was and he thought again of Leah, poor, tormented Leah of Prydd, a woman who had touched his heart, a woman who, beaten, raped, and nearly killed by Darton of Erbyn, had entered a nunnery where she would be safe from the evils of all men and would devote herself to God.

Bjorn believed not in the Father. Especially not in this wretched cell that smelled of urine, dung, and human fear.

"Who are you?" he asked the calm voice.

"A friend."

Bjorn snorted. "I have no friends at Dwyrain."

"Nor I," Cormick agreed from the next cell.

A cat slunk through the shadows, its eyes reflected in the fading light from the torches mounted on the wall. Silently, the rail-thin cat stalked rats and mice that crawled noisily through the straw and damp rushes strewn in a bare layer upon the floor.

"Wolf comes to free you," the smooth voice said in a tone that only Bjorn could hear. "You must be ready."

"How know you this?"

A pause. "I see it as clearly as I do you."

Cormick coughed. "Well, I see nothing in this damned place! 'Tis darker than pitch at midnight."

" 'Tis not with my eyes that I see," the strange one protested.

"Then ye're addled," Cormick decided with a grunt, but Bjorn had experienced many unexplained things in his life. Had not Sorcha of Prydd brought him back to life from the very brink of death? Had she not done the same for her sister, Leah? Aye, he trusted her witchcraft more than he trusted any faith in God.

"Believe me," the odd one insisted. "He comes."

"I'll be ready," Bjorn promised, eager to have a chance to kill Holt with his bare hands. It mattered not whether he lived or died, only that he fought bravely. He only hoped the half-brained sorcerer was not a fraud, for this time, he was certain, he would fight to the death.

Holt fingered his whip lovingly. The leather pommel fit his grip perfectly, and the resounding crack when he flipped his wrist could cause a faithless man to suddenly fall on his knees and pray for God's forgiveness. Aye, the whip was a weapon of power and fear, one that took long to kill a man, but gave the owner time to savor the killing.

Connor and Kelvin were with him as he entered the dungeon, and their footsteps no doubt caused dread in the hearts of the wretches chained within the prison. A thrill of power, not unlike the excitement he felt each time Dilys, the milkmaid, was hauled into his room, scorched through his blood. She was a tiny thing, with only the smallest of breasts budding, and Holt had not bedded her; in truth he thought her not ready, but he bared those tiny breasts of hers and made her play with them, her eyes downcast, as he fondled Nell in her presence. She was too young to be a decent whore, but in time she would learn to pleasure him and his men, for soldiers, if not given a bit of feminine pleasure, were a surly lot. Holt had picked out the girls he planned to use to service them—Dilys was the youngest—but in time, two years or less, he planned to deflower her and show her what it was to pleasure a man. She was already learning from Nell, whose ripe, full breasts and fat, round rump were a willing source of pleasure.

Though she was not Megan. His guts tightened again, for 'twas Megan with whom he wanted to lie and with whom he wanted to beget children. More than anything, he wanted her submission, he wanted to thrust his body into hers and see the surrender in her eyes. He could not think of her now without his damned cock bulging in his breeches.

Holt planned to be a strong ruler. His men, allowed to wager on dice, cockfights, and the baiting of bears, would also enjoy the women he provided and the wages he paid. In return, he would demand and receive their undying loyalty.

At the final bend in the stairwell, he held his rush light higher and made his way through the stench to the farthest cells, where the jailer sat on a stool, his mouth open as he snored, drool gleaming in his gray-flecked beard.

"Wake up, you dolt!" Holt kicked at the man, who started and blinked.

"Eh—wha—oh, Sir Holt, er, m'lord, 'tis sorry I am ye caught me nappin'. I was jest restin' me eyes and—"

"Don't bother with excuses, man," Holt said, his skin crawling. He hated dark places, and being on the right side of the cell door didn't keep him from feeling as if he couldn't breathe. Biting back the urge to flee, he stared at his three most recent captives. "Have you anything to say of my wife? Where is Lady Megan being held?" He waited, then, his fingers curving over the handle of his whip. The men in chains stared at him but held their tongues.

"You have but twelve hours to change your minds," Holt said. "Tomorrow, before noon, I'll haul your sorry hides to the bailey, where you'll be tied and your shirts removed. I'll flog you within an inch of your miserable lives and then you'll tell me what you know!" He waited, half expecting one of the men to break down, beg his forgiveness, and cleanse his soul by spilling the truth, but he heard nothing but the steady drip from the cistern and the rustle of the grimy rushes on the floor. "So be it," he finally said, rage firing his blood as he cracked the whip, and the sound reverberated against the stone walls. "But think not I'll have pity on anyone who helped the outlaw bastard steal my wife!"

Megan's teeth chattered and her fingers and feet were numb with the cold. She'd been riding over a week and had fought the urge to pull on the reins and turn around. Unable to feed herself or the animals, she sold the smaller horse and had enough money in her pocket for several nights' lodging and warm meals, but she didn't dare stop, not until she reached her destination, not until . . . dizziness swept over her, the same sensation she'd had for two days. Oh, what she wouldn't give for a cup of hot cider or some of Cook's venison broth . . .

Swaying in the saddle, she clung to the reins and tried to keep her wits about her. Snow fell from the sky, collecting and freezing on her mount's mane. Though she wore gloves, her hands were clenched over the reins and couldn't feel. She could barely move her fingers. Undaunted, she kept on, certain she was nearly to Erbyn. If only she could talk to Lady Sorcha, find out the truth about Holt, and return to Wolf . . .

Wolf! Her heart cried for him and she bit her lip. Where was he now? Did he think she had betrayed him? Would she ever see him again? She had to! She was a woman with a mission, a woman who was determined to choose her own fate, a woman who—

The blackness threatened to overtake her again. Moving from the outward corners of her vision, slowly encroaching, it advanced. Squeezing her eyes shut, she tried to clear her head and clung to the saddle pommel, but no matter what she did, the dizzy sensation continued to overtake her and she could no longer tell which was up and which down. The earth tilted.

"God help me." Reining in her horse, she attempted to dismount. The blackness threatened again. She was halfway off the horse, her foot searching for ground that wasn't there. With a cry, she fell, toppling to the ground in a heap. The last thing she saw was the clouds swirling wildly as her head banged against the hard, icy road.

Then there was nothing.

Eleven

Crack!

The whip buckled, then hissed forward. Like a snake, the tip bit into his flesh, stinging. Bjorn's body jerked. Pain exploded in his muscles.

"What know you of Megan?" Holt demanded, standing behind him and ready to flail again. "Speak, outlaw!"

Bjorn bit hard on his tongue and closed his eyes, bracing himself for the next blow. His body was on fire, his legs weak, his wrists raw and bleeding where they were bound by leather cuffs and ropes. The outer bailey of Dwyrain swam before his eyes. Dark clouds, swollen with rain, rolled across the sky, and the wind was chill and harsh, cutting through his soul as easily as the whip sliced through his flesh.

"So be it, criminal. Just remember, you chose your own fate!" *Snap!* The thin rope of leather slapped hard again. Bjorn convulsed, pulling at the straps that held his hands. Numbing blackness threatened to swallow him and he prayed it would be so. Around him, peasants, servants, and soldiers stared at him, some with faint smiles, others holding hands over their mouths as if they were about to be sick, still others with lifeless eyes, as if they cared not. Work had stopped in the castle and he and Cormick had become the main attraction.

"Speak, damn you!" Holt thundered, and Bjorn felt a small measure of satisfaction at the vexation in his tormentor's voice. "For the love of Christ, tell me!" Another flick of Holt's cruel wrist. The whip cracked, then sizzled as it flayed another strip of skin off Bjorn's shoulders. With all his strength, he held his tongue and didn't look to his side, where Cormick was already sagging against his restraints, blood oozing from his mouth, eyes closed, his skin split open from more than a dozen brutal bites of the whip.

"Stop!" a woman's voice—the blond girl Cayley—yelled from a window high in the keep. Bjorn could barely see her. "For the love of God, Holt, stop this!"

"Bloody Christ," Holt muttered, then turned to face the keep. "If what I do offends you, m'lady, do not watch. I only make an example of those who are disloyal to Dwyrain!"

"By beating them until they die? This man was only a messenger, who wanted to help you find Megan—"

"I barter not with the demon outlaw!" Holt said, his temper snapping. In a softer voice, one she would not be able to hear, he growled to one of his men, "Go up to her chamber and keep her away from the window until I'm finished."

The fat-necked soldier was quick to run to the keep, but not before Cayley yelled again.

"Stop this torture now! The baron would not approve. This is still his castle, his soldiers, his prisoners, and—"

"I spoke with your father this morning, m'lady. 'Twas his idea to flog the truth from these men in an effort to find Megan. 'Twas he who insisted the traitors not go unpunished."

"Nay, my father would not . . . Who are you? Stay away!

Nay! Leave me be! Unhand me, you brute!" she cried, and then there was silence in the bailey once again.

Holt, grumbling about hardheaded women, advanced to the brace where Bjorn was bound. With the handle of his whip, Holt bashed the side of Bjorn's face, rattling his teeth. Pain, in a blinding flash, ripped through Bjorn's jaw. "I'll find out the truth, you know. One way or t'other. You'd better talk while you can, you dirty, lying dog."

Bjorn spit blood and hit Holt square in the face.

"You stupid bastard." Again, the whip handle crashed against his face. With a sickening pop, his nose broke. Blood spurted. Pain screamed through Bjorn's brain, but he managed to look Holt square in the eye.

Through rattling teeth, he muttered, "Go to hell, you son of the Devil!"

Several peasants laughed and Holt's face turned red in rage. White lines edged the corner of his mouth. "You first," he growled and struck another blow. A flash of blinding agony flared behind Bjorn's eyes and the blackness that he welcomed came at last to claim him.

Cayley shoved her trencher aside. Ever since Holt had banished her to her chamber, she'd seethed. Treated like a wayward child! Not trusted even to take meals in the great hall! Restrained by a big, burly, stinking knight while the outlaws were being flogged! She glanced at Megan's bed and felt a deep pang of sorrow for the sister she'd tormented and teased.

Climbing into the window, she stared down at the bailey and felt sorry for herself. Even the girls plucking eggs from nests, milking cows, or herding the geese had more freedom than she.

From her position, she heard the pounding of the carpenter's hammer and the clank of steel as the armorer forged new weapons. Smoke drifted to the sky and a thin, cool mist shrouded the forest far beyond the castle. The chapel bells rang and she watched Father Timothy and Holt, heads bent against the wind, hurry down the steps and into the bailey. They were arguing, Holt's face stern, the priest's worried.

She shivered and felt as if death were near. If only Megan were here or her father were well or her brother hadn't died. But idle wishes helped no one. For the first time in her life, she had no one to turn to, no one to take care of her. "Please, please help me," she murmured, hoping God was listening.

Wringing her hands, Cayley tried to think of a way to see the crippled sorcerer again. Though she'd once hated him, she now believed that he was good, that his interests in Dwyrain were pure, that he, if anyone, could help break Holt's horrid death grip that was clamped firmly over the throat of the keep.

The door opened and a soldier allowed Rue, wearing an apron and carrying a basket of herbs and eggs, into the room. The door closed with a thud. Rue crossed the chamber in surprisingly swift strides. Sighing loudly, she took Cayley's fingers in her own bony hands.

"Something's wrong," Cayley said.

Rue slid a glance at the door. "Aye," she admitted in a soft whisper.

"Father!"

Rue gripped tighter. "He is not long with us, aye, but he no longer drinks fouled wine. 'Tis you I fear for," she said. "Holt has sent a messenger to Rolf at Castle Henning, offering you to be the old baron's bride."

"What—?" Cayley could hardly breathe and her legs

threatened to turn to mush. Rolf was an old man—an enemy of her father—one who had been married many times and whose wives either died or disappeared. "Nay—"

"Aye, 'tis true," Rue said, finally releasing Cayley's grip and rubbing her arms as if she were cold from the inside out. Cayley's strength gave way and she fell against the bed. Marriage to Baron Rolf? Her stomach turned over and she had to fight the urge not to retch.

"It could be worse," Rue said, avoiding her eyes.

"How?"

"Holt—he's already promised you to Sir Connor, but he wants not to marry you, because . . . well . . . you know . . ." She fluttered her fingers in the air. "But Holt wants to marry you off and not to Gwayne of Cysgod, though I know you wanted to be his wife."

"Gwayne is of no matter," Cayley said quickly, her head spinning. Her love for Gwayne was not deep, she now knew, just a childhood attraction, but Gwayne would be a much better mate than either Rolf or Connor. Her skin pimpled in goose bumps from fear of the dead-eyed knight and the sick old man. "I have to get out of here," she said. "I—I have to find Megan, to get help from a baron who is friendly to my father . . . or a priest of—"

"Slow down, child. You be rattled and—"

"But there is no time!" she said, feeling as if a cold, hard hand was slowly squeezing the life from her. "You must help me."

"Aye," Rue said, nodding. "I know. I asked Holt to set you free and he laughed at me. Told me 'twas not my place to even make such a suggestion." Her jaw tightened so hard that the bone showed white against her chin. "He's loathsome, Cayley, and cannot be allowed to rule Dwyrain." Then, as if feeling the need to explain herself, Rue glanced down at her hands. "He's taken a fancy to Dilys," she said and shook her head. "Poor girl. My only granddaughter. A comely, sweet lass, but sometimes slow." She swallowed hard and her eyes narrowed with injustice. " 'Tis difficult for me not to pour the poisoned wine I steal from your father's chamber into Holt's mazer. 'Twould please me to see him sputtering and gasping for his life."

"Aye, and I would slit his throat if I could," Cayley agreed, surprising herself, for she'd never been a savage woman, had never felt the need for revenge, never wished a man dead except for the sorcerer before she'd met him. When she'd blamed him for the deceit, sickness, and pain at the castle, she'd thought she'd like to see him dead, but now, she knew differently. He was a kind and good man—a strange one with near-magical powers. But not so Holt. He was the very Devil incarnate.

Rue reached into her basket, beneath the eggs and a soft cloth, to the small dagger she'd hidden there. "For your protection and escape," she said, handing the knife to Cayley. Its handle was carved from wood, its fat, short blade straight and deadly.

"Escape?" she repeated, gnawing on the inside of her lip as she twirled the tiny weapon in her fingers. "There is no way I can escape."

"I will help you," Rue vowed. "Now, I must leave or the guard will become suspicious. We will both think, and when I return, we will have a plan for you to escape Dwyrain, find Megan, and warn her of the horrid beast her husband is."

"And what then?"

"I know not," Rue admitted. "Pray your father does not fail." Adjusting the eggs and herbs over the towel in her basket, she left the room quickly and Cayley heard the bolt being slammed over the door. She could not break down the thick planks with her bit of a knife, nor could she carve her way through the stones of the floor. Her only means of escape was through the hole in the roof for the fire or the window, which was far above the frozen loam of the bailey. Oh, would she were a sorcerer, then she could find a way to escape. At that thought, she rounded her bed and walked to the window, where she could see the north tower. 'Twas there, deep below, where the sorcerer was held. She had only to set him free and he would help her escape and find Megan.

Oh, cursed fates, what could she do against an army the size of Holt's?

'Tis not the number of men who fight for a cause, but the convictions of those who do, lass. Her father's words swam in her mind and she knew that there had to be a way to leave these castle walls behind and find Megan.

"Ahh . . . she awakens . . ." a gentle female voice, one Megan had heard in her dreams, whispered.

"Praise God," another, deeper, voice intoned.

"Maybe now we'll find out who she is." Another woman, one with a slight lisp.

Those soft, soothing voices surrounded her and Megan blinked several times against the light of a candle being held near her face. "Where am I?" she asked dazedly as the women, several of them, exchanged glances. Only then, when her eyes adjusted to the yellow candlelight, did she realize that they were nuns, dressed in their somber habits and wimples, staring at her as if she were some oddity—a freak of nature. The room was a dark chamber with a single window and cavernous ceiling.

" 'Tis the Sacred Heart Nunnery where ye be," one of the women said. She laid a smooth hand to Megan's forehead. "I'm Sister Leah, and you . . . ?"

"Megan of Dwyrain," she said without thinking, and then gave herself a swift mental kick. Kind as these women were, they believed in God and truth and all that was holy. They wouldn't look kindly on a bride who had been kidnapped from her husband, then refused to return to him after lying with another man. A cold blush stole up her face and she tried to lever herself up from the hard pallet on which she rested. "I . . . I must not tarry."

"You're ill," one of the sisters said. "A farmer found you on the road not far from here two days ago and you have not once opened your eyes or taken any nourishment."

"Aye," she said, her voice scratchy, her throat dry as flour, her mouth tasting foul. Foolishly, she ran her tongue around her teeth and nearly retched.

"Be quiet," Sister Leah suggested with a patient smile. "We will bring you food and fresh water and you'll feel better. Then you can tell us why you were traveling alone."

"My horse?" Megan asked.

"Horse?" The nuns exchanged knowing glances, which Megan read much too easily. They thought she was not fully awake—that her mind was playing tricks on her.

"My destrier." *Wolf's* horse. "A black stallion with three white stockings and a small white patch on his forehead."

Three heads slowly wagged side to side. "The farmer brought you in his cart, and 'twas pulled only by a brown workhorse with a back that looked near broken."

"This is a warhorse, a steed that . . ." She let her voice drift into silence, for what could she say? That she'd stolen the horse off an outlaw who had kidnapped her and then eventually loved her, as a man loved a woman? That the horse was probably stolen from some nobleman the outlaw had robbed? Swallowing any more arguments, she said instead, "I am on my way to Erbyn."

"Erbyn?" The first nun, Sister Leah, stared at her with puzzled eyes. "Why?"

" 'Tis the Lady Sorcha I must see." Her voice was weak and she could hardly remain half sitting. With a sigh, she fell back on the small bed and the chamber spun before her eyes.

"I'm Sorcha's sister," Leah said. "Erbyn is close by."

With what small amount of strength she had, Megan struggled to sit up again. "Then I must go there. I have to find her and talk to her . . ."

"Shh. 'Twill all come to pass. First, Megan of Dwyrain, you must get your strength back so you're able to travel."

Ice surrounded the edges of Hag's End Lake, a smooth body of water rumored to be haunted by the ghosts of dead Welsh warriors. Wolf drew up on the reins, motioning for Jagger and Robin to remain silent and invisible in the shadowy forest surrounding the banks. Closing his eyes, Wolf tilted his head. From his mouth came the harsh shriek of a hawk's cry. The scream split the cold forest air. Jagger blew on his hands. Robin bit on his lower lip.

Wolf waited.

Stillness whispered through the dry leaves and steam seeped from the horses' nostrils as they breathed hard and stamped impatiently.

" 'Tis no use," Jagger finally said.

"Shh!"

They were close to Dwyrain, less than a day's ride away, and Wolf wasn't turning back. 'Twas time to face his old enemy and end the burn for revenge that fired in his gut. *And time to find Megan,* his mind tormented him again. There had been but a few minutes when he'd not thought of her and, in truth, it wasn't revenge that spurred him on so much as the need to see her again. *What if you do see her again? What then? Will you steal her away once more? Bed her ruthlessly? Try to hold her close when she wants nothing to do with you?*

Bittersweet agony ripped through his soul. How foolish he'd been to let himself care for her, to let his emotions become entangled with her when he'd vowed years ago never to let a woman close to his heart.

Now he had no choice but to follow his convictions. He could offer her nothing, but he could save her from a marriage that was certain to kill her spirit and dull her bright mind.

So now you're a god—or a priest? his mind taunted, and Wolf ground his teeth together in frustration. Though she had stood before the altar and pledged her troth to Holt, Wolf believed in his heart that she didn't love the cur and never would.

Since when do you believe in love?

Ignoring the demons in his head, Wolf lifted his hands to his mouth once more, raised his chin to the sky, and gave the hawk's mournful cry.

Again, nothing.

"Why not howl like a wolf?" Jagger said and was rewarded with a hard glance.

"And announce to everyone within earshot that I be here?"

Jagger chuckled at his joke or Wolf's consternation, Wolf knew not which. Robin, swallowing a smile, stared at the ground. Around his neck he wore a strand of bear claws from the beast that had nearly taken his life.

An answering cry split through the forest, so loud it nearly parted the shroud of fog that clung low to the hills.

"I'll be damned!"

"No doubt, Jagger. Come." Wolf leaned forward in the saddle and urged his mount to the edge of the lake where another rider appeared through the icy mist. "Jack."

"Aye, and how d'ye be, Wolf?" the hunter asked, his eyes dark and worried.

"I've been better."

"Haven't we all? Haven't we all?" Jack said. "And the lady? Is she safe?"

"Megan?" Wolf asked, alarm causing the hairs on the back of his neck to rise. "Is she not at the castle?"

"Nay, the messengers came in peace, bringing your letter of ransom, but Holt turned on them." Quickly, Jack explained about the capture of Bjorn and Jagger, as well as the return and imprisoning of the sorcerer. According to the hunter, Holt had control of the castle and sent search parties out patrolling for his wife, but his two most diligent men, Sir Connor and Kelvin of Hawarth, had become disinterested.

Holt had reprimanded them and they'd laughed in his face. Furious, he wouldn't give the men any more chance to snigger at his foolishness. He planned not to pay ransom for his wife and had declared it a sign of weakness to give in to the demands of criminals. His answer was that he intended to flog the truth from Bjorn and Jagger and any other poor soul who might have some knowledge of Megan's whereabouts and happened to wander through the gates of Dwyrain.

"But Lady Megan, no one has seen her?" Wolf asked again, fear congealing his blood.

Jack scratched the whiskers on one cheek and shook his head. "Yer men claim she is with you."

"She escaped," Jagger said with a wide grin. "Think on it, a tiny woman like that, slippin' away from Wolf."

Robin's smile was smug, as if he thought it a great joke that the bit of a woman he adored had tricked Wolf.

"She's not returned to Dwyrain," Jack said.

Desperation took a stranglehold on Wolf's throat. 'Twas possible she was safe with friends somewhere, that she had decided not to return to her father's castle and her husband's ire, but 'twas unlikely. She could have been captured by another band of outlaws—there were many in the surrounding woods—but Megan was smart, an accomplished horsewoman, and was riding the best steed in the land. Also, he was certain that she would be more careful than she'd been on her wedding day, when Wolf had abducted her.

"So there has been no sign of the lady, but my men and a strange sorcerer are being held captive?"

"Aye." Jack studied the rocks and ferns on the ground. "Not only being held, but beaten as well. Two days past, they were flogged within an inch of their lives and when I left the castle on this hunt, one, the dark-haired one—"

"—Cormick."

"Aye, he be the one. He . . . well, he was lingering near death. The priest had already been called to his cell."

"Nay!"

Jack lifted his eyes. "Aye, Wolf. 'Tis the truth I speak."

Robin's grin disappeared and he swallowed as if with difficulty.

Guilt galloped through Wolf on sharp, steel-shod hooves that ripped at his heart and soul. He should have expected this, he decided, fingers clenching around the reins, but there was an unwritten law—a code of honor that outlaws and noblemen alike respected—that messengers were not to be handled as prisoners, though he knew some of his men had at times attacked the bearer of bad news rather than the source.

Torn, he glanced behind him, as if in studying the undergrowth he could determine what had happened to Megan. Surely she was safe and, after hearing of Holt's reign of terror, he was grateful she hadn't returned to Dwyrain . . . but where was she?

"We needs save Bjorn and Cormick," Jagger reminded him, as if reading his pained thoughts. This was his fault—everything that had gone wrong could be laid at his own feet—but he could undo nothing, and if he followed his heart, he would chase down Megan wherever she was and demand that she become his wife—the bride of an outlaw of the forest. The thought was like salt water on a wound, for he physically jerked when he imagined giving up his freedom for a woman. But not any woman, he reminded himself bitterly—Holt's wife.

Jagger cleared his throat and glared at Wolf as if he suspected him of some deep treason. "Aye," Wolf agreed reluctantly, "we must save the men and then we will find Lady Megan. Dwyrain is but a day's journey from here." That thought, too, was worrisome. Mayhap Megan was indeed still trying to return to Dwyrain. Mayhap her horse was stolen or lame and she was on the road. If 'twere so, she had to be stopped afore she walked innocently through the gates of the keep, like a calf to the slaughter.

The knock on the door was firm. "Cayley, child," Father Timothy greeted her as he let himself through the door. "I've come to pray with you." He closed the door behind him and Cayley shivered at the thought of being alone with him. She was also expecting Rue soon; the nursemaid had promised to help her with plans for her escape. Time was passing much too quickly and if Cayley were to help her father, she had to ride for help soon—tonight, for the moon was full and bright in a cloudless sky. Drat and spit that this was the night the good father chose to come to help cleanse her soul.

"Kneel beside me," he ordered, and Cayley lowered herself onto the rushes, where the priest was already positioned so that he could face the door. "Aye, that's good," he said when she was beside him. Clearing his throat, he held his breath for an instant, then said so softly she barely heard him, "I have a confession to make."

"You?" she replied, sensing a trap.

"Aye. I've not always been faithful to my vows." He clasped his hands in front of him as if he were praying. "I—I have strayed, been lured by the temptations of the flesh rather than traveling down the path that leads to the purification of the soul."

She bit on her lip, refusing to be drawn into this unlikely confession. Father Timothy was a shrewd and not particularly pious man; she believed he had broken his vows a hundred times over, but she didn't trust him enough to admit as much. He could be a spy sent by Holt to trap her into saying something incriminating. "Mayhap you should pray for God's forgiveness," she said.

"I have, child. Many times, but I feel that God is asking more of me than a simple confession. I think he wants me to prove myself, to show Him that I will not fall prey to the lust and greed that sometimes afflict me." He was looking at her no longer, instead staring at the door over the fingertips of his tented hands, as if he expected someone to burst through at any second.

"Why are you confiding in me?"

"Because your heart is pure." He swallowed hard, his Adam's apple bobbing nervously in his throat. " 'Tis true I've harbored a feeling akin to love for you . . . and not the love of a priest for one of his flock, Lady Cayley," he said hesitantly, his eyes sliding her way for just a second. "Nay, I've wanted you as a man does a woman."

She recoiled at the thought. "No, Father Timothy, do not say any more, please."

But her words fell on deaf ears, for his words tumbled freely and more quickly from his mouth, like a stone gathering speed as it rolled downhill.

" 'Twas vexed I was that I had pledged myself to God and the rules of the priesthood; aye, the vow of chastity became a burden, and I . . . I was jealous of those who did not have to abide by its rigid rules."

"You need not tell me this—" she said, trying to scoot away, but he grabbed her hand and his eyes flared with a newfound conviction.

"Oh yes, I do, but 'tis not all that I must suffer," he said as if humiliated beyond words. "I must offer myself up as a sacrifice to cleanse my soul."

"Nay," she said, trying to draw away, but his grip was strong and the fire in his gaze convinced her that he would not be denied. Whatever sacrificial torture he'd planned for himself, it somehow involved her. "You needs seek counsel. Mayhap the abbot—"

"I know the way to my salvation," he said and reached beneath his vestments. Cayley nearly swooned. Was this man of God going to disrobe before her?

She yanked back her hand just as he pulled a long length of rope from beneath the folds of his robe. "What?"

" 'Tis for your escape," he said, and her heart turned to stone. If the priest knew of her plan, thin though it was, who else had guessed that she had plotted to break free of the castle walls? Fear pounded in her heart. She had no idea how she was to escape, only that she would swallow her pride and ride like the wind to Cysgod and beg Gwayne and his father, Nevin, for their help in overthrowing Holt and saving her father. Once that was accomplished, she would search for Megan. If, God forbid, she was refused help at Cysgod, she would ride to . . . where? Erbyn? Abergwynn? Ah, but 'twas nearly a week's journey to Abergwynn. Pennick was closer . . . oh, 'twas too much to think of.

The priest, eyes fixed on the door, continued. " 'Tis to Rue I spoke, and she told me of your plan." He rubbed his chin with the tips of his fingers. " 'Tis a prideful, blind, and ambitious man I've been, Cayley. Now I must atone."

"By helping me?" she asked, not daring believe that she could trust him.

"Aye, 'tis one of my penances." He reached deep into a pocket in his vestment and withdrew a small leather pouch. " 'Tis money. Take it."

"Money?"

"From the chapel." He blushed. "Do not ask how I acquired it; 'tis yours now."

"Another of your penances?"

"Aye." He slapped the bag into her hand and she dropped it as if her flesh had been seared. The coins clinked loudly and Father Timothy shot a glance to the door. "Do not warn the guards," he ordered.

She didn't dare ask him if he had more penances. He could be either addled or trying to make her prove her disloyalty to Holt. He swept up the bag of coins and forced it into her hand, folding her fingers over the soft, worn leather. What if this was only a ruse? What if he hoped only to gain her confidence, then expose her to Holt? Nay, she could not trust him.

"I've made poor allegiances here in Dwyrain," he admitted. "Today, when the men were beaten, I realized how badly

I've chosen my friends, the men in whom I've trusted. I . . . God in heaven, forgive me. I've witnessed human suffering and felt that it was right, that I, as a priest, could mete out pain in the name of the Lord, that I had the right to be the judge of men whose only sin was they were as weak as I was. I was wrong."

He sounded sincere, in his own guilty hell, but he could be a fine actor, playing his part well. His eyes didn't meet hers and he was shaking, but she remembered too many times when he'd enjoyed the belittlement of a sinner, the superiority he wore like a halo bestowed by God.

Swallowing hard, she shook her head. "I plan not to leave the castle," she said, resting on her knees and beginning to sweat anxiously. Moisture collected beneath her hair and on her spine.

"Do not lie, child. Rue said—"

"Rue is kind, aye, but old and sometimes her mind strays. If you want to pray, Father, I'll pray, but believe me, I plan not to go against Holt's wishes. My father named him as the next baron and I would not go against his word."

Timothy's lips pursed. "One of the prisoners is near death," he said.

Just as the sorcerer predicted! "Nay."

"You might pray for his wretched soul." He wiped his hands on his robes and sighed loudly. "For that of your sister, too, for if she returns to Dwyrain and has not been faithful to Holt, he will kill her."

"No, please—"

The priest's face was somber. "Say what you will, child, but mind, if you need my help, I'm at your service." Climbing to his feet, he left the rope in the middle of the floor. " 'Tis not that far to the bailey from here, and one of the stable boys left a hay cart filled with straw beneath your window. 'Twill be there until morning. Rue will be in to see you before you sleep, and, should you find a way out the window, she'll untie the rope and drop it into the cart."

"I told you I plan not to—"

Holding up a hand to silence her, he said, "I blame you not for how ye feel, Cayley. My thoughts of you haven't always been pure, I've enjoyed too much the Lord's wine, and I've been a prideful man worried about earthly things. I've . . . I've forgotten my purpose. But no longer. I pledge you this, my lady, I am your humble servant, as I am the servant of God." He laid a cool hand on her shoulder, muttered a short prayer, and then hurried out of the room, leaving the length of rope and small sack of coins behind. She tucked the coils beneath her bed, hid the pouch in the thick fur coverlets piled over the mattress, then walked to the window and peered down the sheer rock walls of the keep.

As Father Timothy had promised, a farmer's cart filled with hay was positioned beneath the window of her room. If she were brave and if she could trust the priest, she could secure the rope on one end to the foot or post of the bed, throw the coil through the window, slide down the thick hemp snake, and sneak to the stables.

Before fleeing, however, she would have to try to free the outlaws, and the sorcerer, to aid her. If Holt found her, he'd kill her or flog her as well. She cringed inside and wished that someone, anyone, would come to her rescue. She wasn't cut out for danger and would rather be weaving or embroidering than doing anything so rebellious as plotting this escape.

But she had to work fast, before the prisoner died. Whether she wanted to or not, she was forced to trust the priest.

* * *

" 'E's dead, fer sure," the jailer said. "Barely alive when we brought him in."

Holt scowled down at the body. The stench and squalor of the dungeon turned his stomach and the glassy-eyed body, battered from the flogging, lay curled in a ball in the corner. Holt hadn't intended to kill the man, not so soon, not until his tongue had been loosened, but the shorter, dark-haired outlaw had given up the ghost and died before uttering a word, not even his name.

"You'll pay," a deep, rolling voice warned.

Holt's head snapped up at the ominous words coming from the next cell. The blond outlaw sat cross-legged in a corner, his eyes burning feverishly bright as they bored into Holt.

"Upon my mother's grave, I vow, Holt of Dwyrain, I'll kill you with my bare hands."

"You're in no position to start handing out death sentences." Then why did his insides turn as weak as jelly? The man was locked and shackled, he could do nothing but talk, but Holt felt a tremor of trepidation slide down his backbone in this dark part of hell. "You're the prisoner, not I."

"All in good time."

Through soggy rushes, Holt advanced upon the barred wall separating the cells. "But your time isn't good now, is it?" he said with a nasty sense of satisfaction. "Your time is spent healing in this rat-infested hellhole. You're in no position to bargain or threaten me."

"As long as you live, I will be your enemy."

"Nay," Holt said, his temper snapping, "as long as *you* live, which, judging from your friend's length of time on this earth, won't be long. If I were you, my *friend,* I'd be less inclined to wag a tongue that could easily be cut off and be more interested in telling the truth so that I would be set free."

The blond one had the audacity to laugh, sending Holt's anger screaming through his blood. He was tired of being laughed at, furious that men—even this lowly prisoner—had the audacity to snicker at him. "You have one day to change your mind, and then, piece by piece, I will cut you apart. First, a finger or a toe, then part of your ear—even your balls—until you loosen your tongue."

Furious because the man was not intimidated, he motioned to the body. "Burn or bury this and tell me when our prisoner changes his mind!"

The blond prisoner's silent rage followed him up the steps like a shadow and Holt felt an unlikely tremor of fear. Outside, the night air was cold but fresh, and he shook off the dark images of the cells.

He had to do something. Things were not happening rapidly enough. Though there were men searching for the outlaw and Megan, it had been weeks since her capture. Wolf and his band had quite successfully eluded them. Since the day when they'd come upon the old camp by the creek where Connor had discovered Megan's wedding ring, there had been no sign of the outlaw.

Until now when Wolf's two messengers had appeared. Now, because of Holt's harsh need for justice, one of the two men who knew where Megan was hidden was dead. The other—that big blond brute—had to be kept alive no matter what.

There was too much disloyalty in the castle as it was. Many of the men were beginning to doubt him. Oh, they'd been only too happy to swear their allegiance to him when they realized that Ewan of Dwyrain was failing, that his mind was no longer sharp, that he was not the dauntless and feared leader he'd once been, but now, ever since Megan had been captured and the men had been tested, their loyalty questioned, Holt had felt that the tides of allegiance had shifted from him and to the dying baron. Curse the old apothecary; had Jovan been right in his dosage, the old man would have died weeks ago, but instead Ewan of Dwyrain lived on, lingering in his bed, muttering his thoughts to a wife who was already in her grave.

Well, Holt was tired of waiting. Everyone expected news of the baron's death and now they would get it. 'Twas only a matter of laying a thick robe over the elderly man's face. He was too weak to struggle and he'd die quietly. Then Holt would summon the guard and the castle would learn the news that the old baron had left this earth to join his wife. Holt would become the new ruler.

Swiftly, he mounted the stairs, and with a nod to the guard, entered the baron's room. He closed the door firmly behind him and saw in the quiet light the face of a once-strong man. He hesitated only a second, calling softly to the baron. Ewan's blind eyes turned in his direction and he managed a weak smile.

"M'lord," Holt said. "I've come to help you."

"There's news . . . of my daughter?" Hope brought a smile to his weathered face.

"Soon."

"Ahh. 'Tis a pity."

"That it is, m'lord. That it is." Without another word, Holt snatched a fur coverlet, and using every ounce of his strength, held the once-comforting blanket tight over Ewan of Dwyrain's face.

Twelve

"Come," the calm voice ordered.

Bjorn, seething with injustice, spit on the floor of his cell. His muscles were on fire, his face throbbing, his jaw swollen, perhaps broken.

"Come." Again, the soft-spoken command.

"Go to hell," Bjorn growled.

"Am I not already there?"

Bjorn's jaw tightened and made a horrid cracking noise, but he didn't budge. The prisoner in the next cell was certainly half crazed. Though everyone here thought him some kind of magician, what lord of darkness would allow himself to be caged like a pathetic animal? Nay, he was just a half-wit who spoke in a kind turn of phrase.

"Do not let your friend die for naught."

"My *friend* will be avenged," Bjorn vowed, his lips pulling tight against his teeth. Fury and injustice beat fiercely through him and he blamed himself for Cormick's death. Had he been more cautious, been ready for the men they approached to turn on them, they would not have been captured and beaten and Cormick would not have been killed. He should have known there was no honor in Holt of Dwyrain and both he and Wolf had been foolish to think that Ewan's good word would still be law.

"Aye, but Cormick will not be avenged by a beaten, savage man who wants only fast justice. Nay, the way to win this battle is to destroy Holt by more than fists and swords."

"Ah, ye speak as if ye've got only half a brain."

"Shuddup in there," the jailer shouted. A rotund man who sat half the time at his post and walked the halls and stairs the rest of his shift, he glowered at the prisoners as he polished the blade of his sword. "There'll be no talkin'."

I can soothe your wounds. The words came to him, though he wasn't certain the sorcerer had spoken. Bjorn glanced to the jailer, who hadn't looked up and was busying himself with cleaning his weapon.

Through the flickering, smoky light, Bjorn stared into the next cage and was certain that he could see the sorcerer's kind face. There was not a trace of malice, no evil, but his eyes glowed a deep summer blue. *Come!*

Bjorn jumped. This time he was certain the man had not spoken. His lips hadn't moved and the noise that rattled through his brain sounded as if it had traveled a long distance, even through a long tunnel.

Do not be afraid.

"I fear nothing!" Bjorn stated fiercely.

"Yeah, and bully fer you," the jailer said. "Now, hush! Jesus God, do ye want another beatin'? That's what ye're askin' fer."

The lady Cayley comes and will save you, but you must be strong to help her; a weak man will only slow her on her quest to find her sister.

"By the gods!" Bjorn thundered, standing and stepping

to the other side of the cell, tripping on his shackles and falling against the screaming muscles of his back.

"Enough from ye!" The jailer jumped from his stool, forced his sword into its sheath, and strode to the door. "Sir 'Olt, 'e's got no love fer ye. If ye were to 'ave a mite of an accident, 'e wouldn't be cryin' a river of tears over yer body, let me tell ye."

"Untrue." This time the strange one spoke. "Holt needs this man to take him to the outlaw who stole his wife, and if he is harmed, Holt will surely punish whoever it was who let the 'mite of an accident'—I think you called it—happen. Think you twice afore you hurt the one man who can help Holt find his wife."

"I'll never—" Bjorn started, but that faraway voice stopped him.

Hush. The guard will leave us be.

"Bloody Christ," the jailer muttered, but returned to his seat and removed his sword from his sheath again. With one eye on the cells, he snagged his rag and began to rub the blade with renewed fervor. Soon, with only the drip of water and sound of mice scurrying through the crevices in the walls for noise, the guard was caught up in his work.

Bjorn turned to the cripple.

Come to the cell wall. I will help you. Do not be afraid.

"I fear nothing," Bjorn whispered, but, in truth, his heart was thundering loudly, his face and back throbbing in pain, and it took most of his courage to walk the few steps to the rusted bars separating his quarters from the sorcerer. Not long ago, he'd been nearly killed by a rampaging horse and Sorcha of Prydd had used some of the spells from the old ones to heal him. He'd been brought back to life from the brink of death. But this man—this cripple who could not heal himself—was different. Oddly reassuring and yet . . . By the gods, what did he have to lose? He was in prison, sure to be tortured again, probably killed. He had no choice but to place his trust and his life in the strange fellow's hands. Squaring his inflamed shoulders, he shot his hands through the bars, and the sorcerer, who appeared to move without sound, placed his soothing fingers on Bjorn's torn flesh.

"So, Lady Megan, you've traveled a great distance to see me," Sorcha of Erbyn said as Megan slid to the muddy ground within the gates of the largest castle she'd ever seen. Thrice the size of Dwyrain, Erbyn rose like a great yellow-gray dragon from the very cliffs on which it stood. The battlements were high and wide, the towers strong, the keep massive. Servants, pages, and peasants scurried through the bailey; carts pulled by old workhorses and travelers on swifter palfreys and jennets passed through the gatehouse. Chickens clucked and squawked, cattle bawled, and children ran through the few flakes of snow that fell from thick, slate-colored clouds.

Sorcha held a forest-green cloak around her. The hood was trimmed in rabbit fur and the hem flapped loudly in the wind. "Come into the keep and have a cup of wine by the fire. You, too, sister. 'Tis much too cold a day for travel."

Leah slid down from her spotted mare and embraced her sister. "So good to see you."

"Aye, and you." Sorcha held her sister at arm's length and studied her face, as if searching for traces of unhappiness.

"How is my niece?" Leah asked.

Sorcha laughed, the sound ringing over the pounding of a carpenter's hammer, the creak of the windmill's sails, and the cursing of the master mason who was unhappy with one of the freemasons' cuts of stone. "Bryanna is as beautiful as her aunt and mean-tempered as her father."

"I heard that!" A big man with sharp eyes the color of ale, thick brows, and a vexed expression approached. By his dress and manner—that of pride and arrogance—Megan guessed him to be the baron, Lord Hagan of Erbyn. "You're ever a witch, Sorcha."

"And you'd not have it any other way," she teased, clasping his hand. "Lady Megan of Dwyrain, please meet my husband, the ogre."

Laughing, he placed an arm possessively around Sorcha's small waist. "Forgive my wife; she sometimes forgets her manners." He caught a page's eye. "Have rooms prepared and tell the cook we have guests!"

The lad with straw-blond hair and crooked teeth nodded heartily, anxious to please. "Aye, m'lord." He turned and ran toward the keep, while another boy of eight or nine appeared and, without a word, took the reins of their mounts and led the tired horses toward the stables.

The big man with tawny eyes smiled. "Now, Leah . . . so good to see you again."

"And you, Lord Hagan."

A pang of loneliness tore through Megan when she thought of her own family, so small now, but so close. Her father near death, or so she'd been led to believe, and her sister, fair and giddy, never thinking about the morrow—how did they fare? It had been weeks since she'd seen them and though she'd often fought with Cayley, now she wished to be able to sit down and talk to her, to confide in her.

Great snowflakes fell from the sky in earnest. Scowling at the dark clouds, Hagan shepherded them into the great hall. Once seated near the fire and drinking wine, pleasantries aside, Megan explained her reasons for riding to Erbyn. She told of marrying Holt and being kidnapped by an outlaw who, he claimed, was Ware of Abergwynn.

With the three sets of eyes steadily upon her, Megan barely touched her wine as she spoke. "... I am worried that my father and I have been deceived by the man I married, a man I do not love. If it be true that he rode with your brother, Lady Sorcha, if he lied to my father, if, indeed, he committed the horrid crimes that Wolf claims, then Dwyrain is in jeopardy and ... and I would want my marriage annulled. I need to know the truth and return to Dwyrain." *And to Wolf*, she thought miserably, knowing that he would never again touch her, never speak to her, as she'd deceived him by lying with him, feigning sleep, then stealing his horses and leaving him stranded. That thought brought with it a deep ache in her heart, and her hands shook slightly as she took a long sip of wine.

"Everything Ware has told you is true," Sorcha assured her with a thoughtful frown. "Leah knows." The sisters' gazes touched and they shared a silent painful moment before Sorcha looked at Megan again. "My brother was a cruel man with no thought but of his own wants. He cared not for Prydd, nor his family, nor the servants or peasants who lived within the castle walls." She swallowed and stared at her hands before squaring her shoulders and tossing a mane of wild black hair over her shoulders. "Aye, Tadd raped Mary, the fisherman's daughter. She was not his first, nor his last. On that day, there were several soldiers with him. Holt was there."

"You remember him?"

"A bit." Sorcha shivered. " 'Twas a bad time in our lives." She glanced at her sister.

"Aye. Our darkest hour." Leah made a swift sign of the cross over her chest and blinked for a few seconds.

Relief that Wolf hadn't lied came to her but the truth was damning, for she was married to this monster of a man.

Leah said, "Megan has traveled a long distance and was ill when she was found by a local farmer who brought her to us. Now that she knows the truth, I think she should rest."

"Nay, I must return to Dwyrain. My father—"

"Would want you to be well. Let us eat and rest. Tomorrow we can talk of traveling to Dwyrain," Hagan interjected, his face a mask of hard determination.

But each day so far from home—away from Wolf—was an eternity to Megan. Since she knew the truth, she was eager to return, to face the man who had lied to become her husband.

"When you are strong enough to leave Erbyn, my best men will ride with you," Hagan decided aloud. Though he stared at the fire, his eyes were trained on a far distance only he could see. "I have waited long to purge the land of anyone who rode with Tadd or my brother Darton. I, too, will ride to Dwyrain." A cold smile crossed his square jaw. " 'Twill be a pleasure."

A piercing cry rang from the rafters. Megan jumped.

"Ah," Sorcha said with a smile. "The lady Bryanna is hungry. If you'll excuse me."

An ancient woman with gray hair descended the steps. Smiling and wizened, lines of age etching her skin, she was carrying a small, howling bundle. "I've never seen a babe with such lungs in her."

" 'Tis a sign for strength of character, Isolde," Sorcha said as she took the crying infant from the old crone's arms, and the nursemaid cackled affectionately. One little fist had escaped from the blankets and a head of black curls was visible as the babe let out another lusty cry. "Come, little one," Sorcha cooed, kissing the child's soft crown. " 'Twill be only a minute. I know . . . I know."

Hagan watched his wife ascend the steps and a kind,

nearly reverent expression changed the hard contours of his face as his gaze followed her. The love in his eyes touched Megan. Here was a man who would lay down his life for his lady and child, a man devoted to her, a man, upright and law-abiding, who wanted only to provide for and protect his family and castle.

Unlike the renegade outlaw to whom she'd given her heart.

"Did Wolf kill Tadd?" she asked once Hagan had turned to her again.

"Aye. After Tadd nearly killed me." He finished his wine and set his mazer on the hearth. Then he told her the story of Sorcha of Prydd, his wife, born with the birthmark of the kiss of the moon, an ancient prophecy stating that whosoever was born with the mark would become the savior of Prydd. Many had scoffed at the thought of a woman becoming a leader, mostly Tadd, Sorcha's older brother, but in the end, she proved herself to be uncommonly brave and determined.

Megan withered inside. Sorcha had done so much for those who depended upon her, while Megan had brought only fear, distrust, and now, by marriage, the reign of a cruel baron. Unwittingly, she'd become the curse of Dwyrain. And now she was in love with a wild man, an outlaw of the forest, who used her only for revenge against a sworn enemy.

As if reading her thoughts, Hagan said, "Wolf breaks the law without a thought, he takes refuge in the forest and disdains life within a castle, he makes his own rules and lives by them, but he is a good man, Lady Megan; his heart is pure."

"I—I believe you."

"Good. Then eat the food that Cook has prepared and rest. We'll talk of riding to Dwyrain tomorrow."

Megan didn't argue as a page brought in a trencher filled with eggs and eels, a round of cheese, and a few tart winter apples. The cold seeped from her bones and she realized how badly she missed a part of her life at Dwyrain. The adventure of living in the forest was appealing, though, and she thought of the outlaw band—grizzled Odell, innocent Robin, even-tempered Peter with his one eye—but she knew that the source of her fascination with the life of the thieves was their leader. Where was he now? Was he following her? Would he even now burst through the gates of Erbyn? If he asked, she would eagerly give up the comforts of the keep to be with him.

Silly girl. Foolish heart. He was probably glad to be rid of her and the problem of returning her to her husband.

Holt.

Her blood curdled at the thought that she was, in the eyes of the church and in accordance with the laws, bound to him for the rest of her life.

She'd finished eating when Sorcha, carrying the tiny babe, swept down the stairs. No longer wailing, the infant's face had lost its scarlet hue and was as smooth and white as her mother's. "She'll not be an easy lass," Sorcha said proudly. "Headstrong."

"Like her mother." Leah swallowed a last bite of eel and sighed contentedly. Fluttering her fingers, she indicated that she wanted to hold her tiny niece, and Sorcha reluctantly gave the swaddled babe to her sister.

"I know of Ware of Abergwynn," Sorcha said. "I knew him first as Wolf, the outlaw. But he is Baron Garrick's younger brother who, in his youth, was overly confident and eager to prove himself a man. Unfortunately, when his brother trusted him to rule the keep, he was overthrown by a traitor, his own cousin, Strahan." She crossed her legs and laced her fingers over a velvet-draped knee. "Ever since that time, Wolf has been a man haunted by his past, an outlaw who is forever chased by the demon guilt. Though Garrick blamed him not for losing Abergwynn years ago, I think that Wolf has never been able to redeem himself in his own eyes.

"At the time he and Lady Morgana's—she is now married to Garrick—anyway, her brother, Cadell, escaped from Strahan only to be forced over the cliffs at Abergwynn and into the sea far below. Their bodies were never found. They were both thought dead for years until the outlaw Wolf turned out to be Ware of Abergwynn."

"What happened to Morgana's brother?" Megan asked.

"Never heard from since. 'Tis presumed that he died in the fall off the cliffs or drowned in the sea."

"And Ware blames himself for this as well?"

Sorcha lifted a shoulder. "I say only what I've been told by those who were there. 'Twas a long time ago. Over ten years." She cleared her throat, dispelling the dark mood that clouded her eyes. " 'Tis late and you need your rest, Lady Megan."

"Nay, now that I know the truth, I must return."

"Tomorrow," Sorcha said. "With Hagan and his army."

"Curse your bones, Megan," Cayley growled under her breath as her fingers curled more tightly over the rope. Fighting a fearsome dizziness, she climbed out the window, swallowed back her qualms, and began to lower herself slowly into the waiting cart filled with straw. If only her sister hadn't gotten herself into such a mess, then she wouldn't have to go through this torture. Her arms and shoulders ached from holding up her weight, her shoes slipped on the stones of the castle wall, and the rope felt as if it were shredding the skin off her hands even though she was wearing gloves.

Finally, she was close enough to the cart to jump. Silently counting to three, she let go and fell, landing in the piled straw with a soft thud. The night air was crisp and cold, her breath fogging, the moon shining bright and nearly full to give some light. Rolling off the cart, she alighted on the hard ground and twisted her ankle. Holy Mother, she wasn't any good at this!

Biting the urge to cry out, she hurried onward. Fear crawled up her spine, and she was constantly looking over her shoulder, certain she was being followed. As she passed the fish pond, she heard a splash in the water and nearly screamed. Her hasty footsteps echoed down the path near the beehives and through the bedraggled gardens.

Beneath her black-hooded mantle, deep in a pouch strapped around her waist, was the small knife Rue had given her, and she prayed that she didn't have to wrestle with the guard and his huge sword. Dear God in heaven, what was she doing?

Tamping down the dread that stole the spit from her mouth, she opened the door of the north tower and tiptoed quietly down the steps. A few rush lights still burned, fouling the air with their oily smoke and causing shadows to shift in the narrow, dark halls. This was no mission for a lady—no mission for a sane person—but she continued downward, half expecting some burly guard or ghost of a dead prisoner to jump out at her. *God be with me,* she silently prayed as she rounded the final corner.

She comes. Be ready! The unspoken words charged at Bjorn from the next cell, and he saw the stranger arise. Using some small piece of metal, the sorcerer silently unfastened the manacles over his wrists, then did the same with the shackles at his feet. *Come closer.* As Bjorn edged closer to the barred wall, a hand shot through the metal slats and a nail was dropped into his palm. Sweating nervously, Bjorn glanced up at the guard and worked at his own bindings.

The man was so strange, he frightened Bjorn, but Bjorn was thankful that the fire in his back had faded to a dull ache, and his face, swollen and no doubt bruised, was stiff and sore but no longer throbbed in agony. Whatever magic this man possessed, 'twas powerful.

Now, lure the guard into your cell and we will steal his keys. You are stronger than I if he resists.

Bjorn no longer questioned the sorcerer's commands. As if he were a knight who had pledged fealty to this peculiar baron, he climbed to his feet and felt a new freedom in his ankles and wrists. Revenge tainted his blood and he wanted nothing more than to seek out Holt and slit his traitorous throat.

Later.

He had to appear weak, he had to appear as if he needed assistance, he had to worry the simpleton sentry. Grabbing a handful of the foul rushes on the floor, he shoved them into his mouth. Straw and hair, dirt and all manner of grime and refuse clogged his throat, and as he coughed it up, he began to retch violently, his body racking against the putrid matter.

"Hey—what?" The guard glanced up.

Bjorn kept coughing, spitting, and vomiting.

"Oh, ye gods, what's 'appened to ye?" Disgust and worry edged the jailer's words. He climbed off his fat rump and grabbed his keys, as well as a candle for light. "Don't ye be dyin' on me, ye hear? Sir 'olt, 'e wouldn't like it if ye did somethin' as infernally stupid as leavin' this life." Keys jangling, he opened the cell door and slipped through, slamming the heavy bars into place behind him. " 'Ere now, what's got into ye?"

Bjorn waited until the man was near, then he grabbed with both hands the manacles that had bound him, and with a quick lunge, forced the sentry backward. The candle dropped, hot wax sprayed on Bjorn's legs, and the soggy rushes on the floor caught flame, only to sputter out.

"Hey! Wha—?" the startled jailer yelled as links of chain wrapped around his thick throat. Using his weight, Bjorn jammed his heavy body against the wall of bars that separated his cell from that of the stranger.

Coughing, choking, swearing, and stumbling backward, the guard kicked forward, attempting to wound Bjorn between his legs, but Bjorn, finding some sort of sweet justice, only tightened the noose. The guard wound his meaty fingers around the steel coil cutting off his wind, but Bjorn pressed harder until the man was backed against the bars, and the stranger wrapped his own manacles around one of the jailer's legs, looping the chain through the bars and clamping on the other cuff to his free leg.

"Hold him," he ordered. With deft fingers, he tore a strip of cloth from his tunic and forced it into the guard's gaping mouth. Only when the man sagged against the bars, his legs wobbling, did Bjorn release him and snap his manacles over the man's thick wrists. The jailer-turned-prisoner struggled, shaking his head and throwing himself against his bonds, but to no avail. Bjorn grabbed his keys, sword, and dagger, then hurried through the door, unlocked the stranger's cell, and ran toward the stairs, nearly knocking over Lady Cayley, who was hastening soundlessly down the steps.

"You're free?" she cried, stepping backward, surprised.

"Aye. Let's go."

"But how—?" she asked as she squinted into the darkness.

"Later, woman!" Bjorn insisted. "Now hush."

"He's right. Come quietly," the sorcerer agreed.

Bjorn grumbled, "I don't know why we need her!"

"Trust me. She is on our side."

He felt, rather than saw, the woman's back stiffen. "You doubt my integrity?"

"Nay, lady, only your ability." Bjorn had no time for a woman—a rich, pampered daughter of the baron—getting in his way.

"Even though I risked my life to come down to the dungeon to save you, even though you are a common outlaw, you doubt me?" she said, her voice filled with indignation.

A woman would only slow him down, but Bjorn would not question the sorcerer, not when the man had healed his wounds and shown him how to gain his freedom. Now, if only he could sneak into Holt's room and—

Enough! We must flee the castle before we're discovered! Trust this woman; she needs us as much as we need her.

The cripple, even with his limp, was swift enough, and Cayley led the way to the stables, where no guard lingered. Inside, the horses snorted and rustled when they sensed the intruders. But each animal quieted as the magician touched its coarse winter coat. 'Twas too dark to see much, but Bjorn found his stallion and Cormick's fleet mare for the woman while the sorcerer untied a quick horse to claim as his own. No bridles were in evidence, but Bjorn cut lengths of rope with the jailer's knife. He fashioned the twine into halters with reins, and soon they were leading their steeds out of the stables and into the moonlight.

Don't worry about the guards, the strange one intoned without words. *I shall handle them.*

The horses' hooves rang through the bailey as they

approached the main gate. Bjorn thought 'twould be easy enough to lure the guards from their posts and pounce on them, but he sensed that the magician had another plan.

Be ready!

The sorcerer rode his horse into the middle of the bailey and threw his head back to howl like a dog at the moon.

"Wait!" Bjorn commanded. "Do not—"

But the deed was already accomplished, and men were beginning to awaken and shout.

"What's he doing?" the lady asked, horrified.

"I know not! Shh!" Bjorn kept his horse in the shadows of a hayrick. The main gate was open, the portcullis not yet dropped for the night.

"Halt! You in the bailey! Who be ye?" one guard asked.

"Know ye not?" the magician asked.

"Speak up, man!"

"I be the voice of the Devil. Lucifer's my name."

"Holy Mother," Cayley whispered, swiftly making the sign of the cross over her ample bosom.

"For the love of Christ, he's either drunk or as mad as a dog!" the guard growled. "He'll wake up the whole damned castle."

"Who is it?" another sentry asked, and he, too, was lured into the inner bailey, where the magician, arms spread wide, began to bay soulfully again. In a rustle of feathers, a great owl hooted and landed squarely on the man's outstretched arm. Bjorn watched in fascination as the wizard didn't flinch when the curved talons bit into his skin.

"Come," Bjorn ordered and kneed his mount. The horse took off like a thunderbolt, leaping forward, in its anxiety running toward the gatehouse. Cayley's horse gave chase.

"Stop! For the love of God, what's that?" one of the guards yelled.

"Who goes there?" another demanded as Bjorn's steed raced under the portcullis, steel hooves clattering over the drawbridge.

" 'Tis the prisoner! 'E's escaping!"

"Nay, it couldn't . . . God's blood, there'll be 'ell to pay now!"

Bjorn heard no more. Over the ringing of hooves, shouts of alarm, and that horrid, soul-scraping, keening wail, he heard only the sound of his own heart beating a wild tattoo in his chest. "Run, you bastard, run!" he yelled at the horse, who was already nearly taking flight.

Down the road they sped with only a ribbon of moonlight as their guide. He glanced over his shoulder and saw that Cayley was tucked low, her black mantle billowing like a dark sail behind her as Cormick's game mare swept across the night-darkened countryside. The wind whipped past them, bringing tears to his eyes, and Bjorn's heart beat stronger, for this was the first taste of freedom he'd had in days, and oh, 'twas sweet.

The road forked, and they turned south, toward the nearest woods.

Zing!

An arrow hissed past his ear.

Thwack! Another landed in a tree to his right, and he heard the shouts of men on horses, already giving chase. A hasty look over his shoulder confirmed his worries; whatever advantage they had was surely fading.

"Bloody hell," he grumbled. Without another thought, he turned off the road and into the blackness of the woods. Cayley's horse didn't break stride, and together they slowed, moving silently and doubling back, delving deeper into the woods as they crossed a stream and peered through the leafless branches to the starry sky. In a thick copse of pine, he stopped and grabbed hold of the reins of Cayley's mount. Silently, he pressed a finger to her lips and felt her hot breath on his skin. The forest shivered with the rapid thuds of hoofbeats pounding over the frozen road. The soldiers passed not 20 feet from them, their horses galloping swiftly to the south, their torches held aloft, blinking like evil red-gold eyes before disappearing in the distance.

Once they could no longer be heard or seen, Bjorn pulled on the reins of his mount and headed north, to the camp near the old chapel where Wolf had said they'd meet.

"Oh, dear God in heaven," Cayley murmured, her voice trembling. "They'll find us."

"Not if we shut up and hurry."

"But they'll send dogs and—"

"Just ride, woman. Do not cry, do not beg, and do not whimper, or I'll leave you."

"You wouldn't!" she said, and he sensed her bristle. At the very least, she had some backbone.

"Not if ye behave yerself. Now, hush!" He felt her need to sputter and hiss at him, but she didn't utter another word. "We'll find Wolf."

Wolf. The man he'd trusted with his life. The man whom he'd revered. The man who'd nearly sent him to his death. The man whom Cormick had considered his family.

Angry with himself, with Wolf, with the damned martyr of a magician, he glanced at the woman huddled on her steed. She trembled from the cold, and when she glanced his way, there was pain and anger in her gaze. "We should have left him not," she finally said.

"Who? The wizard?"

"Aye. He gave up his life for us." Her gaze, filled with blame, cut him to his bones.

" 'Twas what he wanted," Bjorn muttered, but couldn't

stop the blade of guilt that twisted in his heart. What the lady was saying had already crossed his mind. "Shh. Be still. As you said, Holt's men could have dogs with them and find us." He clucked to his horse, urging the stallion through the undergrowth, but his thoughts were at Dwyrain with the sorcerer.

God be with you.

As if he'd heard a scream from the dead, Holt awakened with a start. But the blood-chilling wail didn't stop with his nightmare; no, it echoed through the castle, tumbling off the stone walls.

'Twas Ewan's ghost returned to haunt him!

Guards shouted, footsteps thundered through the hallways, someone began pounding on his door.

"Sir Holt!" Red shouted. "The prisoners have escaped!"

"What?" Anger tore through him. "But how?" He threw on his breeches and tunic, then opened the door to find the rotund knight breathing hard and sweating despite the cool temperature of the castle at night.

" 'Tis true. We were tricked, we were. By the magician!"

Another keening wail raced through the corridors of the castle. Holt's heart nearly stopped, for it sounded to him as if the very beast from hell had been unleashed in the bailey.

"What in the name of Jesus is that noise?"

"The sorcerer, Sir Holt. He's . . . he's possessed! Call the priest."

"The man's a fraud. As you said, he's used his magic to confuse you," Holt sneered, hiding his own fear. Was he the only man in the castle with any brains? Strapping on his belt, sword, and dagger, he strode out of the room. Whatever trick the cripple had played, 'twould be his last!

Guards and servants were scrambling through the hallways, muttering oaths, whispering prayers, causing the rush lights to flicker as they passed. Outside, the noise was louder, a piercing, haunting scream that turned Holt's insides to water. The sorcerer sat on his horse, his arms thrown wide, a huge ruffle-feathered owl sitting on his shoulder.

"Stop!" he commanded, but the man continued his screaming as if he heard nothing other than the demons in his head. "Do you hear me, man? Stop this infernal—"

"Hey! Halt! Stop!" Out of the shadows, two horsemen spurred their mounts through the untended gates. "Oh, for the love of Jesus. 'Tis the prisoner! He's escaped!"

"What?" Holt's eyes narrowed on the fleeing horsemen. Not one, but two of them. "The prisoner—?" His mind spun backward to the flogging. No man he'd beaten so hard would be able to ride, and who was the other one—the smaller rider? Certainly not the dead man, returned to life like Lazarus. Nay, that criminal had been buried in the woods outside the castle—the maggots were feasting on his flesh already. A cloud crossed the moon, casting a shadow on the land, and Holt felt as if the cold hand of death had grabbed his heart and squeezed so hard he couldn't catch his breath.

"Stop them," he yelled, but his men stood transfixed, staring as the sorcerer howled at the damned moon like a wolf from the depths of hell. *Like a wolf—sweet Jesus, the man is mocking me.* "Red, Oswald! Get some men together and stop those two!"

"Oh . . . aye." Red snapped out of the spell that had disabled him.

"After them!" Holt ordered. "After them!"

Red's gaze swept the gatehouse. "Damn it." Drawing his sword, he sprinted toward the stables, hitting men on the shoulders and hurling orders. Several men managed to break the spell and took off after him, their boots thudding on the frozen mud of the bailey.

Father Timothy, rumpled and cross, strode out of the chapel. Befuddled by the wailing and the crowd, he demanded, "What's the meaning of this?"

"Prisoners have escaped!" someone in the crowd yelled.

"The sorcerer is possessed!" Nell proclaimed.

Timothy's steps faltered. "I think not."

"Listen to him, Father," the candlemaker insisted. " 'Tis what he said, that the Devil had control of his tongue!"

"Nay, this I do not believe." But the priest was more ashen-faced than before and trepidation contorted his fleshy features. His fingers anxiously rubbed the beads of the rosary hanging from his pocket.

Holt drew his sword and made his way through the crowd that had gathered, forming a crescent of onlookers near the center of the spectacle.

"You there, hush!" Holt commanded as he approached.

The shrieking didn't stop; 'twas almost as if the man took no breaths. Children were crying, women on their knees, men staring at the sorcerer as if he were the Christ arisen again.

"Stop now, or I'll kill you."

"Nay!" one woman, the baker's pregnant wife, cried. "Sir Holt, you cannot. He's but a half-wit or . . ."

"Pull him down!" Holt ordered his soldiers.

"Oh, please, no. He means no harm."

"Do you not remember that he cursed Dwyrain?"

"That's right," the miller said, his frown deep. "We all suffered much. I lost a son."

"And I a sister," a woman said, but there was no conviction in her voice.

"My boy lost his leg," another woman said with a catch in her voice. They stared at the man as if he were a saint rather than the hellmonger he was.

"Show some mercy," Father Timothy pleaded, and Holt saw that his misgivings about the priest had proven true. Holt had always doubted the man's allegiance to him. Timothy was weak in his faith and in his convictions. Holt had no use for him.

"The sorcerer is not a man of God, but practices pagan magic," he reminded Timothy.

"He's misguided."

"As well as being a traitor to Dwyrain. This man helped the prisoner escape," Holt said. How had the magician managed that? Who was the second rider? Several men appeared at his side, and while the man screamed, he was dragged from his horse, and the owl, startled, flew away with a great flapping of his wings. Feathers fluttered to the ground. Two huge, burly soldiers held the prisoner fast, and the sight was pitiful, for he was a thin cripple who struggled not and would become a martyr if Holt wasn't careful.

"Who are you?" Holt threw at him, asking a question that had never before been answered. "Why are you here?"

The screaming suddenly stopped and the man's fevered, mindless eyes once again were eerily intelligent, more frightening than when he appeared riotously insane. "I, Sir Holt, am your conscience, that nasty prick of worry that you've hidden deep but sometimes keeps you awake at night."

The moon appeared from behind a cloud, bathing the sorcerer's face in a silvery, nearly angelic glow. Holt shivered in his boots.

"What say you?" Holt asked again. The man was truly addled, but a drip of fear slid down Holt's spine.

"I'm your conscience, for I know what you've done."

There was no reason to listen to this. "Take him away!" Holt roared, trying to stem the dread that was slowly scraping at his soul.

"Is not the baron dead?" the cripple demanded.

Holt rounded and crashed his fist into the madman's face.

Several women gasped and fell to their knees, praying loudly. The wind picked up, scattering dry leaves and playing with hems of surcoats and mantles.

"Ask him," the prisoner said to the crowd. "Ask him if he hasn't been poisoning Baron Ewan each day, and when the old man didn't die quickly—"

"Enough! Take him to the dungeon. He'll be hung at dawn!"

The magician had the audacity, the sheer, stupid insolence, to laugh. "Is that what you do to your adversaries, Holt? Kill them? Sneak into their chambers and place the skin of a bear over their faces until they can no longer draw a breath, as you did with the baron? Or do you marry them off, as you plan to do with Lady Cayley? Are you not planning to have her wed an old, cruel man who will kill her?"

"Take him away!" Holt swallowed hard. How had this . . . this addled half-wit known what he'd done? If anyone found out about the death of Ewan or if Connor discovered that Holt planned to betray him . . . He felt a tremor of fear, for Connor was a coldhearted bastard.

The guards pushed their captive roughly toward the north tower, but the sorcerer laughed again, the sound hideous to Holt's ears. "Enjoy your short rule as baron. Holt of Prydd," the sorcerer said with a patient, knowing smile. " 'Twill soon be over!"

Holt's temper exploded and he caught up with his captive. "You fool," he uttered as he smashed a fist into the cripple's gut, causing the man to double over. If not for the guards holding him upright, he would have fallen to the ground.

"Did you see that?" a man's voice, one he didn't recognize, yelled loudly.

"A brute, he is," a woman murmured. "Lady Megan is lucky that she escaped becoming his bride."

"Thank God Baron Ewan is alive."

If you only knew, Holt thought, but he held his tongue. 'Twould look suspicious if he alone knew that Ewan had already left this world and joined his dead wife and children. That thought warmed him. Soon enough, come the morning, no one would any longer question his authority and refer to Ewan as the rightful baron of Dwyrain. 'Twas his now.

"Sir Holt!" Mallory yelled as he ran, ashen-faced, down the keep steps. " 'Tis the baron."

"Did he call for me?"

"Nay," Mallory replied as he crossed the mashed grass of the inner bailey. " 'Tis Lord Ewan. I'm afraid . . . 'tis dead he is."

"No!"

Gasps and wails met the soldier's announcement.

" 'Tis true . . ." Mallory searched the crowd. "Father Timothy, please—"

"Did not the magician say—?" a woman asked.

"Shh!" her husband commanded.

"Say no more." Timothy held the skirt of his robes high and marched soberly to the keep.

"The baron? Are you sure?" Holt asked. He started toward the keep.

Mallory placed a hand on Holt's arm, restraining him. "There's more," he admitted, staring at the ground and tugging on the end of his moustache. " 'Tis Lady Cayley."

"Yes, yes, what about her?" Holt shoved the man's hand off him and strode toward the great hall.

"She's missing, m'lord."

Holt whirled so swiftly he nearly fell over. "Missing?"

"Aye." Mallory paled and his Adam's apple wiggled nervously. "She escaped down a rope from her window."

"For the love of God," Holt growled, looking at the gate where the *two* horsemen had escaped. The tall blond outlaw and *Cayley*? Ewan's weak, whimpering, and flirtatious second daughter? His blood boiled. Not only had his own wife eluded him, but her simpering younger sister as well. Every muscle in his body grew taut as a bowstring and his eyes narrowed on his pathetic troop of soldiers. "Can't we hold anyone in this keep? Now, if you don't want to be flogged, beaten, or hanged, I suggest you take off after the prisoner and return him dead or alive. I care not which." Though a few troops had left, too many stood idle. "Go!"

"And . . . and the lady?"

His jaw clenched so tight it ached. Both Cayley and the prisoner were worth more to him alive than dead, but he cared not. "Kill her if she won't return peacefully."

"But she's the baron's daughter!" the cook proclaimed, unable to hold his tongue.

"Nay," Holt snarled to the pathetic people clustered around him. "If what Sir Mallory says is true and Ewan has given up his life, then I'm baron of Dwyrain!"

Megan stirred and reached for Wolf, but her hand found only an empty place on cold linen sheets. Opening her eyes, she blinked in the darkness and wondered where he was, what he would be thinking. Her dream of holding him close, of feeling his warm body and demanding lips, had been so real, so vivid, and she'd thought for just an instant that he was here with her.

"So ye're awake." The voice, that of the old crone, startled her and she scooted upward in the bed, holding a blanket over her chest.

"Aye," she said as the woman lit a candle from the dying embers of the fire.

"I know ye be worried about yer man, the outlaw Wolf."

"How would you know . . . ?"

"I see things, lass. 'Tis my curse." Rubbing the huge knots that were the joints of her fingers, the gnarled woman lowered herself onto the foot of the bed and gazed out the chamber's single window to the star-studded sky. "Something's amiss tonight," she said, as if to herself. "The gods are not happy."

"Gods—you mean God," Megan said.

"Aye, Him, too." Sighing, she placed a candle on a small table near the bed and the flame flickered in the breath of wind stirring through the castle. "There's good and bad in the world, m'lady. Everyone has a share of each."

"What is it you're trying to tell me, Isolde?"

"There was a death tonight," the old one said, her eyes far away. "At Dwyrain."

"Nay—"

"Your father, lass."

"Nay! Nay! Nay! I believe you not!" Megan cried, though the lines of sadness around the old woman's eyes and etching over her forehead half convinced her.

" 'Tis true. He was helped to his death by your husband."

The world jolted and spun. Megan's breath stopped dead in her lungs. "No," she cried, but sensed the woman would not have come here if she did not believe it.

"I sensed a tremor, child, a rending in the air. 'Twas Ewan giving up his life."

Megan's bones no longer supported her. She felt as if the world had stopped, as if life itself had withered. Her father, her wonderful father, now dead? Though she'd told herself that his death had been imminent, that there was a chance she wouldn't see him alive again, she could not believe that he was really gone. Tears gathered in her eyes, but she held them at bay, refusing to break down. "Leave me alone. I—I believe this not."

"There is more."

"I do not want to hear it."

Isolde reached forward and grabbed Megan's fingers, still clutching the coverlet. "Aye, this news is sweet," she said with a smile. "For every death, there is new life, and you, m'lady, carry new life in your womb."

Megan couldn't speak. Her words jumbled and clogged in her throat. *A baby?* Is that what the woman was saying? She was going to have a child? *Wolf's* issue? "How . . . how would you know?"

Isolde sighed. " 'Tis a gift," she said.

"You practice the dark arts."

"Aye," she admitted. "Some say I be a witch, but 'tis not true. I'm a nursemaid. 'Twas I who helped Lady Sorcha come into this world."

Megan glanced down at her flat abdomen, now covered with thick blankets. Could this be true? Could she believe this glorious gift had been given her and deny the woman's death sentence for her father?

"As for the babe growing within you, 'tis early yet, the child only just conceived."

Megan swallowed hard. *A baby!* Though she felt a deep grief at the loss of her father—if the old woman spoke the truth—the thought of bringing Wolf's child into the world brought with it a joy she'd never before known.

Isolde placed a warm, aged hand over the furs and blankets that covered Megan's abdomen. A small smile played at the edges of her thin lips. "I know not what it will be, 'tis much too soon. But ye must be careful, Megan. This babe was created by great love. You must take care of yourself and of it. Now"—she reached for her candle—"sleep well. Both of you."

Megan slid lower in the bed and placed a hand over the skin stretched between her hipbones. Could she believe this old woman? Was Ewan really dead? Did a child grow deep inside her?

Tears slid down her face and she knew not if they came from grief or happiness.

Thirteen

"Isolde told me you were with child," Sorcha said as her husband gathered together a small band of men to accompany Megan to Dwyrain. Leah had already left Erbyn with a sentry and was riding to her duties in the nunnery.

Now Sorcha and Megan stood on the steps of the keep, cowls pulled tight around their necks, hems caught in the stiff breeze. From the armorer's hut came the clank of a metal hammer repairing broken links of mail; from the outer bailey could be heard the slice of saws and chop of axes chewing through timbers for firewood and beams. In a lean-to near the farrier's hut a wheelwright pounded new spokes into a broken cart wheel.

Smoke filled the air and icy rain drizzled from the heavens.

Megan glanced away from the questions in the other woman's deep blue eyes. "Isolde is only guessing. 'Tis too early to tell."

"But 'tis possible."

"Aye." Megan nodded, biting her lip, mentally calculating

and realizing that her time of the month should arrive soon, or mayhap was already a few days late.

"She is rarely wrong in these matters." Sorcha laid a hand on Megan's shoulder. "The babe. Is it not Holt's?"

Megan sighed, but didn't answer.

Sorcha persisted, "If you are with child and that babe is not your husband's, will he not know it?"

How could she possibly explain? Lord Hagan and his lady had a fine marriage where they teased often, touched intimately, and ruled together as one. Their love was deep and strong, their marriage as solid as the castle built high on this cliff. "I detest my husband and wanted to marry him not, but my father would not hear my protests. Then, on my wedding day, I was abducted . . ."

"By Wolf."

"Aye."

"And you fell in love with him," Sorcha said as if reading Megan's thoughts.

Pain clawed its way through Megan's tortured soul. "Aye."

"So you gave yourself to him."

Megan's spine stiffened and she lifted her head proudly, her hood falling away and her hair waving wildly around her face. "I would do it again if given the chance."

"Holt will not be pleased."

"Nay."

"He might want to harm the child," Sorcha said, her gaze clouding.

"He will never have the chance!" A fierce new fire grew within Megan and she knew she would do anything to save the life of her unborn infant. Should Holt try to harm her child, she would kill him.

"If, as Isolde says, your father has passed on, you must find a priest or abbot who will annul your marriage."

She thought of Father Timothy, a weak man with no convictions, a man who only wished people punished, and knew she could not speak with him. Nay, she needed someone with power, someone who understood her precarious position, someone who could strike down the marriage vows.

"Hagan will help you find the right abbot," she assured Megan. "Now, does Wolf know of the child?"

"Nay." She shook her head and bit her lip.

"Does he . . . does he love you, or was your seduction part of his plan to embarrass your husband?"

"I know not," she admitted, though she clung to the hope that he'd lain with her not because she was Holt's bride, but because he could not stop himself, that he, as she, was compelled to kiss and touch, to caress and bond.

"You must tell him."

'Twas not the first time the thought had crossed her mind. Wrapping her arms around her waist, as if to protect the fragile life growing inside her, she nodded. Should she meet Wolf again, what would she say? How could she tell him he'd unwittingly become a father of a bastard child? "I will, but not before I am free."

Instead of condemnation in Sorcha's gaze, there was silent praise. "God be with you, Megan of Dwyrain," she said, adjusting Megan's cowl again and kissing her lightly on the cheek, "and with your babe."

" 'Tis time," Hagan said, astride a large gray destrier. He led a smaller horse, a bay with a notched ear. Climbing down from his mount, he handed Megan the bay's reins, then kissed his wife so passionately, Megan had to look away. "I'll be back," he promised.

"Ride safely," Sorcha said, kissing him lightly on the cheek and blinking against tears. A blistering howl rose from inside the castle. "'Tis your daughter, m'lord," Sorcha said with a smile. "Methinks she is hungry again." She shot Megan a glance that said, *See what you have to look forward to?*

"Take care of her and worry not about me!" With a final look at his wife, he signaled for his small army to move out. Megan climbed onto the bay mare and tugged on the horse's reins as Bryanna wailed again and Isolde, carrying the loud, tiny bundle, appeared in the doorway. Waving, Megan urged her mount forward and joined the soldiers in their march to Dwyrain. She silently chided herself for leaving the ragged outlaw band, with its well-meaning criminals and brooding rogue of a leader.

What would you do had you stayed with them? Tell Wolf that he will be a father? Hope that he would marry you? Even if you were not already wed to Holt?

Wolf, the outlaw, was not a man to marry.

Aye, she told herself, clucking to her mare, *but surely Ware of Abergwynn is.*

"Something's wrong," Jack said, eyeing the crenels of Dwyrain's north watchtower. "See there—one of the shutters is closed; the others are open." He, Jagger, Robin, and Wolf, astride their sweating mounts, were hidden in the forest and watching the castle through the wintry foliage that remained. The wind was biting, the clouds dark, sleet starting to fall. "The baron's standard is not flying . . ."

Wolf felt a stab of fear deep in his soul. His gaze moved to the flagpole. 'Twas true. The new colors waving vividly against the dawn sky were a deep blue field with a red chevron . . . the symbol Wolf had seen upon Holt's shield. A sickening dread stole over him. "Baron Ewan is dead. Sir Holt has proclaimed himself the new ruler of Dwyrain."

"So it appears." Jack spit on the ground. " 'Tis cursed we are."

"Unless we defeat him," Wolf said, his eyes narrowing on his enemy's lair. His fingers clenched over the hilt of his sword. What pleasure he'd find in running the bastard through. Was Megan somewhere in the stone keep? A prisoner, mayhap, or Holt's willing wife? Had she returned to Dwyrain to her father, only to find that he'd died and she was forever married to the new baron? Had she shared a bed with the bastard? Given herself willingly to him? Been forced into submission? Had she suffered a beating at Holt's hands, and was she now his prisoner?

Guilt clawed at him. Had he not sealed her fate by stealing her from her husband? If Holt's wrath was aimed at Megan for her betrayal, was not Wolf responsible? Had he not incited Holt, humiliated and taunted the man in an effort to belittle him? Pray that he would not hurt her!

Rage stormed through his blood. Horrid, painful images of Megan being used by Holt brought a snarl to Wolf's lip. 'Twould be so easy to kill Holt and taste sweet, long-awaited vengeance. "Let's go!" he growled, eager to find Megan, to kidnap her if 'twas what it took to keep her safe.

"Be ye mad?" Jagger asked. "We can't ride through the gates, now can we?"

"Why not?" Robin, impatient for battle, demanded.

"I'll go ahead," Jack offered, "and I'll take with me the kills that I've got—" He motioned to the stag and boar he'd slain this morning and now were lashed to a sled built of poles. "I'll tell Cook that I'm taking a hunting party out this evening, and when we return, late, there may be three more men with me. No one will notice."

"And the men who leave the castle with you? Will they not wonder?"

"I'll choose my party well. 'Twill be made of those who detest Holt as much as we do," Jack said with a wicked smile. "There are men within the gates of Dwyrain who would follow you blindly on only my word."

"Good. While you're inside, learn what you can about Megan—if she's within the keep."

"I will," he promised. He rode through the underbrush to the road to join a small procession of carts and horsemen moving to and from the castle through a curtain of icy rain that washed away any lingering traces of snow and added to the chill that had already settled deep in Wolf's bones. 'Twas all he could do to remain where he was and not steal into the thick walls of Dwyrain to see for himself if Megan had returned.

'Twas simple enough to sneak into the castle with the hunting party. Once inside the walls, several of the men carried the kills of badger, pheasant, boar, and stag to the butcher and the tanner, while Jack and Tom, the carpenter's son who so often was in the north watchtower, led Wolf, Jagger, and Robin down a dark, winding staircase past the brewery, where the alewives stirred oaken vats of ale, and into a small chamber used for the hoarding of grain. With a few candles for light, the men rested on sacks of grain and watched shadows play on the rock walls.

Tom, about the age of Robin, peered over his shoulder as he spoke. " 'Tis as if the beasts of hell have been let loose," he said, his green eyes wide in the shadowy room. "The baron drew his last breath last night and Holt proclaimed himself the new ruler of the keep." Tom's tongue rimmed his mouth nervously. "He sent men to chase after Bjorn, who escaped with Lady Cayley."

"What of Cormick?" Wolf asked, grateful that one of his men was free.

"Dead. Killed when he was flogged."

"Mother Mary," Jack said under his breath as he crossed himself hurriedly.

Wolf flinched and again guilt was his companion. Because of his own need of vengeance, he'd sent a trusting, faithful man to his death. Back teeth grinding together, he silently cursed the demons who drove him. If only he'd let things be, Cormick would be alive, Bjorn would not have been flogged, and Megan . . . oh, sweet spitfire of a woman . . . would be serving her time as Holt's wife. Nay, he could never accept that.

"Lady Megan has not returned?" he asked.

"Nay, neither Holt nor his men have found her."

Where was she? A dozen horrid thoughts crawled through his mind, but he pushed them aside. At least she was not suffering as Holt's wife.

"But when Bjorn and Cayley escaped, Holt was in a rage, and he plans to hang the sorcerer who was with them."

"Sorcerer?" Wolf said.

"Aye, the same man who is said to have cursed Dwyrain years ago, the cripple that Lady Megan met in the woods when her mare came up lame two years ago."

Wolf had heard the tale, of course. It had spread throughout the countryside like wildfire.

" 'Twas as if he wanted to be captured again," Tom insisted as he anxiously picked at his teeth with the nail of his thumb. "He raced not to the gatehouse but stayed his horse, threw his hands wide as if to heaven, and screamed as loudly as if he were trying to wake the souls of the dead. An owl bigger than I've ever seen landed on his arm."

"He is being held prisoner here?"

"Aye, in the north tower dungeon."

"And is scheduled to hang?" Wolf asked uneasily.

Tom nodded. "My father was told to build a new gallows. Holt is said to want to make an example of the man and to prove that he is a strong baron even though his wife was stolen from him and neither he nor his best men have been able to find her."

Footsteps scraped upon the stairs. Wolf's hands curled over the hilt of his sword and Jagger flattened against the wall at the base of the steps, ready to jump the intruder. Robin and Tom hid behind sacks of grain, their weapons unsheathed, while Jack waited in the shadows.

" 'Tis only me," a woman called.

Tom grinned widely. "Rue. Thank the saints."

An old, thin woman appeared with a pitcher of ale, loaf of bread, and round of cheese. " 'Tis not much, I know," she said, setting her fare on an upended cask. "But 'twas all the cook would give for fear the steward or one of Holt's spies might see him." She turned tired eyes on Wolf and offered him the pitcher. "The baron is dead, both his daughters are missing and, I fear, Dwyrain lost."

"Nay—" Tom argued, but Rue persisted, staring pointedly at Wolf.

" 'Tis said you are Holt's sworn enemy."

Wolf took a long draft from the pitcher, wiped his lips with his sleeve, and nodded. " 'Tis true."

" 'Tis also thought that you are much to blame for the trouble here. If ye had not stolen Lady Megan, mayhap Holt would have been less angry and cruel."

Wolf passed the pitcher to Jagger, who took a long, healthy swallow. "What do you think, woman?" he asked.

"Holt is bad to his bones. I would waste no tears if Holt were found murdered," she said, as if she hoped to find the new baron with a sword run through his heart in the morning, "but I'm grateful that both Lady Megan and Lady Cayley are far from his grasp, even though this keep is theirs by rights." She sliced the cheese with a large knife and sawed off hunks of bread, which she passed to the men. "I think ye, Wolf," she said, wagging the tip of her blade at his nose as he sank his teeth into the crusty bread, "should see that both of the baron's daughters are safe so that someday they might reclaim Dwyrain. Ye started this, so I think ye should finish it."

"I intend to," he agreed, reaching for the ale pitcher again. "I'll start by freeing the magician this night. Mayhap he'll help me find Megan and Cayley, and then, I swear, once they're safe, I'll come for Holt."

"Will ye kill him?"

Wolf thought of Megan and how she might suffer at Holt's hands should he ever find out that Megan had given herself to his sworn enemy. Something deep in Wolf's heart stirred; he couldn't bear to think of her with another man, especially not a cruel cur the likes of the man who had willingly held down a fair maid so that she could be brutally raped. The ale and bread suddenly tasted sour and stuck in his throat. When he lifted his eyes, he found Rue staring at him and he nodded. "Aye," he vowed, "if needs be, I'll send him to hell, where he belongs."

"We cannot stop!" Megan said, though every bone in her body ached, her head throbbed, and her legs were sore from three days of riding.

"The men are tired and you, m'lady, need to rest." Hagan's eyes searched the dusky countryside, looking for a spot near the road to make camp.

"Nay! We are too close." Though she dreaded facing

Holt again, she'd felt drawn to Dwyrain, knew she had to return to her home. Hagan had sent word ahead to the abbot of St. Peter's in the hope of annulling her marriage, and Megan had been restless and eager to ride under the portcullis of Dwyrain. Despite her feeling of despair, she had been whispering prayers that Isolde had been wrong about Ewan, that he yet lived. Though Isolde had sworn that she'd seen him in his grave, the old woman could surely make a mistake now and again. Megan refused to believe that because the nursemaid had been correct about the baby growing in Megan's womb, this meant that she was never wrong.

"Here!" Hagan indicated a small field not far from the road. "We'll camp for the night."

She wanted to argue, to insist that they travel on, but she held her tongue. Hagan of Erbyn had been good to her and his men; she would not thwart him, but she couldn't shake the feeling—the dread—that something dire was happening within the stone walls of Dwyrain, that if only she were there, some kind of tragedy could be averted.

'Twas but a feeling, although 'twas so real. Goose bumps crawled up her arms and she refused to give in to the fear that gnawed at her insides, the fear that somehow Holt had caught up with Wolf and that even now, the outlaw might be dead, killed by her husband's hand. Shivering, she dismounted, and as the men started a fire and skinned the squirrels and rabbits they'd killed on the journey, she found the bucket tied to the saddle of her mare and walked to the stream. Dipping into the dark water, she was reminded of her stay with the sorry band of criminals she'd grown to love. She wondered about Robin. Had his wounds healed? Had Odell learned to cook any better? Was one-eyed Peter ever the quiet voice of reason whenever there was a fight? Did Wolf think of her as often as she did of him?

A knot tightened in her throat as an image of Wolf with his brooding dark looks, the pain of his past, the silent anger that drove him, crossed before her eyes. She lifted the pail, but in the ripples of the water she saw his face, handsome, arrogant, and proud, his smile as hard and cunning as the beast from which he'd taken his name. As she drew her bucket through the clear water, she heard the men behind her as they staked out the tents and told jokes. She absently rubbed her abdomen, trying to comfort the child growing deep within her womb. Would this tiny person ever meet his or her father? Would the outlaw Wolf ever learn that he was a father?

Rather than dwell upon the thoughts that were forever tormenting her, Megan squared her shoulders and sent up a prayer for his safety.

In a few days, they'd arrive at Dwyrain and then . . . then somehow she'd find a way to untie the dreadful knot of her marriage and become a free woman.

Why? To what end? So that Wolf will marry you? He's an outlaw, Megan, a criminal running from the law! Is that what you want your child to grow up with, knowing that his or her father is a common criminal?

Not common. Far from common. A nobleman turned outlaw.

She lugged the pail back to the fire and set it on the rocks surrounding the crackling kindling.

Aye! My baby will know the wonderful rogue who gave him or her life. By the gods, if it's the last thing I do, Wolf and his son or daughter will meet!

The moon was cloaked in clouds and no campfire guided them as they picked their way through the woods. Cayley was bone weary, her back sore, her spirits sinking with each plod of her mount's hooves. It felt as if it had been years since they'd seen civilization. The naked trees of the forest were gloomy and protected them little from the icy mist that drizzled from the sky. Wet branches slapped at her face and vines clawed at her cape.

Bjorn, the broad-shouldered outlaw brute, rode on and outwardly appeared not to notice the cold or feel the sleet, rain, or snow. Proudly, he sat astride his mount, moving onward, pausing only once or twice to hunt some small forest beast or rob an unsuspecting traveler. Since leaving Dwyrain, Bjorn had stolen two blankets, food for themselves and the horses, and several weapons. He never asked for gold, silver, or jewelry, didn't bother with anything more than they needed or could carry. Cayley had never actually seen him stalk his human prey; he'd done most of his thievery at night, and when she'd awakened, there had been a loaf of bread, a new thick blanket tossed over her, or a knife to keep in her boot. The horses had eaten well and Bjorn had refused to explain whom he'd had to threaten in order to survive.

'Twas thrilling, and had Cayley been a stronger woman, she would have insisted upon going with him on his nightly marauding. She thought he made camp close to his intended victims, for she knew that he would not leave her long alone in the woods with only a fire and her own small knives to protect her.

She'd imagined that she'd never sleep a wink, but each morning, 'twas Bjorn who placed a huge, callused hand on her shoulder and shook her awake. She'd slept without dreaming, her head resting on a root of a tree or a flat rock, her fingers curled over the hilt of her dagger.

"Holy Christ, Odell, what've ye done?" Bjorn muttered as

the overgrown trail broke into a clearing near a river. The rushing sound of a waterfall greeted her ears; the grass and weeds of the small clearing had been trampled by horses, carts, and people.

From the tone of Bjorn's voice, she knew that something was wrong—very wrong. Cayley clucked to her mount, reaching Bjorn's side. "What?"

"They've moved."

"Who—what?"

"Wolf's band. The sorcerer told me that the band was ordered to stay here, but Odell, curse his flea-riddled hide, decided to move on." He slid from his mount, and still breathing fire and swearing, he kicked at a circle of stones that had once been the rim of a campfire.

Cayley, too, dismounted, and for a second, her tired legs were unable to hold her, but she steadied herself, stretched, and viewed the night-darkened landscape. Aside from the fire pit, there was evidence that people had recently been here, the broken grass, wheel ruts, and discarded bones from meals still visible. A huge skeleton of a building, half standing, half in rubble, loomed near the river.

"Used to be a chapel," Bjorn said tightly as if reading her mind. "We stayed here with your sister and Wolf told Odell not to move camp." He spat loudly. "That slimy little cur!"

"Where would he go?"

"Good question." He thought for a second. "Odell's a bit of a coward. He talks much, acts as if he's braver than the other men put together, but the truth of the matter is that he would do nothing to incite Wolf's wrath."

"So he was forced to move."

"Mayhap."

"What would cause him to leave?"

Bjorn rubbed the back of his neck. "Holt's army," he decided, and then, as if determining that they, too, might not be safe, said, "Come, lead your horse into the old chapel."

"A beast in the house of God?" she said, shaking her head at the blasphemy of it. "Nay, I don't think—"

"Hush, woman! 'Tis no longer a chapel and God will not care if one of his four-footed creatures stumbles upon the altar. Methinks all manner of beasts have already crept their way through the windows and open doors." His patience was nearly gone—that much was obvious—and the argument that simmered between them, which was her forever doubting or second-guessing his orders, flared again. He'd told her once that he thought her nothing more than a pampered, rich pain in the backside, and she'd let him know that he was an uneducated criminal brute. They were at a stalemate, stuck with each other until they could find Wolf and Megan.

From what Cayley had gleaned, and it wasn't much from this quiet, stubborn giant, Wolf and several of the men had fallen half in love with her sister.

"Come, m'lady," he said as she crossed herself with practiced fingers. "If ye want to save yer pretty skin, you'll do as I say and guide yer horse through the door!"

She had no choice and tugged on the reins, leading the animal through the icy mist to the shelter of the chapel. God forgive her, she had no choice but to depend upon this blond criminal to help her find Megan.

Tom and Robin's job was to open the gates, Jack's to guide Wolf to the dungeon where the sorcerer was held, and Jagger was to guard the door so that no one would surprise them as they made their quick escape. Wolf held his knife in his teeth and had one hand on his sword. The other trailed along the wall of the dank-smelling stairs that wound downward.

He had to fight his fear, for this was not the first time he'd been in a prison. Years before, he and his friend, Cadell, brother of Morgana of Wenlock, had been locked in the bowels of Abergwynn. 'Twas only through their quick wits and the guard's stupidity that they were able to flee the castle walls, only to be chased down by enemy men. Wolf—Ware at the time—had watched in horror as his friend had pitched over the cliffs to the black sea. Then, rather than be captured and imprisoned yet again, he had followed Cadell, throwing himself over the edge. . . . Wolf shivered inwardly. He *hated* dungeons, detested confinement. Tight places with locked doors made his skin itch and his head pound.

The guard was awake and held a knife in his hand as if he expected someone to try to help the prisoner escape. "Who goes there?" he demanded.

" 'Tis only me. Jack, the huntsman."

"Oh, and what is it ye want, Jack?" the sentry, suddenly more at ease, wanted to know. While Wolf hung in the shadows, Jack, holding his candle high, approached the sentry.

"I'd like a word with ye. I saw yer son, Ian, in the forest the day before last. He was trackin' a stag on the baron's land without permission. Got off one good shot, but the deer sprinted away and the arrow missed its mark, landing in the trunk of an oak tree instead."

"For the love of Jesus." The guard made a hasty sign of the cross over his thick chest.

"I told Holt not."

"Thank ye for that much. I'm tellin' ye, Jack, that boy will be the death of me and his ma. Always gettin' into trouble, that one, not like his older brother—hey! What the—"

Jack sprang and Wolf lunged from his hiding place in the dark corner near the stairs. Together, they knocked the guard off his feet and wrested the knife from his hands. He fought, kicked, and swore as Jack lashed his hands behind his broad back. "I thought we might make a trade, Theodore," he said, holding his knife to the guard's thick neck. "I'll not tell Holt about yer boy and ye keep yer mouth shut about this."

"Nay, I cannot."

"Then ye'll die." Jack appeared about to slice his throat open, but Wolf stopped him.

"No more bloodshed."

"What?"

"Holt's blood is all that needs be spilled. This man has done nothing wrong."

"He'll sound the alarm."

"So be it."

Theodore listened to this exchange with bulging eyes. "No good'll come of this, Jack. What the hell d'ye think ye're doin'?"

"Saving the castle."

"By gettin' me killed? Holt'll have me hide when he finds out what ye're up to. Yer skin will be worthless, too!"

"Like as not."

Wolf reached for the guard's key ring. He saw the sorcerer in the corner of the cell, standing peacefully, though he was chained with thick links to the wall. "You're to be a free man," he assured the magician as he swung open the gate and held a torch aloft, throwing flickering illumination through the cell. When the light touched the cripple's eyes, Wolf's blood turned to ice, for standing before him was not the sorcerer he'd heard so much about but his old friend, the boy he thought had lost his life on the rocky shoals beneath the cliffs of Abergwynn.

"I knew you'd come," Cadell said in an even tone. "What took ye so long, Ware of Abergwynn?"

"For the love of Jesus. Cadell."

"Aye. 'Tis I."

"What happened to ye—where've ye been?"

"We have no time for this."

"Let's go!" Jack said.

"Aye," Wolf said, grateful that his old friend had survived. He wasted no time, but opened the cell. "Right now, we must leave." He unchained his old friend, then slapped a small dagger into his hand.

"I use not weapons."

Wolf's eyes met Cadell's in the darkness. "If we escape without battle, praise God. But if we run across anyone who wants to kill us, please, do them the honor first."

"Come!" Jack yelled. "We've lost too much time." He had gagged and bound the guard and now tossed the frightened man into Cadell's cell. Slamming the door shut with a distinct clang, he led them up the slippery stairs.

The air became clearer and Wolf, holding on to the hilt of his sword, breathed deeply. Within minutes, they'd ride through the gates of Dwyrain and into the forest. Once back at the camp, he'd start looking for Megan, sending his men out to the villages and keeps until he found her. Cadell could help . . .

And what then, Wolf, his mind sneered. *What do you plan to offer her? The life of an outlaw—a man with no castle, no house, his only possession a sword? Or are you willing to give up your freedom?*

Pale light filtered through the open door, and Jack

stepped cautiously out of the tower. Wolf was behind him, his eyes searching the bailey for Tom and Robin, who were nowhere in sight. They might have been waylaid trying to raise the portcullis in the gatehouse. Or . . . the hairs on his nape raised and his fingers tightened over the hilt of his sword. The castle was still as death. Stepping onto the packed mud near the door of the tower, he began to sweat in the cold mist.

"Wolf! Watch out!" Jack's voice cut through the silence, then there was the clang of steel striking steel. Swords clashed, ringing through the bailey.

From the corner of his eye, Wolf saw a glint of metal, a silent, swift movement near the side of his head. He ducked, spinning fast, sword drawn, as a battle ax cleaved the air and sliced heavily into the earth. The ground shuddered.

Wolf rolled onto the balls of his feet, slicing around him as men, 8 or 10 of them, ran, swords drawn, from the shadows. Within seconds, they'd surrounded the doorway of the tower. Bloody Christ, what had gone wrong?

Tom and Robin were both with the soldiers, their wrists lashed, their faces pale as the moon. Blood ran from one of Robin's nostrils and caked his lips. Tom's eyes were round with fear, blood staining his tunic.

Jack spun and struck, but a huge man swung a mace and it caught Jack midsection, sending him to the ground with a sickening thud.

"Halt, outlaw!" a gravelly voice ordered as a soldier lunged at him, and Wolf's sword was swift, severing the man's arm and sending him reeling. With a hideous roar, he fell against the tower wall, blood spurting and spraying as he slid down the stones. Another man, big and burly, rounded on Wolf, only to feel Wolf's blade slash him through the ribs. As a third came at him from behind, he whirled, intending to draw blood.

Bam!

Pain exploded in his brain and he fell to his knees.

Thud!

Another blinding jolt of pain. Wolf cried out, dropping his sword. The world tilted. His head slammed into the dirt, the stars and moon spun wildly. He tasted his own blood, and suddenly there was nothing.

Megan woke with a start. Heart pounding, she sat bolt upright. *Wolf!* Dear God, she'd been dreaming of him, touching him, feeling his skin upon hers, his lips brushing her eyes and throat and breasts, when suddenly he'd jerked, like a puppet on a string, his body wrenched from her. She cried out and the battlements and walls of Dwyrain came into her view.

'Twas only a dream, she told herself and tried to slow her racing heart, but she couldn't shake the feeling that Wolf was in trouble, that he needed her. But that was silly. Restless, she crawled out of the tent Hagan had staked out for her, and walked to the stream. A sudden chill turned the marrow of her bones to ice and she rubbed her arms.

Pausing at the stream, she heard the sound of wings, the rustle of feathers, as a huge owl landed on the bare branch of a willow tree over her head. She swallowed hard and remembered seeing such a bird with the sorcerer when he'd predicted trouble at Dwyrain, then again in the woods at the camp with Odell, and now here.

The owl stared at her with round, unblinking eyes that caused another shiver to race through her blood. He didn't settle down, his head never lowering into his neck, and he flapped his great wings several times, as if straightening his feathers. She tried to ignore the winged creature—he was probably resting from the hunt—but she felt his eyes upon her and thought that his presence could only be a sign, and not a good one.

What had old Rue said so long ago? That the creatures of the forest had a sense unlike those of man, that the beasts could smell trouble before it appeared, feel a storm before it broke, sense the movement of a fire before the smoke had met human nostrils?

The horses were close by and she saw her notched-ear jennet resting at her tether, one hoof cocked in slumber. 'Twas quiet in the camp, aside from the gentle snoring of the man who was supposed to be tending the beasts.

Praying she was not making a huge mistake and inviting the wrath of another baron when Hagan awoke, Megan stole to the horses and untied her mare. The horse awoke with a snort. "Shh," she murmured, knowing she was inviting doom.

But because of Wolf, she could wait no longer. As sure as the moon rose in the sky, there was trouble at Dwyrain, and she, as the baron's eldest daughter, had to return.

Cold water splashed over him in a wave and Wolf coughed and sputtered, his eyes opening slowly, his head thundering in pain. He didn't remember where he was or how he'd gotten there. A second after he saw the smooth leather shoes and gold braid of a surcoat, he lifted his eyes farther to find his old enemy Holt standing before him in the inner bailey. There were people everywhere, the sun was rising through a gray fog, and geese, ducks, chickens, and children scrambled out of the way of the new, imposing ruler of Dwyrain.

"How dare you," Holt said. One of the guards hauled

Wolf to his feet and he stood, between two burly men, swaying. Stripped to only his breeches, he tried to stand on his own and failed. His muscles flexed as a blast of northern wind cut through the bailey, chasing the last hint of fog. "How dare you sneak into my keep and try to steal one of my prisoners? Did you not think my soldiers were told to watch and wait, that your coming here was inevitable?"

Even in his pain, an insolent smile curved Wolf's lips. "How dare you presume to be baron?"

A glimmer of recognition flashed in Holt's eyes and Wolf knew he'd struck a sensitive nerve.

"Ewan chose me as his successor."

"Was that before or after you started poisoning him?"

Holt's fist crashed into Wolf's body, the metal studs on his gloves cutting into Wolf's flesh. "Impudent whelp!" he roared, then, as if realizing dozens of pairs of eyes were upon him, Holt drew in a long, ragged breath. "Bring him to my chamber," he growled.

"What about the others?"

"Leave them to rot for now. They'll hang later."

Surcoat billowing behind him, Holt stormed up the steps of the keep, and Wolf was half pushed and shoved behind him. He caught several men's eyes, and their expressions varied. The carpenter, Tom's father, gritted his teeth against his fury, the armorer slid Wolf a knowing look, several soldiers spit as Wolf was hauled roughly through, and milkmaids and laundresses looked upon him as if he were an amusement. An old woman, weathered and gaunt, crossed herself, though her piety seemed forced.

"Move!" one of the guards ordered as he elbowed Wolf forward.

On shaking legs, he followed Holt up winding stairs, past

rush lights that cast shifting gold shadows upon the walls, and into the lord's chamber. A fire roared at the grate and tapestries draped the walls. Above the curtained bed, the horns and antlers of beasts the lord of the manor had felled in years past were mounted proudly.

As the guards held Wolf, Holt sat in a huge chair. A page brought him wine and dates, which he plucked at as he stared at his enemy. "Where is my wife?" Holt asked, a vein throbbing across his temple.

Wolf managed a sneer. "Have trouble keeping her?"

With a motion of one finger, Holt gave a silent command to the guard and a fist, hard-knuckled and bare, crashed into the side of his face. Bones crunched. Blood sprayed. Wolf's knees buckled, but the sentries held him upright. "Why is it you stole her from me?"

"Know you not, Holt?" Wolf asked. "Do you not remember me when Tadd of Prydd had his way with the fisherman's daughter in a village east of Prydd?"

"I remember not. . . ." But his voice faded and his jaw grew tight. Clearing his throat, he glared at Wolf.

"Now," Holt said, dismissing whatever thoughts chased through his evil mind. "Let's start again. Where's my wife?"

"Go to hell."

Holt's lips flattened over his teeth. "Hell? Interesting that you should bring it up, because I think, when I'm through with you, you'll wish you were there." Rubbing the stubble on his jaw, he said to a thick-bodied knight, "Throw him in the dungeon, but not in the same cell with his friends. Torture him slowly, until he tells us what we want to know. When he finally confesses, see that all the rest of the prisoners—the damned sorcerer, the two who rode with this cur, Jack, and Tom, the carpenter's son—feel the noose tighten around their necks."

Wolf felt sick. Because of his love for Megan, he'd brought Robin and Jagger to their deaths.

Another flick of Holt's finger. A fist splintered Wolf's nose and the world swam again. Wolf felt as if he were drowning, but before he slid beneath the balming waters of unconsciousness, he sputtered, "I'll see you in hell, Holt."

Holt shuddered at the words. Why would this man not break? How deep was his need of vengeance for a woman who had been raped . . . a woman Holt did not remember? "Take the Judas to Ivor and see that his tongue is loosened," Holt commanded, his nerves jangled. How could one man, beaten and battered and half dead, dare defy him?

Holt had felt a rush of ecstasy when he'd heard that Wolf had been captured in the north tower. Finally, his luck had turned, and he planned to prove Wolf for the traitor he was. There had been too much gossip in the castle, too much speculation that Megan had not been found because she didn't want to be located, that she'd taken up with her abductor and willingly slept with him, that she was dirtying her marriage vows and laughing at him.

Holt's stomach turned at that thought. True, he'd not been celibate since his wife had been stolen from him, but with his vexation, he'd needed some comfort. Nell had willingly provided her lush body to him, but it wasn't enough. Even when Dilys was forced to watch them couple to add to his delight, 'twas an empty union. As he'd gazed down upon Nell's freckled and gap-toothed mouth, it had been Megan's face he'd seen and he had nearly tasted her total and complete surrender. He wanted to mount her like a stallion and trumpet in primal lust that she was his and his alone.

Except for the outlaw. If the cur of the forest had bedded her, then Holt planned to cut off each of Wolf's balls slowly, drawing out the process and savoring the gelding of his enemy.

He finished his wine and met his guards in the chamber deep beneath the north tower that Ewan, the fool, had rarely used. Wolf was deep within the bowels of the keep, spread-eagled upon the floor, still unconscious. More icy water was used to awaken him, and when his eyes blinked open, Holt stood before him.

"Now," he said, "let's begin again."

Wolf felt as if a thousand destriers had trampled upon him. Every muscle ached and his bones felt as if they'd splintered from his joints. Pain, deep and feral, pounded on his body and he was aware that he was in a dark, fetid chamber surrounded by Holt and his men. A huge fire burned bright in one corner, a boy fanning the flames with a bellows.

Holt reached for a long-handled clamp with his gloved hand, and using the tool, dug in the flames until he found a coal that glowed like a red eye in the night.

"You will tell me where my wife is," Holt said, advancing slowly, the red ember menacingly close to Wolf's face.

Wolf raised his head, and mustering his strength, spit on the toe of Holt's boot.

Rage sparked in the new lord's eyes. "So that's the way it is, eh? Fine. You're a fool, Wolf, and I brand you as such." With that he dropped the coal onto Wolf's back. White-hot pain seared into his body as flesh singed and burned. Wolf convulsed and bit down on his tongue. They could burn him, slice him, set the beasts of the forest upon him, nearly drown him, but never would he betray Megan.

"Lord Holt!" a soldier cried as Wolf struggled with consciousness.

"Not now. I'm busy!" Holt walked to the fire again, his wicked weapon in his hand.

"But, m'lord—"

Spinning fast, Holt pinned the soldier with harsh, unforgiving eyes. "I said—"

" 'Tis the lady Megan," the soldier announced, his gaze moving from Wolf's singed back to Holt's face.

Wolf swallowed to keep his stomach contents from spewing from his mouth.

"What of her?"

"She's here, m'lord, at the castle gates, and she's demanding to be let in!"

Fourteen

"So my wayward bride has returned!" Holt's eyes gleamed as the winch was turned and the portcullis grated open. Dressed in a crimson velvet surcoat befitting a king, Holt was surrounded by soldiers holding torches and drawn swords. Though he forced a smile, disapproval edged his mouth and brought deep furrows to his forehead. A dozen accusations sizzled in his eyes—questions Megan didn't want to hear or have to answer.

Astride the bay, Megan shivered but refused to show any sign of weakness. Fear could never be her companion, for courage was her shield. This keep, with its familiar stone walls, tall watchtowers, and wide battlements, was her rightful home, the castle she was to inherit once her brother, poor Bevan, was pronounced dead. Squaring her shoulders, she stared straight at the husband she loathed. "I needs speak with my father," she said, bracing herself for the ugly truth.

"Well, that's a bit of a problem, you see." Holt glanced from her and shook his head slowly. Despair burrowed deep in her soul and she knew before he spoke a word that the old crone had been right. "Baron Ewan passed on a few days ago, I'm afraid."

Megan thought she'd steeled herself, but when the dreaded words rolled so easily off Holt's tongue, her insides turned to jelly. A mind-numbing wave of grief washed over her, extinguishing the solitary flame of hope that had burned so brightly in her heart. *Oh, Father,* she silently cried, *I abandoned you. Had I returned sooner, mayhap I could have forestalled your death.* Swaying upon the mare's back, she grabbed the saddle's pommel, blinked for a second, and fought the tears that blocked her throat.

Dawn was breaking over the walls of the keep but the joy she should have felt at returning to her home, the castle where she'd grown up, withered away. Father, mother, brother, and baby sister, nearly everyone gone. Only Cayley remained, and that thought brought her a ray of happiness. At least she was not alone.

Do not forget that you carry Wolf's child in your womb. You will never be alone or without one you love. She took a small bit of comfort in that thought.

"I've upset you," Holt said, with feigned remorse as he lifted a hand to her, and the sun, fettered by a thin layer of clouds, offered some illumination to the winter-cold castle. "I'm sorry about your father's death—'tis a tragedy." Holt motioned to her horse, and receiving the unspoken command, one of his men, Elwin, a gangly youth who nearly tripped over his own feet, charged forward and grabbed her mount's reins. The thin straps of leather slipped through her fingers and she silently cursed herself for letting down her guard.

"Come in, wife, and warm yourself."

'Twas time to set matters straight. "Make no mistake, Sir Holt, I'm not—nor will I ever be—your wife!"

"Did I not hear you vow in front of God, country, and everyone in this keep that I was to be your husband?"

" 'Twas my father's bidding. He's gone. I no longer have to try to please him."

"Too late, Megan," he said without the slightest inflection as his jaw turned to granite. Determination flickered in his gaze and Megan knew more than a moment's fear. This man—heavily muscled and ruthless—was not about to be denied. "Surely you've not forgotten that the priest married us, and by the law of the land, as well as that of the church, you are now and for the rest of your days bound to me."

She didn't move, but the words crashed over her, echoing through her brain over and over again, like a monk's damning cadence. "Come, Megan," Holt said with a hard, unforgiving smile as he motioned for her to climb down from her mare. "You're tired and need rest. I trust you were able to elude the outlaw who ransomed you."

Feeling like Judas, she nodded woodenly, telling herself not to think about Wolf and her love for him, that if she pushed him to a far corner of her mind, the pain in her heart would lessen. She could never be with him as wife to a husband—not that he would want that—nor could she be his wench, not as long as she was married to Holt. Bitterness crept into her soul and she prayed for an end to a marriage that had never begun, a marriage that should never have existed. Her heart belonged in the forest with the outlaw who wore the name of the beast of the night. Though she'd tried to turn her mind against him, to pretend that he was nothing but an uncivilized rogue, a criminal who hid in the woods and preyed upon innocent travelers, she couldn't. She loved him far too deeply. 'Twas her curse.

Holt was staring at her and she forced the image of Wolf's handsome face from her mind. "Has . . . has my father been laid to rest?"

"Aye. This morn. In the chapel cemetery."

Pain ripped through her, as she was unable to say good-bye or see again the man who had sired her, taught her to ride and shoot a bow and arrow, the man who had taught her to look for the finer points of a horse, and, in the end, thinking he was doing what was best for her, insisted she marry Holt. Heart heavy, she said, "I need to visit his grave and speak with Cayley."

Holt's eyebrow quirked upward and he smiled, opening his hands to her. "Then come into the keep. She's not been well and—"

"What?" Megan's head snapped up and she stared at Holt. Her pulse pounded a dread-inspired tempo. Cayley was the last living member of her family. Nothing could be wrong with her. Nothing!

" 'Tis true," he said, frowning thoughtfully. "Since your father's death, the lady has been beside herself and the physician knows not if 'tis something within her or only her grief causing her so much pain."

"For the love of Jesus, take me to her," Megan said, her own sorrow forgotten in the thought that she might be able to help her sister. Every muscle in her body ached from days of riding without much rest, but she needed to see the one remaining member of her family. Though they'd often fought as children, she and Cayley were close and had shared many a secret between them.

Dismounting in one swift motion, she was grateful her legs held her, for she wanted not any help from Holt. Though 'twas early, the castle was coming to life with the approaching morning. Peasants, soldiers, and servants alike began to cross the bailey, and she smiled at the faces she recognized—the baker and miller, wheelwright and ale conner. Boys of every age lugged firewood, sacks of grain, and baskets of stones. Girls, too, were busy gathering eggs, tossing seeds to the chickens, carrying laundry to the creek, or checking the eel traps in the pond. Water was being drawn from the well and the farrier's hammer was already clanking against his anvil.

"Hey, look! 'Tis the lady!" one of Cook's helpers, who was hauling a side of venison, said.

" 'Tis!" Nell, this time, carrying a pail of milk.

"Wonder what 'appened to her with that outlaw?" the miller's wife asked.

A giggle. " 'E was a handsome devil, 'e was."

"Look at her. Wonder what she's thinkin'? Poor lass, losing her father while she was gone."

"Lady Megan!" Rue cried out, and Megan smiled as she spied her old nursemaid. Never had there been a kinder-hearted soul than Rue. Plucking her skirts upward so the hems would not become soiled, the old woman started across the bailey, but at a signal from Holt, one of the men detained her.

So this was how it was going to be.

"Come, Megan, Cook will fix you something warm while you see to Cayley. Mayhap you can make her feel better," Holt said, and Megan caught the unspoken messages being exchanged among some of his men. Something wasn't right in the castle, and 'twas more than her father's death that caused the eerie feeling to settle upon her.

But she had to see her sister.

As she hurried across the bent, frozen grass, her stomach rumbled at the smell of smoke mingling with the scent of sizzling meat. A side of pork roasted on a spit over an open fire, turned by a dog rigged to the contraption as it ran in circles.

Chapel bells pealed softly, reverberating in Megan's heart and reminding her of her mission to untie herself from this unwanted marriage. Father Timothy hurried across the bailey and Megan stiffened. She trusted not his piety or his words. "Welcome, m'lady," he said with a worried smile. He'd become thinner since she'd seen him last and his air of superiority was missing this morning. " 'Tis sad news you've come home to."

"Aye," she said, nodding.

"The lady needs her rest," Holt said swiftly while clamping possessive fingers over Megan's forearm.

"Of course." Timothy nodded, but his eyes never left Megan's face. 'Twas as if he was trying to silently speak with her. "I've said the Mass for your father and I prayed that you or your sister would have been there when he was laid to rest. 'Twas a pity he had no family at his bedside near the end or at his burial—"

"No family? But Cayley . . ." Dread strangled the words in her throat while Holt glared at the priest. ". . . was she too ill to attend Mass?" she asked, fear and suspicion mingling in her mind. Had Holt deceived her? "Do not tell me that my sister is on her deathbed."

"Oh, no, I only meant that she wasn't in the chapel during Mass when your father—"

Holt coughed loudly and the fingers tightened over her arm. "Excuse us, Father," he said, "but the lady is tired from her journey and we've not had any time together as husband and wife." His voice was soft and filled with suggestion. "You understand."

Timothy blushed. "Aye—"

"Wait!" Megan whirled on the hated man who was her

husband. “Why would Cayley not attend my father’s funeral Mass?”

“She was not here,” Holt admitted.

“Where was she?” Megan’s heart blood turned to ice. Something evil was happening here at Dwyrain, something she didn’t understand, something that involved her sister.

“Lady Cayley left.”

“Left?” She turned to the priest so quickly that a gust of wind caught her hood and tore it from her head.

Father Timothy stared at her for a heartbeat, cleared his throat, and nodded. “Aye.”

Holt scratched his upper lip. “I did not want to worry you—”

“So you told me she was ill?” Megan spat. Vile, treacherous man!

“She was kidnapped by a prisoner who escaped. A big yellow-haired brute who used her as a shield as he made his way out through the gates—”

“Bjorn?” Megan said, her mind spinning in restless worrisome circles as she recalled him at the outlaw camp. Shaking her head, she said, “Nay, he would not . . .”

“He was desperate,” Holt inserted, shooting a look at the priest as if to stop any disagreement from the man of God. “He and the other man—”

“Cormick,” Megan said under her breath, unable to hear over the painful hammering of her heart.

“—aye, they tried to escape. The one you call Cormick was killed in his attempt to flee the castle, but the other used Cayley as his hostage and was able to elude my men.”

“Liar!” she said, feeling revulsion as the earth shifted beneath her feet. Not only was her father dead, but Cormick, gentle, gruff Cormick, as well. Because of Holt. “Bjorn would never use another’s life to save his.”

"So you know him well?" Holt was not pleased. Several deep clefts appeared in the skin between his eyebrows.

"Aye, and he's a good man, a—"

"Criminal. Wanted by the law. A robber, thief, pickpocket, murderer, or rapist, most likely. Your precious criminal is no better than the scum of the earth."

"No, Holt, methinks you alone retain that honor," she argued, thankful that her sister was free from the rein of terror that was sure to ruin Dwyrain and everything Cayley held dear. *Run, Cayley,* she silently thought, *run fast and never return!*

Holt's jaw clenched and the fingers around her arm dug deep into her flesh. "So my wife has come home only to defy me."

"And annul the marriage."

Holt laughed. "Christ Jesus, you be a saucy tart! 'Twill never happen." He leaned closer to her, his voice low and rough to her ear. "I've waited long for you, wife, but tonight the waiting ends and I will get you with child. Then, not even God Himself would dare break our union."

A wave of sickness climbed up her throat. She could never give herself to this cur who wore her father's robes, stole his keep, and lied through his teeth. "What do you want of me? You have the keep!"

Holt eyed her reflectively. Hesitating a second, he touched her hair and sighed. " 'Twas true, as well you know. I wanted the castle and the wealth that was Dwyrain, and I worked close with your father so that he would choose me as his successor, but that wasn't enough, Megan. I wanted you as well." She could hardly believe her ears. His voice was firm, his chin set in determination. "I hoped that you would care for me, that you would agree to become my bride."

She tried to step away, but his grip was harsh, and as he

drew her closer, the tip of his tongue swept over his thin lips. “Since you defied me and rejected my courtship and proposal, I wanted you more than ever.”

“Why?”

His grin stretched into a seductive leer. “Because, dear wife, the taming of you will be that much sweeter.”

Without thinking, she slapped him. The sound of flesh striking flesh echoed through the bailey. A woman gasped. The priest crossed himself and all work ceased. The farrier stopped pounding, the carpenters stayed their hammers, even the windmill quieted.

Holt’s expression changed from leering seduction to rage. “That,” he said through lips that barely moved, “was a mistake.”

Two soldiers stepped forward as if to take her off his hands. Every eye in the keep turned in their direction. Holt’s patience was stretched to the breaking point. “Careful, wife, or our joining will be rougher than you might wish.”

“You sick, lying bastard! You told me that Cayley was ill, that you were taking me to see her!”

“A small deception, I’m afraid. I did not want to worry you.”

Her eyes narrowed. “What would you have done once I was in her empty chamber?”

“Detain you.”

“As you would a common prisoner?”

“You leave me no choice,” he said with measured calm, “for you said yourself you do not think of me as your husband. Until I can convince you otherwise, you will be locked in your room and—”

“Nay, m’lord,” Father Timothy interjected. “You cannot jail her as you would a traitor.”

“She’ll have her own room, food and water, a guard at

her door, and be allowed visitors of my choosing—treated much better than those held captive in the north tower." Yanking on her arm, he half dragged her toward the keep.

Megan felt like a fool. She dug in her heels, trying to stop him, knowing that dozens of curious eyes were cast in her direction. The men and women who watched her being pulled into the keep against her will, would they help her or damn her for not living up to the forced promises of her wedding day? "Nay," she cried, "unhand me!"

Holt's face changed from a mask of determined impatience to one of leashed, ugly fury. "Tell her," he ordered the priest, anger creasing his words. "Tell her she is my wife."

Father Timothy fingered the cross at his neck. His eyes, once so superior and condemning, now held only pity. " 'Tis true, m'lady. Your marriage vows are sacred."

Despair threatened her and she turned her gaze upon the man with whom she was doomed to spend the rest of her life. "Would you want a wife who loves you not?"

Holt stopped dead in his tracks and whirled on her. "Love?" he repeated. "What in the name of Christ has love got to do with marriage?"

"Everything!" she cried.

"Megan, Megan," he said, clucking his tongue. "What happened to you in the forest to make you think that love is so important? I never took you for such a fool—" His words stopped suddenly and his eyes narrowed as if a great understanding had come to him. "Wolf," he said, his teeth grinding together. "You did not come here to flee him," he said, his nostrils flaring in silent rage, "but to find him."

"I—"

"Everything that was said, about you leaving with him willingly, about your giving yourself to him like a common whore, 'twas true," he said venomously, as if wounded to his very soul. Then, as if finding an inner strength, he spat and said, "It matters not."

She tried to jerk her arm from his deadly grasp, but he only tightened his grip and pinned her hand behind her back, forcing her to face away from him and stare at the carpenter's hut, where a platform and scaffolding was half finished. "Merciful God," she cried, realizing that the structure was a gallows, nearly finished. "What is this?"

"For your friends," he said. "Wolf, the sorcerer, a boy and man who rode with him, and the traitors in the castle."

"No," she said and thought she might be sick. The skeleton of the gallows swam before her eyes and her knees buckled, but Holt's firm grip kept her upright. "You cannot," she cried and panic raced through her blood, thundering in her brain. "Nay, nay, nay!"

" 'Tis true enough," Holt said. "They all will hang. I was only waiting until one of them told me where to find you, but now that my willful wife has returned, there is no need to delay the event any longer."

"Holt, please," she begged. "Please, do not send them to their deaths."

" 'Tis too late to bargain, m'lady," he said, smiling at last. "They'll be hanged tomorrow at sunset, every one of them, including the leader of the outlaws—your precious Wolf."

Awaken.

The voice sounded odd, as if it were spoken from a great distance.

Ware of Abergwynn, awaken and I will heal you.

Wolf opened an eye and sucked in his breath. Gritting his teeth, his body clenched from the pain, he held his tongue. For the first time in his life, he welcomed death.

She is here. Lady Megan has come searching for you.

What? With every ounce of strength he could summon, Wolf struggled to a sitting position and found himself in a hideous, smelly cell deep in the dungeons of Dwyrain. His head ached wildly, the pain behind his eyes was intense and blinding, and his back stung as if it were on fire.

" 'Tis over," he said, though no sound came from his voice.

You cannot give up on her.

Megan. His heart ached at the thought of her, her warm, golden eyes, easy laugh, and wild curls. The few hours of bliss he'd had on this earth were when she'd been with him, giving of her body and her spirit. His throat ached, but not for water. Nay, though he was thirsty, 'twas not for drink. If only he could see her before his spirit left this earth.

You will only die if you so wish it, the voice reprimanded again, and finally his head was clear enough to understand that Cadell, the sorcerer, was speaking to him through his mind—or was it that he was addled himself?

For the love of Christ, look at me!

Wolf raised his eyes and his gaze connected with the intense, outwardly serene stare of the magician. *Now, friend, pay attention, for I will heal you and you will be strong again, but for our plan to work, you must pretend to be weak and feign that you are near death. Not even Megan can suspect that you be whole; elsewise, all is lost.*

" 'Tis lost already."

"Say what?" the guard asked, looking up from his post.

I've never thought you were a coward, Ware. Prove me not wrong! Lady Megan's life depends upon you.

Gritting his teeth and closing his eyes, Wolf inched himself across the cell. Through fetid rushes, scraps of bone from previous meals, rat dung, and spiders, he forced his battered muscles and broken bones to move. Each bit of space he crossed felt as if it lasted forever, but he set his jaw and decided that if he was going to leave this earth, he'd do it while trying to save the woman he loved.

The thought jolted him, for he'd vowed never to love another woman, not after giving his heart to Mary and watching her be destroyed. Now, years later, he'd fallen for another woman, a beautiful, headstrong baron's daughter who had married his worst enemy, and his actions had started a chain of events that might cost Megan her happiness as well as her life.

Nay, he could not die with her death on his hands. If there was a way to save her, he'd find it, no matter what the cost.

That's better, Cadell intoned without words. He stretched a hand through the bars and clasped Wolf's frail fingers with his own strong hand. *Heal, friend.* Cadell closed his eyes and a warmth the likes of which Wolf had never felt before swept from the magician's body to his. *Be strong and you will see your beloved Megan again.*

"I demand an audience with my husband!" Megan yelled, the word tasting foul on her tongue as she pounded on the door. "Do you hear me, guard? Fetch Lord Holt, for I needs speak with him!" She'd been deceived and locked in her chamber for nearly a day. In that time she'd slept fitfully, prayed constantly, and eaten only a bite or two of the food sent her way. She was allowed to speak to no one but the guard. Not even Rue was permitted to visit her.

She'd waited, standing for most of the day upon a stool to look through the window and watch as the gallows was constructed. Every thud of the carpenter's hammer drove a nail of fear deeper into her heart. She'd heard snippets of gossip from the laundress and milkmaid as they'd passed under her window. Not only were Wolf, Jagger, and the sorcerer to be hanged, but young Robin and a boy named Tom—the son of the man building the hated structure—as well. But the builder did not slack in his work, and the horrid wooden structure was taking form.

"Did you not hear me? I demand to speak to Lord Holt!" she cried again, pounding on the thick oak of the door until her knuckles began to bleed.

"I heard ye, m'lady, but the baron's out for a while."

"Then am I not in charge of the castle?"

There was a soft laugh on the other side of the heavy oak beams and Megan leaned uselessly against those imprisoning timbers. "Lord 'Olt, 'e said ye'd try somethin' like this. Nay, Sir Connor is in charge while the baron's out 'unting."

"Hunting?" she repeated, feeling the horrid talons of defeat swipe at her courage. *Holt is out hunting while Wolf and Robin are doomed to breathe their last breaths?*

"Aye—oh, ye do 'ave a visitor."

With a clank of locks and the scrape of the heavy bar being lifted, the door opened and Father Timothy, a look of vast superiority pinned neatly on his face again, swept into the room on a cloud of pious pomposity.

"Please, m'lady, if you would pray with me," he said, his voice cold and distant, "for your husband has pointed out to me that you may have sinned in the days since your capture and you may need to confess." He lifted his eyes to the sentry still standing at the open door. "This is private," he said, "between a woman and her God."

"Aye." Crossing himself, the sentry scooted quickly out of Megan's chamber. The bolt slid into place.

"I have nothing to confess."

"On your knees," Father Timothy commanded in a rough voice. "Fold your hands and pretend to pray, so that if the guard opens the door, 'twill look as if everything is right. Now, listen, I care not about your confession, nor about your sins."

Falling to her knees, she wanted to believe him, but this man had lied before, his piety second only to his own needs.

"Cayley did not leave the castle as Holt would have you believe. Nor did your father die quietly in his sleep." Solemnly, in the cadence of a chant of prayer, the priest unburdened himself, telling of his part in Cayley's escape, Holt's murder of Cormick, his torture of Wolf, and finally, the sorcerer's claim that her father was sent to his grave early by the man who was her husband. "He is a fiend, the very spawn of the Devil," Father Timothy admitted, "and I placed my trust in him. I was a fool and God is punishing me. As part of my atonement I helped Lady Cayley flee, and I will do my best to see that your marriage is annulled."

She should have been relieved but she was stricken by the depths of Holt's treachery.

"Alas, I cannot save you from your husband unless you, like Cayley, leave and give me time to speak to the abbot and the bishop on your behalf."

"I cannot leave," she said firmly. As long as Wolf and Robin were alive, she would stay and try to help them. "But if you need atone, then help me find a way out of my chamber so I can visit the prisoners."

He shook his head. " 'Tis impossible. The guards have instructions."

"You are a man of God. Surely you can convince a dull soldier that 'tis the will of the Lord that I visit the poor wretches in the dungeon, as part of my duties as the baron's wife."

Sighing, he glanced to the window and shook his head, as if seeing, in a distance visible only to him, his own ruin. "I'll try," he said, rising from the floor and crossing himself. At the door, he spoke with the guard, who argued with him for a few minutes, then left, only to return and argue again. Megan heard only parts of the conversation, but it had to do with the soldier's doomed soul and the will of God. Father Timothy was adamant that God wanted the lady of the manor to visit the prisoners, to speak with the men who had kidnapped her and to, in good Christian manner, forgive them before their black souls left this earth.

Eventually, after many words and much debate from the dullard who stood by her door, Timothy was allowed to take her to the dungeon as long as the guard himself joined them.

Megan steeled herself for the worst. Though she'd never been to the prisons of Dwyrain before, she knew they were cruel cells that were built to hold only the most dangerous criminals and traitors to the baron. Her father used the dungeon rarely and she trembled inside as she followed the priest down the staircase and outside the great hall. A rush of wind tore at her cloak and brushed her cheeks with its icy breath. Shivering with dread, still she smiled at the people who greeted her, the steward and tailor and a farmer who had sold sheep to her father.

Inside the north tower was worse than she'd feared. Aside from reeking of a foul stench, the stairs were dark and uneven. The prisoners were held on the lowest level, the same dark hell where they'd been tortured, according to the priest, a place she'd visited only once as a child on a dare from her brother Bevan.

Clutching her cloak, she followed the priest to a guard station and the surrounding cells, small rooms with walls of rusted bars.

Wolf lay within one cell, his back to the door, and her

heart, traitor that it was, soared at the sight of him before she saw the new welts upon his shoulders, the bruises showing beneath his dark skin, and the fresh scars of burns where he'd been tortured. The contents of her stomach, meager though they were, threatened her throat, and she swallowed hard as she made her way to the cell door.

"Let me inside."

"Nay." The guard on duty shook his head. "Father Timothy, these men are not to have any visitors."

" 'Tis the lady of the manor. She is here only to see that the prisoners are treated fairly."

"But—"

"Hush, man!" Megan ordered, taking Timothy's cue. "Elsewise I'll report to my husband that I was mistreated."

Wolf's head rolled her way. His eyes, once bright, were glassy and vacant. *Oh, God, no! Let him not be in pain. Help him, please!*

" 'Tis Holt's wife," he sneered, his voice gravelly and foreign.

"Wolf!" she cried.

"What is it you want?" he snarled with no trace of kindness—no hint of the gentle man hidden deep beneath his hard exterior. His eyes were feral and slitted; he appeared a beast she didn't recognize.

"I—I—wanted to know that you were treated well."

His laugh was a ruthless bark. "Your husband's hospitality, m'lady, leaves much to be desired."

"Why are ye speaking to her so?" Robin, in the next cell, demanded. "Lady Megan, we were worried about you. We tried to find ye for fear—"

"The lad's addled with fear," Wolf said in that same hoarse, cruel whisper. "And half in love with ye. Stop it, boy, the lady's a married woman. The new baron is her husband."

Something deep in her heart withered. "Why be you so cruel?"

" 'Tis my way," he said, and for a second she thought she saw another emotion flicker in his eyes, a pain she didn't recognize, but it was fleeting, and when he stretched to his feet and limped slowly to her, her heart tore open. How had she thought he might ever love her? The shackles on his feet chinked as he moved and his face was tight, his lips flat, his gaze steady and hate-filled. His grimy fingers circled the iron slats of his cell and she reached forward to touch him, only to have him draw away. "Return to the keep and leave us in this hellhole, woman," he said, his lip curling in disgust at the sight of her. "We need not your pity."

"I'm tellin' ye, m'lord, he acted as if the sight of her disgusted 'im, as if he couldn't bear to see her," the guard told Holt. " 'Twas wicked he was to her. Father Timothy he stayed on, asking for confessions, offering to pray with the prisoners, but they turned their backs on 'im as well."

"And the lady?" Holt asked, suspicion still pounding through his brain. When he'd heard that Father Timothy had disobeyed him and had taken Megan to the dungeon, he'd been furious, but now, upon the second guard's word, which was as strong as the first sentry's, he felt some sense of relief. Was it possible that the outlaw had at least a shred of honor and hadn't stolen Megan's virtue? Or was he protecting her? Or did he actually loathe her?

As Holt sat in Ewan's recently vacated chair in the great hall, with one boot propped on the hearth and the servants scurrying through the keep to see to his every need, Holt felt a second's peace.

The hunt today had been rewarding—a doe and one fawn, though the other wounded yearling had escaped, its trail of blood leading nowhere. Now, it appeared that his stubborn wife might not be tainted, and he so loved to enter a virgin. Lifting his mazer to his lips, he sighed. "You were speaking of my wife," he said, savoring the word. Marrying Megan had given him this keep, and aside from the pleasures of her body, which he planned to soon sample, his newfound wealth was gratifying.

"Aye, she's been askin' to see ye," the guard proclaimed.

More good news. He'd been patient with her, hoping she would see that there was no use in resisting him, but he could not wait forever.

"Bring her in." As the sentry hurried up the stairs, Holt clapped his hands and felt immense satisfaction when a page, his eyes round with fear that Holt wasn't satisfied with the performance of his duties, listened in trembling silence, then retrieved another cup of wine.

Life, indeed, was good.

Within minutes, he spied Megan walking slowly down the stairs and he couldn't help the small catch in his heart at the sight of her. She was beautiful, with her bright, ale-colored eyes and quick smile. The bridge of her nose boasted a few freckles and her thick hair curled in russet-colored waves. She'd dressed in a deep blue tunic and amber mantle and looked as if she were truly the mistress of the keep. One day she would bear him strong sons and beautiful daughters, and if only he could teach her to rein in her wicked tongue, she would be a good companion for him.

" 'Tis said that you want to speak with me," he ventured, waving toward a chair and sliding a cup of wine across the table toward her.

"Aye," she said, and he waited until at last she muttered, "m'lord."

"What is it you wish to discuss?"

"The prisoners," she said, hitching her chin upward in defiance and refusing to take the seat he offered. Nor did she show the least inclination to pick up the cup of wine. Willful. Stubborn. A woman who would be a challenge in bed.

"I heard you went to visit them and were not well received."

"Let them go."

He laughed. Surely she was joking, but the serious expression on her small face convinced him otherwise. "They are criminals and needs be punished."

"Because I was stolen from Dwyrain," she said. "But I've returned."

He ran his finger around his mazer thoughtfully. "How can I be assured that you will stay?"

"You have my word," she said without the slightest hint of hesitation. "Did I not return when I had the chance?"

Lifting a shoulder and mindful of the servants who were within earshot, including Nell, who was taking her time polishing the candleholders while pretending not to listen, he said, "Aye, but how am I to know that 'twas your first attempt at escape from the outlaw?"

"It wasn't. But I was caught every other time. The last time, I took the leader's destrier."

Holt laughed. "That must have stolen the piss from him."

"Unfortunately, it was stolen by the farmer who found me and took me to the nunnery."

"Aye, the nunnery that was far from Dwyrain. It appeared you were not returning here so much as fleeing," he said, watching for any hint of reaction in her smooth features.

Her eyebrows drew together. "Aye, 'tis true, but I could not chance riding to Dwyrain without the outlaws catching up to me, for 'twas what they expected."

"So you want me to believe that you led them on a wild chase that took you to the nunnery."

"Believe what you will, Holt. Know you that I did not come to be your wife willingly. I wanted you not. But now"—she turned defeated palms to the ceiling—"I cannot pretend to love you or even care for you, but . . . I . . . I am willing to be your wife day and night if you let the prisoners go free."

He laughed again and this time felt a mite of joy. "Silly girl. Why would I agree to this? You are already my wife. You will do what I say, eat what I tell you, sleep with me when I want you, hold your tongue when you disapprove, and bear my children. This you have agreed to do."

"Not willingly. I'll fight you every step of the way."

"But if I release the prisoners?"

"I will be your servant."

He nearly choked on his wine. "Ah, Megan, a fine liar you be, but I think no man would ever be your master." The thought caused his blood to heat a bit, and seeing her standing before him in her tunic as blue as midnight, color high in her cheeks, her lips quivering slightly, he could barely restrain himself.

" 'Tis a deal I wish to strike with you, Holt."

"And you'll promise to do anything I ask?" he jeered.

She closed her eyes and her fingers clenched into tight fists. "Aye," she agreed. "Anything."

Twirling the stem of his mazer in his fingers, he considered her proposition. Was she sincere? The skin drawn tight over her nose and the lines around the corners of her lips convinced him, and had she not always been true to her word? Firelight gleamed against his silver cup. 'Twas pleasant to think her malleable and fearful of his power. If he agreed, he would finally have her where he'd wanted her—under his thumb and groveling to do his bidding.

Unless she was lying.

"You will not argue with me?"

"On my word."

"You will lie in my bed and give me sons?"

He watched her swallow. "As many as God allows."

He couldn't resist seeing how far she would go. He'd been humiliated in front of his men and 'twould be good to get a little payment in kind. Since he was made to look the fool by her capture and rumors of her ardor for the damned outlaw, Holt wanted her to taste what it felt like to be utterly mortified.

"What if I wanted to bed you in front of some of my men—or mayhap share you?"

"Dear God," she cried in dismay, her face flushing with color, her eyes blinking wildly.

"Well?"

She bit down hard on her lip, drawing blood. "Aye," she consented and faltered a bit as if she were about to keel over.

"So tell me, Megan," he said, unable to push aside the horrid thought that had been nagging at him ever since she made her first request. "Do you love the outlaw so much that you would suffer complete shame and indignity to save him?"

She hesitated, but when she opened her eyes to stare at him, he was awed by the strength in her gaze. "I've said I would do what you ask. Why I do it is of no matter. Now, Lord Holt, will you spare the men?"

"Each one but Wolf. The other men, including the boy and traitors in mine own castle, will be allowed their freedom, but Wolf must remain in the dungeon. His sins of kidnapping, traitorous insubordination, and murderous intent must be atoned for." She nearly lost her balance, but leaned against the table for support. "Wolf's punishment will be an example for those who dare think they could defy me. The gallows, though they are nearly finished, will stand for a week, as a reminder of what happens to those who betray me. Then, at week's end, he'll be hanged by a rope until he's dead."

"You cannot do this!" she cried, her calm exterior cracking and tears of genuine fear filling her eyes. "Holt, please, I beg you . . ."

" 'Tis no use."

"But—"

"Hush! 'Tis done," he said, his lip curling in disgust when she revealed how much she cared for the forest thug and his motley band of thieves. "Guard!" he called, then turned his anger to Megan. "Prepare yourself, m'lady, for I will come to your bed tonight. Rest now."

She started to protest, but held her tongue.

"So you be a smart girl. Asides," he said with an ugly chuckle, "your friends will go free. Except, of course, for your beloved, doomed Wolf."

Fifteen

"So where were ye for the years we thought ye dead?" Wolf asked, eyeing his friend through the iron slats of the wall separating them. "You never once sent word to Garrick or Morgana that you'd survived the fall."

"Aye, nor did you," Cadell reminded him.

"I had reasons."

"As did I."

Cadell stared up at the small hole where a breath of fresh air sometimes filtered into the dungeon. "Nearly drowned and broken I was when I washed up on the shore. An old woman, one the townspeople called a witch, Fiona of the Hills, found me. There was barely a breath left in my body, nary a hint of life, but she took me in, healed me with her spells, herbs, and runes. I remembered nary a thing, my mind was near gone, but in time most of it returned. By then, 'twas years and many miles later."

"So how did you come to be a magician?"

"Again, 'twas Fiona. She saw that I had the gift, as did my sister Morgana, and my grandmother, Enit. Fiona was a patient woman and childless; she was grateful to find one who could be nurtured and taught. She showed me how to use what the gods had bestowed upon me."

"And you became a sorcerer."

"So some say."

"You can heal."

"Sometimes."

"But not yourself? You still are lame."

Cadell stared deep into Wolf's eyes. " 'Tis wise to remember we are only people, even those of us who have been given special powers."

"So you stay crippled by choice?" Wolf asked.

" 'Tis not so bad."

"Cadell, 'tis nonsense ye speak!"

"Shh! 'Tis time." Cadell's gaze shifted to the stairs and Wolf felt it, that tiny rush of air stirring through the cells before the first scrape of a boot was heard. "Holt approaches." With a twisted smile, Cadell turned his attention to the staircase and his lips moved not, though his words reached Wolf as surely as if he shouted. *Do not forget, Ware, ye are injured so badly ye may not survive.*

Like an emperor visiting paupers, Holt strode through the shadowy caverns that were the dungeons of Dwyrain. His mouth was compressed against the foul air, but he carried himself as a conquering king and walked steadily, only to stop in front of Wolf's cell. Four soldiers stood behind him, their hands on their weapons as if they expected the prisoners to attack through the bars.

"Lord Holt!" the jailer exclaimed, jumping to his feet from the stool where he'd been nearly napping. "I knew not that ye'd be visitin' the prison."

"Be still!" Holt ordered as his eyes slitted in the darkness and settled on Wolf. "The lady has bartered for your pathetic lives."

Wolf's nostrils flared and his muscles strained. Glaring at his captor through the bars, he prayed for one more chance to place his bare hands around Holt's neck and strangle him until the bastard could not draw a breath. Megan, sweet Megan, would be better off widowed. "Bartered with what?" he snarled.

"Her subservience." Holt's smile was smug and Wolf's insides turned to ice.

Megan? On her knees before this lying, murdering cur? Never! Not as long as there was a breath of life in his body.

Holt studied his fingernails for a second, as if thinking. "She cares about your flea-riddled hides. Because I want to please my wife, I listened to her pleas, but granted not everything she wanted. 'Twas my decision, as an act of good faith, Wolf, that I would release everyone but you."

Wolf felt a second's relief. At least those he'd dragged into his personal mission of vengeance would be safe. But there was Megan to consider. He could not allow her to spend the rest of her life living as Holt's doormat.

"The traitors will be banished, of course, and they will be freed one day at a time to prevent them from banding together and plotting against the castle. But you, Wolf, will hang for your treason."

Wolf felt no fear and managed a smile. He was about to tell Holt that he'd meet him in hell, but Cadell's unspoken voice called to him. *Hold your tongue, Ware. Do not mock him. Play the victim.*

The thought was revolting. "I cannot!" Wolf announced, and Holt laughed.

"But you have no choice. You'll swing by your neck until

it breaks or until you can no longer breathe. Either way you'll be dead."

Wolf rolled onto the balls of his feet, ready to lunge.

Stop! Remember, you are weak and ill from the beating and the torture of the coals against your skin. Do not give him the advantage of seeing that you are healed, or all will be for naught. If ye care for the lady, Wolf, pretend that ye can do nothing to help her—that the bastard has nothing to fear from you.

"I'll not—"

She is with child, Ware. Your child.

"What?" he cried, and Holt laughed.

"Are ye daft, Wolf?" Motioning toward the dingy cells, Holt said, "Has being locked away stolen yer mind? I blame ye not. 'Tis not easy to be a prisoner, is it? The mind sometimes leaves us."

Gnashing his teeth in frustration, Wolf pretended to try to lunge at the bars, only to fall to the floor as if in great pain. With an agonized whistle, he dragged air through his teeth, then cursed Holt roundly. "Go to hell, you sick bastard."

A child? Megan was with child? Was it possible?

'Tis true.

"Why did ye tell me not sooner?" he demanded.

"He's gone mad," Holt said, clucking his tongue.

'Twas not necessary and should be something a woman tells a man, but I had no choice.

Wolf closed his eyes. A baby. His child and Megan's, and she was now married to Holt. His fists curled into balls of frustration and he pounded uselessly on the grimy floor. He had to protect her and their unborn child. Nothing else mattered, not even his own life.

"Save your strength, fool." Holt laughed. "You'll need it when the hangman comes for you. Now, you, magician, leave this castle tonight and never return. 'Tis banished ye are, and I have guards posted outside the walls of the keep. They have orders to kill ye on sight if you come anywhere near Dwyrain." He glanced to the connecting cells and said, "This goes for the rest of you. If any of my men spies your faces again, 'twill be the last time."

Wolf, determined to defy Holt and steal Megan from Dwyrain again, watched as his enemy turned and hastened from the dungeon, his bodyguards following after him like trained dogs. "Trust him not," he warned Cadell, but the sorcerer was smiling to himself, as if he alone knew all truths.

"Worry not about me. 'Tis your own skin that is in danger."

Holt cared not about his own life, but he'd fight the very Devil himself for Megan and the baby she carried.

Riding through the gatehouse with the magician tied and bound on the horse behind him, Connor decided Holt was a fool. Not only had the big outlaw—the one he'd heard called Bjorn—escaped with the woman Connor had planned to seduce, but now Holt was letting his prisoners leave the castle unharmed, or so it was to appear. The magician's well-being was for show because some of the peasants and servants—aye, even the soldiers—had begun to believe that the man had mystical powers, and Lady Megan had demanded his release.

'Twas Connor's mission to kill the wizard once they were far from the view of any of the sentries who might still be scouring the woods for Lady Cayley and her captor.

Glancing to the dark sky, Connor cursed his luck. He'd given what small amount of trust he had to Holt, and the man had deceived him. While playing dice and drinking too much ale, one of Holt's bodyguards had admitted to hearing the new baron conversing with the priest about marrying Cayley off to Baron Rolf of Castle Henning. The thought was disgusting, even to Connor, for Rolf was a withered old man, blind in one eye, who took pleasure in the torment of others—not that Connor didn't understand the old man's needs, but Rolf was past his prime, with a limp cock and a thirst for killing his wives, or so 'twas rumored. Connor could have accepted this, but the fact that Holt had lied to him by promising him Lady Cayley, then planning to barter her to a rich baron, was too much.

Mayhap it was time to deal with Holt.

A fine mist seeped from the ground, rising upward as Connor turned into the woods and stopped beyond a copse of oak, where a small clearing was surrounded by trees, ferns, and brambles. "Here," he said, hopping easily to the ground. His quiver pressed between his shoulder blades and he thought that killing a crippled man was not much sport. He would rather have had a shot at Wolf or one of the younger, agile prisoners—Robin or Tom—but Wolf was sentenced to hang and the boys were locked in the dungeon.

Why not kill Holt for betraying you, his own mind said to him—or was it his mind? He felt a shiver like tiny footsteps crawl down his spine.

"Get down," he ordered, and pulled roughly on the man's tied hands. The cripple toppled to the ground, lost his footing for a second, but managed to scramble to his feet, such as they were.

Connor slid an arrow from his quiver and hoisted his bow. "Run!"

No.

God's eyes, he hadn't said a word, but Connor had heard the answer clear as a bell. Perhaps 'twas his mind playing tricks on him again. His hands weren't as steady as they usually were as he drew hard on the bowstring with the arrow. "Move, sorcerer, and ye've got a chance."

And your soul will rot forever in the depths of hell.

"Say wha—?" Connor jerked as if someone had struck him. This time he was certain it wasn't his own mind chiding him. Nay, but the prisoner hadn't moved his lips nor used his voice. 'Twas as if the sorcerer had talked to him mind to mind.

He looked over his shoulder, half expecting another to have joined them. What kind of devilment was this man conjuring?

Go on, kill me if you can.

"For the love of God, I will!" he said, nearly pissing in his breeches.

Overhead, through the rising mist, came the sound of great wings flapping wildly. An owl, the same huge ruffled-feathered bird who had landed on the prisoner's arm the night he'd been recaptured, settled onto one of the cripple's shoulders.

"So ye've found me, Owain," the magician said in his calm voice. He turned his haunted eyes to Connor and the soldier felt a shiver cold as death crawl through his bowels. "Give Holt a message," the cripple commanded, spreading his arms wide, his wrists no longer bound, as the mist, like a thick curtain of fog, began to rise from the ferns and grass surrounding him. "Tell him that the Devil wants his due."

The forest became engulfed in the icy haze and Connor let his arrow fly. He waited for the scream, or the sound of running feet, or the angry flap of huge wings, but silence greeted his ears and the fog was suddenly thick as Cook's tasteless pea soup.

"Where are ye?" he called, striking out after the sorcerer, assured that he'd stumble across the man's corpse. "Hey! Where are ye?" He walked across the clearing thrice before stopping to scratch his head and fight the dry fear that had settled in his mouth. His arrows never missed; his aim was straight and true. A split second before the mist rose, he'd had the sorcerer in his sights, but . . . Then he realized that not only had the man disappeared, but so had the owl and both horses as well. Without a sound, they'd been swallowed by the forest.

Unnerved, he whistled sharply, hoping his mount would respond, but there was no answering whinny, no snort of recognition, no pawing of a hoof against the forest floor. Nor was there any other sound. The shrouded woods were completely silent and he heard neither the call of a winter bird, the scramble of some rodent hurrying through the bracken, nor the whir of a single insect's wings. No breeze rustled the dry leaves and no water splashed over stones in a nearby creek. 'Twas as if he were truly alone on the earth, and for the first time in years, fear—as dark as the middle of a winter night—bored deep into Connor's black heart.

Walking backward, he expected the sorcerer to appear and kill him on the spot, and when he reached the edge of the clearing, he turned and ran, not knowing which direction he took and not caring. He knew only that if he was to escape with his life, he would have to run as far and as fast as his feet would carry him.

"Well, I'll be jiggered!" Odell's smile stretched from one side of his craggy face to the other as Bjorn rode into the shifting circle of light thrown by the campfire. "Find us, did ye?"

"Where's Wolf?" Bjorn demanded, blowing on his hands in an attempt to warm them, then motioning for Cayley to urge her horse forward and join him. He searched the faces of the men, looking for the man who had sent Cormick to his death.

"Ain't 'e with you?"

"Nay."

"But he and Jagger and Robin left days ago to find Lady Megan and collect the ransom. Leastwise, that's what he claimed!" Odell's grizzled face squinched and he scratched his bald head thoughtfully. "Where's Cormick, and who's the woman?" he asked as if suddenly suspicious. "Ye know the rule."

"Aye, and I had no choice but to bring her," Bjorn said, hopping lithely to the ground before trying to help Cayley from her saddle. She would have none of his assistance and he held up his hands as if in surrender and allowed her to dismount. Rubbing the kinks from his shoulders, he was grateful to have finally found camp and the men he knew and trusted. Women, especially rich women, were trouble to deal with and difficult to understand. He wanted to despise this headstrong blond woman he'd been forced to ride with, but he'd found, as they'd spent so many long hours together, that she'd proved herself stronger and quicker witted than he'd ever thought possible. "This, lads, is Lady Cayley, Megan of Dwyrain's sister."

"Another one!" Odell rolled his eyes as if searching for divine intervention.

Bjorn took the time to introduce each man, but Odell was impatient.

"Tell us all everything," Odell demanded as Peter saw to

the horses. "Sit down by the fire and I'll get ye somethin' to eat, but tell us what happened."

The strips of eel and shanks of rabbit were far overcooked, but it had been long since Bjorn had eaten. As he gnawed on a rabbit bone, Bjorn told them of his capture, Cormick's death, and his escape with Cayley. The men were grim-faced throughout and in the end, they voted, by throwing their knives into the fire, to seek vengeance for their comrade's death.

"Holt will rue the day he killed one of us," Odell crowed.

"Aye," Heath agreed, the skin beneath his beard stretched tight. The thirst for vengeance glinted in his eyes.

As the men swapped stories about how they intended to find Wolf and kill Holt, Bjorn watched Cayley from the corner of his eye. She wasn't repulsed by the outlaws' promises of revenge. She ate heartily and without complaint.

When she was finished, she eyed each man, opened her mouth to say something, then closed it decisively. Bjorn swallowed a smile as she licked her greasy fingers, then wiped them on her mantle. She was a pretty one, though spoiled, and she'd been far less trouble than he'd expected. But her tongue—how she could give a man a lashing with it!

"I had trouble findin' ye," Bjorn admitted as Heath passed a jug of ale. Bjorn took a long swallow. The brew was bitter, but he was grateful for a draft and drank his fill before wiping his mouth with his sleeve. He handed the jug to Cayley, who licked her lips and seemed about to decline. Then, gaze fastened to Bjorn's, she hoisted the dirty vessel to her lips and took a swallow, only to end up coughing so hard she had trouble catching her breath and nearly dropped the jug.

"Careful!" Odell warned.

Tears streamed from her eyes, spilling on red cheeks. "What *is* that?" she asked.

Odell sniffed, offended. " 'Tis me own brand of mead."

" 'Twill burn out yer insides if ye're not careful," Peter said.

"Even if you are," she said, struggling with her voice.

"I don't see ye passin' the jug too often without takin' more'n yer share, Peter," Odell grumbled, his pride wounded.

"Shh. 'Tis of no matter." Bjorn glanced at Cayley. "The lady is fine. Mayhap she'd like another sip."

"Later," Cayley said, her voice a raspy whisper, and she patted her chest with the flat of her hand.

"Good." Bjorn couldn't hide the amusement he felt as she tried to regain her composure and hide the fact that her face had turned crimson. "Now, we must find Wolf. Since he's not returned, he's at the chapel waiting for our return, or on the road, or at Dwyrain."

He's in the prison, Bjorn, where you were once chained. Bjorn turned swiftly, reaching for his sword as he saw the crippled sorcerer step into the golden shadows of the campfire. A speckled owl sat on his shoulder and he held the reins of two fine horses in his hands. "Hagan of Erbyn has a small army of men that we can join," he said, the men staring at him as if he were the ghost of some great Welsh warrior. "The lady left him and rode day and night to Dwyrain. His soldiers moved more slowly but they will reach the gates of the castle soon." No one had heard him approach, nor had they heard the sound of his horses' hooves.

"God be with us, ye've got that flappin' beast with ye!" Odell exclaimed, leaping backward at the sight of the sorcerer and his winged friend. The bird's head swiveled to pin the wiry man in his wide-eyed stare. "Owl stew is what ye're good for, and nothin' more! Git!" Odell waved his arms at the bird, but the owl only settled in and gave a soft hoot. "Bloody Christ, just what we need!"

The magician heeded him not. 'Twas as if he hadn't heard a word of Odell's chatter. "Wolf needs our help. If we hurry, we can join Hagan of Erbyn's army and try to save him." The sorcerer somehow locked his gaze to that of each and every person gathered around the fire. "If we do not come to his aid—and soon—I fear that he, Robin, Jagger, and those in the castle who have been his spies will surely die."

"Jack?" one man asked.

"Aye."

"Anyone else?"

"Yea," the sorcerer said sadly. "The Lady Megan as well."

" 'Tis time to collect my part of the bargain." Holt swayed slightly as he glanced over his shoulder to the hallway. Leaning against the doorway, he said, "Leave us be, guards—I want no one to disturb us." Then, weaving, he entered her chamber and closed the door behind him.

Dread clamped around Megan's lungs. Throughout the gloomy day she'd watched from her window as the gallows was finished, nails pounded into place, a thick noose swinging ready from a crossbeam. The thought that Wolf would lose his life on that monstrous scaffold turned her stomach, and now, facing the man who was her husband, the self-proclaimed baron who had ordered Wolf's death, she recoiled. "All of the prisoners have not been released."

" 'Tis only a matter of time." He fumbled with his belt and she smelled wine souring on his breath. "You and I, wife," he said, his eyes finding hers, "have wasted too much time already."

"Nay, I—"

His head snapped up and his lips turned bloodless with rage. "Do not dare defy me, wench, for we struck a deal and you, if you want to see any more of that sorry lot of prisoners released, will do as I say."

She bit down hard on her tongue rather than telling him to fly straight to the portals of hell. A breeze swept through the half-open window, rattling the shutters and causing a stir in the fire. Amber coals glowed brighter and flames crackled.

"Or would ye rather see the young one—Robin, I think he's called—hanging from the end of a rope? Is that what ye want, his death on your head?"

"He's but a boy," she protested, knowing that Holt had her cornered.

"And a traitor to Dwyrain." His jaw grew tight, his countenance unforgiving. Fury flared his nostrils. "Now, Megan, test me no more." His belt dropped to the floor, the buckle smacking the stones with a heavy chink. She jumped. Oh, God, this was really going to happen. She would have to lift her skirts to this . . . this monster she detested. Frozen for a second, she watched as he tossed his surcoat onto the foot of the bed and began working the laces of his mantle. "Did you hear me, woman? If ye do not strip yourself of your clothes, I'll do it for you and I'll make you watch while not only Wolf but his band of thieves and Judases are killed one by one!" With a final tug, the mantle fell free and dropped to the floor.

Megan's heart beat in fear.

Advancing upon her, his eyes gleaming bright with the reflection of the fire, Holt stretched out a hand and ran one long finger over the slope of her jaw. Her skin crawled and she fought the urge to slap the damning hand away.

What did it matter if he touched her tonight or later in the week? She was doomed to lie with him, to pretend that the child within her was his progeny. She had no choice if she was to protect Wolf's babe, but she'd never been the kind of woman who let her fate be decided for her. For as long as she could remember, she'd been vocal and demanding about what her life should be. Her independence had been her undoing in the end, and her father, deciding she could not make the right choice, had betrothed her to Holt.

Now her enemy of a husband bent closer, the stench of consumed wine with him as he pressed his lips to her cheek and neck. Her skin prickled in revulsion and she couldn't imagine the torture of letting him bed her.

Could she lie with him night after night? Nay! 'Twas unthinkable, but she had only a few days and then each of the prisoners would be released. If she allowed Holt to think that she enjoyed him, that she couldn't wait to be with him, there was a chance he would no longer lock her in her chamber. He might even remove the guard from her door. If he were duped into believing that she'd accepted her lot as his wife, he might not have her watched so closely and she would be allowed to roam the castle freely. She knew more about Dwyrain than anyone within the castle walls, for she and Bevan had, while growing up, explored every staircase, attic, loft, and cellar. If given a tiny bit of freedom, she could find a way to release Wolf.

She had allies, she thought, as Holt's hand reached for the tie holding her tunic over her breasts and his hot breath feathered across her collarbones.

Father Timothy, and surely the carpenter, the nursemaid Rue, and others loyal to Ewan. Surely the outlaws would come for their leader, and Hagan of Erbyn was due to arrive on the morrow unless he, infuriated with her for deceiving him and stealing away into the night, had returned to his family.

The tunic opened and she shivered with loathing. "That's better," he breathed against her skin before looking up and pressing hot, insistent lips to hers. She couldn't kiss him back, but neither did she push him away. His tongue slid into her mouth and she nearly gagged. *Please God, no!* she silently screamed as his weight pressed her down to the bed. Tears burned behind her eyes as he stripped off her clothes, ripping them in his hurry, dropping them onto the floor by the bed along with his own tunic, breeches, and purse.

With great effort, she closed her eyes and pretended that she wasn't in the room, that what was happening to her body had naught to do with her. His hands were rough against her breasts, tweaking and pushing them, giving her no pleasure, and when he slid his knees between her own bare legs she scooted upward on the bed, as far from him as she could get.

"Do not try to escape from me, wife," he ordered. " 'Tis time to give up your virginity."

Oh, God, soon he'd know! There would be no blood, no ripping of her maidenhead. Then he'd realize that she'd been with another man. Surely he was not so stupid that he would not discern who that man—the father of her child—was. Eventually, he would know the babe wasn't his.

Holt growled into her ear, "I have waited long for this, planned for it, dreamed of it, been more than patient since you arrived at the castle. Taking your virtue will be more satisfying than killing your brother—"

She gasped and cried out.

" 'Tis true," he admitted drunkenly, his tongue loosened by wine. "Your brother as well as your father. Neither would hurry to his grave fast enough." With a belch, he laughed, and Megan wanted only to do him harm.

"I detest you!" she spat, giving up her plan to dupe him and play the willing bride. She could never, would never . . .

He clucked his tongue. "I would have done anything for this time with you," he said and she spat up at his face.

"Get off me!"

"Too late. Now, wife," he said, rising above her, his white, naked body poised between her legs, "watch as I make you mine."

She stared up at him, but she would not touch or caress him. One of her arms was flung over the side of the bed and her fingers touched his garments, the velvet and leather and . . . something metal. Her fingertips scraped the hilt of his knife.

A gift from God. She licked her lips as her fingers wrapped over the carved handle.

"Now and forever, Megan of Dwyrain, ye belong to me!"

He thrust forward. Her fingers wrapped around the weapon and with a swift shifting of her body, she brought up the knife and plunged the wicked blade deep into his side.

Blood sprayed the bedclothes.

Holt let out a hideous, timber-rattling roar. Rage and pain contorted his features. "I'll kill you!"

"Go to hell, you murdering beast!" Megan squirmed away as Holt tried to reach for the knife that stuck beneath his ribs.

Rolling off the bed, she grabbed her chemise and landed near the fire and basket of logs. She had to get out of here. Now! Escape!

"You'll pay for this," he charged, but was sweating and breathing hard. Stumbling to his feet, he yanked out the knife. More blood splattered. Holding the dripping weapon, he dove forward. She sidestepped his attack and he fell on the floor with a thud and a pained grunt.

" 'Tis Wolf I love," she said, wanting to wound him, to make him feel some of the pain she felt now that she knew that he'd taken both her brother's and her father's lives. She threw her chemise over her head.

"The thief."

"But not a murderer."

"He killed Tadd of Prydd." Holt was struggling, his arms levering his torso upright. Blood ran from his side. "Now, you are my wife and—"

"In name only," she said, as she gathered up the rest of her clothes. Holt's skin was pale, but as Megan tossed on her tunic and backed toward the door, he sprang to his feet with renewed strength.

"You'll regret you ever crossed me, woman." He thrust at her with the knife and she spun away, knocking over the basket of firewood. Small logs rolled free.

"Keep far from me!"

"Not until you beg for mercy."

Without thinking, she snatched up what had once been a branch and heaved it at him. He ducked, but the corner of the log caught him on the edge of his jaw and sent him spinning into the wall, where he cracked his head on a crucifix hung near the door. Megan, certain she'd killed him, dropped a second piece of oak and stumbled backward. "Oh, God, please help me," she cried.

He groaned and lay still.

Never before had she taken a life, and though she hated Holt with all her heart, she'd never truly believed that she'd have to kill him. She nearly retched, but told herself to keep going, this was her chance. Grabbing her mantle and boots, she stepped over his bleeding body. Fingers fumbling, heart pounding, she threw on her mantle, pried the knife from his fingers, and bolted for the door. It opened without a sound and soon she was in the corridor for the first time in days.

"God be with me," she whispered, thankful as she locked the door behind her that Holt had dismissed the guards.

The air in the corridor was cool. The rush lights flickered dimly, casting shadows against the walls, but Megan's steps were sure. She'd grown up in this castle and knew connecting routes to back stairs and seldom-used passages. Walking barefoot and noiselessly, she slipped unseen through the hallways. Most of the castle was asleep—only a few nodding guards stood their posts—but Megan hurried down a curving staircase, through the gallery, past a door leading to the priest's quarters, and finally down another set of steps to the kitchen.

A cat lurked near the door, but it only watched with amber eyes as she stole outside where the moon, not quite full, bathed the bailey in its silvery glow. The gallows, with its noose swaying softly, loomed like a huge, ungainly beast, casting a horrid shadow over the grass. In her mind's eye, Megan saw her beloved Wolf swinging from the hangman's rope, and she sped forward, past the evil structure and the pillory to Rue's hut.

Quietly, she tapped on a window until it was opened by a sour-faced Rue, who grimaced as if she were about to give whoever was bothering her a tongue-lashing.

"Megan," she said in surprise, "come in, come in." Within seconds, the door was open and Megan threw herself into the nursemaid's outstretched arms.

" 'Tis worried I've been. Holt, he would not let me visit ye and I feared . . . oh, Lord, child, don't worry about what I feared." Her small hut was warm, a banked fire radiating heat. From the rafters hung bundles of herbs that Rue had collected and had suspended to dry.

"I've not much time," Megan said, her words coming out in short, wild bursts. "I killed Holt and now—"

"Killed him?" Rue crossed herself. "What were ye thinking, child? The punishment for murdering a baron is—"

"—what he deserved. *He* killed Father *and* Bevan. He admitted as much to me." She was suddenly shaking, her teeth chattering as she talked, the cold in her soul deep and mind-numbing.

"There now, lass, worry not about it. What is it ye want from me?"

"I want to know who is loyal to my father, who would rise against Holt's soldiers; and then I need a disguise, for I'm going to set Wolf and the rest of the prisoners free."

"Holy Mother," Rue said, her face wrinkling in concentration and worry. "Think ye it's wise to—"

"I killed Holt!" Megan said again. "I have no choice."

Rue nodded and rubbed her hands, with their big knuckles, together nervously. "Many in the castle despise Holt, but would they take up arms against his men? I know not." Shaking her head, she said, "There is Ellen, Tom's mother; she would do anything to free her boy, for she's certain that Holt will make him hang from the very structure her husband built."

"She has many children—boys," Megan said. "I need one of their—George's, as he's near my size—his tunic and breeches."

"His clothes?"

"For my disguise, of course."

"Oh. Of course." Rue looked more worried than before.

Megan rattled on. "And I'll need someone to go with me to the dungeon."

"Yes."

"And more—I'll need my own guards posted to warn me of any soldiers approaching."

Rue bit her lower lip and grabbed both of Megan's shoulders in her long, bony fingers. "Ye should have been the baron, ye know, if the king would allow a woman to rule. Ye'd be as good a ruler as your father and far better than Bevan would have been." Tears sprang to her old eyes. "Ewan, proud he'd be of ye."

"Aye, but we have not time for this now," Megan said, her throat growing thick with the sorrow she held back. "Hurry!"

"Come. We'll talk with Ellen," Rue agreed, reaching for the door. Before she stepped into the bailey, she turned and her face softened. She touched a hand to Megan's crown. "God be with ye, lass."

"Halt!" the guard commanded as he heard the sound of footsteps on the stairs. "Who be ye?"

" 'Tis only me, Ronald, and me helpmate Stanley," a boy answered, and Wolf recognized the voice as belonging to one of the peasant children whose job it was to bring down buckets of food and water as well as empty pails in which he and the other prisoners were supposed to relieve themselves. Stanley was younger, with a pockmarked face and a stutter that was so difficult to understand, he rarely tried to speak.

" 'Tis late ye be," the guard said with a yawn. There was an edge of suspicion to his voice.

"Aye," Ronald replied. "Cook fergot to give us these buckets of slop earlier."

"Could not it have waited 'til morn?" The guard was on his feet to greet the boys. A nervous man, he'd been watching Wolf most of the night, as if he expected some plot to set him free. The sentry was a big man and one who had sworn to Holt that there would be no attempts at escape under his watch. Too many times lately had a prisoner tried to flee. To strengthen his words, he was heavily armed with two daggers and a sword lying unsheathed upon his table.

"Ye'd have thought morning would be soon enough," Ronald agreed around a yawn as he and his friend set the heavy pails on the guard's small table. "But ye know Cook. 'Waste not, want not,' 'e's always preachin'. Worse than Father Tim, he is."

The guard chuckled. "Right ye are about that, boy." He motioned toward the cells. "Come, we'll feed the animals, then we both can get some sleep."

Wolf felt something in the air, a breath of breeze laden with a familiar scent, and his heart jolted as the boy Stanley turned and faced him. Amber eyes held his for an instant and his throat was suddenly tight with fear. Megan! What was she doing here? She'd only get herself killed! Frantic, he shook his head quickly, trying to discourage her. Whatever she had planned, she should not be risking her life or that of their child.

" 'Ere we go," the guard said, starting with Jack's cell. "Come, huntsman, for some of the leftovers." Keys jangled loudly, rattling Wolf's nerves. The rusted cell door squeaked open on old hinges. Wolf's heart thudded as slop was poured into a bucket on the floor. Did the others not know? Were they not ready to ambush the guard?

Wolf had never been a man of strong faith, but now he prayed to God and watched as the small trio moved to the next cell. *Robin's* cage. Holy Christ, the boy would surely recognize her and blurt her name, and everything would be lost. Sweat ran down Wolf's arms as he saw Robin meet the silent boy's eyes and his mouth drop open, but before the guard noticed, he fell into a squatting position next to the pail, staring at its unappetizing contents as if starving. To the next cell, Tom's, the guard and his helpers moved, and now Wolf could see her plainly, a few wayward strands of mahogany hair poking from her cowl, her small upturned nose. How much she appeared as she had at the camp when he'd tried to disguise her female curves from his men. His throat went dry and love beat wildly in his heart.

Wolf's mind screamed for her to be careful, to forget her plan, whatever it was, that 'twas not worth risking her life for his, but he held his tongue and as the cell door swung open, he was on the balls of his feet, every muscle in his body strung tight. As "Stanley" poured the slop into his pail, the guard watched him. "Be careful," he said. "This one—Wolf, they call him—is truly a beast and would gladly rip out both yer throats, but he's calmer now, in pain from the beatings he's been given."

"Is that so?" Ronald asked, and Megan, in her disguise, feigned tripping over the pail, sending slop everywhere.

"Oh, son, look at the mess ye've made! Bloody Christ!" the guard reprimanded.

Reacting by instinct, Wolf caught her and felt her body close. She clutched his hand but for an instant, leaving a small knife in his fingers.

"Come on, ever'body out!" the guard ordered. "Wolf, 'e won't get to taste any of Cook's fine—"

Wolf leaped onto the man's back.

"Hey! Stop!" He whirled and Megan, grabbing a bucket

from the floor, slammed it against the guard's big head as Wolf plunged the knife into the man's shoulder. They fell against the cell walls, rattling the bars, the guard starting to yell.

"Say a word and I'll slit your throat!" Wolf promised, his blade at the sentry's thick Adam's apple as he still rode the burly man's back.

"He—"

The blade pressed closer and blood oozed. The sentry's voice suddenly failed him.

"That's better," Wolf said as Megan lifted the man's keys from his belt.

Within seconds, the guard was bound and locked in Wolf's cell, the other prisoners released. The weapons—two buckets, two knives, and a sword—were distributed as they headed for the stairs. "This was foolish," Wolf reprimanded her in a low whisper.

"I could not let you die."

God, how he loved her! "So you risked your neck and that of our babe?"

"How—how did you know?" she asked, and a small smile tugged at the corners of his mouth. Was she not the most beautiful woman in the king's lands?

He glanced at her abdomen covered in tattered clothes and placed his hand over her flat stomach. "Cadell—the magician—he told me."

Her fingers folded over his and he melted inside. "The sorcerer is Lady Morgana's lost brother?" she asked in wonder.

"Aye, but let us not tarry. I will tell you everything once I have killed Holt and we have fled Dwyrain." Reluctantly, he turned to the task at hand. They were not yet free of the walls of the dungeon.

"Do not worry about Holt," Megan said, and then crossed herself in the dim, flickering light. "He's dead."

"Dead?" Holt hardly dared believe his good luck.

"Aye," she said and he felt her shake. Her golden gaze was troubled, her chin jutted out defiantly.

"*You* killed him?"

" 'Twas either that or share his bed."

Wolf's heart warmed for this woman. He held her close for a second, then brushed his lips over hers. " 'Twould have been all right," he said, reassuring her. "Nothing is worth your life."

She shook her head vigorously. "Nay, I could never—"

"Let's go!" Jack growled.

Jagger, carrying a knife in one big hand, agreed. "Aye, there's time for talk later. Now listen, Robin, Jack, and me—we'll take care of the guards in the gatehouse. You, Wolf, and Megan and Tom, get the horses from the stables. We'll open the gates as soon as we see you with the beasts."

Wolf nodded. 'Twas as good as any plan they could conjure without more time. "We'll meet in the shadow of this very tower."

Without another word, they hastened up the stairs. At the door, Wolf motioned for everyone to wait. He stepped into the moon-washed bailey first, the guard's sword at ready. As his foot touched the ground outside, he whirled lithely, but no one accosted him, and aside for a few sentries positioned as they ever were in the watchtowers, the castle was quiet.

Was it possible? Could Holt be dead, slain by his wife, and no one in the keep be aware of his death? His heart leapt at the thought, for finally he and Megan could be together—as man and wife. If she were widowed, he could surely ask for her hand. Though she had killed Holt, Wolf was certain Megan would be acquitted of any crime and he . . . he would give up living as a criminal in the forest, if only she would be at his side.

He motioned to Jagger and the prisoners split into two groups. Jagger, Jack, and Robin, pressed close to the stones of the bailey wall, hid in the shadows as they hurried toward the gatehouse. Megan, Tom, and Wolf crept into the stables and, sliding through the half-open door, spoke softly to the animals as they chose six swift horses.

Despite their caution, several nervous stallions whinnied noisily. "Damn it all to hell," Wolf muttered under his breath.

A bleary-eyed stableboy opened the door. Wolf set upon him, his sword at the lad's throat. "You'll say nothing," Wolf commanded in an authoritative whisper.

"Nay, nay, nothing!" The boy gulped. "Wolf, is it?" Even in the partial darkness, Wolf noticed the youth's face lit in admiration. "Can I come with ye? I've fancied meself an outlaw for a long time now."

" 'Tis not as glorious as you may think," Wolf said, hoping to discourage the lad. How many boys had he met like this one who thought living the life of a criminal and outrunning the law was a grand adventure? Had he not thought the very same?

His attempts to dissuade the boy were in vain.

"I'd be a good thief," the lad insisted.

"We must be off," Tom said, but the stableboy wasn't finished.

"Ian's me name, and I've stolen from the baker and armorer and poached in the baron's woods and not been caught," he boasted.

Foolish youth! Wolf remembered the guard who had complained of his son getting into trouble. 'Twould be better if he left the boy here, but he had no time to argue. "I wouldn't be bragging of your crimes," he reprimanded. "Now, hush. Come with us if ye will, but understand that if ye be caught, ye'll hang."

"I won't be," he said with the confidence of youth.

"Then keep these beasts quiet and come along!"

They led the horses from the stables, and with Ian along, the horses quieted and were less nervous. Wolf's heart was drumming, his nerves stretched tighter than a dying man on the rack, dread inching up his spine. Surely their escape wouldn't come so easily. Everyone in the castle had suffered Holt's wrath when Cayley and Bjorn had stolen their freedom, and certainly the guards would be doubly vigilant, on the lookout for another attempted break from the dungeons, rather than feel the sting of Holt's anger.

The wind was chill and moist, promising rain, though no clouds blocked the moon, the castle silent except for their muffled tread. Their breath fogged in the night. Freedom was so close . . .

Silently they approached the gate, but the portcullis hadn't been lifted.

Wolf sensed trouble. There had been more than ample time to winch up the iron gate. Holding Megan's small hand in one of his, he silently prayed. The fingers of his other hand tightened around the hilt of his sword. Something was wrong. Looking upward, he scoured the battlements and towers, but nothing appeared amiss.

Come on, come on! Jagger and Jack were strong men; winching up the gate would be no trouble.

Unless they'd been caught.

Unless even now they'd been taken prisoner again.

Dread thudded through his brain.

“Well, well, well.” Holt’s voice, deep and foreboding, rang through the bailey.

For the love of God, no! Whirling, sword ready to cleave anyone who should try to thwart him, Wolf found his old nemesis, not dead as Megan had vowed, but very much alive and standing proudly upon the gallows as he glared pointedly at Wolf and Megan. His voice was deadly as he said to the sleeping castle at large, “If it isn’t my murdering wife and her outlaw of a lover trying to flee!”

Sixteen

"Now, Wolf, outlaw of the forest, you die," Holt announced with some difficulty, and Megan's heart turned to stone. They were doomed, and the glint in her husband's eyes warned her that he would extract his revenge upon each and every one of them. Absently, she touched her abdomen, to the low spot where her baby was growing—so innocent, so perfect. She could not endanger this fragile life.

"Let's kill him," Tom muttered under his breath.

"Aye," Ian said.

Wolf shook his head. "Not yet."

'Twas idle hopes. Lurking in the shadows were soldiers who had been hiding in the towers, behind the hayricks, under carts. They came forward with bows strung tight and arrows aimed at Wolf's heart. *Oh, love,* Megan silently cried, and her mouth was suddenly dry with fear.

The horses, sensing danger, fidgeted, pulling tight on their reins, whinnying and snorting, but Wolf held them firmly.

Holt was not finished. Swaying slightly, standing as if

with great effort, he said, "Before I send you to hell where you belong, you pathetic outlaw"—he ran a hand over the fresh wood of a support beam of the gallows—"you'll watch each of your men die, one by one. Now!" He snapped his fingers and grimaced in the pale moonlight.

Megan shivered, not from the cold of the wind that blew past the thick stone walls, but from the despair gathering in her heart, the fear that she'd never see her beloved Wolf again. "Please be with him," she murmured to a fierce God who, she sensed, had abandoned her this night. "Save him and my child."

Sentries in the watchtower opened the door of the gatehouse and pushed their captives into the bailey. Jack, Jagger, and young Robin shuffled forward, their eyes blindfolded, their mouths gagged, their hands tied in front of them.

Megan's legs threatened to give way, and had it not been for Wolf's strong arm supporting her, she would have swooned on the frozen grass of the bailey.

"For the love of Jesus, what's going on here?" Like a mother hawk swooping from the heavens to save her chicks, Father Timothy, robes askew and billowing behind him, ran barefoot across the bailey. He blinked rapidly, as if fighting to maintain his courage as he shoved his way through the armed men. "Lord Holt, I beg of you, do not shed any more blood!"

"And why not?" Holt demanded, his jaw tight, his skin pale as death. "These men and my own dear wife are traitors of Dwyrain." A dark bruise and bloody cut discolored the skin above his eye, yet the wounds Megan had inflicted hadn't been mortal, and though he was not as strong as he had been, he appeared to be able to survive. "The outlaw turned my bride against me."

"Nay, Holt, you did that yourself," Megan said boldly, finding her courage and pushing off Wolf's restraining arm to step forward to face the man she'd thought she'd killed. All the pain and suffering was her doing, and she would willingly sacrifice herself if only Wolf and his men were allowed their freedom.

"Stop!" Wolf shifted quickly, dropping the horse's reins and throwing himself between her and the soldiers' arrows. "Do not be foolish," he said under his breath, but Holt heard the command and laughed.

"Isn't that touching? The outlaw and his would-be murderess of a lover! Who would have thought that there was such devotion between criminals?"

" 'Tis not God's will that innocent people die!" Timothy proclaimed, his lower lip trembling nervously.

"Innocent?" Holt said with a lusty laugh as he slowly climbed down from the raised floor of the gallows. Grimacing in pain, he repeated, "Innocent? Did ye not hear that my lady tried to kill me, first with my own knife and then with a piece of kindling? Believe me, priest, no one here is innocent this night."

His stride faltered a bit as he strode across the trampled grass. His steps were not firm, and he was still pale as death. A crusted bruise was beginning to show over his temple, where a vein throbbed in anger. "You!" he said, his voice echoing through the castle and in Megan's heart. His eyebrows slammed together and his lips were bloodless and flat against his teeth, his eyes hot coals as they found hers in the night. "You, wife, come with me. We have unfinished business."

"If you want her, then you must kill me first," Wolf invited, his voice smooth as glass.

Megan's heart sank. "Nay!"

"Gladly." Holt's grin was pure and intense evil as he unsheathed his sword. "Why wait?"

"No!" Frantic, Megan tore herself from Wolf's possessive grasp. "Nay, do not kill him," she cried, the ugly thought too horrid to bear. "I'll go with you. Willingly." Tears filled her eyes, and despite the knowledge that she was inviting her own doom, she turned to Wolf and stared into his blue eyes one last time, searing their image into her mind for all eternity. She felt a deep rending in her soul and she fought the urge to break down. Tears streaming from her eyes, her fear suddenly abated, and she sniffed, lifting her chin and refusing to weep any more. In a choked voice, she vowed, "I will love you forever, Wolf."

A muscle worked in Wolf's jaw. His fingers clenched until his knuckles showed white over the handle of his sword. "As I love you, Megan," he said, his voice deep with conviction. "Until the day I die."

"Which will be soon," Holt announced. "Spare me the pitiful scene."

Megan's heart caught. She heard not Holt's scorn, only that Wolf had said that he loved her. She would carry that sweet drop of heaven with her to the grave.

With a howl, the brutal wind swept through the bailey, moaning eerily, as if God himself were watching Dwyrain and voicing his disapproval. A cloud crept over the moon as Holt stalked up to the outlaw.

Wolf's eyes narrowed savagely on his enemy. Fearless, he ground out, "Harm her, and I swear that I or my very ghost will hunt you down like the filthy cur you are, find you wherever you cower, and rip out your throat."

"Bastard!" Holt's fist crashed into the side of Wolf's face.

Pain exploded behind Wolf's eyes and Holt nearly stumbled with the effort. "Take him away," he snarled at his men. "Haul his pathetic hide and the rest of the traitors to the dungeons. I want a dozen of you to stand guard. There will be no escape! Not this time. Do you hear me?"

When no one answered, he clenched his fist. "Do you?"

"Aye, m'lord," a fat knight agreed anxiously, his Adam's apple bobbing in fear.

"They'll be hanged at dawn, and everyone in the castle, every man, woman, and child, from the oldest crone to the newborn babes, will witness how I deal with those who betray Dwyrain and deceive me." Yanking her roughly, he pulled Megan toward the great hall, and though he had lost blood, he was strong, his grip punishing, his strides long.

"Lord Holt, wait!" a sentry in the watchtower shouted, his voice ringing over the commotion that erupted as the doors of several huts began to swing open. Men and women, bleary-eyed and confused, filtered into the bailey.

Holt stopped dead in his tracks and turned, his head uplifted in harsh fury. "What?"

"There are men outside the gates," the sentry yelled.

"Who?"

Megan had to fight a glimmer of hope.

"I know not." Cupping his hands around his mouth, the sentry yelled down to those on the outside of the portal, "Who goes there?"

"Damn it, man," Holt thundered. "I care not if it's the bloody king! Can't you see I'm with my wife?! Leave them be 'til morning!" Strong despite his wounds, he headed for the keep and hauled Megan with him.

"M'lord!" Again, the priest tried to intervene. "Please,

Holt, listen to me. As God is my witness, you must not kill these men, nor harm this woman."

"As God is my witness, you and your false sense of piety bore me, Timothy. You are a traitor." His eyes swept the crowd that was beginning to gather and gape. "Yes, the good priest has betrayed me," he said to his subjects, "as many of you have, and I will not—will never—allow any kind of insubordination." He snapped his fingers.

Hiss! Thwack!

The priest screamed in pain as an arrow pierced him from behind.

Megan gasped in horror.

"Oh, Jesus, Lord, forgive me of my sins!" Timothy fell forward, first to his knees and finally onto his face.

Someone in the crowd screamed. A horse reared and lashed out with its hooves and Holt sneered at the blood staining the priest's robes. "Now I suppose he can speak with God more easily."

"You brute!" Reeling away from him, Megan dove toward the fallen man. "Father Timothy, oh, Timothy—" she said, cradling his head. "Call for the physician or Rue!"

"Leave him be!" Holt commanded as the doctor pushed through the crowd. Reaching down, he jerked Megan to her feet. "Weep not for the priest."

Wolf lunged, but was restrained, and Holt laughed at his futile efforts while Megan again fought tears and fury that such horrors had happened in her beloved Dwyrain.

Groaning, the priest lifted his head and began chanting prayers. Blood spread over his robes, and the bottoms of his bare feet turned upward, showing calluses and corns in the shimmering moonlight. "Make an example of him as well," Holt ordered. "When he's bled to death, gut him and mount his head over the south tower."

"Father, take me now," Timothy prayed.

"Nay!" Megan ordered, whirling on Holt. "You are a fiend!" To the soldiers, she commanded, "I'm mistress of this castle, and I say you let the prisoners go free and see that Father Timothy is seen by the doctor and—"

Slap! Holt's hand connected with her face, sending her spinning. Pain blinded her. Blood slipped from her lip. She started to fall, but Holt caught her before she hit the ground and in one swift motion, hauled her over his shoulder.

The earth swayed and heaved and she caught a glimpse of Wolf, lunging forward, trying to reach her, screaming something she couldn't hear as she pounded on Holt's back and kicked. His laugh was brittle as a leaf in January, and several burly soldiers restrained Wolf.

"You'll find out what happens when a woman defies me," Holt promised, limping and swearing as he carried her up the stairs to the keep. She pounded on his back and kicked wildly, hoping to land one of her blows in his wound, but he shifted his weight so that she could not draw any more blood.

"Bastard! Fiend! Dirty son of a—"

"If you do not want to see your traitor of a lover killed right now, you'll stop!" Holt growled, and she quit moving in an instant. She bit her tongue in her efforts not to scream at him, but she knew she would never accept her fate.

Desperation clawing at his soul, Wolf watched in silent agony as the woman he loved was torn from him and hauled up the stairs of the keep to be raped by the man she'd wed. Rage thundered through his blood, pounding in his brain, nearly blinding him.

Holt's soldiers dragged him roughly toward the prison, but as Holt's hand connected with Megan's cheek, Wolf roared in fury. Pivoting sharply and snarling, he flung off the men restraining him as if they were stuffed with down.

"Hey, what the bloody hell—"

Wolf snatched an arrow from a guard's quiver, then rammed the deadly tip deep into the man's neck. As the soldier squealed and bled, Wolf snatched his sword and began swinging.

Jagger, though blindfolded, heard the sounds of battle and threw his considerable weight at his guard. He sent the man reeling, tore off his blindfold, and with his wrists bound, leaped upon his captor, snapped his neck in his powerful hands, and grabbed the guard's sword. "Now, men!" he yelled.

Jack and Robin tore off their blindfolds. Tom kicked a guard in the shin and Ian reached to the ground, found rocks, and hurled them at a horse's haunches. A destrier neighed in fear and tore through the crowd. Other beasts followed, scattering soldiers and peasants.

"Bloody hell!" one soldier exclaimed.

"Don't shoot. They be the baron's best stallions!"

"For the love of Christ!"

"Watch out—" another guard shouted as he reached for the reins and was knocked to the ground. Screaming in tortured agony, he was trampled by heavy, frightened hooves.

Still swinging the sword wildly, Wolf yelled to the soldiers attacking him, "Those who swore your fealty to Baron Ewan, rise against Holt and his army, for 'twas he who killed the baron and his son!"

Tom ran for the gates as Foster yelled, " 'Tis true! I heard Sir Holt bragging after he drank too much wine!" Several other voices took up the battle cry and joined forces with Wolf. Swords crashed. Arrows zinged. Wolf ducked and saw an attacker running at him, crossbow aimed at his heart. Throwing himself to the ground, he rolled, and before the man could realign his weapon, Wolf's sword sliced his legs. Tumbling to the ground, the guard writhed in agony. Wolf tossed the loaded bow to Ian.

Tom, swinging a mace he'd grabbed from a fallen guard, inched his way backward toward the wall and finally disappeared into the gatehouse. Soldiers fought their own. Peasants found weapons and joined the battle. Blood stained the grass of Dwyrain.

Wolf swung his stolen sword, slicing anyone who came too close as he made his way across the bailey to the keep, to Megan.

With a loud grinding of gears, the portcullis opened, spilling a small army of men into the bailey. Swords unsheathed, they entered with a piercing battle cry and the thunder of hooves. Swords clattered and clashed and horses screamed. Some of the new arrivals were dressed as soldiers bearing the colors of Erbyn, while the rest were those loyal to no baron, members of Wolf's bloody band of thieves. Odell and Cadell rode side by side, but Wolf's heart stilled when he thought he spied another man, one afoot, creep through the open gate.

Connor, whom he'd heard a prison guard say had not returned after escorting Cadell away from the castle walls, was within the keep again.

Hagan's voice rang through the bailey. "Put down your weapons or make ready to die!"

"You die!" a man loyal to Holt said, only to be cleaved by Robin's piercing sword.

Arrows hissed through the air, and Wolf, running

swiftly, turned his thoughts to Megan and the man who was defiling her as he dashed up the stone steps of the great hall.

He was met by peasants and servants racing from the keep, awakened and drawn into the bailey by the sounds of battle. Throwing on clothes, grabbing torches, pokers, swords, and knives, they hurried to defend Dwyrain as Wolf slunk through the dark hallways, as he had once before when he'd started his quest to kidnap Megan, the very journey that had sealed her doom.

Continuing ever upward, running along hallways, opening doors, his eyes scanning each chamber as his heart thudded in fear of what he might find, Wolf stole through the castle, his sword drawn, his mind and body relentless in his search for the lord's chamber and the woman he loved.

Megan swallowed hard against her fear and inched her chin up a notch as she leveled her gaze on Holt.

"You lied to me, wife," he said, circling her as she stood at the foot of the bed. The window was open and the sounds of clanging metal, screaming voices, shouts, and frightened cries of horses seeped into the room. *Wolf, oh, love, please be safe. Take Robin and flee for your life!*

Holt's nostrils flared and he fingered the hilt of his sword as he pointed the deadly blade at her face. "You bartered for the lives of those loyal to Wolf, then you went against your own word." So many memories she had of this, her father and mother's chamber, so many happy thoughts, now destroyed. "You tried to kill me, Megan." Clucking his tongue, he shook his head. He was pale, the wound in his side leaking through his tunic, his head bruised, but he was strong enough to frighten her. "I could have forgiven you, except for the fact that you gave your heart to a vile forest creature and then stabbed me, hoping for my death." His eyebrows lifted in accusation. " 'Twas a mistake, I'm afraid. There was a time when I wanted you to reign beside me, to be mistress of my manor, to bear my sons. Now, I only want to force you onto the bed and mount you, then let you whore for my soldiers before I cut out your traitorous heart."

Her mouth turned dry with fear, her insides cold as the death that would surely be hers, but she squared her shoulders and glared at him. She'd not die without a fight. As long as she was alive and there was a breath of life in her body, she would fight this heathen murderer.

"Strip," he ordered, but his attention was averted as he heard the rattle of chains, grind of gears, and a thunderous battle cry scream through the window. "Oh, for the love of Christ, what now?"

"Could it be that your men have turned against you?" she taunted, and he whirled on her again.

"Take off your damned clothes, woman!"

She didn't move. Defiantly, she stood.

"Did you not hear me?" His mouth was tight against his teeth, his eyes blazed with fury.

Without a sound, she disobeyed, and a vein in his temple began to throb.

"Foolish woman! You have no power over what I do. You will do as I say or I will call for the boy Robin to be brought here. I could start by cutting off his fingers one by one, or his toes, and you could hear him cry in pain and beg for mercy while he bled on the rushes. Or if that be too unpleasant, you could take off your bloody clothes for me *now!*"

Trapped like a cornered dog, she had no choice but to

follow his commands. *Dear God, be with Wolf and the rest of his men. Save them.* Closing her eyes, Megan reached for the ties of her mantle. *Pretend it isn't happening,* she told herself. *'Tis only your body. He will never lay claim to your heart.* She lifted her mantle over her head.

She stopped, and his eyes flashed in the dark room. "Keep going," he said, his voice uneven. Though she didn't want to notice, 'twas impossible not to see the swelling in his breeches as his cock rose in anticipation. Revulsion filled her throat as she untied the ribbons of her tunic and tossed it off. Standing only in her chemise, she shivered.

He motioned with the sword again. "Your underclothes as well, m'lady. Christ, you are beautiful," he said almost in reverent awe as she lowered her chemise and stood proudly before him. Refusing to cover her breasts or the thatch of curls guarding her legs, she waited. "Come forward," he ordered, and 'twas all she could do not to leap at him and try to scratch out his eyes, but 'twould be futile and others would suffer.

Stopping short of him, she didn't move when he set the long blade of his weapon between her breasts. "Now, m'lady," he said, breathing in short, shallow gasps. "Kneel before me as you would your king." When she hesitated, he growled, "I'll bring up the boy," and slowly she fell to her knees. "Unlace my breeches."

Oh, God, no, she silently prayed.

"Do it now, Megan," he said, his voice rough, the pointed end of his tongue rimming his lips, "and do it slowly."

"Sweet Jesus, you cannot ask me to."

"Guard!" he yelled. "Send for the boy—"

"Do not!"

"Then unleash my cock, whore, or see the boy suffer, and if that is not enough to convince you, I'll bring your precious Wolf up here so that he can watch me bed you."

"Nay—"

"And each of my most trusted men will stand in line, waiting and watching for their turn to lay you any way they so wish, and you will service them while the outlaw looks on."

I'll die first, she thought, and decided that she had no choice but to do as she was bid, for though she would go willingly to the gates of hell rather than suffer the humiliation and degradation that Holt conjured, she could not take her child's life. *Be strong, Megan.*

As she reached upward and touched the leather of Holt's breeches, she caught a glimpse of movement from the corner of her eye. She dared not look too closely and pretended interest in the task at hand. Holt closed his eyes and groaned in ecstasy.

The door inched open and Wolf, blood running from a cut in his forehead, rushed into the room. "Run!" he yelled at Megan.

Holt's body jerked. His eyes flew open. Megan ran to the door, and Holt, seeing his enemy's reflection in the blade of his weapon, hoisted his sword high as he swung it round, facing the door. He slashed the air with his weapon, his eyes centered on Wolf. "Die, you bloody bastard!"

"Only if I take you with me!" Wolf said as he swung a bloodied sword at the new baron, twisting from the blows of Holt's weapon. Too late. The sharp blade sliced into Wolf's arm. Blood sprayed the chamber. Megan screamed, and with her horrified eyes trained on the two men reeling, parrying, lunging, and swearing, she stepped away, closer to the fire, searching for something, *anything,* to use as a weapon.

"This is for Mary, the fisherman's daughter!" Wolf cried

as he jammed his sword into Holt's thigh. Holt roared in pain, but struck with his sword, slicing through Wolf's tunic.

"Tadd raped her."

"Aye, but you held her down, did you not?"

Oh, God, they were both going to die! She found a stick used to tend the fire and lifted it, only to have the slender wood cleaved by Holt's sword and her feet knocked out from under her. "You, too, will see the end of this earth," he promised her, spinning to meet Wolf's thrust. Desperate and mindless of the fear, Megan held on to the short end of her stick, and on her knees, stretched upward, plunging the cleaved stake into the wound at Holt's side, the wound she'd inflicted earlier. Holt bellowed like a wounded bull.

"Jezebel!" he roared, but fighting the pain, swiped his weapon at Wolf. Swords clanged, bodies fell against her. Megan, struggling to her feet, lost her balance and fell. The room spun, rush lights glittering wildly. Wolf and Holt locked swords as the rush-strewn floor came up to meet her.

"Megan!" Wolf cried.

Her head slammed into the stones and her body crumpled. The room temporarily went black as she felt a sharp, hard pain deep inside, a tearing, but she bit down against the agony and tried to save Wolf.

"Stay back!" Wolf commanded. He swung fiercely, cutting Holt on the ear.

With fire in his eyes, Holt rushed forward.

Wolf grinned with vengeance and held his sword aloft. "Now, you die, bastard!"

Men rushed into the room and Megan thought that they were Holt's men until she recognized the sorcerer, Robin, and Hagan of Erbyn. Her heart soared for an instant.

" 'Tis over!" Hagan ordered.

"This is still my castle!" Desperate, Holt grabbed Megan, one arm locked around her waist, the other holding his sword outstretched as he used her naked body as his shield. "Leave me be, or she dies!" he screamed.

She kicked him hard in the shins, her heels screaming with pain, but he didn't let go, and to Megan's horror, Connor stepped into the room, a crossbow in his hands. "Everyone step away!" he ordered in a voice as cold as the depths of a bottomless well.

"Thank the saints!" Holt said, his legs unsteady. He shoved Megan aside and approached his knight. His smile faltered as the flat-eyed man watched him. "It's been days since you took the prisoner and . . ." His gaze wandered to the sorcerer and his words stuck in his throat for a second. "Where have you been, Connor?"

"To hell and back." The soldier's eyes narrowed and he let the bolt of his weapon fly as Wolf reacted, hurling his sword at his enemy, the blade driving deep through the muscles of Holt's chest to pierce his dark heart. The crossbow bolt gored Holt in his gut. "This is for lying to me about Cayley, you pig. I know you intended not to give her to me."

"Bloody God, no!" Holt cried out, falling to his knees as he stared blindly at the man who had defied him, and fell into a useless heap, where he surrendered his last rattling breath.

Megan held a fur coverlet she'd snagged from the bed over her body, but she couldn't move. Determined to stand, she closed her eyes, tried to rise, but was suddenly weak. Deep within she felt a rending, and her head spun. She blinked hard.

"Get that mess out of here," Hagan ordered.

" 'Tis over," Wolf said, gathering Megan into his arms. He

was warm and strong and . . . another sharp pain gored her. She bit down on her lip and couldn't stop the tears in her eyes, for Wolf was safe, she was alive, and . . . and . . . oh, dear God, no . . . the baby!

Wolf buried his face in the crook of her neck. "Love, oh, sweet, sweet love," he said, blinking against tears as he lifted her into his arms and carried her down the hallway. He kissed her head, her throat, her eyes, but she couldn't move, couldn't speak, because she knew as he laid her on the bed in her chamber that she was losing his baby. Silent agony tore through her, blinding her, extinguishing the light in her soul.

"Megan?" His voice came as if from a distance. "Megan."

" 'Tis gone," she said and felt the rush of blood between her legs. "Wolf, please listen . . . the babe . . ." Deep racking sobs rose from her lungs, and then he understood.

" 'Tis all right, rest," he said, lying beside her, refusing to let her go. He pulled the blankets over her and held her close, whispering into her hair. Outside, the sounds of battle quieted, but deep in her heart, Megan felt a pain more desperate than ever before. "I will be with you forever," he vowed, but she hadn't the strength to believe him. As she closed her eyes and drifted into sleep, she knew that she'd lost their child, their precious babe, and even Wolf's love couldn't fill that gaping hole in her heart.

The sorcerer came later.

Wolf stood at the window of her chamber, and while Megan lay half in and half out of consciousness, Cadell laid his hands upon her and shook his head. " 'Twill be difficult, friend, for the babe's life has barely started and is slipping away."

"I know, I know. Damn it, would you try?" Wolf muttered through a jaw clenched so tight it ached. The wounds he'd sustained while battling Holt were nothing compared to the agony ripping through his soul. 'Twas as if the Devil himself were chasing through his heart, laughing at him, mocking him, for 'twas he who'd brought this pain to his beloved Megan, he who got her with child, he who inadvertently, while slaying Holt, had nearly killed his own unborn babe.

"Leave us," Cadell ordered, and the candles near the bedside flickered as the great owl who was the sorcerer's companion landed in the window and stared inside.

Reluctantly, Wolf walked through the corridors of Dwyrain, past chambers where the wounded were being tended, through the kitchen, where Cook was attempting to start the morning's meal, and outside to the bailey, where bodies were being hauled through the gates to the graveyard.

"So there ye be, ye black-hearted cur," Odell growled as, bartering with the armorer, he spied Wolf.

"What now, Odell?"

The grizzled outlaw picked his way over the spilled blood to stand below Wolf on the steps. "Ye sent Cormick to his death and nearly took Robin and Jagger as well."

"Aye." Guilt would forever be Wolf's companion. In the distance, the sun was just beginning to rise, sending pale rays through the mist that clung to the cold ground. " 'Twas my mistake."

"All for a woman," Odell reminded him, and spat upon the ground.

"For the woman that will be my wife."

"We have rules—"

"Should they not be bent for Megan?" Wolf growled, reaching for the front of his old friend's tunic and clenching the rough fabric in his fingers. " 'Tis sorry I am about Cormick. Could I, I would trade places with him, but it cannot be."

Odell's mouth opened and closed and Wolf, realizing that he was close to strangling the man, let him go. "I'm giving up the band," he said as Holt's standard was lowered from the flagpole and the old colors of Dwyrain flew once again, for now Megan was truly mistress of this keep.

"Leave us?" Odell paled. "But—who will lead us?"

A cold smile played upon Wolf's lips as he watched Bjorn order the men about, telling the soldiers what to do with the wounded and commanding the carpenter to tear down the rigging for the gallows. "Bjorn will be your leader," he said, and strode down the steps to meet his friend.

"He's not happy with you. He was almost killed as well," Odell said, rotating his neck like a chicken eyeing a fat bug and rubbing his throat.

"Aye, Odell, I know. You needs not screech at me like a fishwife, now do you?"

Bjorn dusted his hands as the last of the dead were carted from the castle. "Wolf," he said, his eyes showing no trace of emotion. "We needs speak." His gaze moved pointedly to Odell, but the grizzled old outlaw didn't budge.

"I'm not movin', if that's what ye're askin'."

"I'm leaving the band," Wolf announced. "And I want you to be its leader."

Bjorn rubbed his jaw. " 'Tis your group of thugs."

"Aye, but they need a new leader."

"Why?"

" 'Tis time." Wolf sighed. "What say you?"

A corner of Bjorn's mouth lifted. "I know not if 'tis an honor to be the leader of so foulmouthed and ill-tempered a group."

"Well, I'll be jiggered. If ye won't be the new—"

"I'll do it," Bjorn said.

" 'Tis thanks I owe you," Wolf said, glancing to the window of Megan's room, where the owl was perched and blinking against the winter rays of the sun. "You saved my life and that of those in the castle."

Bjorn shook his head. "As ye saved mine years ago."

The two men clasped hands and Odell spat in disgust as the men Wolf had been close to—Heath, Peter, Robin, Jack, and the lot—came to shake his hand, forgiving him for the death of Cormick.

"The lady," Robin asked, his cheeks reddening a bit. "How is she?"

The pain in Wolf's heart was great, but he said, "She'll be fine, Robin lad. She'll be fine."

He only hoped it wasn't a lie.

Hagan's troops left on the third day and Cayley, sitting in for the absent baroness, was in charge. She was young and pretty, but stronger than Wolf had ever thought possible, helping tend to the sick and wounded while dealing with the squabbles of some of the peasants and ensuring that the castle kept running.

The only time Wolf wondered about her strength was when she said goodbye to his band of thugs, for she appeared to be fighting for self-control, and as Bjorn and his ragged group filed through the gatehouse, she bit her lips and dashed aside tears that had formed in the corners of her eyes.

Elsewise, she was an able and caring leader. She spent hours with Megan, sitting with her, praying for her, and ordering the servants to care for her.

Cadell had done what he could, and Megan, bedridden,

was still with child. But the days stretched long and she was tired, her face pale, worry shining in her beautiful ale-colored eyes. Wolf didn't leave her side. While Rue and Cayley tended to her, he'd turn his back and stand at the window, but as she regained her strength, he stayed with her. 'Twas as if he was afraid she might slip away again.

'Twas nearly a week before she seemed alive again. There was color in her cheeks for the first time since the battle, and she smiled at him.

"The baby?" she asked, biting her lip.

"Cadell and Rue did everything they could," he said, frowning, "but you lost a lot of blood."

"Oh," she murmured, the pain in her heart inconsolable.

"But the flow—it stopped on the second day—and if you can keep yourself in bed, there's still hope." But she saw the doubt in his eyes. He was trying to give her hope when there was none. *Oh, sweet, sweet baby,* she silently cried, but pushed the painful thought aside.

"Tell me . . . Holt?"

"Is dead."

That much she vaguely remembered, though the days were lost to her and one was like any other. She knew not how much time had passed, nor did she care. "Many of his men were slain as well, and Cayley has not punished their wives or children, but kept them here."

"Is she a wise ruler?"

"Very." Wolf sat on the corner of her bed and held her hand. "Connor is in prison and Father Timothy is staving off death, though 'tis a miracle."

As he talked, Megan tried to shake off the shroud of guilt that had been her cloak ever since feeling her unborn baby's precious life begin to slip away. She'd dreamed of the child, as she had of Bevan, sweet little Roz, her father and mother.

"Cadell has returned to the forest, though he will visit, and Jovan the apothecary is in the dungeon, for 'twas he who gave Holt the poison that killed your father."

"So much treachery," she said and closed her eyes. Wolf placed his arms around her and held her fast against him.

A week passed before she had the strength to rise and walk on shaky legs to the window. The cold breath of winter touched her face as she looked into the bailey and saw that the hated gallows had been destroyed, the timbers broken apart, to be used for firewood.

Wolf had been dozing in a chair he'd brought in. Though he'd held her often during the day, at night he'd refused to lie in her bed, insisting that she needed her rest and knowing that her body and mind needed time to heal. He roused and smiled as he saw her on her feet.

"The lady arises, eh?" he asked, stretching in the chair.

"Aye."

"And how're you feeling, Mistress of Dwyrain?"

"Better."

His blue eyes gleamed and a shock of black hair fell fetchingly over his forehead. "Well enough for a wedding?"

"A wedding?" she repeated. "But whose—?"

"Our wedding, love," he said, standing and circling her small waist in his arms. "The priest, he swears he's able to perform the ceremony. All we need is a willing bride."

"Father Timothy is still recovering."

"Aye, but Hagan rode to the abbey and located another man—Brother Something-or-Other—to help Timothy. He's ready."

"Are you?" she asked, touching his rough cheek with her fingertips.

His smile was warm, his eyes sincere. "I've been waiting for you all of my life, Megan," he said, his lips brushing lightly over hers.

"But your life as a—"

"What? A criminal? An outlaw?" He let out a soft little chuckle. " 'Tis over. Bjorn is the leader now."

"So you're ready to settle down here?"

"At Dwyrain?" He shook his head. "Nay, m'lady, I think we need a new start, and long ago my brother promised me a small portion of land with its own keep. 'Tis time to take him up on his offer. If you'll agree to be my wife."

Her heart was suddenly full and she pressed a soft little kiss to his lips. "How could I deny you?"

"You couldn't." Lifting her off her feet, he carried her to the bed and fell with her on the rumpled coverlets. " 'Tis too early yet for me to show you how much I love you, m'lady, but when you are well and truly healed, I will take my time pleasuring you."

"Mayhap I'm healed already," she teased and sighed as his lips found hers.

"When you are, woman, we will have another child," he promised, "and 'twill be the first of many."

"*How* many?" she asked.

He laughed and the sound echoed off the rafters of the chamber. "As many as you want, Megan. As many as you want."

Snuggling close, she wrapped her arms around the rogue who would soon be her husband and whispered into his ear, "I think we've already started."

"What—?"

"I know not, but the bleeding's stopped, and I . . . I feel that the babe is still with me, that somehow Cadell saved that small soul."

"Megan," he said, shaking his head. " 'Tis too much to believe."

"Trust me," she said and placed a kiss at his temple. "Do you not know that I love you, Wolf?"

"Forever?"

"At least," she said with a giggle.

"And I love you, woman," he vowed. His lips found hers in a kiss that touched her soul and promised a lifetime of happiness for the lady and her outlaw.

Epilogue

Father Timothy sprinkled holy water on the infant's forehead and said a soft prayer over the rising wail of the tiny babe. When the prayer was finished, Wolf accepted the small bundle from the priest's trembling hands, and to his wife's surprise, planted a kiss on the shock of fine red hair. "You be a loud one, son," he said before handing the baby back to Megan.

"And strong," she said as she greeted their guests, those who had attended little Cormick's christening, for the child had indeed survived, despite the deep rending she'd felt in her womb and the fear that she'd lost him.

Throughout the chapel were the people she'd grown to love and trust: Robin, now much taller; Odell; one-eyed Peter; Cayley; Bjorn; and Cadell, the sorcerer. Even Lord Hagan, Lady Sorcha, and Bryanna joined them, as did Morgana and Garrick of Abergwynn. Morgana, tears in her eyes, stood with Cadell, her brother, and would not let go of his sleeve, as if she expected him to disappear from her again.

While little Cormick squealed unhappily, the guests filed

out of the chapel at Dwyrain, where she and Wolf had made their home during most of the past year while waiting for the birth of their child. Cayley was ruler of the castle, and between her and Hagan of Erbyn, all Wolf's sins had been forgiven. Now, 'twas time to return to Abergwynn and to a small keep not far from the castle.

Wolf wrapped an arm around her middle, and urged her toward the steps of the great hall.

"I'll be there in a minute," she said, and while he led their guests into the keep for a feast, Megan hurried through the gates of the castle and up a small hill to the cemetery. As the October breeze swirled her skirts, she laid a small bouquet of flowers from the christening on her father's grave. Finally, Ewan was at peace with his beloved Violet. Bevan's grave and a small one for Roz were nearby. "I miss you," she said, "I miss you all, but Father, finally, at last, I'm married. As you wanted."

"And happy?" a voice boomed behind her. Turning, she spied Wolf, his hair catching in the wind, his face as rugged as the great hills of Wales.

"Where's Cormick?"

"His aunt Cayley was cooing to him when I left."

"She needs a babe of her own."

"First a husband."

"Who would marry her?"

"A man more stubborn than she."

"Is there such a bullheaded man in all of Wales?" she asked, laughing, and the merry sound carried on the wind.

"Now, wife, you didn't answer my question," he said, advancing upon her. "Are you happy?"

"Oh, nay, Wolf, can you not see I'm miserable?" Again, she laughed.

"As miserable as I am."